Extinguish

J. H. Mitchell

Crassula
Press

ISBN: 978-1-925828-00-9 (paperback)
ISBN: 978-1-925878-01-6 (ebook)

First Printing, 2017

Cover illustration by DenaHelmi
https://denahelmi.deviantart.com

Crassula Press
crassulapress.com
crassulapress@gmail.com

ACKNOWLEDGMENTS

DenaHelmi - for your amazing cover art.

Mum and Dad - for your support and (sometimes brutally) honest advice—despite my complaining and defensiveness I appreciate every bit of help you give.

Emily and Chelsea - for being my sample audience, for filling me with praise, and helping me tap back into those teenage years.

Jo - for both having faith in my dream and for helping me to be practical in achieving it; I wouldn't have gotten through the technical side of publishing without you.

Bek - for reading every—and I do mean *every*—one of the dozen or more drafts of my book. For fielding my hundreds of (sometimes inane, sometimes pointless) questions, even if I often answer them myself. For listening to me prattle on for hours on end. For being my soundboard, my mind map, my notebook; but most of all for being my lifeboat through the many, *many* moments of doubt.

And especially Jason - my partner in all things. You may not read, you may not write, but your unwavering faith in my ability to make this happen was the most precious gift you could give. You listened even when you were not interested in the subject matter. You helped even when you didn't understand. You gave me strength, and you never once complained about the expense, about the grumpiness when I was "in the zone", or about being sometimes ignored in favour of my computer. I love you always.

For Rebecca Sutton
For being my own personal BK, for reading my countless
drafts and answering my countless questions;
For always keeping faith, and helping me stay strong enough
to push through my doubts.

And for Bree Harvey
My eighth year English Teacher who encouraged me to
pursue writing in the first place.

CHAPTER ONE

Zach

The art gallery was crowded. Seventeen-year-old Zach Andrews wound his way through the packed bodies, attempting to get from room to room with as little physical contact as possible. His nose wrinkled at the smell that often accompanied large crowds; a pungent mixture of sweat and perfume. His fingers kept up a rhythmic tap, drumming along the soft leather of his book bag.

In a post-party daze that morning, waking between empty cans of V, half smoked joints and scrunched up packets of CC's, Zach had the brilliant thought to go to one of the most crowded buildings in Brisbane and wander around. The thought was more of an urge. An idea that had blossomed from the emptiness of his grumbling stomach, surging up his spine and into his mind in a persistent nag.

Zach had followed the nag, leaving the house in the post-party disaster he had created—half hoping his parents would arrive home early from their cruise and discover the mess. It was just a bit of silly string and party rubbish, but in their eyes he would have destroyed their beautiful house. Serves them right for keeping secrets.

Zach sighed and was jostled sideways. A thin young woman pushed through the crowd, pulling a small, blond boy along with her. The little imp squeezed past, stomping on Zach's foot. Zach winced, muttering a curse that wasn't quite quiet enough. The imp's mother didn't apologise, but rather glared at Zach as if it was his fault the child had trodden on his foot.

Zach put on his best snob face, sneering at the mother and her boy as if they were nothing more than ants under his shoes. Even in the state he was in, disheveled clothes and clearly hungover, the expression was still effective. They scuttled away from him and Zach smirked. Every single time. He'd perfected the look from his mother, who wore it genuinely and often. Funny, how even though they weren't truly related, Zach could still inherit things from his parents. Like arrogance and conceit. He took comfort from the fact his intelligence had nothing to do with either of them, something he was sure drove them insane.

Zach hunched his shoulders, trying to make himself smaller as he slipped through the crowd searching for... something. He paused behind a group clustered in front of a bland and cluttered painting. Whatever he had come for, it wasn't art.

He shook his head and tried to move on. Another couple squeezed past Zach and he resisted the urge to pull them to a stop and explain what personal space meant.

The dozens of murmured conversations made it too hard for Zach to hear himself think. He sighed, closing his eyes and attempting to straighten out his thoughts; to clear away the fog and smoke of the night before. His fingers stopped tapping and slipped into the pocket of his jeans. How tempting it was, as the next tour of ten eased their way into the room, to pull out the pre-rolled joint and light up. Instead, Zach huffed out a breath and turned toward the exit, pulling at the collar of his shirt. He was hot, and he needed space to breathe.

He ended up near the back windows of the gallery overlooking the river. He should leave. He had no appreciation for the chaotic mess of colours and shapes that people called art, so, what on earth was he still doing there?

Yet, he couldn't bring himself to leave. The feeling— that tug that had brought him to the gallery to begin with—

sat deep in his stomach, coiled and waiting.

Waiting for what?

Zach leant his forehead against the cool glass, and the temperature around him rose. It was too hot. The air shifted, and Zach lifted his head, stepping away from the window as it flexed against his hand. The coiled feeling clenched in his gut and he stared out the window. A fresh scent, like the clean smell that preceded rain, filled the air. Zach watched with widening blue eyes as a ripple went across the water below. He almost thought he could feel it through the building, through the glass of the window, even see it through the air; like a shadowy shimmer rippling the very fabric of reality. The bridge, its architectural style more aesthetic than practical with all those needles and spikes, seemed to…to bend.

Boom!

Zach stumbled back. A shockwave burst through the gallery, almost knocking him off his feet.

He steadied himself, accompanied by a string of swear words that would have had made his socialite mother scarlet in anger.

Pictures fell in clattered chaos. Somewhere in another room something shattered. Voices erupted around him, echoing over each other in the domed ceiling.

'Jesus!'

'Oh my god, oh my god, was that an earthquake?'

'Shit, watch it.'

Zach glanced around, trying to steady his breathing. A large frame tipped sideways and fell from the wall.

Faint buzzing tingled along the base of his spine and up through his head. People milled about him on the verge of panic, checking their phones to find out what had caused the earthquake. They'd have been better off joining the people shoving up to the windows.

Pain spiked in Zach's head and he reeled, crying out and throwing out a hand to catch hold of something, anything to keep him standing upright. His hand slapped on the glass and he leaned against it, his shaking knees just holding him up as he clutched at his head with his other hand. A headache of gargantuan proportions blossomed behind his eyes.

He was shoved harder against the glass as people crammed up behind him, clamouring to see outside. On the bridge, caught up in the wires and spikes that made up the bridge's architecture was some sort of…of aircraft.

Was he hallucinating?

Zach's breath came fast and he cast an anxious look around the room.

'Stop pushing!'

'Jesus what is that thing?'

'This is a show, right? It's some prank by the art students.'

'A *prank*? Are you an idiot? That thing shook the whole building!'

'Ohmygod, ohmygod, ohmygod.'

'What is it? What is that thing?'

So, not hallucinating then.

Zach sucked in a deep breath. The air was quickly getting hotter as everyone in the room crowded the windows. People had their phones out and were recording. Zach squinted against the pain behind his eyes and tried to block out the noise of the people around him.

A steady *thud thud, thud thud* was beating hard in Zach's chest. He reached down to clutch at the lighter in his pocket, feeling for the smooth metal, focusing his mind on the warmth against his fingers. It gave him space to breathe. To think through the haze of the pulsing headache.

The cool glass was beginning to warm under his fingers and a flush was creeping up Zach's neck from the rising temperature of the crowded room. Below, where the bridge arched out from the art gallery lawn a figure crawled out of the aircraft. She was just close enough for Zach to make out her bright purple suit as she staggered from the craft onto the bridge facing the museum.

Zach couldn't see her face, but sensed somehow that they were looking at each other. The image of her—head tilted up toward the building, toward him, her silver eyes wide and frightened, yet hopeful—blossoming from within his mind, rather than from his own sight.

The noise in the gallery grew into a roar of frantic voices trying to make sense of what they were seeing. Zach staggered back, clutching at his head. God, would they just stop talking? The pain pounded behind his eyes and along his temples, a migraine in the making, made, already steamrolling its way through his mind. Amidst the pain there was a light. *Get down there!*

He shook his head, trying to clear away some of the pain, or at the very least some of the hazy vision. In a small window of clarity, he watched the girl in the purple suit turn and jump over the edge of the bridge, plummeting down to the water below.

Zach sucked in a deep breath and turned sharply. He didn't wait for anyone else to realise what was on the bridge. He ran.

His sneakers squeaked along the polished wooden floor as he dashed to the left to avoid ramming into a group of teenagers.

He reached the exit just as the panic peaked behind him; Zach was out of the room and in the corridor when the screaming started. Cries of hysteria and disbelief echoed behind him as he sprinted through the building and out the nearest exit.

He skidded on the grass and almost fell over. The migraine erupted, exploding darkness through his head with a single bright thought illuminating his whole being.

He had to get there first.

He had to get to the alien girl first.

CHAPTER TWO

Genie

'…flying over my house last night.'
'And you think it was an unidentifiable aircraft?'
'It didn't look like any plane I'd ever seen!'

The voices were loud, buzzing out of the busted old radio speakers obnoxious tones, determined to wake me up. I sighed and rolled over, pulling my duvet above my head in an attempt to block out the noise.

Old aches tingled along old scars on my chest. I shifted, uncomfortable in the heat under my blankets, feeling sticky and itchy and restless.

Any thoughts of returning to sleep vanished into the muggy warmth of a summer morning. Besides, the voices were still yammering.

With a sigh, I reached out a hand and felt around for the clock. When the voices finally stopped, I lay in bed for a moment longer. Distant memories threatened to pull me back into sleep. Memories I'd rather avoid. Memories of pain and sadness and hope.

Shoving the thoughts away, I dragged myself upright. My uniform was laid over the end of my bed. I struggled into it in a half daze.

Dark, tangled hair fell in my face as I fought with a pair of black stockings. Who made these things anyway? Were they designed to be difficult?

Somehow managing not to fall on my face, I tucked my hair behind my ears and righted myself.

Dull pain shifted through my chest, like a faded memory across my skin. I winced. Massaging the pain never worked, but I rubbed at the old scar anyway. More reminders of what today was. I was heavy and tired and sore.

Deciding to forgo the rest of my morning ritual, I wrangled my tangled hair into a messy bun. It would have to do. I checked the mirror, eyeing the top button of my school shirt and ignoring the mess that was my hair. A faint flash of faded scar tissue peeked out from above the top button. I chewed the inside of my lip and debated wearing an undershirt. The faint sheen of perspiration already forming on my forehead and neck indicated that, in this heat, an undershirt would be unreasonable.

The smell of bacon wafted in from the hallway. Hunger lurched and I abandoned any ideas of changing. I pulled the curtains aside and peered out into the lawn. As I'd suspected, someone jogged across the grass. He stuck to the outskirts of the yard, just on the inside of the garden as he kept a steady pace.

I pushed open the window and called out, 'Breakfast is ready!'

His direction changed and he veered off toward the house. Shaking my head, I turned and traipsed downstairs to find the source of the bacon smell.

BK and I shared the only upstairs room in the house—an old attic bedroom. When BK had been adopted, there hadn't been enough room for us all, so Grandpa decided to remodel the house.

The attic was supposed to become my twin brother's room. Freddie and I had shared a room up until that point, and this was supposed to be some sort of man-cave—recompense for being kicked out of our room—but BK loved the hideaway so much she offered to take it instead.

I could have stayed with Freddie, but Grandma had been insistent I bunk with BK. At twelve, she said Freddie and I were getting too old to share rooms. She was right, of course, so I shifted into the attic with my new cousin.

I didn't mind.

Downstairs, BK stood cooking at the kitchen island and more rich smells wafted my way. Crispy hash browns, creamed corn, fried tomato. I breathed in. Yum.

As usual, BK's hair was even messier than mine. The blonde curls fell around her face in a perpetual tangle, never to be reasoned with. The sight made me smile.

She beamed, green eyes lighting up just at the sight of me. Of course, they instantly furrowed, picking up as she always did on my melancholy.

'You need a hug,' she said decidedly, abandoning her duties as cook to come and throw her arms around me.

I melted into it, forever grateful she'd been brought into our family. BK's hugs were always warm and full of love. How she managed to always be so cheerful and bright, I would never know. I didn't complain. She was comfortingly reliable. Especially now, since Grandma had passed away.

For two months BK had dedicated herself to trying to fill the void Grandma's absence left. It was an impossible task. Grandma had raised us with stern kindness, with passion and humour. She had seemed so vibrant and full of life. Until it had been taken away.

Now we were left just us three, in the big empty house our grandparents had built.

BK pulled away, eyeing me as fiercely as she could manage. 'Time to perk up, missy,' she said. 'I had a feeling you'd need cheering up, so I cooked! It's your favourite!'

I laughed.

'How do you always know?' I asked, and surveyed the options. I grinned and turned away.

'What's wrong?' she asked, her tone dropping in worry. 'Did I miss something?'

'No,' I said hurriedly. 'It's great, really.'

It was great. But it was Freddie's favourite spread. She'd only be upset if I pointed it out, and I was happy enough with the gesture. Besides, knowing BK's sense of intuition, the fact she'd steered towards his favourite foods meant Freddie probably needed cheering up more than I did.

Right on cue, he stumbled into the kitchen, school tie askew and shirt half tucked in. His face was still red from his run, raven hair sticking up in a windswept mess and he was somehow missing a shoe. He kicked the edge of the bench and winced, but didn't slow in his beeline for the hash browns.

Grey eyes flickered up to us girls, and Freddie cocked his head, one eyebrow raised in question at BK.

She crossed her arms and tried to give him a firm look.

'Use your words,' she said.

Freddie sighed and rolled his eyes. He'd always inclined towards body language rather than sign, something that drove our therapist insane. We'd gone through years of therapy, he and I. They thought he was autistic and I was crazy. The boy who couldn't speak and the girl who saw an alien.

What a pair we made.

In an exaggerated motion he crossed his hands, palms open and flat and knocked his wrists together—making the word for 'work'—then cocked his head at her again.

I glanced sideways at BK. She had her stubborn face on, but she relented and answered his one worded question.

'I'm not going in today. We got rained out last night.' She peered out the kitchen windows up at the grey sky above. 'They think it'll storm again today.'

'In this humidity, it'll probably be a big one,' I said, reaching for a hash brown.

A horn tooted outside and I sighed.

'Of course he's early today,' I muttered, and reached out to snag some bacon before Freddie ate it all.

Freddie eyed me shrewdly, eyes as grey as the clouds outside. I recognised my own features in his face. The same eyes, the same arch of brow, the same…well you get the point. The only difference was the perpetual state of mischief Freddie seemed to exist in.

As if sensing my thoughts, Freddie rolled his eyes and looked away. He huffed and stuffed another mouthful of hash brown into his mouth. He made some vague motion with his hands, fluttering them about and gesturing toward the door, before darting out of the room. Hopefully to find his shoe.

'You're not yourselves,' said BK, her green gaze shifting between Freddie's retreating back and me.

I shrugged.

'Sure we are,' I said, trying to smile. 'You just don't normally see us in the mornings.'

Her frown remained, but she didn't say anything else. I leaned around the corner of the bench to give her another hug.

'We'll see you later, okay?'

'Hang on, I'll fix your hair. That'll cheer you up.'

The car horn blasted again, two longer hoots this time. Tim was impatient this morning—Tim was always impatient.

'No time,' I said, shrugging in a "what-can-you-do?" manner.

She sighed but let me go without a fuss.

I slipped into the back seat of the old, faded red Ford. It sat rumbling in the driveway, less a purr and more a sputter, as if it were about to shut off at any moment.

When Tim turned seventeen and passed on his licence, his mother had offered to buy him a second hand car. Something a little better than the car he and Freddie did burnouts in in the middle of the fields when they thought no one was looking.

He'd refused. I don't know why. It was barely more than a glorified paddock-basher, yet Tim loved it.

'Where's Freddie?' Tim barked, glancing up at me in the rearview mirror as I slid in.

'Morning, Tim,' I said with a wry grin.

'Yeah, yeah,' he said, fingers tapping on the wheel. 'We're late, where is he?'

'Coming,' I said. 'And you're early, not late. Who're you avoiding today?'

'Who says I'm avoiding anybody?'

'You're never early.'

'Am so,' he said. 'Sometimes.' A quick grin flashed up in the rearview mirror, but it didn't quite reach his eyes.

I guess we were all in weird moods this morning.

Freddie came barrelling out the front door, BK close on his heels with lunch containers in her arms. As Freddie all but fell into the front passenger seat, she handed one through to him.

'I packed you lunch!'

Freddie grinned at her, and kissed her on the cheek in thanks, earning himself a bright smile.

'Oi,' Tim objected, leaning over to peer out at BK. 'Where's mine?'

BK smiled in at him, far more patient than most girls who dealt with him (and no-where near as smitten).

'I didn't forget,' she said, and handed across another container. 'I added peppers in yours!'

Tim flashed her a toothy grin. 'BK, have I told you a love you?'

'Many times.'

'You're the best sheila in town.'

I rolled my eyes. He thinks he's so smooth.

'You've told me that too,' she said, shutting Freddie's door.

She leaned in the half open back window I was sitting next to.

'Hope you feel better today,' she said. 'I put in something extra for you, so cheer up, okay?'

I smiled. 'Thanks, BK.'

Tim drummed his hands on the wheel, glancing back at us.

'Alrighty,' he said, jamming the car into reverse. 'Let's get this show on the road.'

BK stepped back out of the way as Tim began to roll out.

Right on cue, the car stalled.

CHAPTER THREE

Zach

The alien girl emerged from the water in silence, gliding out as if she were a part of it, leaving little evidence in her wake that she had been there at all. She didn't notice Zach at first. He stood staring at her, at the sheer impossibility of her, unable to speak.

He'd been wrong. Through the haze of the pain exploding in his mind, he'd thought the figure that emerged from the crashed aircraft was wearing a purple suit, but he'd been wrong. So very wrong.

It wasn't that she was wearing purple she was purple.

Now that he was closer, that he had reached her, the pain in his mind had subsided somewhat and his vision cleared. With sharp focus he stared at the figure before him.

Her torso was skinny, and she touched her temples with elongated fingers. She was strangely human, and yet completely and utterly not.

Her skin was a translucent, pastel purple colour that was smooth and hairless. Zach could see her veins, a bright blue beneath the purple, and wondered what colour her blood was. Her mouth had no visible discolouration from the rest of her skin, and her nose, though raised, was flatter than a human nose.

The biggest difference, though, were her ears, and Zach stared at them in open curiosity.

There were two large, curving indents on either side of her head. A thin layer of what appeared to be webbing flexed along the outside of the holes, acting as a shield from the water dripping off her. The ear holes themselves curved along the ridges on either side of the crown of her head. The ridges started out small, then grew wider until they came out of her head into ears that looked more like tails. They were long, thick and smooth.

She was the strangest, most fascinating beautiful thing Zach had ever seen.

So of course, he gaped at her like some gormless high school student at the zoo. He shook his head, opened his mouth, and said the first thing that came to mind.

'Hi.'

She jumped, silvery eyes snapping up to his in alarm, and she tensed as if to dive straight back into the water.

'No, no, no! It's okay!' said Zach, throwing his hands up to show her he was harmless, internally cursing his sudden onset of stupidity. 'I won't hurt you, I swear!'

Her ear twitched, and she tilted her head toward him, studying him with no small amount of wariness.

'I don't suppose you speak English?' he asked.

She shifted, staring at Zach with wide eyes as she stood dripping on the bank. The strange fabric of the clothes she wore was already drying, shifting from the colour of her skin to a lighter hue, then to a darker shade. The fabric had been as translucent as her skin, but appeared to become more solid as it dried. It was a full body suit, thin and clinging like a flight suit straight out of a science fiction movie.

The whir of a siren jolted through Zach, and he looked about again, nervous of how exposed they were.

He shook his head. They didn't have time for this. A sharp hitch of adrenaline shot through his chest.

The urge to be closer to her spiked and he reached for the alien girl, stretching out his hand in the least threatening way he could manage. He wasn't sure what he was doing, why he felt such a persistent need to be with her and help her, but it was something he would have to think about later.

'Come on,' he said, his heart picking up pace as he tried not to focus on the sound of the sirens. They were getting closer. 'It's not safe here. I have a car.'

She tilted her head at him and one of her ears twitched again. Her pupils dilated, blotting out almost all the silver, and the air grew charged around them. Everything become muffled and a light pressure encircled his head, almost like the earlier headache but not quite so painful.

Zach took a hasty step back, and the world snapped back into focus. He shook his head to clear the sudden disorientation and stared at the alien girl.

What had she done to him?

She took a cautious step forward, the silver returning to her eyes, and in a slow, stilted voice said,

'I am look-look …' she took a deep breath and tried again. 'Looking for some-someone.'

Zach straightened, a tingle of excitement shooting up through his spine.

'You do speak English,' he said, then rolled his eyes at himself for stating the obvious. 'Have you been here before? When? Where did you go, and why did you come to Australia of all places? Wait, sorry. You said you were looking for someone?'

She nodded, her long fingers curling into the fabric of her clothes.

'Who?'

'A g-girl,' she said. 'Her name is-is … Genie.'

Zach raised his eyebrows.

'What's her last name?'

She shook her head. 'I'm not … I don't … not sure.'

Zach grimaced and tapped his fingers along his book bag. At least she shouldn't be hard to find. After all, how many girls could there be with the name Genie?

He shook his head.

'What about where she lives? Do you know that?'

She turned and pointed across the river.

'In the city?'

She shook her head again, ears twitching and hairless brows creasing. Zach was struck by the fact that she didn't have eyebrows.

'North,' she said. 'M-much farther n-north.'

Zach glanced back up the hill toward the museum and

wondered how long they had before the bank would be crawling with people. He turned back to the alien girl.

'I can help you,' he held his hand out to her again.

She hesitated, eyes going distant in thought. One of her ears twitched, and her gaze refocused on him.

'You-you will h-help me f-find her?'

That same urge, the nag at the back of his mind, pulled at him. The thought of leaving her alone to whatever dangers awaited made Zach feel sick.

He shook his head again, trying to clear the unusual emotion clouding his judgement. There was something else going on. He knew that. Felt it now that he'd felt her presence around his mind. Telepathy? Zach wasn't sure.

'Sure,' Zach shrugged. 'Shouldn't be too hard, so long as she doesn't live in a lamp.'

The alien girl tilted her head, brows furrowing in confusion. 'A l-lamp?'

His fingers drummed against the book bag again and he attempted a laugh. 'Earth joke. Never mind.'

'Her n-name,' she said, still not moving toward him. 'I-it's Genie Hart.'

'Heart?' Zach asked. Something about the name nagged at him, but the sirens were getting closer.

'Alright,' he said, 'let's get out of here then.'

She looked back up at the bridge, and Zach followed her gaze. There were people all over it, crowding into the strange aircraft above. Some of them leaned over the edge of the railing to stare down below.

The shadow of the bridge and the garden path beneath them shielded them somewhat, but it would only be a matter of time before they were noticed.

A small current of electricity ran along the ridges on the alien girl's head. She turned back to Zach, took a step forward and finally grasped his hand. Her touch was cool and smooth—almost rubbery and he recalled petting a dolphin when he was younger.

His eyes met hers, blue into silver, and a grin erupted over his face.

'Alright,' he said again. 'Let's go find your girl.'

CHAPTER FOUR

Genie

Despite the rain from the night before and the grey sky above, dust still rose up behind us as we headed into civilisation. Like a stubborn cloud reminding us of our origins: *you belong to the country, the dirt, the earth.*

As if we needed the reminder.

Freddie shifted, pulling out a bundle of papers wedged down the side of his seat.

'Shit,' said Tim, reaching over to yank them away. 'Sorry. Don't worry about those.'

He started stuffing them into the pocket of the drivers door, but Freddie snatched one of the loose papers back. I leaned forward to see what it was that Tim wanted to hide from us.

A newspaper clipping.

I glanced over at Tim and caught the flash of guilt in his face. Olive skin flushed red, and his coal-dark eyes turned to the road with unerring focus.

Freddie lowered the paper. He didn't look at Tim, and he didn't look at me. Instead, he leaned his elbow on the jammed window and stared out at the countryside.

'What?' I asked, and reached around to take it.

Girl attacked by older brother saved by neighbour.

I swallowed, my mouth going dry.

'Sorry,' Tim blurted. 'Was Mum. She found them last night. I dunno why she thought I'd want them. I dunno why she even saved them in the first place. It's not exactly a fond memory. Anyway, I'm sorry. I shouldn't've had it in the car. It was stupid, I—'

'Tim,' I said, cutting him off. 'It's okay.'

His eyes flashed my way again. 'Is it? Because you seem like you're in a shit mood.'

'What makes you say that?' I said, leaning back and crossing my arms.

'What makes me say that?' he scoffed, mimicking me. 'A bunch of things, and anyway BK said you needed cheering up.'

I shook my head, hunching down in my seat.

'BK's not right about everything.'

'Sure she is,' said Tim brusquely. 'Especially about you two.'

With a sigh, I confessed. At least a little.

'I'm just feeling a bit down I guess,' I said. 'It's just… today, you know? Lots of…anniversaries.' I rubbed at the scar through the stiff fabric of my school shirt.

'Great,' Tim muttered. 'I'm a dick.'

Freddie nodded, his head tilting sideways to cast Tim an irritated glare before returning to the window. I shoved half-heartedly at his shoulder.

'No, you're not,' I said to Tim, and looked down at the news clipping. 'How can you be? You saved my life.'

Silence reigned. Tim's knuckles went white. His face was set in hard lines, glaring out at the road as memories flashed across his face. Memories of me.

I looked down at the news clipping to see a picture of the two of us. There I was, small, frail and white as a sheet, wrapped in a blanket and Tim's arms. We were only a year apart in age but he was so much bigger than I was. He sat next to me, looking up into the face of the fireman who was walking over to us. He had that fierce expression on his face, even then, at eleven years old. He had one arm around my shoulders and the other arm pressing a towel to my bloody chest. Yet even with his arms preoccupied, he looked ready to take on the fireman if he made the wrong move.

The picture was Tim all over. Soft and caring, and yet fierce and full of fire. Daring anyone to take me away from him. I ran a hand over the image, gaze trailing over to the article detailing how, seven years ago today, my older brother had gone crazy and attacked me and how Tim had found me and called for help.

I'm not sure who took the photo. Tim's call had brought two ambulances, three cop cars and a firetruck. News that a little girl had been carved up in a town as small as ours had brought everyone running.

'Come out, come out, wherever you are.'

I swallowed and squashed the memory.

'I had a dream last night,' I said, attempting to lighten the mood and get their thoughts off my past. Our past. 'About Einstein.'

So far as distractions went, it seemed to work. The two of them lost those dark, faraway expressions and glanced back at me.

'Your alien?' Tim asked. 'He coming back or what?'

'One day,' I said. 'I hope.'

Seven years ago today, my older brother attacked me, slicing open my chest with a kitchen knife in a fit of rage I would never understand. A year later to the day, I was visited by an alien. He was strange and beautiful and impossible.

My shrink said it was some sort of coping mechanism. That I'd hallucinated the whole event in order to somehow deal with what my brother had done to me. Sometimes, I almost believed him. But Freddie and Tim, even BK, never let me doubt myself. They believed my story as if they'd seen Einstein with their own eyes.

'Well then what was this dream—shit.'

Tim braked hard, swerving onto the side of the road as three fire trucks shot past in the overtaking lane, appearing out of no where around a bend.

The car rattled, sending us all jolting along the shoulder of the road. At the speed Tim was driving, the sudden change from road to dirt sent vibrations along my spine, rattling every bone and organ in my body.

'Jesus,' Tim said, pulling back onto the road in a swirl of dust and fading sirens. 'What the bloody hell was that about?'

'Fire in town?'

Tim brightened.

'Hopefully at school. I'd love to have a day off.'

'It's Monday.'

'Yeah, and?'

'We just had two days off.'

'What's your point?'

I shook my head, giving up on trying to make Tim's attendance any better than it was. He'd already been held back a year due to too many absences. I sighed. It was a battle for another day. One with less memories.

Tim accelerated, eager to discover whether or not we'd end up with another day off. Freddie went back to staring out the window, unusually still and broody. I stared at the article.

There was no mention of Freddie. He wasn't there in the photo because he hadn't been there at all. Grandma had taken him out to one of his endless afternoon activities while I was being babysat by our elder brother.

James.

I shuddered. Freddie shifted in the front seat, glancing back at me over his shoulder. I smiled, trying to keep the ghost of memory off my face. He frowned, not buying it, and went back to staring out the window again.

He was so quiet this morning.

Everything was quiet this morning. The clouds were grey, the traffic was light, and though school wasn't on fire, it was empty. There were maybe ten other cars in the carpark when we pulled in as opposed to the usual fifty.

The air was still, as if someone had thrown a blanket over the world, making all sounds muted and indistinct. There was no chatter of milling teenagers, no revving of boys showing off in their cars. Just…silence.

'This is weird,' said Tim, leaning against the door of his car with his arms crossed.

'Where is everyone?' I asked, staring around the empty carpark.

Freddie's only response was to frown up at the school.

'We're not that early, are we?'

'Actually,' I said, glancing at my silent brother. 'I think we're late. Though I don't know how.'

'Maybe there's some sort of mass wagging ploy,' Tim suggested with a shrug.

'If there was, you'd be the one to organise it.'

Freddie signed something in short, stiff movements, his brow creased and his shoulders tense. *Flu?'*

'You think everyone's sick?'

Two days ago the UN had shut down the borders to three countries, declaring a national crises due to an unknown flu pandemic. The news was terrifying and yet, until that moment, I hadn't considered the fact the pandemic might reach us. That it might jump the endless ocean that marooned us on our island in the middle of the Pacific.

A chill crept up my arms, and half a second later I saw Freddie shudder, as if reading my thoughts. It had always seemed to me that Australia was disconnected from the rest of the world. Now, with the gooseflesh spreading over my skin, I thought maybe we weren't so far away from everyone else as I'd imagined.

'Maybe we should just go back home,' Tim suggested.

'If you miss anymore class, you'll get another suspension.'

'Who cares. This is too bloody creepy.'

Freddie's shoulders tensed and he raised his eyebrows, tilting his head toward Tim and shrugging in agreement. I took a step closer to Tim, and snagged the keys.

'Hey!'

They jangled as I shoved them into the inner pocket of my skirt. Tim might make a try for them, if he was up for getting punched by Freddie. He took a step toward me, dark eyes flickering to my somewhat overprotective brother. Freddie wasn't watching, but his shoulders were still taught, hunched in on his crossed arms. He was refusing to look our way.

Thankfully, Tim thought better of wrangling back the keys and took a step back.

'Come on,' I said, trying to channel BK and perk my voice up. 'Let's go.'

As we headed further in, the eeriness only got worse. Teenagers standing in their usual hang outs despondently, not quite sure what to do with themselves without the rest of their friends. It was different from just one or two friends being coincidentally sick. This was...weird. Unnatural.

For years I had watched all those girls in their packs wander around the school yard and felt envious. I wanted to be part of that, to be among them, whispering and giggling and accepted. Now I was glad it was just me and the boys. If I'd been stuck here alone, in this quiet emptiness...I shuddered again.

Freddie glanced my way, his grey eyes dark and his jaw clenched. I could see in his face that he didn't like this.

'We should go home,' I imagined him saying, agreeing with Tim. *'This is too weird.'*

'Come on,' I said. 'It won't be that bad.'

CHAPTER FIVE

Zach

So far as road-trips went, a seven hour drive to Rockhampton with an alien had to take the cake.

Attempting to scramble from the front lawn of the museum without being seen had been tricky. Zach was sure they'd startled more than one passer-by. His path to the underground carpark had taken them across the grass in full view of the river and past the glass windows of the building they were skirting.

Zach just hoped there was some sort of convention on that would help explain why there might be a purple girl running around Brisbane.

He'd dropped his keys in an attempt to unlock the car quickly—ignoring the two women standing three rows over, pointing and no doubt gossiping about his new companion —and gestured the girl inside.

With another nervous look, she slid into his car and Zach raced around the side of the car to jump in before anyone tried to talk to them.

His head smacked into the door frame and he cursed loudly, slamming the door shut as he jumped in. Jamming the keys into the ignition, he jerked the car into reverse and squealed out of the car park.

Two hours of speeding up the highway had yet to calm Zach's nerves.

He hadn't stopped at his house, hadn't even thought about the fact he needed clothes and supplies if he was going to go trekking around the country with an alien. Instead, Zach had pointed the car in the direction she indicated and drove, not entirely sure he wasn't stoned.

Despite that his new companion didn't make much of a conversationalist, Zach remained ultra aware of her, as if he had become attuned to her presence.

She set every fibre of his being on high alert, sharpening every sense into an almost painful intensity. He could feel every stitch in the steering wheel cover against his hands, saw even the smallest of potholes and cracks in the road. Colours were brighter and more vibrant.

As he drove through a less populated area along the highway, Zach wondered if it was something she had done to him. Always her eyes would go out of focus after they spoke as if she were internally processing what he was saying, or translating it … or something else. Occasionally her ears would twitch or a strange current would run along the ridges on her head like lightning, making him wonder what other purpose her tentacle-like ears served.

He glanced over at her. She was leaning against the window, huddled toward the sun patch. Zach frowned. He leaned over to flick on the AC, turning the dial to warm.

'Here,' he said. 'Turn the vents like this.'

She looked up at him, watching as he adjusted the air vents on his side.

'For warm air,' he elaborated when she didn't copy him.

She blinked, two sets of eyelids flashing shut, and then reached out to do the same. She closed her eyes as the warmth reached her, a small smile curving her lips.

'Thank-thank you,' she said.

He nodded watching the car to his left in case it decided to merge in front of him again. He scowled. He hated four wheel drivers.

'No problem,' he replied distractedly. 'You should have said if you were cold. I would have turned it on sooner.'

'I d-didn't know,' she said, and gestured to the air vents.

'Oh,' he said, 'I suppose you wouldn't. Say, how do you know English?'

She thought about this for a moment, playing with the hem of her sleeve in such a human way that Zach couldn't help but smile.

'You would c-call it c-culture studies,' she said.

Zach raised his eyebrows, glancing over at her quickly.

'Culture studies? Really?'

She nodded.

'Did you study a lot of the languages on Earth?'

She nodded. 'A-all,' she said.

'All? All the languages on Earth?'

'And some other p-p-planets,' she said. 'Do you n-not st-study other languages?'

Zach laughed tightly. It wasn't often someone made him feel stupid.

'Uh, I guess,' he said, 'but not quite on that level. I only know five.'

She tilted her head, her curiosity beginning to override her anxiousness.

She bewildered him. For a creature so intelligent, and—he eyed her tentacle like ears—as powerful as he suspected, she was so shy.

He wondered if that was why she stuttered?

She shifted toward the warmth while also attempting to keep in the dwindling sun patch. Clouds were building in the midday sky, and Zach suspected they would soon be driving through a storm.

'Are you still cold?' he asked.

She glanced over shyly, and he was caught by her silver gaze. Zach resisted the urge to roll his eyes at himself. Out of all the strangeness, from her tentacle ears to the purple skin it was her eyes that threw him off. What was wrong with him?

She tilted her head at him, eyelids fluttering shut again. He caught that flicker of a second membrane and was reminded of a documentary he'd watched on crocodiles.

He blinked and came to a sudden realisation.

'You're cold blooded,' he said, glancing between her and the road.

She looked up, startled by his exclamation. A darker

purple crept up her neck and along the tips of her ears. She was blushing.

He waited until she nodded.

'Some sort of amphibian creature, right? You don't have any scales, and unless you're hiding some extra limbs in that suit you're not an arachnid. Unless you're something altogether different, but I'm thinking something similar to our amphibians, yeah?'

After a pause, she nodded somewhat jerkily. As if she wasn't used to the scrutiny. Knowing he was being impolite and far too personal Zach attempted to stop asking questions. Ten minutes of driving and sneaking glances at her, and Zach's curiosity won out.

'You were under that water pretty long,' he said, switching lanes and accelerating. 'Can you, uh, shut your nose off?'

He tapped his nose, just to be sure she knew what he meant. When he glanced back over at her, she breathed in and her nostrils closed together, the sides lying flat against each other. Completely sealed. Her flat nose wasn't so odd, now that he was beginning to understand her.

'I'm guessing you can breathe through your skin, too right?'

Another nod.

Zach grinned. 'That's kind of cool.'

She stared at him, those double eyelids flickering shut, and turned back toward the window. The darker purple colour spread up through her ears. Taking pity on her embarrassment, Zach decided to forgo the personal interrogation, lest the alien take on a permanent blush. Instead, he focused his next question on their quest.

'So what's so special about this Genie girl?'

She was silent and Zach thought she wasn't going answer, but a quick glance told him her eyes had gone distant again.

The air became charged, sending prickles of goosebumps up his arm, like the static before lightning. He was trying to think of another topic, hoping to dispel whatever it was that was causing the hairs on his arms stand up, when she spoke.

'She-she is important t-to us,' she said.

He wanted to ask more, wanted to know what connected this Genie Hart to an alien that had come so far to find her. Instead, he held his tongue.

Every half hour or so he asked if they were still heading in the right direction, and the alien girl would just nod. Chatty.

The clouds swelled and yet the rain didn't fall. Patches of sunlight filtered through, casting bright spots of annoying sunlight off cars and mirrors. Zach scowled again and searched around his centre console for some sunglasses.

'We'll keep going a while longer before we stop,' he said to her.

She glanced over but didn't object, or offer any sort of opinion. The excitement of having an alien in his car had worn off in the wake of all his unanswered questions. Zach sighed and flicked on the radio.

He skimmed through the stations. He paused on one, raising his eyebrows as the presenters answered phone calls from callers saying they'd seen a space-ship crash in Brisbane River.

'A space-ship? You're telling me a space-ship cashed in Brisbane?'

'It was huge, my cousin has footage of it. I'm telling you aliens are going to invade! They're coming. The government's obviously been hiding this from us!'

Zach cast a quick look at his passenger and switched stations again. He frowned, noticing a few recurring words.

'Residents are being reminded to have their flue vaccination shots in the wake of an increasingly virulent strand of flu—'

Switch station.

'Hospitals are overflowing. People presenting with flu systems should first seek medical advice from their GP or nearest clinic.'

Switch station.

'Yet another border closed in Europe.'

Zach swallowed and switched from the radio to his iPod, trying not to think of his parents. They'd been in Italy when it started. By the time Zach's parents reached Paris, they were no longer allowed to travel. Zach doubted he would see them for quite some time.

He sighed and shifted in his seat, then pulled out his lighter and the joint he had been dying to have all afternoon.

'Mind if I smoke?' Zach asked.

She shook her head but watched him as he lit up. He wound down his window a crack, giving the smoke an escape. It probably wasn't a good idea to get his alien companion high.

Big droplets of rain began to fall just as he was starting to relax. Zach sighed and put out the smoke, winding up the window and peering ahead at the ominous clouds.

CHAPTER SIX

Genie

Lunch was like the set up to a horror movie. Not the gory bits where everyone goes missing or dies, but the weird, half-suspenseful beginning where you know something isn't quite right.

'You still reckon we should stay?' Tim asked, tossing his bag on the ground and handing Freddie a coke.

I chewed my lip. The fact was, I *didn't* want to stay. I hated horror movies, and I hated the set up to horror movies. I hated that they couldn't tell when to run and get out of there, even though it was obvious; and here I was, feeling like I was in that exact scenario.

Except that it was absurd. Besides half the school being away, there wasn't actually anything wrong. Horror movies were just that: horror movies. They weren't real. This was nothing more than some freaky coincidence and a couple (okay, a *lot*) of kids being sick. Besides, there *was* something going around. It was all explainable. Simple. *Not* a horror movie.

'You can't miss anymore school,' I reminded him.

Tim rolled his eyes, dismissing the seriousness of the situation. Despite how much I did want to just call it a day and go home, all I could think about was the warning letter BK had pulled out of the bottom of Tim's bag three weeks ago.

I can't remember what she'd been looking for, nor why she'd opened up the letter and started reading (she wasn't normally such a snoop), but what I did remember was the last line of the letter.

If this attitude continues, we will have no choice but to expel Tim from this school, an outcome I am sure none of us wants.

Expulsion.

Tim wasn't *that* disruptive but he had missed a lot of school. Having already been held back for attendance, the school was desperate to make Tim pay attention. He wasn't stupid, he was just…bored. And when Tim was bored, bad things happened.

What followed was usually in-school detention (which he skipped), after-school detention (which he *also* skipped), followed finally by suspension. He was on his fifth for the year, bordering on his final warning.

They really would expel him if he skipped anymore class. He was so close, *so close* to graduating. His grades were finally holding (he may have been disruptive and absent, but he at least handed in all his homework—thanks to BK and me, anyway). I couldn't bear the thought of him failing at the last minute like this.

'We're *staying*,' I said, ignoring the tight feeling in my gut.

Tim sighed, but didn't press the issue. 'Alright, alright. Keep your pants on.'

Freddie was notably silent. Though his attendance wasn't quite so bad as Tim's, he did have just as many warnings. Usually, where one was, the other lurked nearby. Unfortunately, the teachers knew it. They had a tendency to just punish both of them, even if all the evidence pointed only to one.

I didn't blame them. After all, I couldn't think of a single case where the teachers had been wrong.

Without the others—who had graduated the year before —it was just the three of us, making it a bit harder for me to keep the two of them in line.

Freddie, for instance, had already landed himself in detention for the day. Tim nudged him, frowning at his best friend's surliness.

'So what'd you do?' he asked.

Freddie glanced over, grey eyes stormy, and shrugged.

'C'mon, don't give me that,' said Tim. 'Besides, it's the rules. If you do something without me, you have to tell me what it is.'

Freddie scowled, throwing Tim a dark look that clearly said *'back off.'*

I raised my eyebrows.

'What's wrong?' I asked. 'What happened?'

He shifted, leaning back against the brick wall and crossing his arms, hands curled into fists—a clear sign he was not going to be talking. Or rather, signing.

Tim's attempt at cheerfulness dissipated. Dark eyes flicked my way, and in an instant, we both knew what the problem was.

Me.

'Okay, so clearly we have to beat someone up-'

'Tim!'

'But before we get to that, can I at least know what they said?' continued Tim, completely ignoring me as usual.

'You're not beating anyone up,' I said, glaring at him. I sighed and muttered. 'Who am I kidding, you're not going to listen to me anyway.'

'No, I'm not,' agreed Tim, still staring at Freddie. 'Out with it. Who said what about Genie?'

This time it was me crossing my arms. 'It's not always about me, you know.'

Tim and Freddie both looked at me, and I flushed. 'Well it shouldn't be,' I said. 'I don't care what they say, I just want you to stay out of trouble!'

Freddie's hands flashed out, his fingers uncurling to instead make sharp, rapid movements in quick succession. His hands slapped together with more force than necessary, his jaw clenched, and his eyes blazed.

Then they should shut their mouths!'

'Just ignore them,' I said. 'I do.'

Maybe you shouldn't!'

'It's not even that bad, Freddie—'

They called you crazy.'

I flinched, recognising the gesture for crazy before the rest of the sentence had even registered. The single finger to the temple, followed by the sharp flick away of the entire palm. Freddie's movements made the motion seem violent. He was on his feet now, his shoulders taught and jaw clenched. I stared at the ground.

'It doesn't matter,' I muttered, cheeks burning. I clenched my fists, trying to believe my own words. 'I know I'm not crazy, and that's all that matters.'

'Of course you're not,' said Tim, his voice hard. 'Who said it?'

'It doesn't matter!' I snapped, standing up and glaring back at them. 'It doesn't matter who called me crazy or who thinks I'm insane or whatever else they want to say about me, just stop getting into fights! *Please!*'

Freddie scowled at me, grey eyes fierce and angry. I could see it all over his face. The fury, the resentment, the guilt. He couldn't be there to protect me from our brother, so now he'd protect me from all the people who thought I'd lost my mind.

The two of them always fought my battles, trying to convince themselves they could protect me from the past. Like the more battles they fought, the more faded that memory of me would become. Of me, small and tiny and blood-soaked.

Something shifted in Freddie's gaze like a ghost from the past flashing across his face. Hurt and worry and fear all rolled into one. He sucked in a breath, eyes shifting away from my face, loosing their fierceness under the sudden watery quality.

He scowled, resentment flooding in over his anger. *'Fine,'* I imagined him saying, *'defend yourself. Let them call you crazy.'*

He snatched up my bag and, before I had a chance to stop him, was pulling the keys out of my pencil case. I scowled, annoyed he'd known they were there and annoyed I hadn't just kept them in my pocket.

'Where do you think you're goin'?' Tim asked as Freddie dropped my bag at my feet.

I sighed and reached out for him. 'Wait, Freddie…'

He twitched away from me, mirroring my scowl, his movements taught and stiff.

'You're not supposed to drive the car,' Tim called after him as Freddie stormed off. 'Don't get caught!'

Freddie was often stopped by the cops in town (who knew Tim's car by sight) and was sent home with written up ticket-warnings—warnings they never managed to follow through with. I don't know why, but despite Tim and Freddie's obnoxious unruliness, the cops were rather fond of my brother and his best friend.

'Jesus,' Tim muttered, linking his hands behind his head. 'Is everyone in a mood today?'

I paused, glancing after Freddie, though he was no longer in sight. 'He just needs some time to himself. Today is hard for him.'

'Why? Not like he was the one cut up,' he muttered under his breath.

At my expression, he flushed, dark skin reddening in shame. 'Sorry,' he said. 'I didn't mean that. I get it. Today bugs me too.'

'Yes, well,' I said. 'We only have one class left anyway.'

Tim scowled.

'So why can he leave and I can't? We could've gone with him.'

'Oh…go then,' I said, slumping down onto the bench. 'Get expelled. See if I care.'

'Alright, alright, calm down. Gees, one angry twin is enough. If you both get mad I'll have to be the sensible one, and we all know how that ends.'

Despite myself, I smiled. I took a deep breath, resisted the urge to rub the ache in my chest, and blew all the air out of my lungs in one big huff.

'If it makes you feel better,' I said. 'I'm pretty sure you've got a few admirers in class. One of them is a boy.'

Tim perked up instantly.

'Interesting,' he said, a wicked grin forming. 'Who?'

Affecting an air of mystery I said, 'Guess you'll just have to find out.'

CHAPTER SEVEN

Zach

The lumpy mattress was perhaps the worst thing Zach had ever slept on. The sagging pillow and the scratchy woollen blanket (kicked off almost instantly) weren't much better. He twisted and turned, trying to find a semi comfortable position before ending up curled and half hanging off the side of the bed as he scrolled through Facebook on his phone.

Every other news page was filled with stories of people dropping dead, scattered through with the occasional post about the space ship. Zach paused on a few pictures—some of them had clearly been photoshopped to make the ship seem bigger and more outrageous than it actually was. Others showed the real ship, some blurry, some fuzzy, one with the faint blurry image of Zach's new companion diving off the edge of the bridge. Zach stared at it for a long time before scrolling past and focusing more on the spreading sickness.

Some news agencies, Zach suspected those influenced by the government, were trying to tone down the severity of the virus. That hadn't stopped others from throwing around words like "epidemic" and "catastrophe". Zach reached for his zippo lying within easy reach on the old, decrepit bedside table. He'd gone to the stingiest, most run-down motel he could find. The kind that take cash and don't ask any questions.

They were still headed north and even though it was only late afternoon, Zach was tired—still recovering from his party the night before—and his alien companion hadn't looked much better. Apparently travelling across galaxies was rather exhausting, as she'd drifted off to sleep several times in the last two hours.

So, amongst the pouring rain, Zach had pulled off the road and gotten the two of them a room for the night. He didn't plan on staying, but a hotel offered more sanctuary than anywhere else they'd passed. At least they could lock the door.

He offered the alien the bed, but she'd wandered into the bathroom and hadn't come out. When Zach went to check on her, he'd found her curled up inside bath tub, covered by lukewarm water.

He'd panicked for a moment and had staggered forward, almost reaching into the water to pull her out, before his mind had jumped back to their conversation in the car.

Amphibious. She could breathe underwater. Amused, but tired, he'd left her in her strange sleeping position and stumbled back out to flop onto the bed and surf the net.

Zach flicked his lighter open and watched the flame sway, orange light dancing over his hand and the off-white sheets. Smoke drifted up from the now lit joint he held. He rolled onto his back, dropping the phone onto the mattress and staring at the ceiling, inhaling deeply on the joint. He closed his eyes, willing himself to relax, to let the high wash away the stress, the anxiety, the restless thoughts about what an epidemic could mean.

Instead his mind drifted to the why of his current situation. To the impulses that had urged him to the alien girl and help her. Abandoning his parents comfortable, luxurious house with its big fences and large private-property signs. Not to mention his computers.

When the headache had erupted at the museum, all thoughts other than getting to the girl had evaporated. Nothing else had mattered. Running towards danger was very un-Zach like and the idea that something else, some external force, could push him toward a dangerous path disturbed him.

Zach sipped at his joint, allowing his thoughts to drift between the events. He watched himself stagger back from the window and bring his hands to his head. Saw the sheen of sweat on his skin as he whirled about and ran from the building. He watched his own memories, studying himself like he was as alien as the girl he'd stumbled upon—or was lead to?

Telepathy. That was what he had thought of when he had stepped away from her, startled and surprised by the pressure on his mind, so clearly external, so foreign. What if he was right? What if it was telepathy and he was being controlled?

Yet she was asleep now, and he was awake. If he wanted to, he could leave. Abandon her in this dodgy little hide-away while he escaped back to his cushy life in the security of his parents' home. Plague or not, he would survive there.

Would he survive with her?

Oddly, the thought that he wouldn't didn't bother him as much as it should. Of course he was afraid, terrified even, of catching the plague. Of becoming nothing. Fading into oblivion without any contribution left behind that he'd been there, that he'd existed. Yet being with an alien? That was an adventure he wasn't sure he could miss.

How much could he learn from her? What fathomless things did she have hidden in that brain of hers that he could discover? It was tantalising.

For a brief, frightening moment Zach wondered if that feeling was his own. Was he being influenced into thinking this would be exciting? Was someone else playing with his mind, knowing the way he thought and providing the right motives to encourage him to help the girl?

He wasn't sure.

It was the fear that convinced him his thoughts were his own. The tightening in his chest. The dizziness that swept over him as his breath shortened. The sudden urge to throw up that swept over him like a rough ocean wave. His mind went blank and he curled up on his side, gasping for air as the panic overtook him. Don't throw up. Don't throw up. Just breathe.

His hands clenched in the sheets and the smell of burning blazed in his nose.

His eyes shot open. Burning?

The sharp sudden tang snapped his mind back into focus. The nausea dissipated and clarity rushed in.

'Fuck,' he gasped, springing up and stamping one foot down on the smouldering cigarette. 'Ouch!' He yanked his foot up from the hot embers, hopping about on one foot as the underside of his heel began to sting.

The cigarette was out and Zach scooped up the remains and dropped it in the bin, not wanting another fire to ignite.

Bleary eyed, he glanced toward the bathroom door, but there was no movement beyond. Clearly his little incident hadn't woken the girl. He wondered at the sense of sleeping underwater, where you couldn't hear your enemies approaching—or, for that matter, a fire burning.

He snorted. Not that it would matter if the fire had started. She'd have been safe, tucked under the water as she was.

Zach flopped back down on the mattress, falling backwards and bouncing slightly. The springs groaned and shrieked and Zach ignored them. His feet hung over the edge of the bed yet he didn't move. He was oddly comfortable.

The high was settling in and Zach closed his eyes, floating away on thoughts of telepathy and purple aliens and genies with golden lamps of wishes.

When he opened his eyes, Zach thought it had all been a very vivid, very elaborate dream. He shifted around in bed, eyes adjusting to the half-light and reached for his phone. As he did, the mattress moved under him and he frowned. This wasn't his bed.

The thought sparked through his mind. He sat up, staring at the old, faded brown wallpaper.

'Shit …' he said.

He'd gotten high and managed to play out some crazy

hallucination, ending up in some seedy hotel in the middle of nowhere.

He stumbled out of bed, rubbing sleep from his eyes and dusting ash from his clothes. Just to be sure it really was some crazy hallucination, Zach leaned against the bathroom door and knocked. He rubbed a thumb and finger along the bridge of his nose, feeling almost hungover. When did he eat last?

Someone shifted around on the other side of the door, and Zach almost toppled sideways when it was opened. He staggered, regained his balance, and came face to face with a purple alien girl.

He blinked. She blinked back. He gaped. Her ears turned mauve.

She tilted her head enquiringly, eyes flickering to the floor.

'Uhh, sorry,' said Zach. 'You … uh, are you ready to go?'

She nodded. Zach nodded too.

'Right,' he said. 'Okay.'

He stumbled around the room, collecting the few items he'd brought in with them—keys, lighter, a pack of weed and rollers—and headed for the door.

Back in the car the surreal feeling began to fade and the curious anxiety returned. The alien girl curled up in the corner of the passenger seat, ears tucked over her shoulders, and began pointing him in the right direction.

Zach wondered how she knew where to go. His mind went back to his earlier speculations about telepathy. Was she being directed there by someone else? Or could she pin point this Genie girl's mind somehow, and find her like some tracking device out of a video game.

The storm had drifted on during their three-hour nap and the sun was back out in full force. Still, gooseflesh prickled his arms, and a nervous chill had Zach reaching for the heater.

'So,' he said, trying to break the awkward silence. 'Nice ship?'

Her gaze jerked over to him, and this time her whole face turned a darker shade. She nodded quickly, and focused her gaze back out the window.

Zach raised his eyebrows at her. 'Not a nice ship?'

'It…it is o-okay,' she stuttered, flushing so dark Zach thought she might overheat.

He wondered why she seemed so embarrassed and tried to picture the ship again.

'Oh,' he said, as the image of the ship in a tangle of wires and metal came back to him. 'I didn't mean anything about the crash. I was just making conversation. Sorry. Did it malfunction?'

If possible, her face became even more flushed. She shook her head.

'You crashed?'

'I have n-never p-p-p- driven before.'

Zach frowned, glancing back and forth between her and the road. 'You mean, on your own, right?'

She shook her head. 'Ever.'

'You've at least been in one, right?'

She shook her head again.

'Seriously? You mean you flew that thing all the way here without knowing how to even control it?'

She hunched down, and static returned to the air. Zach couldn't help a little grin at her embarrassment, but bit down on it before she saw.

'Well…you made it. That's what counts, right?'

She ducked her head, and Zach turned his attention back to the road. After a moment, while Zach was flicking through the radio stations again, she said,

'It was on auto-auto p-p-pilot.'

Zach snorted. 'Sorry,' he said, biting the inside of his mouth to keep the grin off his face. 'But why'd you come if you didn't know how to drive?'

'He n-needs my help.'

'Who?'

She shook her head. Zach waited but no more information was forthcoming, so he gave up and switched the radio back on.

They drove for four hours. The longer it took the stronger the tight, jittery feeling creeping its way up Zach's legs got. His knee jerked in a relentless motion. He drummed his fingers along the wheel with more intensity, glancing over at the alien every few seconds as she finally directed him off the highway.

He slowed the car to a crawl as she gestured to a turn off onto a narrow dirt road. Zach resisted the urge to light up, instead concentrating on keeping his parents pristine car bumping steadily along the poor excuse of a road.

As he turned up the indicated driveway—still dirt—Zach wondered what would happen to him. Would the alien girl keep him around now she'd found her human?

His stomach knotted, but as he slowed to a stop outside the brown brick house he realised that although it was fear, it wasn't a fear of being disposed of, but a fear of being abandoned. It surprised him to realise he wanted to stay with her.

He glanced over at the girl, who was looking at him with those big silver eyes, a tinge of dark purple colouring the tips of her ears.

'Ready?' he asked.

She nodded.

'Right,' he said. 'Well, here goes.'

Zach pushed his door open and swung out.

CHAPTER EIGHT

Genie

Tim's interest in Ian's crush on him vanished within the first ten minutes of class. He, like everyone else, was too preoccupied with the dwindling numbers of students. Three people had already left sick, and Josie hadn't stopped coughing since we started.

Tim huffed as he slouched over his desk, finally bored with tormenting poor Ian. Sweat beaded on the back of his neck and despite the clouds still hanging outside his face was blotchy with heat. I imagined my face wasn't any better, only my red splotches would be even more pronounced against my fair skin.

'Portable classroom my arse,' Tim muttered. 'More like a tin hotbox.'

Mrs Parker glowered, but said nothing. He was right.

Tim started scrolling through his phone, ignoring Mrs Parker, Amy's none-too-discrete stares, and Ian's shy glances. 'Gees, this bug is everywhere.'

I glanced over at him, trying to pay attention to the lesson, but unable to help my curiosity.

'I've got a mate in Yeppoon who says it's the same at his school,' he said, leaning over to show me his phone. 'No one's there. Everyone's either stayed home or left sick. And Jonathan—my buddy up at St Brendan's—says they've put the whole school in lockdown.'

'Lockdown?' I asked, looking down at his screen. 'Someone broke in?'

'Timothy!' Mrs Parker barked.

Tim didn't pay her any mind. 'No,' he said, his voice even and low. 'They tried to break out. He says they aren't letting any of them leave.'

'The teachers aren't?'

In the background I heard Mrs Parker again, but I was too focused on Tim to pay her any mind.

Tim shook his head slowly.

'They were sent back to their dorms and told to stay there. Even the kids who don't board.'

'What? Why?'

'Timothy, Genevieve!' Mrs Parker yelled.

'Jonathan heard someone talking, and they're saying they don't want it to spread. He says one of his teachers tried to leave and they locked him in a classroom.'

'Don't be stupid,' I said. 'He's pulling your leg.'

'I dunno,' Tim said. 'I thought so too, but it's all over Facebook. Schools in lockdown or closing altogether. Students not being let out, they're all posting it from their accounts. Videos and photos and even hashtags! They're sharing things from Europe.'

'But-'

A ruler slapped down in front of me. Mrs Parker leaned over my table, coming within an inch of my face. Her eyes were wide and her nostrils flared as she spoke.

'I said enough!' she said, her voice a low snarl.

I went still, feeling like I was staring into the face of a bear or some other predator. One that was wounded and scared and ready to start fighting tooth and nail at the slightest provocation.

When I was five, I'd seen my grandfather try to help an injured dingo. It had gotten caught up in some chicken wire and had scratches all along its hide. Every time my grandfather tried to get close, the dingo snarled and barked and tried to hurt him. Even when Grandad offered it food it tried to bite. I remembered how bright its eyes looked. Despite the calm, even tones of Grandad's voice, despite his offering of food, the wounded creature was terrified. It couldn't help lashing out.

That was what I saw as I looked at my English teacher. The hand that held the ruler trembled and her pupils were wide and dark. I swallowed hard, glancing back at Tim to see if he could see it too.

Josie, sitting two seats away from me, chose that opportune moment to erupt into a fit of coughing. It was enough to catch Mrs Parker's attention, and Tim and I were saved from a mauling.

Ignoring Josie, I turned to Tim. 'How do you have reception? I've been trying to text BK, but nothing's going through.'

'It's slow, but it's working. What's wrong with BK?'

'She wanted me to come home.'

Tim's already dark eyes became almost black. He frowned at me, his gaze flickering down to my phone. BK was known for being weird and odd, but when she suggested something, you listened.

I bit my lip. Josie's coughing became harsh and loud, interrupting our speculations. Tim and I, like everyone else, turned to stare.

I watched the scene unfold with a strange sort of detached dread. Almost like my favourite movie on fast forward, I could predict what was going to happen, but couldn't do anything to stop it. Couldn't will my body into action.

'Josie, go to the sickbay,' Mrs Parker snapped in that same snarl of fear.

Josie shook her head, covering her mouth with her handkerchief.

'I'm so sorry,' she wheezed once her coughing had subsided. 'It'll pass, I promise.'

Tim snorted and Michelle—Josie's best friend—glared at him.

'Don't think I don't know what you're thinking!' she said, standing up and glaring at Tim accusingly. 'There's no need to make things worse by spreading rumours.'

'I didn't say anything,' Tim said. He leaned back in his chair.

Michelle rolled her eyes. Once, the two of them had

gone steady. Then Michelle had caught Tim with someone else and that was the end of that. She had known Tim's reputation for being a flirt, but I don't think she'd expected to find him making out with her brother.

Josie bent her head over the worksheet and attempted to muffle the soft coughs that escaped every few seconds. Her breath came out in rasping wheezes. Michelle stopped glaring at Tim and attended to her friend. I was more interested in Mrs Parker's reaction. At the tension in her shoulders and the way she watched Josie, clutching the ruler close to her with both hands. As if it could provide her with some sort of meagre protection against whatever Josie had.

When Josie began coughing again, she didn't stop. They came in big rasping lungful's that shook the tiny girl's entire frame.

Josie stood, one hand covering her mouth as she practically choked on her own breath, and the other bracing herself on the table. Michelle was grasping at her.

'Josie? Josie are you okay?'

Josie shook her head and pulled away. She tripped on the chair and went down, crashing hard into the desk, then tumbling to the ground in a heap as she began coughing up blood. Mrs Parker backed up, still staring at Josie with that terrified expression.

I swallowed, unsure whether to help or to get as far away from the girl as humanly possible. I liked Josie. She was nice in a quiet, unassuming way. She'd never once bullied me, not like the other girls had.

But … but what if it was true? What if there was plague?

Tim grabbed my arm. I jumped, looking up to find him already standing over me. He pulled me to my feet, not saying a word, and yanked me to the far side of the room. No one noticed. The others were transfixed by Michelle and Josie. Mrs Parker looked about to faint.

'Miss! Miss she needs help!' Michelle said, looking around to try and find our teacher.

'She's bleeding,' someone said in a faint voice.

'What's happening?' Michelle asked, still hanging onto

Josie's arm. 'She looks like she's having a seizure. Someone do something!'

The room was loud and hot and chaotic for several moments longer—despite there being so few of us—before everything went still.

Josie had stopped coughing.

'Josie?' Michelle asked, her voice small. 'Josie, are you okay?'

Michelle touched Josie's shoulder, and the small girl tipped over, rolling from her shoulder to her back. Blood seeped from her ears and her mouth, her eyes open and glazed.

'Oh my God,' someone gasped. 'She's dead!'

CHAPTER NINE

Zach

Zach was in the company of aliens and instead of unlocking answers to the universe, he was knocking on the door of some stranger's house—after seven hours of driving complete with a stop over in the seediest hotel Zach had ever stepped foot in—and no one was home.

He scowled and continued to bash on the door. He pulled his lighter and cigarette packet out. The half-smoked joint was still inside. He fetched it out, stuck it between his teeth, and lit up. After several minutes without an answer, Zach decided snooping was in order.

'Come on,' he said, glancing back at the alien girl. 'Let's see if anyone is around the back.'

He headed around the outside of the house, feet crunching in the thick, sun-burned grass as he took another drag on the joint. The yard was nice and wide, rimmed by a garden bed of native flowers. Beyond them, the yard dipped away into tall, sparse trees overlooking the hill below. Zach caught sight of a second road just below the yard—a paddock road, no doubt—and wondered how big the property was as he blew smoke out into the air.

Around the side of the house was a patio with a sliding door that was wide open. Chickens clucked raucously in the yard, paying no mind to Zach and his alien companion.

'Hello?' Zach called, approaching the open back door. 'Anyone home?'

He couldn't imagine anyone leaving their house with the doors and windows open—let alone chickens roaming freely about the yard. Then again, it was the country. What did he know about how things worked out here?

He sighed and contemplated slouching into one of the chairs by the outside dining set. He took two steps towards them, but his alien friend had other plans.

She was by the side door, peering in curiously at the house beyond.

'I'm not sure anyone is here,' said Zach.

She glanced back, before heading inside. Zach deliberated following her. He took a pull, exhaled smoke, and stubbed it out on the table. He winced as a faint smear of ash burned into the old wooden table-top. He brushed at it, shrugged, and followed the girl inside.

The sliding door opened in on a sunroom of sorts. There was a kitchen to the left and a hallway to the right.

'Oh brilliant,' said Zach, darting in to the other side of the room.

A large old juke box sat in one corner. On the other side was a piano forte. Music lovers, apparently. Zach trailed his fingers across the keys, eliciting a startled noise of surprise from the alien girl, before he drifted over to the juke-box. It was huge and ancient-looking. Rectangular, with several options.

To his delight, the machine was lit up, and Zach fiddled with the dials before he managed to select a song.

Tinny music poured out as the faded sound of guitars began. Zach grinned, bobbing his head to the tune. A deep baritone voice echoed out, singing along to the classic tune of jagged guitar.

He glanced back at the girl, lips quirked into a grin. Her ears were perked, pulled slightly away from her back as she cocked her head to one side. The ends twitched as she listened, her gaze riveted on the large old machine.

'You don't have anything like this?' Zach guessed, raising his voice above the music.

She shook her head slowly, still fixated on the machine. Zach grinned.

'C'mon, let's see what else these people got. I like them already.'

He headed down the hallway, bypassing the narrow stairs leading up to a door above. He passed a fish tank, a laundry, and several cupboards before he opened a door onto an actual room.

This was clearly a boys room. There was a double bed pushed into the corner with blue sheets. A bookcase stood opposite the bed, filled not with books but medals. There were kickboxing medals, martial arts, Tai Kwon Do, soccer, football and even archery trophies.

Along with the trophies, were a series of awards.

Zach frowned as he studied one closer. No, not awards. Warnings. Slips of paper warning of disqualifications, suspensions and banning from various sports and activities. Zach raised his eyebrows. This guy had almost as many warnings as trophies.

He shook his head and put back the bundle of detention slips he'd been looking at.

His alien friend had followed him in and was staring at the pictures on the wall. There was a corkboard by the door with a bunch of photo's pinned up. She reached out and touched one. Zach stepped over to look.

Two siblings, a boy and a girl, sat grinning out of the photo. The boy had his arm around the girl's shoulder and was laughing. They both had hair as dark as ravens. The boy's was cut short, yet still stuck up every which way from his head as if he'd tossed and turned all night and never bothered to brush it when he got up in the morning. Her's was in two neat braids on either side of her head, trailing down in front of her shoulders.

There was something familiar about their faces. Zach stared at them, watching as the alien girl brushed a finger down the boy's face.

'Is this the one you're looking for?' Zach asked, still staring at their faces.

They were narrow, with sharp cheek bones, soft noses and bright eyes. Grey eyes. Like storm clouds, and yet without that darkness the often accompanied storms.

Zach frowned and looked over at the alien girl. She caught him staring and her ears went dark purple as she dropped her silvery gaze.

Zach started to ask her a new question, but voices from beyond the room cut him off.

'-sure you didn't leave it on?' came a young soft spoken male voice.

'No,' came an answer, a female voice, light and feathery. 'I'm not allowed to use it when no one is home.'

The music cut off. Next to him, the alien was tense, her entire frame riveted to one spot as she stared toward the open door of the room they were snooping in.

'I'm sure I didn't turn it on.'

'Maybe the twins did, before they left this morning?'

'No,' said the female voice, and Zach could almost hear her pouting. 'They were both running late. I guess it had to have been me. But I'm positive I turned everything off before I left.'

'You were in a hurry. Or, it could've been the cat. She's done it before, hasn't she?'

'I guess so.'

'Right, so don't worry about it, okay?'

'Alright then. Are you hungry? I made muffins yesterday.'

'Mm, what kind?'

'Poppy seed. They're Genie's favourite. I think she's feeling a bit down today.'

Zach perked up at the name of the girl they'd come looking for. He took a step toward the door, keeping his ear angled toward the sound of the voices.

'Yeah?'

'Today is when Einstein visited,' said the girl. 'It's been six years. And the year before that was when James hurt her.'

'Do you…don't you think it's weird how that happened on the same day?'

'Why would it be?'

Zach blinked, bemused by the conversation.

'Einstein?' he whispered, casting a sideways glance at the alien girl. 'Your human was visited by a dead scientist?'

She was staring at the doorway with big silver eyes, her mouth slightly agape. Zach smirked.

'I should have remembered what today was. Of course she's upset.'

'It's okay,' said the girl. 'I have a plan. How are you feeling today?'

'Hm? Fine. Why wouldn't I be?'

'I heard about your mum getting sick. Is she okay?'

The boy's voice became low and subdued. 'She's in the hospital, so I'm not really sure.'

Zach tilted his head, pressing closer to the doorway as fragments of news articles flashed into his mind. If his mother was sick…would he be a threat? Zach cast another sidelong look at the alien girl next to him but she was riveted to the spot, her attention fixated on the door. Her eyes were distant, yet her pupils were pinpoints. She had her head cocked to one side as if to hear better, but Zach couldn't help but wonder…Was she listening, or was she communicating?

The conversation down the hall started up again, distracting Zach.

'Are you going to go see her?'

'I…I'm not sure,' said the male. 'We had another fight. I wasn't even there when she was picked up. I'm not sure she'd want to see me, anyway.'

Zach relaxed. From what he'd seen, this outbreak spread faster than any other sickness Zach had read about. If the boy hadn't been in contact with his mother before she had gotten sick, then he was likely to be uninfected. So far.

'Does she know?' the girl continued. 'About you and Tim?'

A splutter erupted followed by loud, harsh coughing, like the boy was choking on something.

'Oh. Sorry! I didn't mean to surprise you. I just mean, not that you're together but just…I'm sorry.'

'It's alright,' said the boy, his voice hoarse. 'No. She doesn't know that I…about how I feel. I, uh I'm just gonna check Freddie's room for those xbox games.'

'Okay. Do you want another glass of water?'

'Nah,' said the boy, his voice suddenly much closer. 'I'm alright now.'

Zach took a hasty step back from the door, reaching out to pull the alien girl back with him.

'Thanks for letting me come by the way,' said the boy stepping into the room but looking over his shoulder. 'It was just so quiet at…'

Blue eyes turned back to the room as he spoke. At the sight of Zach and his non-human companion the boy's (man's) jaw dropped open, bright blue eyes going wide as his words trailed into stunned nothingness.

'Greetings,' said Zach, and winced. 'Er, sorry. We're um, we're looking for Genie.'

CHAPTER TEN

Genie

'Genie,' said Tim, tugging on my arm.

Michelle was in tears, shaking Josie's prone form. I took a step toward her, reaching out, but Tim's grip tightened.

'Genie, let's go,' he said.

'But—'

He didn't look back, didn't spare the dead girl he'd known for seven years a second glance. He hauled me from the classroom. I turned back once, looking at the pale and frightened faces of people I'd gone to school with as long as I could remember. My throat tightened and I took a deep, shuddering breath. A brief flash of realisation hit me so hard, if it wasn't for Tim holding my arm I was sure I'd have fallen.

I would never see any of them, ever again.

My foot hit a knoll and I almost fell. The two of us stumbled down the grassy hill, Tim just barely keeping the both of us upright.

Someone fled the room after us, and Tim pulled me sideways, well out of reach as they scrambled down the hill and toward the safety of the main school building, running far too fast.

Tim still had that wide-eyed look on his face, but he was focused. He had set his sights and begun to hunt. I let him pull me even though his grip was starting to hurt my arm. The pain was good. It was something to focus on other than what I'd just seen. Josie's wide, blank stare. Glassy blue eyes. The trickle of blood at the corner of her mouth.

I squeezed my eyes shut a moment. A babble of voices caught my attention and my eyes flew open. Tim slowed to a stop at the edge of a hallway leading back into the classroom block. He ducked his head around the corner to look.

Tim had always reminded me of a wild animal, something primal and instinctual, always moving, always prowling for something to play with. He had a predatory grace and he reverted back to it now, relying on it to move us through the school.

He glanced back at me, eyes still wide and black. He gestured with his head at the corridor across from us and I nodded. Quietly, the two of us slipped into the hallway and headed in the opposite direction of the voices echoing down from one of the classrooms.

People were shouting, and somewhere I thought I heard Michelle. For a moment I thought she was following us. Then I realised. It wasn't Michelle. Someone else was sobbing hysterically, calling out a different name, from a different classroom. Tight fear coiled in my stomach like a snake.

'Do you think,' I gasped, trying to make my short legs keep up with Tim's long ones. 'Do you think Freddie got out okay?'

Tim finally let go of my arm and I walked next to him, grateful he matched his steps to mine. He glanced sideways at me.

'I reckon he did,' he said.

His voice was low, with no hint of comfort or consoling. Relief worked itself into my chest.

He stopped and turned to face me. 'Freddie's alright, okay?' he said, and I nodded. 'But we're not. Don't worry about Freddie or anyone else except you, got it?'

'Okay. But we'll get out of here, right?'

His jaw clenched. 'Yeah. I'm gonna—'

A door creaked to my left and half a second later something heavy slammed into my chest. I fell, breathless and my head smacked into concrete. Bells erupted in my ears and stars exploded before my eyes. Somehow I was aware of the danger.

'*Kick!*'

I lashed out, striking at whoever—or whatever—was on top of me.

Then the weight was gone.

'Ricky, Ricky!' Tim was shouting. 'It's me, Ricky, wait, stop-oof!'

Tim went sprawling on the ground next to me. I blinked, trying to turn the blurry figures into actual clear images of people. Ricky loomed above me. All burly six-foot of him. I gulped, staring at the wildness in his face and the…what was that? His veins? What the hell was wrong with his veins?

All around his face were dark, inky lines, standing out unnaturally under his skin.

'Make it stop,' he groaned, pulling at his hair and staring at me with wild, yellowish eyes.

He took a step toward me and I scrambled back.

'Make it stop,' he said again.

'What?'

'It hurts…'

'What hurts?' I asked, still moving backwards.

I tried to get up, but Ricky's entire frame tensed and then he dove at me. I rolled away. He slammed into the ground, his shoulder giving way to an awful pop. It didn't stop him. He was scrambling back to his feet, turning to face me in the same movement.

'STOP!'

He screamed the word in an anguished howl. His eyes bulged in his head and his ears and nose were bleeding.

Tim appeared behind him and he kicked at the back of Ricky's leg. Ricky's knee buckled and he went down, still yowling.

'What the fuck man?' Tim shouted. 'What the hell is wrong with you?'

'I think,' I said, panting as I clambered to my feet and edged away from Ricky. 'He's sick.'

'No shit, do you see-,'

The spray of blood appeared over Tim's face before I heard the sound. The deafening crack of a gun being fired.

I jumped, gaping as Ricky tumbled to the ground, all fury vanishing as the back of his head exploded outwards in a shower of blood and goop. Tim and I stood facing each other on either side of him. My chest rose and fell in short, sharp bursts. My lungs felt tight, my throat more so and I my mind began to drift away from my body, not registering what I was seeing.

Before I could scream or cry or throw up, two men appeared around Tim and me. At least I think they were men. It was hard to tell under all that protective, hazard suit gear they were wearing. Hard to see past the black objects in their hands. Objects I recognised, but couldn't comprehend seeing here at school.

They were each holding a gun pointed straight at our heads.

CHAPTER ELEVEN

Zach

They were at a standstill. The boy—or young man, rather, as he looked about Zach's age, if not older—stared at the two of them, and they stared back.

He took a half step backwards, the top half of his body leaning out into the hallway even as his bright blue eyes stayed glued to them.

'Hey, BK,' he called, his voice hitching. 'You, uh, you should come here.'

'What's wrong?'

'I really don't know how to explain.'

The pitter patter of bare feet on tiles echoed down the hall and Zach glanced nervously at the alien next to him.

A girl stepped into the room next to the young man, looking up at him in worry as she asked,

'What is it?'

He pointed.

Her gaze shifted, travelling in light concern from his face to where Zach and the alien stood. Her eyes were green. Mingled and mossy and bright like grass or a garden or even a rainforest. As if all the world's nature had gathered there in her eyes. Zach was transfixed.

'Oh,' she said, blinking in surprise. 'Hello. I didn't know we had guests.'

Zach almost fell over, not expecting the calm, completely unfazed reaction to finding a stranger—and an alien no less—in her house. The boy next to her groaned.

'Guests?' he asked, his voice still a little too high.

'Why didn't you tell me we had visitors.'

'*Visitors*? BK, they *broke in*—you know, that's not the point. Don't you see that, the um, the…uh…'

'Oh, yes,' said the girl—BK, presumably—shaking her head at herself. 'How silly of me. Do you speak English?' she asked the alien, peering at her intently from the doorway.

Zach blinked, completely nonplussed. BK turned her evergreen eyes on him, raising an eyebrow in question.

'Er,' he said.

'What's her name?' asked BK.

She trotted across the room, and Zach was stunned by her simple grace. She was small and slight, like a child, and yet she was by no means a girl. Her body had all the shapes and curves of womanhood. Her skin was as soft and pale as a porcelain doll. Not the creepy kind his grandmother used to show him every time he was forced to visit, but a beautiful replica of an exotic model.

Her thick, blonde curls were such a tangled mess that Zach wouldn't have been surprised to see a bird take flight from within, and yet they hung with a wild sort of elegance. A thick red band sat around the crown of her head, keeping the curls at bay and stopping them from falling into her wide, unnaturally green eyes.

Zach's stomach did a little flip flop. Despite the grass stained overalls, and the smear of dirt on her cheek, she was gorgeous.

'She does have a name, doesn't she?' she asked.

'Er,' said Zach again, still stunned. He shook himself, dragging his gaze away from her to fix on the boy. That seemed the safer option.

'Well,' said BK, 'What have you been calling her?'

Zach's gaze darted to her, and then flicked away again.

'Einstein?' the boy asked. His voice was still too high, and he coughed, flushing as he tried to bring his voice back to a normal octave. He glanced at BK. 'Right?'

BK laughed, a high, tinkling sound. Like scooping your hand through a bowl of crystal gems.

'No, silly. Einstein was a boy. Or a man, I guess. She's not a man, are you?'

The alien girl, who had been inching further and further behind Zach, froze, caught by the question.

'She's not so fond of speaking,' explained Zach, finally finding his tongue. 'I haven't really been calling her anything. We, uh, we were in a hurry and I guess I never asked. Who's Einstein?'

The boy frowned at Zach.

'You've been travelling with her and you don't know her name?'

Apparently, he had gotten over his shock. Zach flushed, but tried to keep his expression neutral.

'Like I said, we were in a hurry.'

'Hm,' said the boy. He glanced over at BK and then to the alien girl. 'Genie says we can't pronounce your names in our language, right?'

Zach blinked in surprise, and turned to the alien girl. He had thought by their reactions (the boy's, at least) that they'd never seen an alien, and yet, they seemed to have some knowledge of his new companion. Knowledge he didn't have. He frowned, wondering what else she wasn't telling him.

Her silver eyed gaze shifted to him, and then back to the boy and BK. She nodded, a short, jerky motion.

The boy, seeming to sense her discomfort, grabbed hold of BK's hand and pulled her over to the bed. He sat, leaning back on the bed as he gave the alien a reassuring smile. At once making himself smaller and more relaxed—or more importantly, less threatening. Smart, Zach thought. Perceptive.

BK flounced down beside him, tucking her legs up underneath her as the two of them made themselves comfortable.

'Well, my name is Ant,' said the boy. 'This is BK. She lives here. What should we call you?'

'Ant?' asked Zach, raising his eyebrows.

'It's a nickname,' said BK, happy to explain. 'His full name is Anthony, but he doesn't like it much.'

'Oh.'

'So, what do we call you?' BK asked, turning her attention back to the alien girl. 'Are there any names that you like? How about…how about Stevie?'

A slow grin worked it's way onto Ant's face. 'Stevie?'

'Yeah, she looks like a Stevie, don't you think?'

Ant chuckled. 'I guess,' he agreed, blue eyes softening from confusion and nervousness to fondness.

'Stevie's not really a girl's name,' Zach pointed out.

'It can be,' said BK, her face turning into a pout. 'Besides, all that matters is that she likes it. Do you?'

Once again, the girl froze, looking less like the deer in the headlights and more like Dr Grant in front of the T-Rex. Zach tried not to grin. He wondered if that's what humans seemed like to her? Big, blundering, unintelligent creatures that had no consideration for anything around them. After all, *he* hadn't even bothered to ask her what her name was.

'Stev-Stevie?' the girl asked, trying out the name for herself.

Zach felt for the lighter in his pocket, shifting his weight from one foot to the other as they waited for the alien girl to accept or reject the name. Why hadn't *he* thought of giving her a name? At the very least he could've given her something a bit more dignified than *Stevie*. Although, (and he began to grin) BK was right, it did suit her. Stuttering Stevie. He turned his head away, trying to hide the grin, squashing down the laughter that threatened to escape.

'You like it?' BK asked.

The alien considered, tilting her head to the side, her silver eyed gaze flickering to Zach and then away again. Finally, with a twitch of her ears, she gave BK a small, shy nod.

'Great!' BK said, clapping her hands together. 'So, Stevie, what brings you to our house?'

CHAPTER TWELVE

Genie

Guns…why did they have *guns*? More importantly, why the hell were they pointed at *us*. Why had they…they *shot* Ricky. Ricky was dead. Ricky was dead, Josie was dead…how many people were going to die in front of me today?

'What the *fuck*?' Tim exploded.

I jumped but wasn't able to tear my gaze away from the guns. Or the suits. Or the *blood*.

'Stay where you are,' one of the faceless suits said.

The voice was muffled and indistinct.

'The hell I will!' Tim shouted. 'You shot him? You just…you killed him? What the fuck is wrong with you?'

'You need to calm down and stay where you are,' the voice repeated.

'Fuck you!' Tim snarled. 'You just…' Tim ran out of words. The fight was lost amongst his confusion and rage. The fact that they were still pointing their guns at us seemed to be keeping the worst of his temper at bay.

'If you stay calm, you may join the others, and then you'll be transported to safe facility,' said the second suit—this one sounded slightly feminine.

'Liar.'

The word rose up from my subconscious. My inner conscience, who sounded just like how I always imagined Freddie would.

I swallowed. It was hard to spot the signs of a liar when they were covered in mesh and plastic.

'Why are you dressed like that?' I asked.

Tim glanced sideways at me. He narrowed his eyes when they didn't answer.

'You deaf?' he barked. 'She asked you a question.'

'It's not your concern.'

'It is if we're at risk.'

The two suits glanced at each other, exchanging looks. In the quiet corridor their breathing, coming in short rasps through the hazmat suits, was loud and echoing. Like Darth Vada preparing to eliminate a rebel with the power of the force, these men were preparing to kill us. We were just teenagers though, what had we done wrong?

'It's not that simple,' said the feminine-sounding suit. 'You've already been exposed.'

'So what're you saying?' Tim asked, his fists clenched and shaking. 'You reckon we're gonna get sick too? Like Ricky?'

'Once exposed, infection is inevitable.'

'If you think we're sick already,' I asked slowly. 'Why take us to everyone else?'

More silence. My fists clenched. They *were* liars.

'You're going to kill us, too. Right?' I said, my voice low and flat.

'Not bloody likely,' Tim growled, preparing to launch at them.

The guns shifted, both of them focusing on Tim. Tim, who had been my friend for as long as I could remember. Who was like a second brother, a *real* second brother. Who had saved my life when I was ten years old. Who had tormented me and protected me in the same breath. Not a single time when I'd wanted to just sit down and cry and admit defeat had he ever let me give in.

He was my best friend and they wanted to shoot him?

Anger bubbled up from a dark place inside me. A place where I'd locked away all the hurt and pain and fury, keeping a tight hold on those emotions so they couldn't touch me. The anger escaped my hold.

They were too busy looking at Tim. He was the bigger threat. He was taller, stronger and more volatile. A grenade waiting to explode.

Who would focus on little old me over the blaze of fire that was Tim?

My muscles tensed. I felt every fighting lesson Freddie and Tim had ever tried to teach me flash through my muscles. I imagined Tim's fierceness and Freddie's fire. I tried to replicate it, tried to feel it boiling through my veins. To have it flooding through my very pores, as I'd seen it flood through Tim and Freddie whenever they prepared to fight.

A light fixture overhead exploded.

Glass and sparks reigned down on us all. The two suits jolted, guns waving upwards in alarm at the sparking light fixture that had just shattered. I launched in.

They were too busy looking up. By the time they caught sight of me, I was already on them. Tim shouted, half a step behind me even as I barrelled into the feminine sounding suit.

She shrieked as we went down. A gun went off near my ear but I didn't stop grappling with her. My heart banged a steady, painful rhythm in my chest. *Ba boom, ba boom, ba boom.* My vision narrowed into red. Red, red, red. *Survive.*

The instinct saturated me. I tore, I kicked, I clawed. I barely saw what I was doing, didn't feel the punches landing on me. Attack was my only goal. I yanked hard on plastic and tubes and something gave way. A sharp tearing sound broke through the air and suddenly I wasn't sitting on top of a suit, but a woman.

Wide, dilated hazel eyes stared up at me. Red dripped onto her cheek. Startled, I swiped at my face, and a smear of red came away on my palm.

I didn't feel any pain, and it took a moment for me to realise it wasn't my blood. It was Ricky's. Tim's face had been covered in the boy's blood and I'd been even closer than he was.

I looked down at the woman. She had frozen underneath me, her breathing coming in short gasps. Coldness crept into me. I dropped the useless mask next to her, letting it land with a soft thud next to her head. She began to pull her arm up, but I slapped her. The sharp sound echoed in the hall, above the struggle of Tim and the other suit.

'It's no use,' I said, keeping my voice low and mean. 'You've been exposed. Infection is inevitable.'

She froze, like a small rabbit looking up into the eyes of a hungry fox. It was strange. I'd been in this scenario before, but I'd always been the rabbit.

She shoved at me, bucking and twisting like a feral animal. She broke free, throwing me off. I tumbled sideways and got ready to fight her again. Instead, she brought the gun up and fired and I flinched away.

Red splattered the wall behind her. So much red. Why was this happening? Why did I have to keep seeing this?

'Genie!'

I looked up from the dead body of the woman in the hazmat suit. Tim was stuck under the second man.

'Run!' Tim gasped.

The man, who had Tim pinned at the shoulder blades, had his gun pointed at me.

'Run, Genie!'

I swallowed. If I ran, Tim would be dead. There was every chance this other man could shoot me in the back. Then we'd both be dead.

Tim struggled, his eyes wild and desperate. He could see I wasn't going to leave. Not without him. What kind of person would I be if I did after everything he'd done for me? After he'd saved my life?

How could I ever face myself if I left him to his fate.

I clenched my fists.

Above me, the light fixture fizzled and sparked, aftermaths of whatever had made it explode. Dangerous electricity arced out from the base of the destroyed light, distracting my enemy and granting me momentary safety.

I scrambled for the gun, prying it loose from the dead woman's hands, and raised it up.

Before I had time to think about my decision, before the man had a chance to aim his gun, I pulled the trigger.

CHAPTER THIRTEEN

Zach

BK poured iced-tea from a tall jug filled with fruits into four ceramic mugs. Ant drew one close, lifted it and sipped, eyes slipping shut with a sigh of relief.

Zach wrinkled his nose. He was less eager for his cup. When BK had offered tea, he'd thought she meant the hot kind. With milk and honey. Not this cold, fruity stuff.

Zach sniffed at the mug cautiously, and only sipped because BK was watching him expectantly. He swallowed, managed not to spit it all out, and gave her a strained smile. When she looked away he darted Stevie look of warning. She wasn't watching.

'This is really good,' said Ant, peering into the jug. 'What is it?'

'Ice tea,' said BK, smiling broadly as she trotted to the fridge to put the jug away. 'I can't say what flavour, it's a secret.'

Ant chuckled. 'I see. Well, I like it.'

'Really? Because Freddie said it tastes like dirt.'

Ant's low chuckle turned into a laugh of surprise.

'Of course he did,' said Ant. 'Freddie has no taste.'

Zach scrunched his nose, silently agreeing with this "Freddie". Tea was meant to be hot and bitter. None of this fruity business.

Stevie seemed to be enjoying hers, despite his look of warning. She kept swirling it around before she sipped. Her ears twitched incessantly, as though tingled by the taste of the drink. Zach grinned.

'So,' said Ant, placing the mug carefully on the table before him as he looked between Zach and Stevie. 'You're here for a reason, right?'

Stevie was engrossed in her mug, staring at it with big eyes as she licked her lips.

'Erm,' said Zach, tearing his gaze away from her. 'Yes. Well, I'm just a chauffeur. Stevie is looking for someone named Genie Hart.'

Ant and BK exchanged glances. BK sat down, folding her arms on the glass topped table, and gazed at Stevie as the alien took another sip of her tea. Ant focused on Zach.

'Did she say what she wants with Genie?'

'Like I said before, she's not exactly chatty,' said Zach. 'She struggles…a bit. With speaking I mean.'

'She doesn't understand?' asked Ant.

'No,' said Zach, tilting his head and glancing Stevie's way again. 'She understands well enough. I think she's just not comfortable talking. She stutters.'

Ant's eyebrows shot up, and he glanced over at the alien girl in surprise.

'Hm,' he said.

The boy was both taller and broader than Zach, yet he wasn't thick muscled. He somehow managed to make himself seem small. It was in his manner, in the mindfulness of his movements, always being sure to step out of the way or shift aside. Zach watched him shift his arms as BK spread out, not noticing when she spilled into his personal space. Ant said nothing, only smiled and shifted out of the way with a practiced ease.

He was maybe seventeen or eighteen. Eighteen, Zach decided, seeing as he wasn't in school. His bronze hair fell about his face, brown but slightly coppery. For a guy that could take Zach out in a single hit, he wasn't the least bit threatening. His entire manner put Zach at ease, and Zach found himself liking him.

Ant caught Zach staring and tilted his head. Blue eyes asked a question, but didn't glare in hostility or anger at

Zach's inappropriate study.

'Sorry,' said Zach, tilting his head. 'So, uh, where is this Genie? Not in a lamp I hope.'

Ant's smile twitched back into place. It was an understated smile, soft and lurking, nothing at all like BK's broad, blossoming smile, yet just as disarming.

'No,' said Ant (he, at least, appreciated Zach's joke). 'Not in a lamp. She's at school. They should be back soon.'

'They?'

'Her and Freddie and Tim.'

'Oh,' said Zach, and recalled the boy's room he and Stevie had hidden in, and the awkward conversation BK had initiated about Ant and "Tim". 'They live here?'

'Freddie does,' said Ant, watching as BK bounded up from the table and darted off somewhere. 'He and Genie are twins.'

Zach glanced over at Stevie, wondering if she knew this Genie character had a twin brother. She wasn't listening though, too engrossed in the flavours of her drink.

'That was his room earlier,' said Ant.

'Grey eyes?' Zach asked.

Ant cocked his head in curiosity, but nodded. 'Yeah. How'd you know?'

'There were pictures,' said Zach, recalling the photo of the siblings that Stevie had touched. 'So if you don't live here, what're you doing here?' He paused and added, 'sorry, didn't mean that to sound so rude.'

'S'alright,' he said. 'I live down the street. Sort of. Anyway, I only came by to pick up some games Freddie said I could borrow.'

'He rents the barn out from Tim's mum's so he can stay out here instead of living with his Mum,' said BK, flopping back into her seat with an armful of photos, knickknacks and other items. 'She's something called a Bible basher.'

Ant flushed, and cast BK an exasperated look.

'BK,' he trailed off with a sigh.

BK pulled out a stack of photos and handed them over to Stevie.

'These are photos from when Genie and Freddie were little.'

Pushing aside her mug, Stevie accepted the photos. Her ears twitched as she stared down at them, shifting through the pile with her head slightly tilted.

'What do you think?' BK asked.

Stevie paused on one, touching the photo of two young siblings playing at a beach. Smiling faces laughed up at the camera.

'They s-seem hap-happy,' said Stevie.

'They were,' BK said brightly.

Zach noted the use of the past tense. Were they not happy anymore? He was tempted to ask but he didn't want to interrupt whatever was going on between the two girls—one alien and one human.

Stevie glanced up. She focused on Zach before her gaze shifted to Ant in curiosity. She indicated the photo.

'Were happy?' she asked.

'That was before…' said Ant. 'Before she was hurt. About a year before Einstein visited. Exactly a year, actually. He didn't tell you?'

She shook her head, her eyes going cloudy.

'Oh,' said Ant. 'Well, she's a bit quieter now. She's okay, mostly. But I don't think she's ever really gotten over it.'

'Hurt?'

'Uh, yeah. She was attacked. Um, cut. By her older brother. We um, we don't talk about it much,' Ant explained.

'Right. Er, who is Einstein?' Zach asked, changing the subject from the girl's morbid past to what he thought was the more interesting topic. 'Aside from a world famous, long dead scientist, I mean.'

A small grin quirked Ant's lips as his blue eyes flickered back to Zach.

'Sorry,' he said. 'Einstein is the alien that Genie met six years ago.'

Zach started.

Again, Ant's gaze flickered to Stevie, except this time his question was for Zach. 'You didn't know?'

'No,' said Zach, turning to look at Stevie. 'I didn't. I thought you said you'd never been in the ship before?'

She shook her head, still holding the pile of photos. 'N-not me,' stuttered Stevie. 'Just m-my m-mentor.'

'You mean Einstein?' Ant clarified. 'He said he would come back in ten years. You're four years early. Why?'

'It is com-complicated.'

'Well this just keeps getting more interesting,' said Zach, leaning his elbow on the table. 'What exactly do you want with a couple of human teenagers?'

Stevie closed her eyes. Her ears twitched and Zach felt the hairs on his arms stand on end as the air filled with static.

She took a deep breath, as if preparing herself to tell them something huge. She opened her eyes, pure silver with no hint of a pupil.

'We're g-going to s-save them, so sh-she can s-save us.'

CHAPTER FOURTEEN

Genie

Emptiness.

Cold, hard, emptiness. Numbing and wonderful, keeping the panic and the terror of what I'd just done at bay.

Tim scrambled out from underneath the dead man. I had to shoot him three times, not quite hitting him in the right place to kill him.

There was blood all over Tim now. He was drenched. It clung in clumps on his clothes and in his hair, dripping down his face. He tried to wipe some off but only ended up smearing more across his cheeks. He shook himself, scrunching up his nose.

'Sorry,' I said, my voice coming out hoarse and somewhat pained.

Dark eyes snapped to mine.

'Don't worry about it,' he said, and tried to smile. 'You saved my life.'

'I...'

The gun was like lead in my hands, weighing me down, drowning me, and pulling the trigger was like trying to move the ocean that had descended upon me. I stared at it, feeling my own breathing come and go in short, sharp bursts. My vision narrowed, pin-pointing on the black metal in my hands. The weapon shook, trembling like a leaf in a hurricane as the adrenaline fled my body.

Tim stepped over to me and took the gun.

'It's alright,' he said.

I sucked in a breath, unable to take my gaze from the gun, even as he pulled it away from me. I couldn't look at anything else. I couldn't look at the blood splattered walls or the red seeping, *seeping*, out of the hazard suit that was supposed to protect that man.

'Genie,' said Tim as he grabbed my chin, forcing me to look at him. 'You did good.'

'I killed him,' I mumbled, staring at his face—at all the blood.

Blood that was there because of me. Because of what I'd done. Noise rushed in my ears, making the world spin, and blackness touched the edges of my vision. I couldn't get enough air. I couldn't focus. Red kept shifting in and out of the black. I felt dizzy.

'Hey,' said Tim. He let go of my chin and shook my shoulders. 'Genie, calm down. He'd've killed us. You did the right thing.'

'I…I killed him.'

He cursed. He hesitated only a moment before swinging his hand. I caught sight of it just before he struck. The slap resounded in the hallway, echoing slightly. All the air in my lungs whooshed out. My cheek stung and yet my eyes dried up, the tears that had been streaming down my cheeks stopping in the shock of being slapped. I stood there, too stunned to do anything but touch my stinging cheek.

Coal black eyes stared at me, assessing.

'I…I'm okay,' I said. 'I…thanks.'

A wry grin cracked his face, though it didn't touch that dark look in his eyes.

'Anytime,' he said. 'Just don't freak out on me again, okay? At least not 'til we're out of this shithole.'

Cold and numb, I nodded. 'Sure.'

'Great. Now c'mon.' He began to pull me down the hall. 'Let's get the hell outta here before anymore of those assholes show up.'

He gripped my hand, offering me a fierce but grim smile. I tried to smile back, but it was weak. I took a deep breath, and nodded again, more firmly this time.

'What's the plan?'

'Well,' said Tim, pausing around a corner. 'Freddie took the car and I don't reckon the buses'll be showing up. Besides,' he ducked his head around the brick wall before pulling me along after him. 'The front of the school probably isn't an option. Those two won't be the only ones who came here. Judging from the mess.'

He indicated another spray of blood on the wall next to us. I winced. He held the gun slightly in front of him as we inched along the halls. All around us, unnatural sounds of too many feet racing through the school bounced around the hallway. There were screams, and sobbing, and distant gunfire.

'What do we do?' I whispered.

'Teacher's car park,' he said. 'It's at the back of the school, and they probably didn't think to block off that entrance. I reckon that's our best shot.'

I nodded again, trying to keep my breathing even. The woman's face swam before everything I saw. The image of her terrified gaze burned into my mind, her frantic movements as she raised the gun, the nozzle pointed at her own temple. What kind of illness was so terrifying she'd rather die than live with the chance of being infected? Maybe she was right. Maybe infection *was* inevitable?

Tim's hand tightened around mine.

'You okay?' he asked, low and quiet.

I nodded, offering him a weak smile. His dark eyes flickered back at me, seeing through me in an instant.

Two figures flashed across the hallway in front of us. I gasped, pulling back, wanting to flee in the other direction, but Tim held me firm.

He stared after the them, listening to their footsteps career down the intersecting corridor.

'Just students,' he whispered.

Only when we rounded the corner, it wasn't *just* students.

The world dropped away and all I felt was the hot, anxious energy in the corridor beyond, so thick I thought I would suffocate. A knot unrolled in my stomach. My knees shook. The wall felt too far away to grasp.

'The fuck are you doing here?'

Tim's voice sounded too far away as it bounced around the hallway. He was gripping my hand so hard he could've broken my fingers, but I didn't notice. I was too busy staring at the impossibility in front of me. The man in the hallway beyond. My big brother.

James.

His honey brown eyes caught mine, ignoring Tim altogether. They were just like Mum's—from what I remembered of her, anyway—just like Grandma's. Those charming, enticing eyes. Frightening eyes.

He held me there, like a predator held its prey. Like the smiling fox ready to snap me up.

He turned away from the boy he'd been speaking too, letting lose the handful of shirt he'd held in one fist. The boy collapsed, gasping, his lips going blue. There were black veins on his face, just like Ricky's.

James smiled, ignoring the sick, infected boy he'd just deposited on the ground.

My insides felt all mixed up. My stomach was floating up somewhere in my throat, and my heart was beating a rapid beat in the tips of my fingers. My toes tingled.

'Evie.'

The name filled my every nightmare. It was a slice of terror that cut open all the stitches in my mind.

The boy sat gasping on the ground, his hand going to his throat, scrabbling, trying to breath. James stepped toward me, his smile spreading over perfect, straight teeth.

What was he doing here?

I was just a rabbit. I was just a stupid little rabbit trying to be a fox. I wasn't strong or brave. Freddie was wrong. Tim was wrong. It was all a lie. In James' gaze, I couldn't pretend I was more than a broken little girl. A scared little girl. I did the only thing a little girl could, just like I had back then. There was nothing else, just that primal instinct that taught me to run.

So I did.

'Evie, come out, come out wherever you are!'

I ran, and I never looked back.

CHAPTER FIFTEEN

Zach

A hundred questions burst through Zach's mind but he held onto them, sensing Stevie might withdraw. Instead, he nodded, drumming his fingers on the table, and asked just one question.

'You want to save her,' he said, keeping his voice even and calm, like they were discussing nothing more serious than the weather. 'You mean from the plague, right?'

'Plague?' asked Ant looking between the two of them. 'What plague?'

Zach rolled his eyes. He stood up and walked around the table. There was a large archway, offering a good vantage point of the TV from the dining room table where they'd been sitting. He snatched up the remote and flicked it on, switching through the news channels.

Headlines screamed at them: Rising Death Toll, Flu Pandemic, Hundreds Dead, Hospitals Full, Borders Closed. One nightmare after another. Each channel was the same. Coverage of over crowded hospitals and general practices, people falling ill over nothing more than flu symptoms.

He turned back to the table, gesturing at the headlines. 'That plague,' he said.

Ant frowned, staring at the news anchor as she prattled on about cold and flu symptoms and how to differentiate a normal flu from this aggressive strand. Heavy fatigue, anxiety, and unexplained temper, just to name a few.

'But that's just a cold, isn't it?' Ant said, turning his frowning blue eyes on Zach.

'No, it's not. It's something much worse,' he turned to Stevie and added, 'Right?'

She nodded, her gaze fixed somewhere on the glass tabletop as her head dipped down and then back up again in slow confirmation.

'I…' Ant stood up, his expression blank and his eyes far away. 'I have to go. My Mum…I…she's…I have to go.'

'No!' BK jumped up, grabbing Ant's arm with a frantic look in her eyes. 'No, you can't.'

'What?' he asked, his tone bewildered but his expression still closed off. 'I have to.'

'No,' said BK emphatically. 'You *can't*. You have to stay here.'

'But—'

'Ant!' she yelled, flinging her arms around him. 'You have to stay!' Her voice was muffled, her face pressed into his shirt.

'BK…?'

'You have to *stay*. If you go…' She shook her head, wild curls flinging about her.

Ant's blank expression cracked. He looked torn. Zach folded his arms and considered them. He glanced at Stevie, but she was frowning at the two other humans, her silver gaze pin-pointed and…confused?

Zach sighed and ran a hand through his already ruffled hair. 'She's in the hospital right?'

'Uh,' said Ant, blue eyes furrowed, 'yeah.'

'This may sound harsh,' said Zach. 'But BK's right. You shouldn't go. If you go to a hospital, you'll catch it for sure. Even if she didn't have it already, she will now.'

'What're you saying?' Ant asked, his face going pale. He sat down heavily, taking BK with him as she wouldn't let go. 'You think my mother is dead?' he asked, his voice faint.

'It's not your fault,' said BK, releasing him only to take hold of his face. 'It's not your fault at all. She cast you off, remember? She sent you away.'

'But I—'

'No!' BK exclaimed. 'No. She sent you away just because you're different! You told me she thinks you're sick just because, just because you love someone? She wasn't there for you when you needed her. You can't go now! She sent you away. And I'm glad she did. I'm glad. If you were there you'd be sick too. You can't go.'

'Okay. BK, okay.' Ant drew her into a hug, hiding his face in her hair. 'I'll stay. Okay. I'll stay.'

Zach shifted, uncrossed his arms again, recrossed them and sighed. He leaned on the edge of the archway. Stevie stood on the other side of the table, also watching the other two.

BK pulled away from Ant, staring at him with those big, green eyes of hers. 'You will stay?' she whispered.

He hesitated. With a sigh, he nodded.

BK nodded. 'You *need* to stay here,' she repeated, her eyes wide and earnest.

Ant nodded again. He sighed and rubbed a hand over his face.

'So, this…plague,' his gaze shifted and he paused.

He blinked, bemused confusion spreading across his face..

Zach turned and a grin spread across his face. There was a new headline blaring across the screen. *Unidentified Ship Crashes in Brisbane River.* An image—clearer than the ones Zach had seen on social media—zoomed into view, shot from above the pedestrian bridge Stevie had crashed into. Her ship, small and lithe looking, sat amongst the broken wires and poles, quiet and abandoned. Zach ignored whatever theory they were spouting about the aircraft to look back at it's driver.

'You crashed a ship to come and save Genie and Freddie?' Ant asked.

Stevie nodded.

'Why?'

'I think the more important question is,' said Zach, turning to regard her fully, 'can you save us, too?'

'Of course she can,' BK chirped, back to being positive.

Stevie hesitated. Zach held his breathe, waiting for her answer. Her silver-eyed gaze became distant and foggy, like she was recalling a memory. The faint hint of static clung to the air, and one of her ears twitched as it so often did when she got this far-away look in her eyes.

Zach smelt ozone and swallowed.

She nodded, stinted and unsure, but still a nod. After a moment, her gaze refocused and she gave him a firmer nod.

'Yes,' she said, managing not to stutter.

The tension seeped out of the room. BK smiled, though Zach thought he could detect a snippet of relief—as though, despite her confidence, she hadn't been entirely convinced that Stevie would say yes.

'Excellent,' said Zach. 'So I assume we have to get the twins then?'

'And Tim,' said Ant.

'Er, sure. Tim,' Zach agreed, still not sure who Tim was. 'So it's nearly two, when do they normally get home?'

'Half an hour or so,' said Ant.

'Half an hour? Can't we go pick them up?'

'We could,' Ant agreed. 'But by the time we drove out there and came back, it'll have been an hour. We might as well just wait. Besides, you want to go into town with Stevie?'

'Er, no, I suppose not.'

'I think they'll be home soon, anyway,' said BK. She stepped around Ant and headed into the kitchen.

'If you say so,' said Ant, sticking his elbow on the table and watching her go.

'I do say so,' she said. 'Want some fresh bread? I was thinking of making some.'

'Sure,' he said.

He seemed more relaxed now, despite the news he'd been given about his mother. Zach eyed the two of them, confused by their weird relationship. BK's cheerfulness was certainly infectious, but Zach wasn't sure it was positive enough to put his nerves at ease. How was Ant so relaxed? He seemed so sure that everything would be okay just because BK said it would, and yet, from their earlier conversation, Zach didn't think they were dating. She obviously wasn't his type.

Ant got up and moved into the lounge room. He found the remote and switched channels to something less depressing. Some comedy sitcom show.

Stevie glanced between them, staring between BK in the kitchen and Ant in the lounge room. She picked up the photos BK had brought out for her, and followed Ant.

'You know,' said Ant conversationally, throwing Zach a brief grin. 'I never thought I'd be sitting here casually watching TV with an alien.'

'Yeah,' agreed Zach. 'Who would?'

'You'd be surprised,' said Ant, looking from Zach to Stevie. 'Genie always believed you'd come back.'

Stevie flushed, her ears going dark purple. She shifted through the photos again, her expression soft and uncertain, yet also wistful. Long fingers splayed delicately over the photos, hovering just above the glossy surface. She touched one, gaze focused and bittersweet as she brushed a finger across the photo in a hesitant reverence.

Zach frowned and sat down on the edge of the recliner. He started to ask Stevie why them, why these twins? What was so special about them that photos of their childhood put that expression on her face?

He didn't get to finish the question. The sound of tyres on gravel, skidding to a halt outside, distracted all of them.

A door slammed and two heartbeats later the front door was flung open.

CHAPTER SIXTEEN

Genie

'Genie! *Genie!*'

Someone flashed by, skidding to a stop in front of me and forcing me to a halt. They grabbed at my shoulders and I shrieked, trying to pull away.

'Shit!'

A hand came down over my mouth. There was the click of a door and I was yanked into darkness.

'Mmpf!'

For a moment I thought it was James. Terror made my chest constrict into breathlessness as he clamped hand over my mouth but then Tim's hissing voice came sharp in my ear.

'Shut up! It's me. Just…be quiet. There were more of them.'

He was hot, and the rise and fall of his chest was rapid. I'd outrun Tim?

He shifted. 'Can I let you go now?' he whispered, his breath warm in my ear.

I flinched, pulling my head away, and tried to nod. With a slow reluctance, he let me go.

'Why are we in a closet?' I asked, trying to pull my foot out of the bucket it was currently wedged in.

'Hazmat guys. You almost ran straight into them.'

My stomach twisted.

'We should be right in here, until they go past.'

'You're sure the teachers car park is the best option?'

I felt, rather than saw, Tim nod. He edged around me, leaning into the door as he wedged it open a crack. A sliver of light filtered into the room and I could see again. I blinked into the semi-light. Red was everywhere.

'Yes,' Tim whispered, 'I am. Alright, it's clear. Let's get out of here.'

'Wait,' I said, catching hold of his shirt.

It was slick. Blood was seeped into the fabric so thick, not even a thousand washes would remove it. I clutched at it anyway.

'What if…what if he's out there?' I asked, my voice cracking.

Tim didn't ask who I was talking about. He didn't need to. The old scar in my chest itched, a dull ache stretching across it's length.

'Then I'll kill him,' said Tim.

He opened the door. The hallways were quiet. There was no more screaming, no more gun fire, no more shouting. It was eerie. We tip-toed through the buildings, taking random twists and turns rather than the most direct route. I didn't question Tim, only followed. All I could do was watch the back of his head. Any attempt to look around resulted in horror and guilt and sadness. It resulted in fear. Fear that we'd be next, that our blood would be the next to stain the walls. Fear that at the next turn we'd find James lurking there, waiting.

Tim led me out to the edge of the back building. Before us sat the small, teachers' car park, hidden on either side by brown gardens that had once been well cared for and green.

'Okay,' said Tim, pointing at an old, faded Holden wagon sitting in the car park. 'That's our goal.'

I nodded.

'Ready?'

'Yes.'

He glanced back, coal eyes appraising.

'Alright, go!'

Every muscle in my legs released like a spring as I launched after him.

Two minutes later, we both sat on the ground next to

the Holden, panting and waiting for the sound of gun fire to fill the air. The only noise was the wind, rustling through the summer burnt gardens.

'What do we do?' I asked.

Tim grinned. He tapped the side of the car like he was greeting an old friend and I suppose he was. Mr Moore, the principal, owned the ancient, black commodore wagon which had been broken into on a number of occasions. No matter how many times the students got the doors open or hotwired the car, he never upgraded the alarm system—or the whole car. He'd had the car for years and years and went on about how faithful it was and how they didn't make cars like that anymore. At least not ones so easily broken into.

Mr Moore didn't even bother to lock the car after how many times it had been ransacked, and I knew Tim could hotwire it in under a minute.

Hesitating only a moment, I crawled into the backseat, trying to keep low and hidden, and watched as Tim slithered into the front. He went headfirst into the driver's seat, his legs hanging back in the passengers seat. His head disappeared beneath the steering wheel, but I didn't need to see to know what he would be doing.

A few years ago, Tim's delinquent uncle had come to stay at his house. Tim's mother had been firm about him behaving himself and not being a bad influence, but that didn't stop him from teaching Tim, Freddie and me how to pick locks and hotwire cars. I'd always been terrible at it and Freddie had little enough patience for the task, but Tim had been a natural. Just like his uncle.

I heard the little click as he pulled open the panel beneath the old steering wheel and began fiddling with the wires.

'Are we really stealing the principal's car?' I muttered.

'Not like he's using it,' came Tim's muffled retort.

The car coughed and then thrummed to life. Tim wriggled around in the seat until he was the right way up. He jammed the car into drive, took the handbrake off and eased out of the car park. He started slow, inching along the rows of cars at a steady crawl. As if to make our movement less noticeable by the lack of speed. Nothing seemed to move around us. Even the trees were still. We rolled out of the car park and drifted to a stop in the middle of the street.

'What're you doing?' I asked, trying to keep the squeak out of my voice and failing.

The car sputtered, burred, and turned off.

'Nothing,' Tim said. 'I dunno what's wrong.'

'Did it stall?'

'I know how to drive a car,' Tim snapped, adjusting the wires and muttering soft curses. 'It's an automatic, it shouldn't stall at all.'

'Get down!' I yelped, flattening myself against the seat.

Tim slouched, only keeping his head up to stare about, trying to see what I'd seen. Another car had begun to move from the carpark we'd left.

It hummed down the driveway, taking off past us and shooting down the street.

We stared after it, not having a chance to ask for help as it took off.

The car approached the turn at the end of the road—the same turn we'd have taken—tires squealing in desperation as the driver fled.

At first, I didn't understand. One moment, the car was making the turn, the next it was on fire. Flames erupted around it, and the car jammed to a stop, lifting up into the air at the force of whatever it had hit—or whatever had hit *it*.

'Get out!' Tim yelped. 'Get out, get out, get out!'

He was already out the door, flinging it open and diving for the ground. I held my breath as I scrambled out after him. My hands shook. My knees slammed into the ground and gravel grazed up my palms. I didn't have time to feel it.

Tim grabbed my wrist and once again, we ran.

CHAPTER SEVENTEEN

Zach

Zach caught a brief glimpse of the boy that stormed into the house before he disappeared down the hallway on the other end of the lounge room.

'That's not good,' Ant muttered, standing up to go after the boy.

From the kitchen, Zach heard BK's surprised voice.

'Freddie! You're home early, what…Freddie?'

He didn't answer, at least not in any way that Zach could hear.

'Oh no,' BK said. 'Wait, Freddie. Where are you going?' she paused, and then added, 'Ant's in the lounge-room.'

Zach glanced up at Ant, but he was watching the lounge room archway. Right on cue, the boy stormed in, a long shotgun held in one hand.

Zach's jaw dropped and he jumped up, holding his hands up and preparing to explain himself. Ant beat him to it.

'Whoa, easy,' he said, taking a step toward the boy. 'What's going, Freddie? Why've you got the gun? Where's Genie and Tim?'

Freddie made a face, giving Ant a look that clearly questioned his intelligence.

Ant raised his hands again. 'Right,' he said. 'Sorry, sorry. Alright, how about we start with the gun? Are you planning on shooting someone?'

Freddie shrugged, but his gaze shifted and stuck on

Zach. He stilled, his grey eyes narrowing at the sight of the stranger in his house. Zach gave him a little wave.

'Hi,' he said, hoping his voice wasn't as shaky as it sounded to his own ears. 'We come in peace. Please don't shoot me.'

Ant snorted, casting Zach a sideways grin before schooling his face into a more serious expression to deal with the issue that was the gun.

Freddie scowled, still staring at Zach.

Zach sensed something familiar about the boy's face. Freddie shifted, his movement taking him into a patch of sunlight that glanced off his eyes, making them seem more silvery than grey.

There it was. Zach was struck by how much they reminded him of Stevie's eyes, and he stared open-mouthed at the boy until those silvery eyes narrowed again.

There was a tightness around Freddie's eyes and lips. He looked older, as his shoulders deflated and his eyes dropped to the floor.

'Freddie?' Ant asked. 'Where's Genie and Tim.'

'Are they okay?' BK asked, appearing at his shoulder.

Freddie lifted his head, gaze fixing on her in despondency. He shrugged, eyes downcast and throat working.

She stared at him with big disbelieving eyes. 'But…but she was with you, wasn't she?'

Freddie shook his head.

BK took a step closer. 'Are they okay? The radio was just on, there's been problems at some of the schools, but yours was fine, wasn't it?'

Freddie shrugged, the movement slow and arduous, as if he was lifting a mountain instead of just his shoulders.

'You don't know?' Ant asked, his voice soft.

Freddie shook his head again. Zach stared at the three of them, wondering what the hell was up with the twenty questions. Why didn't he just tell them what was going on?

'You skipped school,' Ant sighed.

Freddie nodded again, and made sharp motion with one hand that Zach didn't quite see.

'Lunch?' Ant asked. 'But how were they going to get home? Why didn't you pick them up again?'

Freddie made that face again, as if Ant's question was too stupid to answer, but frustration was etched into his gaze. He took a deep breath, as if about to speak. Instead he sighed and thrust the gun at Ant. Ant took it, unperturbed by the boy's actions as Freddie began making a series of rapid motions with his hands.

'Whoa, whoa, slow down. What're you talking about?' Ant asked. 'Dead? Whose dead?'

One motion with his hands this time, and Zach suddenly understood. Sign language. Seeing as Freddie had no problem understanding everyone's questions, he clearly wasn't deaf. Which meant he was mute. Zach's interest piqued again. Mutism without a cause was rare.

He glanced back at Stevie, bringing his question count into the hundreds, and wondered if she'd known.

'Everyone?'

The word echoed around the room, like a bell tolling at a funeral. Silence reigned in its wake.

'What do you mean, everyone?' Zach asked. 'Everyone at the school.'

Turning that narrow-eyed, silver gaze on Zach, Freddie took a moment before answering. He shook his head.

'You left the school,' Ant said, translating for Zach's benefit. 'And drove around. Wait, why did you leave?'

'Does that matter?' Zach asked.

Ant glanced sideways at him. He considered the question, gave Freddie a wry look and shook his head. 'No' he said. 'I suppose not. Alright, so who was…dead?'

Freddie made that same sharp movement. Crossing his arms in an X and then swinging his arms outward.

'What do you mean everyone?' Ant asked, and a hint of panic was working its way into his voice. 'How could everyone be dead?'

'You mean, everyone that you saw?' Zach clarified.

Freddie nodded again.

'But you didn't see Genie?' Zach asked, getting used to this way of questioning, thinking ahead on how best to phrase his questions in order to find out what happened.

Freddie shook his head, his eyes narrowing further, his brows furrowed in an obvious question. *How do you know Genie?'*

Zach ignored the question, his mind going through the details, flicking back over every news article he'd read in the last week.

'The plague?' he asked. 'They all dropped dead fast, right? Too fast to respond to?'

Again, Freddie nodded.

'Men, were there men? In hazmat suits?'

Freddie's frown deepened and he shook his head, paused and then shrugged.

'Okay,' said Zach, taking over the line of questioning without argument from either of the others. 'So, you were supposed to pick the other two up, but you couldn't?'

Freddie nodded.

'Because people were dying? You were scared?'

Freddie scowled and shook his head emphatically. He made another hand motion that Zach didn't understand.

'Blockade?' Ant whispered. 'Where?'

More hand motions, except this time Zach could tell what it was as Freddie put his hands together, forming an arch. Or a bridge.

'Bridge?' Zach asked, he looked to BK. 'How many bridges are there?'

'Three,' she said, worry etched into her face. 'There's no other way across the river. If there's a blockade…they'll be trapped.'

Freddie shook his head again, and gestured to the gun that Ant had placed carefully on the couch.

'You can't go around shooting people!' Ant said, his voice a mixture of exasperation and worry.

Freddie's expression said he was willing to give it a go.

'Okay, we can't just run into town with the plague running rampant and killing everyone. If there's a blockade, that could mean the military is involved and, no offence, but one shotgun isn't going to make much of a difference.'

Freddie's shoulders remained stiff, and he looked like he

was going to argue with Zach. Maybe if he could have spoken the words he would have. Instead, the stiffness melted away as his shoulders slumped. He looked lost all of a sudden, a flush of shame creeping up his cheeks, and he dropped into the couch. Almost immediately, as if the chair had sent an electric current through his whole body, he jumped back up.

His head snapped to the side and his gaze fixated on Stevie. His eyes went wide, his mouth dropping open into an 'o'.

'Hello,' she said, staring up at him with eyes as big as saucepans, as if she was just as awed by him as he was of her.

Freddie gasped, a quiet exhale of air, and his hands flew up to his head, his eyes squeezing shut in pain.

Alarmed, Zach held a hand out to Stevie. 'Whoa,' he said. 'What're you doing?'

Stevie's gaze broke away from Freddie and he swayed. Ant stepped in, catching Freddie's arm and steadying him.

'Easy,' said Ant, helping him sit back down in the chair. 'It's a bit of a shock.'

Freddie shook his head, still staring at Stevie in bewilderment.

'This is Stevie,' said BK brightly. 'She's here for you and Genie.'

CHAPTER EIGHTEEN

Genie

It took us over an hour to make our way through the south side of town to the river. We darted from building to building, dashing from car to abandoned car across the streets.

Sometimes there were bodies and I turned my head away sharply. Most the time, it was dark enough for me to avoid catching sight of their faces. It didn't matter. My mind supplied the images for me. Josie's vacant eyes. The frantic gaze of the woman in the hazard suit. Ricky's anguish. The feel of the trigger. The rising taste of bile in my mouth made me shove the memories away.

I kept my breathing even as we ran.

'Do you smell that?' Tim panted.

I nodded. 'Burning.'

We jogged towards the bridge, but even in the fading light of the street below we could see it was a heaped mess.

Tim cursed and slowed his pace to a walk.

'No use trying to cross now,' he said. 'It's too light. Doesn't look like anyone's up there, but that doesn't mean much.'

'Maybe they left?' I asked hopefully.

'Maybe,' said Tim, eyeing the bridge. 'Or they could all be dead.'

We watched a little longer, scouring the bridge for movement. There was no sign of light. I glanced at Tim and saw the distrust on his face.

'What do we do?' I asked.

He shrugged. 'We could swim?'

'What?' I squeaked. 'We can't *swim*.'

'Why not?'

'There are crocodiles in that river!'

Tim shrugged again. 'Not many.'

I rolled my eyes and shook my head. I turned away from the barricaded bridge and scoured the riverside for a tinny or any sort of mooring we could steal. Instead, my gaze focused somewhere else.

The rail bridge.

Six months ago, Tim nicked some alcohol from his uncle, dragged us all down to the park in town—a massive playground that had just been done up. The idea was that we'd all have a taste and a play around on the new equipment. Except Tim got bored. And when Tim gets bored…

'Let's go swimming!' he'd announced, leaning forward to stare down at the rest of us from his perch up on the monkey bars.

He jumped down, somehow managing to land on his feet, and proceeded to drag Freddie off toward the river. But not toward the water, instead he headed to the train tracks.

The memory drew my eyes to the thin and narrow bridge further up the river as I recalled how difficult it was to crawl over the tracks.

'What about the rail bridge?' I asked Tim, pointing towards it. 'Doesn't look like it has a blockade.'

A grin split Tim's face. He slung an arm around my shoulders and yanked me in close, planting a kiss on my temple.

'You're a genius, Genie,' he said. 'Why didn't I think of it sooner?'

'I don't know,' I said wryly. 'Seeing as you gave me the idea.'

He raised his eyebrows and pointed to himself. 'Moi?'

'Yes, you,' I said, shaking my head. 'Come on. We should get going. The others will be worried.'

I shrugged him off and headed up the street, picking up the pace. A faint fluttery feeling had settled into my gut. I felt like a rabbit in an open field, waiting to be caught by a dingo or a fox.

'Wait,' he said, jogging to catch up to me. 'How did I give you the idea?'

I shook my head. 'If you can't remember, then I'm not telling you,' I said, trying not to think of it—the incident terrified me. 'I certainly don't want to repeat it.'

I remembered the loose panels and the slippery metal rail that we'd all crawled over at Tim's behest—the alcohol doing its very best to make us our least sensible selves. I recalled the wicked expression that had crossed Tim's face as he'd turned to us, arms spread wide.

'Want to see a magic trick?' he asked, and without waiting for an answer, he'd stepped backwards *off* the edge of the bridge, plummeting down into the water below.

Tim grinned at me now, nudging me as we neared the tracks. 'Oh come on, tell me you didn't have fun?'

I glanced back at him. 'So you do remember?'

The banter made things normal. It took my mind off the too quiet streets, where no one stirred, not even the usual afternoon traffic. The shops remained open but abandoned. No shop clerks, no customers. I wondered why Tim didn't venture off into one of them to snoop around. The fact he didn't told me he was just as nervous as I was.

He scoffed. 'Of course I remember. That was one of the best days of my life.'

'It wasn't for me,' I muttered.

'Oh come off it,' he said and shoulder bumped me. 'Tell me that wasn't the most thrilling thing you've ever done? The wind in your face and your hair, the rush in your blood, the sharp cold of the water. Doesn't it make you even a little proud that you jumped? That you were brave enough to do that?'

'I didn't jump,' I said with a sigh. 'I've told you, BK slipped and I fell off the bridge with her.'

'Potato, tomato,' he said and I laughed. 'Same difference. You still did it and it was still awesome.'

'Whatever you say. If you don't realise it was the most stupid…' I trailed off, stopping in the middle of the street.

A group of apartment buildings rose up in front of us. There was a small park bench on the other side of the road. Balloons swayed in the afternoon breeze and I could hear the faint whisper of music echoing out from a small speaker somewhere. My throat closed up, and I stared, unable to breathe and unable to look away.

A pram sat just next to the picnic table, surrounded by four women, each one collapsed on the ground. From where I stood, I could just make out the pink, lace shoe resting limp on the footrest of the pram.

Deep breath in. I squeezed my eyes shut, not letting the tears form. *Now let it out.*

Freddie. The cool afternoon air sent goosebumps up my arms and I hugged myself, wishing desperately that he was there. *Please be safe.*

Arms encircled me. Tim shook as he drew me into a hug, all sign of mirth gone from his face. His eyes were squeezed shut just as hard as I'd had mine, and he dropped his forehead to my shoulder.

He didn't say a word. We stood there, locked together, clinging to each other as we desperately tried not to fall apart. What was happening? How on Earth were we ever going to survive it?

Tim sucked in a sharp breath and took a step back from me. When he opened his eyes, there was no hint of the fear or pain of what we'd just seen. He took my hand and continued on toward our goal. He didn't look back at the pram again.

Crossing the rail bridge wasn't as frightening as it had been the first time—especially since this time we weren't jumping off. We clambered down off the other side of the tracks, and Tim made a beeline for a nearby car park.

'Time to find a new ride,' he said, keeping his gaze fixed straight ahead. 'After all, the others will be worried about us.'

At the corner of the carpark, a military truck sat silent and unmoving where it had jumped the curb. Tim ignored it, not even glancing in its direction as he stomped through the carpark towards his chosen vehicle. He didn't even stop to look at the little gold pellets clinking against our feet as we walked.

I swallowed hard as they scattered away from me across the road, clattering against the tar. I knew without looking what they were.

Bullet shells.

CHAPTER NINETEEN

Zach

Freddie stared at BK for a long moment, grey eyes wide and unblinking as he processed what his cousin had just said. His expression seemed to ask a question, but Zach couldn't quite figure out what.

'She got here about an hour ago,' explained Ant, sitting back down on the couch next to Stevie, careful to avoid the now forgotten gun. 'We've been waiting for you and Genie and Tim to get home.'

Freddie tensed back up again at the mention of his sister. He signed something quickly, his movements too rapid for Zach to even guess what he was saying.

Ant began to speak, but Stevie shook her head, interrupting him.

'He is-isn't here,' she said. 'I am a-alone.'

There was a tremor in her voice, but Stevie kept eye contact with Freddie, her ears twitching over her shoulders.

Surprise lit Ant's face. 'You know sign language?' he asked her, interrupting whatever Freddie was signing.

Stevie's silvery eyes flicked to Ant and back to Freddie. Zach noticed rather than watching his hands, her gaze was on his face. He guessed it was less about her knowing sign language, and more about her being an alien. She ignored Ant's question in favour of answering Freddie's.

'He c-called me here,' she said. 'T-to find you.'

Her voice was quiet and Zach had to strain to hear it. There was shame in her tone and her eyes, and Zach's chest fluttered with curiosity. There was a pause as Freddie asked another question. His expression darkened when she nodded, her ears going blotchy and bruised in colour. His fists clenched on his knees and she hurried to explain her side of the conversation.

'I- we…that is…Ein-Einstein… he is t-try-trying…I, I want t-to,' her voice caught, her throat working until the whole next word was thrown out in a rush of breath. 'Help.'

Freddie wasn't signing anymore, but Stevie continued speaking, more forthcoming with this silent, angry teenager than she had been with any of the others.

'Y-You were our p-p-priority. B-But I do n-not, d-did not— I want t-to help,' she repeated. She was leaning forward, gravitating toward him, her eyes big and locked on his in earnest hope.

Freddie scowled, his face clearly indicating he didn't believe her.

'I want to f-f-find Genie,' she said.

Freddie made an odd, quiet noise. A huff of protest, maybe? It was hard to tell without the added inflection from vocal chords.

'I *do*, but n-not why you-you think,' Stevie said, shaking her head, her ears swinging.

The air was becoming charged, like it had when Zach had first found Stevie by the Brisbane River, when she had become nervous. Zach inched his feet toward her, worried about what would happen if Freddie upset her.

Ant was looking between his friend and the alien girl, eyes lingering on Freddie's still clenched fists. He frowned, and Zach wondered if he'd noticed too. They were having a conversation, but only one of them was actually speaking, sign language or not.

'I p-promise, I d-don't want to hurt you, I would-would never,' Stevie was saying, wringing her hands, practically begging for Freddie's acceptance.

Freddie made a sudden sharp movement with his hand and Stevie flinched back. The flash was blinding. A bright, blue bolt arced from Stevie's temple, along the ridges of her head, before sparking and crackling into nothing at the ends of her ears.

Zach swore, jumping back even though the light was gone as quick as it had appeared, the afterimage of the blue light shimmering as he blinked. He could smell ozone, and a waft of something else—smoke—like something was burning.

'S-Sorry,' Stevie stuttered, her voice hitching and eyes dropping.

She was blinking rapidly, two pairs of eyelids closing over shiny silver eyes. She wrung her hands again, picking at the hard, dark nails on one hand. They were all such human gestures, human emotions. It made her seem more like them than she really was.

Ant, looking concerned, reached out to touch her shoulder, trying to reassure her. She flinched, and he dropped his hand. He threw Freddie a look, not quite reprimanding, but close.

'Don't be too hard on her,' he said in a soft voice.

Freddie scowled at him a look of *'who's side are you on?'* etched into his face.

'She doesn't understand,' Zach said, having a good idea of what had happened.

Freddie made a face, hands moving again in short, sharp jabs. His brows were furrowed in angry lines, but there was something else there in those grey eyes. Something wary and reserved. He held himself back from her, almost as if he were afraid.

Zach rolled his eyes as Freddie continued to sign. 'I don't speak mute.'

Freddie glowered, eyes stormy and grey, no longer like Stevie's at all. Zach was glad. It made it easier to dislike the boy.

'He said "that's no excuse",' said BK, her voice soft and worried. 'And that she does understand.'

'She doesn't,' said Zach. 'She's never been here before. She's studied us, sure, but that's it. She's read about our languages and our cultures, studied them even, but that's not the same as comprehending. It's not the same as being here.

Besides, you were signing too fast and then not at all. What else was she supposed to do to understand you?'

Freddie's face twisted into a silent snarl and Zach got the message loud and clear. *Not read my mind.*

'It's normal among her people,' Zach said, though this was purely a guess. 'They communicate telepathically. It's perfectly normal for them to be in each other's heads. It's also something she probably can't control. You can't un-hear me speaking to you. It's the same.'

Freddie raised one eyebrow, his mouth set in a thin, sceptical line. He crossed his arms, leaning back into the couch to regard Zach and Stevie. After a long moment he turned to BK, who was crouched by his recliner, and she leaned forward to watch his hands.

'He wants to know how you know all that?' BK said.

Zach crossed his arms. 'Common sense,' he said. 'I already know she's telepathic, the rest of it just makes sense.'

Freddie signed something else to BK, but Ant interrupted. 'Hang on, just … hang on. Telepathic? She can read minds?'

Freddie's scowl deepened and Zach opened his mouth to start arguing again.

'It's oh-okay,' said Stevie, her eyes still on the ground. 'He is, is right. It was wr-wrong of me.'

Freddie gestured, pointing at her and raising his eyebrows pointedly at Zach. *There, see?*

Zach rolled his eyes, getting the hang of interpreting Freddie's meanings. It helped that he was so expressive; his body language, from the smallest tilt of his head to the positioning of his hands, made it obvious not only what he was saying, but the *tone* of his meanings. It was almost like reading a book.

Zach shook his head. 'Is that really what's important right now? I thought you wanted to get to your sister?'

Freddie's face twitched, fighting to keep hold of his scowl, but unable to prevent the anxiety and fear from seeping through. Zach regarded him. The boy really *was* worried about his sister.

'We n-need to f-find her,' said Stevie, raising her eyes

again to look at Freddie in earnest worry.

'We do,' Ant agreed, nodding as he stood up. 'They're both out there still and if it's as bad as you say…'

For a moment Zach was confused, until he remembered the other boy Ant kept mentioning. Tim.

'We should probably be prepared though,' Ant added, standing up. 'You should change, Freddie. BK, you too. And, er, we should probably get Stevie something a little less… obvious.'

Stevie blinked and looked down at herself. She surveyed her clothes, the thin, skin-tight space suit made of the strange, shimmering material, before comparing them to the human clothes the rest of them were wearing. In an instant, her ears turned dark and splotchy. Zach grinned.

'Yeah,' he said in agreement. 'The suit is a bit ostentatious.'

Freddie snorted, shaking his head as a small, reluctant grin twitched into place. *No kidding.*

Well, Zach thought, what did he expect? She *was* an alien.

CHAPTER TWENTY

Genie

Six months ago I'd received my first suspension. Tim's genius idea to jump off the rail bridge had gotten us all in a lot of trouble. Partly because there was a very real chance we could have died (plenty of hidden rocks in high tide), but— not that they'd admit this—mostly because we were wearing our school uniform.

Generally, the school tried to avoid giving Freddie and Tim the same punishments, but this time they wanted to send a clear message—they did *not* condone this sort of activity.

So, the five of us ended up on suspension. I thought it was unfair on BK and Ant, who were in the final months of their last year at school. Grandma was furious.

'What am I going to do with you lot?' she asked when she hung up the phone to the school. 'And to drag Genie and BK into it? Did you even *think* about what would happen if you hit those rocks?'

Freddie and Tim both winced.

'I don't suppose I can convince you not to call Mum?' Tim quipped hopefully.

'Ha!' Grandma barked. 'I will, too. You better make yourselves scarce before I do. Your mother won't be too pleased when I tell her what you've done this time, Timothy.'

Tim winced.

'Go on, off with you. Before I change my mind and belt the lot of you. I'll have a fresh loaf of bread cooked in an hour or so, so get back before then. You'll want it while it's warm.'

Tim and Freddie exchanged knowing grins, not at all bemused by the abrupt shift from 'lecture' to 'I'm making you snacks'.

Tim nudged me, his bony elbow sharp as it dug into my side. 'Thanks Grandma Hart,' he said, grinning as he stepped over to her. 'You're the best.'

He gave her a kiss on the cheek and a sly grin as he darted away. At seventeen, he towered over my wispy grandmother, but that didn't stop her trying to whack him as he danced away from her, crowing with laughter.

'Oh, go away,' she grumbled, but I saw the smile she tried to hide as she turned back to the house. 'Just don't go jumping off anymore bridges. Or I'll skin your hide.'

Tim saluted her. 'Wouldn't dare,' he said.

No one believed him.

'What do we do now?' Ant asked when we reconvened outside.

Tim slung an arm around Ant's shoulders, the wicked grin returning. 'Pool party!' he said. 'C'mon, the neighbours have just finished lining the dam.'

Ant flushed, his gaze sliding sideways to the arm around his shoulder. 'O-Okay,' he said, blue eyes flickering up to Tim's face.

'But we just went swimming,' BK said.

'*This is better*,' Freddie signed to BK with a grin. *'Flying fox.'*

Tim clapped his hands together. 'Exactly! What's better than a flying fox in a dam on a hot, summer afternoon?'

'Is that a trick question?' asked Ant, brushing himself off, his face returning to it's natural colour now that Tim was focused on someone else.

Knowing Tim, there probably *was* something better (not to mention more dangerous).

'Oh, just go get changed, will you?' said Tim, shoving at Ant's shoulder. 'C'mon, we'll meet back here in ten, alright?'

Freddie grabbed my arm and hauled me back into the house. BK trailed along behind, her hands linked behind her back. I glanced back at her, rolling my eyes at Freddie's burst of energy. She smiled back at me.

Freddie yanked open my top draw, dug around, and pulled out the swimsuit BK had bought me for Christmas. He threw it my way, before heading over to BK's drawers and rummaging around for hers.

I held the suit, unable to do anything but stare at it with wide eyes as Freddie pulled out another pair of togs for BK. He turned around, starting for the door, before catching sight of me and hesitating.

It wasn't the lack of privacy, it wasn't that he'd rummage around in my things, it wasn't even that he'd picked out something for me to wear.

Freddie's gaze fell on the beautiful red and white swim set. I held each piece in one hand, and as he looked between my shaking fists, he registered what was wrong.

One in each hand. A two piece. Pretty, but *exposing*. I'd never worn anything other than a one piece halter since I was…well, since I was ten.

Freddie's mouth dropped open in a little 'o'. His eyes rose up to my face, wide and then narrowed in frustration at himself. His jaw set and he crossed the distance between us, grey eyes burning fierce and determined as he stopped before me and wrapped me up in a hug. We were the same height, his chin resting comfortably on my shoulder, and mine on his.

I stood there like an idiot, still holding the two piece suit, and shook while he held me. He pulled back, holding me by the shoulders and staring at me fiercely.

He took one of my hands, and pressed it to my chest.

'You're strong. You're brave. You're beautiful.'

He nodded. Telling me in his own way that I should wear the suit. That it didn't matter that it was revealing. Didn't matter that anyone who saw me would also see the scar, stretching wide and hideous across my chest.

To Freddie, that scar didn't mean that I was small and fragile and weak. To him, it meant I'd survived. To him, it meant I'd fought back. To him, it meant I hadn't left him alone, and that he hadn't failed me.

I sucked in a deep breath. 'Alright,' I whispered.

He nodded, lips quirking up in the barest of smiles. He shoved my shoulder playfully. Then he was gone, disappearing out the door to meet the others.

'Alright,' I said to BK, who had watched the entire exchange in wide eyed silence. 'Let's get this over with.'

She beamed, her own brilliant smile reassuring me. She didn't say anything, but her smile told me she agreed with Freddie. She'd bought me that two piece because she thought I'd like it. Because she thought I would look pretty in it. Yet it had been months and I hadn't even tried it on.

Now, I did.

When we walked outside to meet the boys there was silence.

Tim's jaw dropped open, his eyes almost bulging out of his head as he gaped at me. I flushed, wishing I'd grabbed a towel or a shirt or something to at least cover up with.

Ant, recovering from his own shock quicker than Tim, elbowed Tim hard in the ribs.

'Sorry, Genie,' said Ant with a soft, encouraging smile. 'You just took us by surprise.'

Freddie rolled his eyes, shaking his head at his two friends as if he couldn't understand why they were so stunned.

'You look good,' Tim blurted, his eyes still a little too wide.

Ant nudged him again.

'Ow, what?' Tim asked, glaring. 'What, am I not allowed to say she looks good? She does. I didn't really know she could look like that but- ow, Jesus Ant, what's your problem?'

'Ugh, you're an idiot.'

Despite myself, I giggled. BK grinned at me. There was confusion in her gaze, like she didn't really know what all the fuss was about or why Ant and Tim were shoving each other; but she was happy that I was happy and that was good enough for her.

Tim crossed his arms, annoyed he was being laughed at. 'What's so funny?'

Freddie smirked.

'You really are idiots,' I laughed.

'Pfft,' said Tim. 'Well if you're going to be like that, I won't let you be part of my new idea.'

Ant shook his head. 'Don't worry about it, you're not missing out,' he said. 'His new idea is insane.'

Freddie cocked his head.

'What's the idea?' BK asked, her gaze fixating on Tim in that strange way she sometimes had.

Tim grinned, mischief glinting in his eyes. He clapped his hands together and leaned forward, as if he were about to impart some big secret, forgetting all about my suit.

'We're going to make a blood pact!'

Silence.

Ant sighed and shook his head. 'I told you it was insane.'

'Oh come on,' said Tim, straightening up and staring around at us. 'I mean, we're all pretty much related by now, anyway. We should make it proper. Become blood brothers.'

'And sisters,' said BK, nodding emphatically.

'Right,' said Tim, waving his hand like that was a given. 'That too.'

'How do we do it?' BK asked, infected—like always—instantaneously by Tim's exuberance.

Ant gave me a sideways look, and shook his head.

'It was in this movie I watched the other day,' Tim explained. 'I think the generally accepted ritual is that we all cut our palms, and shake hands, and then we have to make some kind of promise to each other.'

'What kind of promise?'

'Sure,' said Ant, 'just skip right over the whole "cut your palms" bit.'

BK ignored him, her attention focused on Tim. Tim was grinning, even more eager now he'd gotten an audience. Freddie was listening avidly, a slow, sly smile forming on his face.

Ant's shoulders drooped, and he looked to me as the only other voice of reason.

'Well,' said Tim, 'that's what we gotta figure out. But nothing too stupid or complicated.'

Freddie stuck his hands up and signed something so

rapidly I almost missed it. I raised my eyebrows.

Tim cocked his head, considering. 'Short, simple. I like it.'

Ant, who'd always struggled with sign language, frowned. 'What?'

'Us first,' I said. 'First to each other. No matter where we are or who we become, we'll always be there for each other. We first, always.'

Tim raised his eyebrows, and glanced at Freddie. Lips quirked, he said, 'You got all that from what he signed?'

I flushed, eyes dropping.

'I like it,' said BK, beaming at me. 'We already belong to each other, don't we? So we should make it official. Let's do it!'

'BK,' Ant groaned. 'Come on, do you really want to belong to this idiot?'

'Of course,' she said, face bright and earnest. 'You're all my idiots.'

Ant sighed. He glanced sideways at me again and I could tell his resolve was waning. His eyes drifted down to my chest. To the reason I'd never worn a two piece before. The large pink scar glistening in the summer sunlight, stretched tight across my skin.

'It'll leave a scar,' he said softly.

With a start I realised Ant's problem with Tim's plan had nothing to do with the risks of what he was proposing. It was Tim. There were always risks where he was concerned, this was no different.

Just as soft, I said, 'that's the point, isn't it? So we remember.'

Ant's gaze shifted from me, to BK, to Freddie—who nodded, his gaze dark and serious—and finally to Tim. Blue eyes softened, something far stronger than fondness melting away his resolve and his sense. He didn't sigh, didn't make any other argument or sign of resignation. He just nodded.

'Okay,' said Ant, glancing back at me to make sure.

I nodded. 'Okay.'

Tim beamed. 'Right,' he said, turning to Freddie. 'Do you have a knife?'

CHAPTER TWENTY-ONE

Zach

Genie's room was not what Zach expected. Not that he knew what to expect of a sixteen-year-old girl's room. He paused in the doorway. As BK rummaged around in a dresser, Zach surveyed the room with bemused interest.

They'd gone up a small, narrow flight of stairs into the only upstairs room. The ceiling was arched. An old attic transformed into a bedroom with two beds pressed against opposite sides of the room.

The bed on the left was covered with a fluffy, pink duvet and numerous stuffed toys. The combination of pastel pinks and forest greens created a rather dizzying effect. There were three small, vase-like glass structures hanging from the ceiling over the bed, with various sorts of plants overflowing from the openings. Beyond them, on the wall, were numerous bird, insect and plant pictures that looked to be hand painted. He looked closer, noticing small scribblings beside each one.

'The pink is BK's.'

Zach jumped, jerking further into the room and spinning around to see Ant and Freddie standing on the stairs outside the door.

Ant smiled, not unkindly, and gestured to the other side of the room. 'The aliens are Genie's.'

Zach turned back, eyeing the bed opposite the pink and green catastrophe. It was small and understated, with several throw blankets piled over the end. Surprisingly, the only toy on that bed was a small, golden dragon. Compared to BK's bed, it was bare. Instead, it was the large, handsome mahogany bookcase that caught Zach's gaze.

He stepped closer to it, noting how very different it was to the bookcase that had been in Freddie's room. There were no trophies on these shelves. Instead, two large astronomy tomes sat on the middle shelf and beyond those, book after book about UFO's, aliens and the unexplainable. Zach had never seen such a large collection of the strange and abnormal.

The walls around her bed were littered with astronomy posters and—contrary to the general theme of her side of the room—music bands. A large poster of the solar system was tacked to the sloping roof above her bed, right above a large, signed photo of a band Zach had never heard of.

A music book sat on the bedside table. Zach picked it up and flicked through. There were pages and pages of song lyrics and music notes. Zach paused on one page to read, but the book was yanked out of his hands before he got two lines down.

Freddie's glower was fiercer than ever, his eyes blazing a clear message, his jaw clenched around words he couldn't speak. *That's private.*'

Zach shrugged. 'Sorry,' he said. 'Was just curious about who I've come to find.'

Freddie turned, folding the music book in half and shoving it into the pocket of his cargo pants. He'd already changed out of his school uniform. He took two steps toward BK and Stevie, pushed himself between them to rifle through the draw. Within a minute held a pair of jeans and a t-shirt.

He gave BK a wry, exasperated look loaded with affection, and handed the clothes to Stevie. He made a swift motion at BK.

'Okay, okay,' she said, waving a hand at him. 'We'll get changed. Meet you down at the car.'

Freddie held up his palm, all five fingers spread out, and gave BK an expectant look, one eyebrow tilted up in scepticism.

'Five minutes,' she said. 'I *promise*.'

Freddie nodded. There were faint lines of worry around his eyes, and his shoulders were still tense despite his attempt at a smile. BK beamed back, obviously trying to reassure him just as much as he was trying to reassure her. Zach shook his head. This was why he stuck to himself. Trying to make other people feel better seemed so exhausting.

Ten minutes later, trees and properties whizzed past as Zach manoeuvred his parents expensive, luxury car around the twists and bends in the road. Freddie had wanted to take Tim's car, but it had stalled three times before they got out of the driveway, and Zach had vetoed any further attempts to get it going.

He drummed his fingers along the steering wheel, not really paying attention to where he was going unless Ant or Freddie (who kept leaning in from the back seat to make motions at Ant) directed him otherwise.

'Maybe you should slow down,' said Ant, gripping the handle above his door with no small amount of trepidation.

Zach eased off the accelerator, giving him a sheepish look. The speedo dropped from 140 kilometres per hour to a hundred.

'I, uh, didn't see the limit,' said Zach by way of explanation.

He hadn't seen much of anything, really. Nothing except the winding black road before him. He ignored the paddocks, and the infrequent houses that popped up every few minutes along the endless road and tried to piece together what was happening.

Ant's lip twitched up. 'It's Eighty,' he said.

'Eighty?' Zach asked incredulously. 'Isn't this a highway?'

'They dropped it two years ago. Four fatalities on this stretch of road in twelve months and the locals started to get a bit upset.'

'Oh. Speeding?' asked Zach, still sticking to a hundred.

'Cows,' said Ant. 'There's a few cattle farms up ahead.'

This time Zach did back off. Speeding he could handle; cows were another matter. He had no interest in seeing who would come off better: the cow, his parents Porsche, or the five of them inside. It didn't take a genius to work that equation out.

Stevie made a small noise. Glancing into the rearview mirror, Zach caught the faint glow around her ears, almost like she was charging up for another one of those electric strikes. He swallowed, and backed off even more, the hum of the car dropping away as it slowed.

Freddie was watching her. He leaned forward, signing something for Ant to see.

'Huh?' Ant asked. 'Close to what?'

'What did he say?' Zach asked.

'We're close,' Ant said. 'Except that we're not. The school is still a good fifteen minutes away.'

'Twin thing, maybe?' Zach asked, but he thought it was more likely an alien thing.

Stevie's glow was intensifying in the back seat. Zach only hoped she was using whatever telepathy powers she had to find Freddie's sister.

The houses were becoming more frequent. Popping up in closer and closer intervals until there were three in a row, then four, then five. Large Queenslander properties with big balconies and airy rooms built to withstand the summer heat.

He rounded the corner and almost slammed on the breaks, jerking the wheel to the side to avoid hitting the overturned ambulance taking up most the road.

The lights were shattered and the siren was a pitiful half-wail that Zach could only just hear.

'Bloody hell,' said Ant, staring at the wreckage before them. 'What happened?'

Beyond the crash scene was devastation. A car sat through the front of one house, while three more sat smoking—burnt husks of what they used to be. There was a fire truck in the yard of one house, hose out, having succeeded in putting out the flames but the fireman lay motionless in the grass.

'They need help!' BK gasped.

She moved to open the door, despite the fact the car was still moving. Zach yelped and jammed his finger on a button in his door, locking every door with an audible click.

'Don't get out of the car,' said Zach. His voice trembled slightly, and he wanted nothing more than to floor it out of there. Instead he tried to explain. 'We don't know how the plague spreads.'

'But it's a fire,' said Ant. 'BK's right. We should check on them. We might be able to help.'

Zach shook his head, knuckles turning white under the force of his grip. 'He had his suit on, which means he was sick before he got here. Whatever he has, we can't help him.'

The hum of the engine was loud in the quiet of the car, and Zach resisted the urge to turn on the radio. He hated silence. Freddie leaned forward, touching Ant on the arm. He shook his head, his face grim but his jaw set in a determined line. Zach was grateful the boy was so worried about finding his sister.

They headed away from the fire and Zach could see the billowing clouds of black in the distance behind them. The summer sun was starting to dip down on the horizon. Zach cursed, worried they'd be stuck out here in the suburbs when it got dark.

'It's so quiet,' said Ant, blue eyes wide and staring. 'There's no one.'

Zach's jaw clenched, he thought about mentioning they were probably all dead, but a single glance in the rearview mirror told him he didn't have to. The haunted look in Freddie's gaze told Zach they were already aware of what had probably happened to all these people.

It struck Zach that everyone they knew probably lived in town. Friends, family, co-workers, teachers. How many people in this town did they know, had they seen on a day to day basis? Who they would never see again. They might have gone to parties on this very street, had sleep-overs in one of these houses. How lonely, that must be, driving into the remnants of what had been their town.

'Car,' said Ant, straightening up.

Zach leaned forward, squinting out into the fading light. A glint of blue was speeding toward them. A low, dull throb began in the back of Zach's mind. The car drew closer, and Zach could almost make out two figures in the front.

'Is that-?'

'Look out!'

BK's scream came a second before Zach saw them. He slammed his foot so hard on the break he thought he must have broken something. Zach's gaze snapped back to the other car, hearing the squeal of tyres as the little blue hatchback struggled to avoid the dozen or so cows that had galloped onto the road, eyes rimmed white in fear.

Zach had a moment to wonder what had spooked them onto the road, when an awful crunch echoed through the air. The sound of a little blue car slamming into one tonne of beef.

Ant and BK cried out as the car rolled, the bonnet crumpled. By some miracle, the car came right way up again, only now it was on the wrong side of the road, facing down the bank. The car began to roll forward, unresisted, straight into the murky water of the river.

CHAPTER TWENTY-TWO

Genie

It was the cold that woke me from my memories. Everything was blurry and indistinct, and I squinted into the half darkness. My head throbbed in time with my heart beat, and I raised a hand to touch my head. Pain lanced back into my skull and I winced, dropping my hand. Red stained my fingers.

Water splashed onto my thighs, and I gasped with the shock of the cold.

'Shit,' I whispered, pushing up on the seat as the water rose around me.

It was gushing up from somewhere beneath the seat. What...? Were we...in the river?

'Tim!' I cried, turning and getting caught on the seatbelt.

It struck hard against my chest but I ignored it. Tim was slumped forward over the wheel, the half deflated airbag keeping him up out of the water—but not for much longer. I grabbed at him, trying to pull him upright.

'Tim,' I gasped again. 'Are you okay? Tim?'

He groaned. Blood coated the side of his face and dripped down onto his jhoulders. A frown of pain and confusion pulled at his brows and he tried to sit up properly but his hands slipped on the wet, deflating airbag and he fell forward again.

'No, no, no, no.'

Somewhere by my feet, I could feel the water rushing against my school. My toes curled in the squish of wet socks, attempting to find warmth as the rest of my body panicked. It was so cold. How could it be so cold? It was summer!

I leaned forward to peer out through the windscreen. The car was half submerged in the river, the water washing over the bonnet and up onto the windscreen. There was a lurch, and the car slid forward another metre or so into the river. I swore, jerked forward by the motion and yet held in place by the seatbelt. I thought it might cut into me soon, adding to the scars I already held.

'Tim,' I whispered, teeth chattering in a combination of cold and fear. 'Please wake up.'

He groaned again, but his eyes remained shut. I whimpered. Droplets of blood dripped into the water, creating little pools of red. Fear coiled in my gut.

'Think, *think* Genie!'

Shoving my hands into the cold water, I yanked my seatbelt off, sucking in a deep breath as the pressure released from my chest. The water splashed higher and a shiver went through me, wedging itself in my throat. Gasping, I sloshed around for something to put on Tim's head. Nothing. Gooseflesh erupted over my arms.

A sob worked its way out of my throat, and my vision went blurry.

'No,' I said, shaking my head. 'Concentrate. Stop the bleeding.'

I turned back to Tim and contemplated pulling his shirt off. No, easier to use my own. I yanked at the front of my shirt, ripping the buttons away in an attempt to get the thing open. For a moment, I got caught in the thin, soaked fabric. It clung to me, refusing to release me from it's hold, and panic wedged tight in my throat.

With a sharp yank, the shirt came free.

I twisted the shirt diagonally, wringing as much of the water out of it as I could, and tied it around Tim's head. It was awkward. I had to lean over the centre console to reach him and his head kept lolling to one side as I tried to tie it.

Once that was done, I sat back into my flooding seat and wondered what on earth I was going to do next. I looked around. I could break the windows with something, but we'd probably get cut by the glass or pushed back by the force of the water.

'Not like you have a lot of options,' I said aloud to myself.

I thought of Freddie. Of what he'd do in this situation. I remembered the afternoon we came across an old abandoned car out in one of the neighbour's fields, left there by someone who hadn't wanted to deal with getting rid of it themselves. Freddie and Tim had gladly taken it off the neighbour's hands. They spent some time trying to fix it, before giving up and tearing it to pieces. I remembered them breaking the windows. How Freddie had yanked out the headrests and smashed the metal ends into the glass.

'You can get out,' I imagined him telling me. *'You have the tools. Just get out of the water.'*

Sucking in a breath, I felt calmer.

A faint scar marked the skin on my palm. A shallow cut, compared to my previous wounds. The scar had healed better, fainter. Few people noticed it when faced with the more prominent scar on my chest.

Yet this was the scar I bore with pride. It had been my choice. My way of showing that I could be strong. That my wounds didn't define me. I had people I loved and cared about and would do anything for—who didn't care what I looked like or what marred my skin. It seemed such a silly, inconsequential thing, and yet, it gave me strength. Us first.

I clenched my fist, trying to take hold of my courage. 'Be brave,' I whispered. 'You have to get Tim out. So be brave.'

The water was up around my waist, slowing down now there was more of the car to fill. Turning to the back seats, I searched for a way to get into the boot. If I could climb through, I could figure out a way to get the boot open and drag Tim out. The surface was right there, with fresh air and the bank not far away.

With nothing but my bra to protect me from the cold, I shivered and shook. Gooseflesh spread across my stomach and chest, except for the smooth, pale skin of an old wound.

I swallowed, and shut my eyes. Where had that courage gone?

'*Be brave, Genie.*'

I opened my eyes and shook myself.

'Get to work, Genie,' I said.

For the moment, Tim was stable where he was, so I crawled into the back seat and worked at the flimsy, fabric-covered board that acted as a cover to the boot. I just had to get the thing open, and then we could get out. The boot cover came free with a sharp tug, giving way so suddenly that I fell back. Water engulfed me, drawing me in.

My head broke the water, and I gasped out a sob. 'Tim!' I cried, blinking water out of my eyes. 'Tim, *please.*'

'*Don't give up,*' said my inner conscience in Freddie's voice. '*Be brave. You're stronger than you think. Be brave, Genie.*'

My teeth chattered and I felt miserable, but I wasn't giving up. I turned back to Tim. With some grunting and swearing and a lot of shivering, I got him free of his seatbelt. Somehow, I got him into the backseat. It was so cold, I barely remembered how I'd managed it. With him slumped over the backseat, I clambered over the back and into the boot.

The ends of the headrest were pointed and sharp. I didn't wait or pause. We'd been in there too long. I turned, the water up around my shoulders, and smashed the sharp points against the windscreen.

The shatter and rush of water combined into one, terrifying sound. It consumed my soul, crushing me before I had a chance to scream. I gulped at the roof of the car, desperate to get one last breath before the water encased us.

CHAPTER TWENTY-THREE

Zach

For a moment, everything was still.

Then Stevie gasped, 'Genie!' and the boys erupted into motion.

Freddie and Ant almost fell out of the car in their desperation to get out and BK scrabbled after them in a flurry of limbs.

'Shit!' Zach said, and shoved open his door to follow them.

The cars had been a hundred or so metres apart when the cows had burst out. Now, the little blue car was a metre or two off the bank, the back end only just poking out of the water. It had rolled off the edge, crushing the grass and small saplings along the river, as it slid in at an angle.

Freddie and Ant were both faster than Zach, and had raced up the street toward the crash without a backwards glance. BK flew after them, and Zach, left with Stevie anxiously biting at her fingers cursed again and followed.

By the time he reached them, they were struggling to get over the trees and branches clinging to the edge of the embankment.

Zach halted, eyeing the edge of the bank and the muddy water. Freddie toppled into the river, and came up gasping. He shook himself, ignored Ant's hand for help, and waded in after the car. He sunk in three places, and was pushed back by the current each time.

'Freddie,' Ant gasped, slipping and sliding down after him. 'Wait!'

BK made to dive in after them, but Zach grabbed at her. 'Whoa, wait, you can't go in.'

'But Genie-?'

'It might not be her,' said Zach.

She cast him a skeptical look that he ignored. The boys both looked like strong swimmers, certainly stronger than Zach could hope to be, and yet they struggled against the cold current swirling down the river and around the car. Their shoulders only just broke the water's surface and they moved with painful slowness. If BK tried to go in, she'd be swept away with ease.

'We have to stay here, and help them get back up the bank,' said Zach. 'Can you do that?'

'Yes,' she said, never taking her eyes off her cousin.

Each minute dragged out, and Zach felt his heart thudding in his chest as Freddie reached out for the car. He jerked back suddenly, losing his footing and almost going under again. He came up spluttering just as the back window of the car collapsed inwards. Zach swore, and took a half step forward without thinking.

Freddie surged towards the car, grabbing hold of the boot and dragging himself to it. He got his feet back under him and reached into the flooding car. A head poked up, then a pair of hands.

Ant was still a few paces behind, and shouting out to Freddie. BK took a few more steps forward standing right on the edge of the bank. Branches and tree roots moved beneath her feet and Zach reached out, ready to yank her back from the edge.

The boys pulled a body out of the car, limp and unconscious, and Zach sucked in a breath.

'Oh no,' BK gasped, her hands flying to her mouth.

Ant held the unconscious boy up, bracing himself against the car as Freddie reached back inside. A girl emerged like a ghost. Her dark hair was matted to her head and shoulders, and she was wearing nothing but a skirt and bra as she clambered out of the back of the car. She kept her footing, holding onto Freddie's shoulder for support as the four of them began to wade back.

'Here,' Zach said, dropping down and reaching out a hand without even thinking about it.

The girl's skin was colder than ice, and she trembled as Zach tried to haul her up. BK was on her knees, pulling at the girl's shoulder. Together, she and Zach dragged the girl onto the embankment.

She collapsed, coughing and shivering, while Zach turned back to help the others. Freddie brushed aside Zach's offered hand, scrabbling up the embankment by sheer force of will. Once up, he turned and reached back down for the unconscious boy Ant was still supporting.

A few minutes of hauling and yanking, Freddie and Zach pulling and Ant pushing, they managed to get him up.

'Why,' Zach panted, sprawled on the patchy grass beside the river. 'Why on Earth…does he…weigh…so much?'

'He eats a lot,' Ant muttered back.

'But he's so skinny!'

Someone was humming some soft tune that Zach half recognised. Was it a TV intro?

'Tim, you okay?' Ant asked.

He was somewhere to Zach's left, but he just couldn't summon the strength to move. A few metres down the road, the herd of cows shifted restlessly along the road, calling out to one another with mournful cries.

The humming broke off, and a slurred voice said, 'She broke the window. She threw a vase at me.'

'I think…I think he has a, a concush…' the feminine voice trailed off, and there was a short gasp of alarm.

'Genie!'

There was a flurry of motion, and Freddie and Stevie converged on the girl. Zach tried not to think about the absurd string of coincidences that had led them all to being on this road at exactly the right time. What if they'd taken longer to leave the house? What if Zach *hadn't* been speeding? What if he hadn't slowed down? If they'd even been a minute sooner, there was a good chance there'd be two ruined cars in the river instead of one.

'She n-needs to lie d-down. She's g-going to need st-stitches.'

Zach struggled up, rolling onto his side and pushing himself to his feet.

'She's going to need to get warm,' he said. 'They both will, but her especially. She's barely dressed.'

Freddie scowled at him, and Zach hurriedly looked away from the girl to instead study the boy they'd pulled from the car. Tim.

The dark-skinned boy drifted in and out of consciousness. He peered up at the sky with glazed, coal black eyes, mumbling words of nonsense as he struggled to come to. He had a strip of white material that Zach suspected might have been a shirt—Genie's, from her undressed state—wrapped around his head. Red was seeping through the thin white fabric.

Zach caught sight of more blood on the leg of Freddie's pants. He must have cut himself either during his fall into the river or on the hasty climb back up. Either way, it would need attending to.

'I think they might all need stitches,' he said.

'We need to get back home,' said Ant.

He was sitting beside Tim, staring at his friend, deep worry lines etched into his face.

Zach gestured around. 'Why,' he said. 'There are plenty of empty houses right here.'

'You want to break into someone's home?'

'You have two options,' Zach pointed out. 'Let your friends bleed to death while you hum and har, trying to work out how to fit us all in that car and get us back to the house in one piece. Or, break into one of these unused houses and get them better.'

'They're not exactly unused.'

'They are now.'

Zach could see that Ant wanted to object. But he wasn't stupid; he could see that his friends needed help *now*.

Not that it mattered, because Freddie took matters into his own hands. He scooped up his sister and stomped off toward the nearest house without a glance in their direction.

CHAPTER TWENTY-FOUR

Genie

The room was cool. A fan whirred overhead, blowing soft gusts of air over me. The sheets were stiff and the blanket scratchy and unfamiliar.

Opening my eyes, I looked around. There was a glass of water on the bedside table. I reached for it, then decided I had to go to the bathroom instead.

Throwing off the covers I swung my legs over the edge of the bed. Pain spiked. I gasped, clutching at my right side. Why was I in pain?

The room was dark, but sunlight streamed through the gap in the curtain, giving me enough sunlight to see that this was *not* my room. Where was I? What had happened? The warmth and the sleepiness dispersed to be replaced with a disorienting feeling of claustrophobia.

Crisp morning air sent a chill across my bare arms. I had no shirt on. I had no shirt on because I'd taken it off. To save Tim. Memories flooded in faster than the car I had been trapped in.

I took a deep breath. Okay. So I knew what happened, the question remained, where was I?

Getting up, I winced from both the cold tiles and the itch of pain. I turned about the room and when I saw no clothes, riffled through the chest of draws in the corner.

I found a loose shirt two times too big for me and pulled it on, conscious that I was probably stealing but not wanting to leave the room without clothes on.

Wary, I pressed an ear to the door, listening intently. Silence. The door swung open easy and silent, and I shuffled slowly down the hallway beyond, finding the bathroom in the first doorway on my left.

I paused in front of the mirror. I was pale. There were purple rings of exhaustion around my eyes. My hair needed a wash, dangling about my shoulders lifelessly, and a multitude of bandages were wrapped around my waist. They went from my hips all the way above my chest, though not high enough to cover the old scar. My gaze flicked over it. It stood out, shiny and stretched, a lance of lightning going from my right shoulder, across my chest, disappearing under the baggy shirt. A real vision of beauty. I looked away from it, twisting to where the bandages were raised, just above my hip. I prodded at it, wincing a little. There was no blood, though. Someone had been taking very good care of me.

I cleaned up as best I could, washing my face and brushing my hair. It was too painful to braid. The wound the bandages covered stretched tight when I raised my arm, making me stiff and sore. I settled for tying my hair in a bun, away from my face.

I peeked my head out into the hallway again, turning my head in each direction to listen. Still no one. I ventured out, tiptoeing along the hallway, my throat dry and scratchy. I had to concentrate hard on walking, wincing every time I lifted my right foot and leaning heavily on it when I stepped with the left foot. Thankfully, no one was around to watch my ridiculous shuffling progress.

When I reached the lounge room I stopped, gaping at the scene like an idiot.

Ant and BK sat on a large, fuzzy rug on the floor playing some sort of card game. There was a jar of coins to each side and they appeared to be betting, though the game looked to be something like Go Fish.

Ant was wearing BK's bandana, wrapped around the top of his head with a bit of white gauze poking out from underneath it at the temple. A rush of relief swept over me so strong, I swayed with it.

My grip tightened on the door and I searched the room, looking for Tim, the relief becoming an empty, hollow feeling in my stomach before I caught sight of him.

He was sitting on the couch with Freddie, the two of them on either side of a third person. A purple person. With long, tentacle-like ears trailing back over bony shoulders.

I swayed more, using both hands to hang onto the doorway in case my legs decided to give out beneath me. My whole world tipped sideways, and my vision blurred.

Blinking rapidly, I refocused on the couch, trying to make sense of what my eyes were telling me. Déjà Vu flashed across my mind, layering another image of a purple person over this one. As purple as a sunset sky, emerging out of the evening glow in our backyard. Like an angel, or a ghost. Yet somehow, that image was so much *less* surreal than the one I was staring at now.

Freddie was shaking his head, signing something rapidly to Tim, his brows pulled together in disbelief, his mouth twisted in scepticism.

'No, no, no,' Tim was saying. 'You're wrong. Thor's power comes from the hammer, he couldn't beat a fly without it!'

I paused, the world rocking back into sharp focus as I registered exactly what it was they were arguing about. Freddie was gesturing at the TV while the alien girl sitting between them looked more and more lost with each word.

The sound was down on the TV so I hadn't even noticed it was on, but there on the screen was the thunder god in all his glory. It was so typical, so utterly normal, that the fact I was dressed in a stranger's clothes, in a stranger's house, standing across the room from an alien ceased bothering me.

'You know that's not what she asked about, right?'

Tim and Freddie paused their argument, turning to look as yet another stranger entered from a kitchen doorway I hadn't noticed. Both Tim and Freddie looked at the boy as if he were stupid, before returning to their argument.

The boy shook his head. He caught sight of me standing in the hallway and his amused expression melted away to something oddly unreadable. I stared back, frowning.

Growing up with Freddie I'd gotten pretty good at reading people. More often than not, I knew what a person was thinking—even Ant, who hid his emotions from just about everyone.

Yet this boy, this stranger, was indecipherable. He blinked, tilting his head as he regarded me with bright electric-blue eyes. As if he'd just been struck by lightning and the electricity hadn't left his body yet.

'Hi,' the stranger said, still staring at me with those shocking blue eyes. 'I'm Zach. I brought you your alien.'

CHAPTER TWENTY-FIVE

Zach

Zach wanted to smack himself. He couldn't help staring at her. At her scar. The baggy, green shirt she wore did nothing to hide the jagged line that sliced across her chest, like some distorted pink vein. It carved a rugged path from her right shoulder, angling down on a soft yet sawtoothed path to the tender skin above her left breast, where it tapered away to nothing.

She shifted, her shoulders hunching forwards as she crossed her arms. Zach jerked his gaze upwards, looking instead into those storm grey eyes that were so like, yet unlike, her brother's. It was remarkable how similar they looked, even for fraternal twins.

'Sorry,' Zach said sheepishly, dropping his gaze. He pulled the lighter and joint out of his pocket. 'Mind if I smoke?'

Her eyebrows rose, but she nodded and since no one else objected, Zach flicked the lighter open.

'You okay?'

The brusque question came from Tim, who watched the girl with a serious expression.

She nodded. 'Sore, but yeah, okay.'

'You were asleep for a long time,' said Ant his voice low and concerned.

'What time is it?' she asked, looking around, grey eyes taking in the lit room and frowning.

'Ten in the morning,' Ant said. 'You passed out just before seven last night.'

Exhaling smoke, Zach leaned his elbows on his knees, watching the girl before him. She was… unexpected. The scar. Her guarded gaze. Her eyes weren't bright like the green of her cousin's, or expressive like her brother's. They were shaded, inscrutable, and Zach felt drawn into their depths, curious of the shadows and memories hidden within.

She nodded again, and those stormy eyes found their way back to Zach. Her head tilted, and she asked.

'You brought me…my alien?'

Zach grinned. Now they were all out of danger he felt more relaxed. He sipped on the joint, flicking ash onto the floor in the way he knew his mother hated.

'She needed a ride,' he shrugged and leaned back into the couch. 'I had a car.'

Her gaze drifted back to the lounge. Tim grinned, his gaze shifting rapidly between her and the alien girl. Freddie just watched his sister, his own face guarded and—for once—unreadable.

'You're …' Genie trailed off and swallowed.

Stevie was gazing at Genie, silver eyes sharp, head cocked on one side. One of her ears twitched, reminding Zach of a dog responding to something it heard.

Genie stepped closer, slow and unsteady. Zach considered reaching out to help her, but Freddie was already there. He'd moved without sound, rising from the couch to be by his sister's side. He guided her by the elbow back to the lounge where Stevie now stood and the two girls regarded each other.

Zach frowned. The faint buzz of electricity fizzed in the air, but there was no sign of the blue light along Stevie's ridges. Still, something was off. The twins, standing before the alien that had searched for them, were in sync with each other. Their movements had flowed together, over one another, adjusting to each other. Like they were each an extension of the other person. Zach had never met fraternal twins that looked so alike. Not that he'd met many sets of twins. Still, their similarity was unnatural. But there was something else, something that bothered him.

Stevie's gaze flicked to him and—

Zach blinked, remembering the silver shine in Freddie's eyes the day before. Their eyes were the same colour as Stevie's. The alien.

The hairs on his neck prickled and gooseflesh erupted over Zach's arms. He shivered and brought the joint to his lips in an effort to hide his discomfort.

A sudden smile blossomed on Genie's face, her eyes becoming soft.. 'You look just like him.'

Stevie's eye's wined in surprise and her lips twitched up into a shy smile. The flush—of pleasure, rather than embarrassment—spread along her ears.

'Einstein?' Stevie asked, drawing the word out into careful syllables.

Genie nodded, leaning closer to peer at the alien girl. She turned her head, smiling at her brother.

'I told you,' she said, her voice soft and yet filled with awe, as if she only just now believed it herself. 'I told you he was real.'

Freddie shifted, his weight falling sideways to bump into her, a faint smile on his face as he gave one simple encouraging nod.

'I wish you could have met my grandmother,' Genie whispered to Stevie, the sheen of tears glistening in her eyes. 'She'd have liked you.'

Stevie's blush deepened, her ears lighting up in dark splotches of deep purple. 'I have wait-waited a…a long t-time to m-meet you.'

'The question is,' said Zach, inadvertently making them jump. 'What do we do now?'

'Now, she saves us,' said Tim. 'Doesn't she?'

Genie swiped at her eyes, trying to hide her tears, and turned to Tim. 'Saves us?'

'There's a sickness,' said BK, still sitting on the floor with Ant, though she seemed to have forgotten about her card game. 'Like a plague. It's killing everyone.'

'The school,' Genie breathed, her eyes widening in realisation.

Something dark flickered in her gaze, and her breathing quickened. Freddie touched her arm and she flinched, jerking away from him with a brief look of fear. She blinked, her gaze refocusing on him as the fear receded.

She took a deep breath. 'I...I'm going to get some air,' she said. She turned, gaze searching the room for an exit. Her eyes latched onto the front door.

'You shouldn't go too far,' said Zach as she made her way to the door. 'It's not safe out there.'

She paused, that black ice returning. 'I know,' she whispered, and headed out.

Freddie cast an enquiring gaze to Tim, torn on whether or not he should follow her. Tim swallowed, and refused to look at his friend.

'I, uh, may have left something out,' said Tim. 'When I explained about the school.'

He shifted his weight from foot to foot, his voice low and guilty. Zach frowned. Since Tim had woken up that morning he'd seen his first alien, reunited with his closest friend, and retold the horrifying experience of the day before. Yet he'd been unflappable. Now, he fidgeted under Freddie's hard gaze.

'James...he was at the school.'

Freddie went tense all over.

'Nothing happened though, I swear,' said Tim. 'She took off and I went after her. I mean, I could've stayed and shot the bastard but I didn't wanna lose her. So I went after her. I kept her safe, Freddie. I swear.'

Freddie didn't answer. He stomped through the room, gaze fixed on the front door his sister had just vanished through.

'Wait!' Tim called, but Freddie was already gone, the front door slamming behind him. 'There's more...' he finished lamely, his shoulders slumping. Tim ground his teeth.

Zach sighed and took another pull on the joint.

'James was at the school?' Ant asked in a small voice.

'Who's James?' Zach asked.

Tim's gaze flicked his way, but instead of answering, he began to pace. Stevie shifted out of his way, her ears beginning to glow again. Zach wondered what thoughts she was picking up from Tim.

'James was their brother,' said Ant.

'Was?'

'I should've killed him,' said Tim, still pacing, his scowl fierce and violent.

Ant sighed. 'Killing doesn't solve anything.'

'You don't think he deserves to die?'

'I…I don't know,' said Ant. 'Maybe.'

Zach paused, his joint smoking between his fingers as he stared at Ant. He just couldn't picture Ant wanting to hurt anyone. Tim's scowl only deepened as he stomped a path into the carpet.

'What else?' asked Ant in a soft voice. 'You said there was more?'

Tim glanced at his friend, eyes dark, his steps heavy and yet somehow silent.

When Zach was ten, his parents had taken him and his siblings to Africa to help build a new school for the underprivileged. They'd spent one day out in the heat and the dirt, giving out lemonade to the workers before retreating back to the five-star hotel for the next ten days, sipping ice cold drinks by the crystal blue pool; sending their three children off on every activity the hotel offered. One of which was a day safari.

After hours and hours of driving around in the sun, they headed back toward the hotel with nothing but some pictures of giraffe. Except, in the last hour, the driver was forced to take a detour.

A leopard traipsed the road ahead, dragging a dead antelope in it's jaw. With no tree around to drag her prey into, she laid down the carcass and stared at them, amber eyes watchful and calculative. As the jeep circled around, the leopard began to prowl, pacing back and forth in front of her kill.

Tim walked with that same feline prowl, that same set to his shoulders.

Zach made a mental note to never test just how predatory Tim was. He had a feeling he'd come out of that test a little mauled. Zach brought the joint to his lips again and waited for Tim's answer.

Tim took a deep breath, his fists clenched by his side. 'She killed someone.'

CHAPTER TWENTY-SIX

Genie

The pain rose up from the pit of my stomach so suddenly I thought I was going to faint. I doubled over.

The heaving never came though, and I stood panting in the bushes with nothing but the sharp, bitter taste of acid stuck in my throat.

Swiping the back of my hand against my mouth, I straightened and took a few cautious steps. Heat swarmed down my head and shoulders and I swayed, feeling lightheaded and far away. Blood rushed in my ears, and for a moment I was back in that hallway, the sound of gunfire and screams echoing in the distance as James leered at me from a bloody corridor.

A hand grabbed my arm. I yelped, turning sharply only to see Freddie. He stared back at me, a face full of worry lines and creases. His grip on my arm was tight and a little painful, but strong enough to help me balance.

Tim had once asked me what I thought Freddie would sound like. 'When I try to imagine what he says, it sounds like me,' he'd said, head tilted back to the sky, reflections of clouds in the brown of jhis eyes. 'It's almost like having a conversation with myself.'

It wasn't like that for me. Freddie didn't sound like me, and he didn't sound like Tim. He just sounded like Freddie.

'Head between your knees,' I imagined him saying, as he helped me lower to the ground.

I crouched down and let my head hang toward my feet,

hands clutching at my ears as the rush of panic began to pass. Strands of hair had slipped out of the bun, and he swept them back out of my face. Perspiration clung to my skin, though I wasn't sure if it was because of the panic, or the summer sun.

'*Wanna puke?*'

I shook my head, then paused. 'Maybe.'

A bull-ant crawled across the broken pavement I was standing on. Then another, scuttling between the cracks.

Freddie tried to grin. '*Trust you to hurl on an ant nest.*'

The grin didn't reach his eyes though, and he watched me carefully, still brushing back my hair.

When I could lift my head without dizziness threatening to overwhelm me, he helped me stand. His arms were around me in an instant, tight and warm and fierce as he was with all things. A shudder rippled through my chest, and it took a moment for me to realise it was Freddie, trembling against me as he crushed me in a bear hug.

'Freddie?' I asked.

He shook his head against my shoulder.

'Freddie, it's—'

His grip tightened, cutting me off. I felt him swallow. Felt his Adam's apple bob against my shoulder as he clung to me. As if he would fall if he let go. He shook his head again.

I tried to pull away but he wouldn't let me. So instead I clung back to him and ran a hand through his hair, the way I remembered Mum used to do.

'It's okay,' I whispered.

He shook his head again.

I paused, wondering what had set Freddie off. 'Is it… Freddie, it's okay,' I said, taking a guess at what had upset him. 'I'm okay. No one hurt me. In fact, no one hurt *me* at all.'

His breath hitched. He shoved away from me, turning away so I couldn't see his face. I held a hand out to the side, the sudden lack of support causing me to lose my balance.

'*I left you!*'

The words came to me, floating out of my subconscious like the luminance of a lightbulb. Of course he felt guilty. It was in the set of his shoulders and the slight tremor of his closed fists.

'Don't be silly,' I said, my voice catching as I thought about the events at the school.

About Josie, and the woman in the suit and the man I shot. The man I killed. I swallowed hard, trying not to tremble.

Freddie shook his head sharply, dark hair falling around his face, still shielding it from me. His shoulders were shaking.

'Freddie…'

He shuddered, kept his face turned away so I couldn't see his expression. So I couldn't tell what he was thinking. It didn't matter. The words came to me anyway.

'I won't let him hurt you.'

James. Of course. Once again, he hadn't been around to protect me. It had been left to Tim to make sure I was okay. That James hadn't damaged me beyond repair.

I paused, watching his back, watching the way he stayed turned away. He was afraid, but he'd never been shy of letting me see him afraid before. Wasn't he the one who came sneaking into my room after a nightmare, too afraid to sleep on his own? No, the fear wasn't what he was trying to hide. He was afraid that I would see what he was really feeling.

Shame. Shame for leaving me? Shame for running away? Shame for…for what, not fighting James? I straightened, staring at Freddie's back, feeling selfish and stupid. Sometimes I forgot that James was Freddie's brother too. That James had been Freddie's idol. He had admired him, wanted to be *like* him.

The dead man's face flashed before my eyes again. Was *I* like James? I shook my head, trying to chase away the thought.

Before James was sent away, Grandma had agreed to let Freddie see him. Freddie couldn't understand, couldn't fathom why James had hurt me. He'd never told me what they spoke about, but Freddie had begun to change after that day. He became harder, rougher, he fought to win—no matter if it was fair or not. For a while, he had even tried to teach me to do the same.

I had always thought he fought that way because he was angry, but I was beginning to understand that Freddie was afraid. Had always been afraid.

'You're scared he'll hurt you too,' I said, realisation hitting all at once.

Freddie flinched, turning guilty eyes on me. I put my hand on his shoulder but he jerked away. His eyes were red and angry, but not with me. With himself. With his own fears and shame. Tears flooded his cheeks and silent sobs shook him.

'Freddie,' I said, but had nothing else to follow.

He swiped at his eyes, kicking at the pavement. *Don't comfort me. I don't deserve it.'*

'It's okay to be afraid.'

He shook his head again, but his shoulders had slumped. I understood. I sighed, and this time I didn't let him shake me off.

'We're the same,' I said, trying to show him I wasn't upset. How could I be angry at him for being scared? I was always scared. 'If I'm afraid, you're afraid. If I'm angry, you're angry. If I'm sad, you're sad. Just…you've always been better at controlling your fear than I have. You hide under that explosive fire of yours.'

He grinned a little through the tears and scrubbed at his face. *Just not from you, right?'*

'No,' I said, hugging him tight. 'Not from me. Come on, let's go back inside.'

He nodded, pulling back and casting me a sideways look. *'I miss Grandma.'*

My chest felt heavy as I sucked in a careful breath. 'Yeah,' I said softly, trying not to wonder what she would think of my actions. 'Me too.'

Inside, the others had scattered. It was just Tim left in the lounge room, and I looked about for the others.

'They went to explore,' said Tim, answering my questioning gaze. 'Hey, Freddie, wanna play poker?'

Freddie shrugged, eyes still downcast, and crossed over

to where Tim sat. Tim nodded at me, his expression telling me to relax. He had it covered.

'Hey,' Tim called after me. 'BK took Stevie outside to look around. You should see what they're up to.'

Right. The alien girl who had come to find me. It was time to get acquainted with my newest alien encounter.

CHAPTER TWENTY-SEVEN

Zach

Zach knew he was snooping.

He also knew whoever had lived in the house before was never coming back. They could have been at work or on an outing, or even just down the road; but it seemed more likely they were away on some sort of trip. There was a single car parked out the front and no other evidence of anyone at home. No milk or produce in the fridge, nothing that could go off.

Although, they could have just bought a lot of take out. When Zach's parents went out of town, he lived off pizza and Thai food. He paid his father's driver to go thirty minutes out of town just to get his favourite chicken fried rice. Maybe they were like him? He didn't hold much hope for it though.

Besides, it wasn't like Zach was nosing around just because they weren't coming back. He'd have done it regardless. He was inherently nosy. His mother blamed his rebelliousness, which was partly true, but mostly he was just curious.

Zach liked to know things. He also didn't particularly like talking to people. Thus, snooping.

It was a nice house. Three bedrooms and an office—in Brisbane, someone with that kind of space would have a lot of money. Judging by the huge map the owner had covering the entirety of one wall in the study, Zach hazarded a guess the same could be said here.

Zach took a step closer, investigating the map. There were little green and red pins stuck into it. Places the owner had been, or maybe places he wanted to?

Zach wasn't sure, but the map gave him an idea. He turned to the desk, sitting down in the small swivel chair and pushing the power button on the computer tower. The fans inside the machine began to whir and Zach sighed.

'This thing is ancient,' he muttered and sat back in the chair to wait for the computer to boot up.

'What're you doing?'

Zach jumped. Tim stood in the doorway, Freddie peering over his shoulder, like a shadow, or two parts of a greater whole.

Zach's fingers stopped drumming on the table top. 'I have an idea,' he said, gaze shifting back to the desktop. 'I want to try tracking the virus.'

Tim frowned and prowled further into the room, Freddie on his heels. 'How?'

Zach gestured at the map on the wall. 'Internet should tell me what I need to know.'

'Will it still work?'

'What? The Internet?' Zach asked.

Freddie nodded, while Tim just raised an eyebrow.

'Should do,' said Zach. 'It's only been a few days. Things like that won't start shutting down until the bills stop being paid. And that'll be a while yet.'

Freddie turned and began investigating the map. Tim leaned on the side of the desk, watching Zach work with a hooded gaze. The room was musty and hot in the late morning sun, and Zach felt an uncomfortable trickle of perspiration form on the back of his neck. Tim made him uncomfortable.

'Someone could've turned it off on purpose, right?' Tim asked, one eyebrow arched in question.

Zach paused.'Yeah, that could be possible, but I doubt it.'

The computer dinged on. Zach searched the desk, lifting the keyboard and mouse pad and riffling through any loose sheets of paper.

'What're you lookin' for?' Tim asked.

'Password. Most people keep them written down somewhere near the computer.'

Zach pulled open the top draw and found a sticky note stuck to the inside of the front panel. He plucked it off and waved it at Tim.

'How d'you know that's it?'

Zach shrugged and began typing in the letters. The computer dinged again and logged on.

Zach threw a wry grin at Tim. 'That's how.'

He began opening search programs.

'Now what?' Tim asked.

Zach's fingers raced across the keyboard. 'First, I'll try tracking social media and news outlets. They'll be the best indication for when this all started. Though, it won't be completely accurate.'

'How's that help us?'

'Figuring out where it came from might help us figure out how to stop it. All we have to do is find the earliest mentions of unexplainable deaths, and *where* they were.'

'Seems pretty far-fetched.'

'The whole thing is far-fetched.'

'What d'you mean?'

Zach paused, glancing up at the dark-skinned boy. He'd finally changed out of his blood-stained t-shirt, having presumably gone rummaging through the owner's clothes. The shirt was baggy and loose, the pants even more so. He looked like a well dressed homeless person. Despite the clothes, his stance still struck Zach as somewhat intimidating. Zach wondered if Tim realised he was standing over him, leaning on the desk with both hands, staring at the screen Zach was working on.

Dark eyes shifted to Zach's face, and that eyebrow rose up again. His expression became questioning and irritated. Zach dropped his gaze, refocusing on the screen.

He cleared his throat. 'Er, what I mean is…well, there simply aren't any virus's that act this fast.'

'So it's a super bug or something?'

'Er, no. That's something you see on TV, not real life. Something like this doesn't just…happen. A death toll on this stage, in such a short amount of time…it's not plausible.'

A piece of paper hit Tim in the side of the head. Zach blinked. He turned to look at Freddie. Tim seemed unbothered.

'What?' he asked.

Freddie signed something. At the end he gestured to Zach and gave Tim an expectant look.

'What about the Black Plague?' Tim asked, translating Freddie's question. 'Didn't it wipe out half of London or something?'

Zach wondered what kind of school these two had been to. 'Not…exactly. It did kill a lot of people but…well, the circumstances aren't really relatable. While it *was* highly contagious, it only spread the way it did due to poor hygiene and worse medical practices. We have way more advanced medicine now. This sort of thing just doesn't happen out of no where.'

'So what are you saying? This was on purpose or something?'

'Maybe,' said Zach. 'Hey, Freddie, could you move some of the red pins to Russia? Seems to be one of the earliest points of outbreak.'

'Wait a minute,' said Tim, waving a hand at Freddie. 'You *do* think this was on purpose. Why?'

'How would I know?'

'I dunno, you're a nerd, aren't you?'

Zach raised his eyebrows. Tim flushed, surprising Zach as his coal black eyes dropped away from Zach's in abashment. He scratched at the side of his nose, gaze drifting back to Zach.

'Sorry, I mean, you seem smart.'

'I do?'

'Sure,' said Tim and gestured at the computer. 'You worked all that shit out, didn't you? I'd've never thought of it.'

By the map, Freddie nodded. He'd already begun to pull

out all the pins, making colour coded piles on a chair. Now he stood, a handful of pins in one hand, and nodded in agreement with Tim.

'Plus,' said Tim. 'Freddie said you knew all that stuff about Stevie. Like how she's telepathic and amphibious or whatever. So, you must be smart, right?'

'Er, I guess so.'

'Stevie says you know five languages,' said Tim.

Zach blinked. 'She did?'

'She asked Freddie how many he knew, as if we should know more than one,' said Tim, as if this was explanation enough.

Zach wondered when on Earth they'd had time to discuss the matter, and wondered if Freddie and Stevie had been engaging in silent conversation while the rest of them had been sleeping.

'Freddie also said you and Stevie are gonna help save us from this thing.' Tim's voice took on a hard edge as he delivered this next bit of information.

Zach got the distinct impression that if he denied this claim, Tim would personally see to his undoing. He swallowed. While he *had* asked Stevie if she could help save the group—seeing as she was already here to save the twins —he hadn't *technically* offered his help. He supposed there were worse things to do than collaborate with an alien on saving the human race.

Who was he kidding? With his education and experience (not to mention his choice of genre in, well, anything), this was basically a dream come true. He tried to resist a grin.

'What do you think I'm trying to do?' he asked, gesturing at the map. 'Now, are you going to ask me more questions or are you going to help?'

He half expected Tim to hit him. Instead, he and Freddie exchanged roguish grins. As one, the two of them turned to Zach and nodded. Tim straightened up from the desk and clapped his hands together.

'Right,' he said. 'Where're we stickin' these pins?'

CHAPTER TWENTY-EIGHT

Genie

When Einstein had come to find me six years ago, he had been so…well, alien. He was intense, yet aloof. His gaze had been cool and calculative, with a hint of danger. He was clever and poised. Dignified. So unlike anything or anyone I had ever encountered. He was ancient. He was majestic.

This creature before me was more like a frightened mouse. She may have looked like Einstein, but she was no more like him than a mouse was like an elephant. She was meek and mild. There was no poise in her timidness. Looking at her—despite the purple skin and lightning blue veins and her strange rubbery ears—was too much like staring into my own reflection.

People always commented on how alike Freddie and I were. How we looked so similar. How our eyes were the same.

They weren't. When I looked into Freddie's eyes I saw strength and compassion and courage. He was my opposite. The brave half of our duo.

No, looking into Freddie's eyes was always like looking into the future, at the endless possibilities of all that could be.

Stevie was my mirror. I saw my own doubt shining back at me, sinking into me, searching out for the cracks and crevices where I hid my pain. I dropped my gaze.

'You're blushing again,' said BK.

She was taller than Stevie and I and was leaning over to

look into Stevie's face, her hands clasped behind her back as she smiled at the alien girl. Stevie *was* blushing, but not on her face. The tips of her ears were no longer the soft, translucent purple. Instead, they were splotchy and dark, the veins hidden as the rush of blood flooded the ends of her ears. At BK's announcement, the dark flush spread further up her ears, almost reaching to the base of her neck.

'BK,' I said, shaking my head.

BK pulled back, a faint flush of her own spreading. 'I'm doing it again, aren't I?' she asked, taking a step back from Stevie. She twirled a curl around her finger, her lips forming a sheepish smile. 'Sorry, Stevie. I was being too personal, wasn't I? I'm always forgetting.'

'BK doesn't have a filter,' I said, trying to explain for her. 'She doesn't always understand what's socially acceptable. It doesn't help that she hangs around Freddie and Tim so much, they're just as bad. Though I'm pretty sure they do it on purpose.'

Soon after my encounter with Einstein, BK was adopted into our family. Freddie and I had thought she was strange. There was this green eyed, frizzy headed oddball who spoke in riddles, couldn't comprehend the simplest of things, and yet somehow knew everything that was going on around her.

An awkward silence descended. Stevie wasn't much for talking, but unlike Freddie, she was also hard to decipher. With Freddie, I always knew what he was thinking.

Stevie wasn't like that. She was like reading street directions in a foreign language to a part of town you'd been to once as a child. Foggy and indistinct, yet somehow familiar.

Unsure how to proceed, I sat down in the grass, looking about the small, understated garden. The grass wasn't so long that it came up around our ankles, but it was enough that our feet sunk into it with every step. As I sat down, it was like sinking into a scratchy, ticklish cushion.

'Oh, good idea,' said BK, and all but threw herself down into the grass. 'I love sky gazing.'

Shielding my eyes from the sun, I leaned back and squinted up at Stevie, who was staring down at BK with that questioning head tilt. She reminded me of a shepherd, the way her head cocked to the side, her ears twitching over her shoulders. A curious and shy shepherd.

'Lay down with us,' BK said.

After a long moment, Stevie settled into the grass beside me. I laid back, flopping into the grass with a whoosh and a smile.

'You have to put your arms out like this,' I said, turning my head and showing Stevie my wide open arms. 'It's better that way.'

'Don't look at the sun either,' said BK from my other side. 'I forget sometimes, and it hurts.'

Stevie shut her eyes.

I smiled and looked back up at the blue sky. There were few clouds, which made for poor cloud watching. Without anything else to focus on, I closed my eyes too. We lay there, stretched out and eyes closed, soaking in the sun until our skin became warm and toasty. A sheen of perspiration began to form on my skin, and I smiled as the cool autumn wind brushed over us.

'Are you b-better now?' Stevie asked.

'Better?' I asked. 'From what?'

'Tim s-said you were up-up-upset,' she said.

Gunshots and screams and far too much red. My eyes flashed open, the blue sky filling my vision and easing away the nightmares bubbling just out of reach.

'I'm…okay,' I said. 'I guess I was upset, but I'm alright now.'

'What happened?' BK asked. I heard her rustle about in the grass. 'At school?'

She leaned up on one elbow, peering at me with unusually serious eyes. She always seemed to know when I was holding something back. She had a sixth sense about these things, seeming to know ahead of time someone would need cheering up. It made pretending to be cheerful rather hard.

'A lot happened. I…I saw my brother.'

There was a moment of silence. Stevie had her head turned towards us, her eyes open and watching.

'You mean…James?' BK asked.

I sighed and closed my eyes again. 'Yeah.'

Silence. The grass was scratchy, but in a good way, and I began to doze off in the mid-day heat. Until I heard BK begin to sniffle.

I cracked open an eye. 'Don't cry.'

'I'm not,' she said, hiccuping.

Big tears dripped down her face. A small bubble of snot was peaking out of her left nostril.

'Everything's gone wrong. Everyone we know, everyone we love, and him being there trying to hurt you again.' Her eyes dropped to my chest, where the big, baggy shirt revealed my scar.

Stevie touched my shoulder and I turned to look at her, having nothing to say to BK that would comfort her. She was right, after all.

'C-can I see?'

With a small grimace, I sat up and faced her. She leaned in, silver eyes focused and more like Einstein's. I flushed and looked away. She was so close I could feel her breath on my chest. Talk about awkward.

Stevie shook her head. 'Sorry,' she said, 'I can't f-f-fix-fix it.'

My lips twitched, growing into a fond smile. 'That's what Einstein said, when he first saw it. He said he would send someone to look after us.' My gaze rose to hers and I tried to give her a smile. 'Better late than never, right?'

Stevie's looked away quickly.

'Look, I…I know things are bad. And maybe it could get worse. But…if we're going to get through this, I guess, we have to learn how to be strong, right?' I looked between them, and they both nodded, BK still sniffling. 'Right, well, I think…I think being strong is kind of like being calm. So, if we lie back down a while and close our eyes and let the sun soak us up, well, we might feel a little stronger.'

'Like Superman?'

'Superman?'

'The sun makes him strong,' said BK.

Despite it all, a smile worked its way onto my face. I felt

it pulling at my cheekbones, and tugging at the pain in my chest, making it release just enough to breathe a little easier.

'Yeah,' I said, flopping back down into the grass. 'Like Superman.'

'Genie,' said BK.

'Yes?'

'Did…did you really have to kill someone?'

My eyes snapped open and despite my little speech, every ounce of strength I'd gathered around myself vanished.

CHAPTER TWENTY-NINE

Zach

The map was a disorganised mess. Tim stepped back, crossing his arms as he surveyed the patches of red and green pins.

'This isn't working, is it?' he asked, glancing back over his shoulder at Zach with irritated eyes.

Zach frowned, scowling at the map. He'd attempted to colour code the pin placements, starting with red at the origin point, and moving to green where it had spread. Yet the spread of the red pins (any mention of the virus that was more than two weeks old) was just too random.

There were six clusters in six different countries. The first deaths happened in each of those six points, all with frightening quickness. The further from each point the virus spread, the longer it took to infect and take hold.

'It doesn't make sense,' he said, drumming his fingers and glaring at the map, willing it to form some sort of pattern he could make sense of.

Freddie took another step toward the map. His fingers trailed around the pins centred in Australia—the seventh cluster, made only of green pins. The main group centred around Northern Queensland. Freddie's shoulders hunched as he touched one of the pins. Zach heard a faint sigh and wondered what was going through the other boy's mind. He was about to ask, but a shout from the hallway interrupted him.

'Tim!'

Genie's voice. The sound of it, high and stressed, spurred the two boys into action faster than Zach imagined possible. They were out the door before Zach had even registered what was going on.

He blinked, and jumped up to join them. He reached the doorway just in time to see Genie pull back her hand and deliver a resounding slap across Tim's face.

Zach stopped, gaping at her. Her skin was flushed and her breathing came in short bursts as she glowered at Tim with fierce, frightened eyes.

Frightened?

'Why?' Genie shrieked, pulling her arm back again.

Tim stood staring at her, shock making him immovable. Before she could bring her hand around again, Ant was there, appearing out of thin air to grab her arm.

'Genie! What're you doing?'

She pulled back from Ant, trying to yank her arm free, grey eyes big and wild and fixated on Tim. 'Why would you tell them?' she shouted. 'I keep all of your secrets! I lie for you and cover for you and get you out of trouble and you couldn't keep *one thing* to yourself?'

'What…?' Tim stared at her, eyes black and confused and hurt.

Zach glanced between them in confusion. He tried to recall anything Tim might have told them that would cause her to get so upset, but couldn't think of a single thing.

'Genie, what're you talking about?' Ant asked, still wrestling with her as she tried to pull away. 'He hasn't told us anything! Freddie, give me a hand, will you?'

Freddie stood just beyond the door to Zach's right, eyes shifting between his sister and his best friend. He didn't move. He crossed his arms and frowned. Zach raised his eyebrows.

'I don't know what you think he's told us,' said Ant to Genie. 'But I doubt it's anything worth attacking him over.'

'Of course you'd defend him,' she shouted, yanking so hard Ant released her and she went staggering back. She got her footing, glared at Ant and snapped, 'You *always* do!'

Ant's jaw clenched. He glanced sideways at Tim. The

other boy was still gaping at Genie, apparently too stunned by her outburst to do anything else. Ant dropped his gaze and took a step back out of the way.

'Fine,' he said, his voice low and subdued. 'If you really want to hurt him, go ahead.'

Genie paused. Fear once again burned bright within her eyes. She seemed to really look at Tim. See his surprise, his stillness, and the red handprint stinging the side of his face.

'I…I didn't…' and then she was crying. 'I don't want to hurt you,' she sobbed, covering her face with her hands so her words came out muffled. 'I only did it to help. I didn't want to kill him.'

Tim started. Realisation struck them all, like simultaneous bolts of lightning. There was a moment of quiet, save for Genie's noisy sobs, and then Tim found his voice.

'Jesus Christ! *That's* what this is about? You slapped me over that? Of course I told them! This is exactly *why* I told them! If you weren't so, so…'

'So what?' she asked, swiping at her face and staring at him, some of the fury returning. 'So *what?*'

'Pathetic!'

'I'm pathetic? I only had to kill him because I was trying to save you!'

'And I'd only gotten caught because I was trying to save *you*! Save yourself next time! I told you to run, didn't I? Don't blame this on me. You chose to stay all on your own.'

'What else was I supposed to do!'

'Run away!'

'Then you'd have *died*!'

Tim leaned closer to her, his own fiery temper glowing in those black eyes of his. 'Then at least you wouldn't've killed anyone.'

Zach winced.

Genie stared at him a moment longer, before she turned and fled back out the way she had come, the back door slamming behind her.

Ant ran a hand over his face and turned those baby blues back on Tim. 'Really?'

Tim crossed his arms, grinding his teeth. 'What?'

Freddie finally moved. He uncrossed his arms and Zach caught sight of his clenched fists about half a second before he punched Tim in the face. Tim went sprawling, letting loose a string of foul—and rather creative—swear words.

'Oh for heaven's sake,' Ant scowled, crossing his arms and glaring at Freddie. '*Really?*'

Freddie shrugged. Apparently satisfied with his retribution, he turned and stuck out a hand, offering to help Tim up. Tim glared up at him, rubbing his jaw where Freddie had clipped him.

'You two need therapy,' he muttered, reaching out and accepting the offered hand.

Freddie's face cracked into a grin and he hauled Tim to his feet with practiced ease.

'Alright,' said Tim, brushing himself off. 'I need a drink.'

Freddie signed something, his expression wry as his hands moved at a pace too fast for Zach to decipher. Ant rolled his eyes, exasperation and defeat meshed together in one simple expression. He muttered something about work weeks and being friends with idiots before stalking back off toward the lounge room, clearly fed up with the lot of them.

Tim waved Freddie off, staring after Ant's retreating back. 'Extenuating circumstances, end of the world and all that. What do you care anyway? You hate alcohol.'

'Aren't you guys in high school?' Zach asked.

Tim began to move down the hallway after Ant. 'Yeah, so?' Tim asked, glancing back at him. 'You gonna quibble about underage drinking *now*, while the world is ending?'

'Er, I guess not?'

'Good. Besides, I turned eighteen three months ago. Held back a grade. Only ones who are underage are the twins and neither of them can hold their booze.'

Zach glanced back down the hallway at the door Genie had disappeared back through.

'Shouldn't someone see if she's okay?'

'BK's out there,' said Tim brusquely. 'Besides, I don't think she wants to see any of us.'

Freddie glanced back and shrugged again, tilting his

head toward Tim in agreement.

Zach had to wonder how long they'd been friends. While Genie never seemed to need to watch Freddie to know what he was saying, Tim seemed to walk at a permanent angle, his body half tilted toward Freddie, his head always angled in his friend's direction, in easy sight of Freddie's hands.

Freddie didn't seem to notice this attentiveness, as if this way it had always been. They conducted their conversations with an ease Zach had never seen between two people. In the lounge room, Ant was no where to be seen.

Tim and Freddie seemed unconcerned. Tim raided a cupboard, letting out a triumphant shout and producing a bottle of amber liquid. He poured himself a glass and threw himself onto the couch.

'Zach,' he barked, making Zach jump. 'Tell us how you met Stevie.'

'Uh, okay,' said Zach, dropping into the recliner. 'It's not that exciting…it was…well I guess it was only yesterday. Gees.'

It was hard to imagine so much could be crammed into a single day. Zach rolled his eyes. What a cliche. Next thing he'd be saying *it was like a memory of a dream*. He snorted.

Freddie and Tim raised their eyebrows, exchanging amused looks at Zach's expense. He ignored them.

'I was at a museum when she crashed,' said Zach.

Freddie and Tim laughed. 'Of course you were,' said Tim.

Zach rolled his eyes again. 'I don't just randomly hang out at museums. It was an accident, alright.'

'Really? How do you accidentally go to a museum?'

Freddie signed the question at the same time Tim said it. Zach sighed and rubbed the back of his neck.

'Trust me,' said Zach, leaning back into the couch. 'It happens.'

'How?' Tim asked again.

Freddie waved his hand, *'Come on, then, spill.'*

'I was hungover, for starters,' said Zach. 'Er, that is, a high headache. Not alcoholic.'

Tim snorted again while Freddie just grinned, bobbing his head in some form of agreement, though Zach didn't know what he was agreeing to.

'In fact, it's all still a bit fuzzy. When I try to think about it, everything gets a bit hazy. I remember thinking that I should go to the museum, except I hate museums. There's too many people and if there is anything actually worth seeing, you can't appreciate it because the person next to you is in your personal space and apparently they don't know how to bathe; so of course all you can focus on is their stench and basically the whole experience just goes down hill from there.'

Freddie glanced at his friend. This time his question only required one hand. He made a motion, pushing his hand outward from his chest with two fingers raised; followed by a circular gesture with all four fingers tucked in and the thumb sticking out. His eyebrows were raised in question as he eyed his friend.

'What did he say?'

'He thinks you're mental,' said Tim with a grin, taking another sip of his drink.

Freddie tossed a cushion at him, his questioning gaze turning into a glare of annoyance.

'Sorry, sorry. Gees. He asked if you were okay. Guess your babbling worried him or something.'

Zach flushed. 'It's just hard to think about is all,' he muttered. 'I'm pretty sure I was led there.'

'Led there? What, like…mind control or something?'

'Or something,' said Zach.

Tim straightened, all amusement vanishing from his face. 'You think Stevie can make us do stuff like that?'

'I…I'm not sure it was her. Or if it was, I don't think she know's she did it. It wasn't exactly like I was *forced* to go to the museum, but the urge was definitely strong. And it wasn't my own. But if I hadn't gone, I'd have never found her. She crashed right outside the building.'

'Wait,' said Tim, holding up his hand. 'This isn't some bad sci-fi movie. She actually *crashed*? I thought you were joking.'

'Uh, no. She says it was on autopilot and she wasn't sure how to turn it off.'

Tim's grin was back full force. 'Oh that is *awesome*. An alien who can't drive a spaceship. Wicked.'

Zach blinked and then shook his head. 'You are very strange.'

'Oh, *I'm* strange? This coming from the guy who followed an *urge* to go to the museum, went for a seven hour road trip with an alien, and has a crush on the weirdest girl I know.'

Freddie sniggered, an odd huffing noise that distracted Zach from what Tim had said. For a moment, at least.

'Wait, what?' Zach asked. 'Crush?'

'Don't deny it,' said Tim, downing the rest of his drink and pouring another. 'It's obvious.'

'On *who*?'

'What did I just say? BK, of course. Look, don't worry about it. Happens all the time, and not just with boys, either. Something about her just…I dunno, draws people in.'

'I don't…I barely even know her!'

Freddie waved a dismissive hand at him, clearly not listening to Zach's protests.

'What, you don't think she's hot?' Tim asked, cocking an eyebrow in disbelief.

Zach spluttered. How was he supposed to answer that? 'I…I mean, I guess she's pretty.'

'Right, and the fact she's so ridiculously clueless isn't just a little bit adorable to you?'

'Well, I mean, she's a bit naive, sure…'

Tim nodded as if Zach had got down on his knees and professed his undying love for the strange girl.

'Look,' Zach said, feeling his face burn but not willing to back down. 'I don't even know the girl. She's pretty, sure, but that doesn't mean I have a *crush* on her. Anyway, aren't you supposed to be warning me off her or something, instead of encouraging me?'

Tim laughed and exchanged a glance with Freddie. 'Alright, listen closely, 'cause this is all the warning you'll get.' He leaned forward to stare intently at Zach and said, 'The second BK says she's got a problem with you, you're out; but until then, chase her all you like. She can handle herself just fine.'

Zach blinked, surprised by the total lack of concern by the two friends. Curious, he asked, 'What about Genie?'

Tim's eyes flashed dark. His grip tightened around the top of the glass he'd been holding loose in one hand. The amber liquid swirled, but Tim's gaze never wavered from Zach's face.

Freddie, likewise, had gone still. All mirth had vanished from his face. His gaze shifted from Zach to Tim, and he signed something short and sharp, and then gestured to Zach.

Tim grinned and translated. 'Stick with BK,' he said.

CHAPTER THIRTY

Genie

The air was hot. Sweat beaded on the brows of those at the table. Freddie's lip twitched. Zach shifted in his seat, eyes flickering around suspiciously. BK chewed the inside of her mouth. Tim smirked at Ant, who gulped in response.

Ant's eyes flickered over to me. He knew me too well. Whatever he saw in my expression caused him to mutter something under his breath and place his cards face down on the table.

'Fold,' he said, blue eyes flickering to my face again.

His jaw clenched, and blue eyes dropped to the table.

I sighed, and tossed two chips into the pile. 'Raise.'

On my other side BK was frowning at the cards in her hand. 'I'm confused,' she said. 'What's a full house again?'

I tried not to roll my eyes, placing my elbow on the table and leaning my chin on my hand. The game had been her idea—in fact, she had been insistent. No doubt wanting to rectify the tension my little outburst had ignited amongst us. Of course, then she had remembered that she didn't know how to play.

'A pair and a set of three,' said Zach, frowning at his own cards and counting his chips.

BK's face brightened. 'Oh. Then I raise!'

Freddie huffed, slapping his cards face down on the table and scowling. He slumped back in his seat, arms folded and glaring at his dwindling pile of betting chips.

Tim's face twitched. Dark eyes met mine across the table. There was a faint tinge of splotchy purple cresting his jaw. I dropped my gaze to my cards, leaning back in my seat to shuffle them around.

Tim matched BK's bet. Zach didn't even glance at his cards as he placed his bet. He was watching Stevie. She was making notes on some paper Zach had dug up for her and he kept getting distracted by whatever she was writing. Not that he could understand it. None of us could. She wrote in a weird scribble of lines and dots.

'Getting the hang of it?' Zach asked.

Stevie glanced up from her notes. She pointed at me.

'Next b-bet,' she said, and then pointed to the pile. 'I f-flip one?'

Zach nodded, grinning. 'Right, you're getting it. I reckon you could play the next round.'

'No fair,' said Tim as I put another chip in the pile. 'She can read minds.'

Freddie tapped the table, and then mimicked plugging his ears. He pointed at Stevie and cocked his head to one side.

Zach nodded. 'Right, we'll give her headphones,' he agreed.

I raised my eyebrows, surprised Zach was catching on so fast. Freddie's method of communication was a strange mix of Auslan (Australian Sign Language), his own variation of sign language, and facial expressions. Most people didn't bother trying to understand him, going through either Tim or me to communicate with him. But Zach seemed to be making a real effort at understanding my brother. I smiled at him, feeling warm tingles as Freddie grinned and nodded, pleased at being understood.

'BK, you have to place more coins in the pile,' Tim reminded her, leaning over to make her bet for her.

BK frowned at her cards and at the piles of chips on the table. 'Wait, how do we finish?' she asked again.

Zach, distracted from trying to convince Stevie to join the game, began explaining the rules to her…again. Freddie and I shared a grin. He tilted his head toward Tim and shot me a questioning look.

'Think you can beat him?'

I shrugged, glancing back down at my cards again. Knowing Tim, I probably *could* beat him. But after how I'd treated him this morning I wasn't sure I wanted to.

Freddie grinned. *'Take him down, sis.'*

'Take who down?' Tim asked, catching sight of Freddie's hand movements. 'You're not talking about me are you?'

He cast me a quick grin and, his expression turning sly, winked. I flushed, but tried to smile back.

Freddie rolled his eyes and signed something.

'What was that?' Tim asked, turning a shrewd gaze on my brother.

'He says, "Quit flirting with everything that breathes and place a bet",' said Ant, supplying the words with a grin.

'I don't understand…' BK said, her voice pitching high into a whine.

We glanced over at her and Zach. Zach was leaning over, pointing to her cards and trying to explain the process of the game.

'You might as well give up,' said Tim, grinning. 'She's no good at these kinds of games.'

BK pouted and Zach made a face.

Freddie caught my attention again, but this time it was to gesture at Ant. I glanced sideways. Ant still had his chin in his palm. A faint smile twitched at his lips and his eyes had that happy glaze they only ever had when he was staring at Tim.

Freddie waggled his eyebrows.

'We should lock them in a room together.'

I shook my head, trying not to think about the nasty thing I'd said to Ant, and signed back. *'Tim wouldn't understand. We'd have to skywrite it.'*

Freddie shook his head, sighing in exasperation. *'He's Blind.'*

'What're you two talking about?' Tim's suspicious voice made us both jump. 'Who's blind?' He asked.

'Love,' I blurted and bit my lip to keep from laughing.

Freddie's grin was broad in response and we both kept our gaze anywhere but on Ant.

'Oh!' said BK, straightening up. 'If you want a love game, I can read your future!'

Zach stared at BK as if she'd just announced she wanted to be a fish and stuck her head in a fishbowl. Tim's suspicious gaze didn't waiver, it only shifted from Freddie and me to BK. He'd been on the receiving end of BK's fortune telling on numerous occasions and was experienced enough to know to be wary.

Freddie, naturally, was nodding like a maniac, grinning from ear to ear. He threw me a wicked grin, and pointed at Tim.

'Do him!'

Once again, he was keeping his gaze away from Ant.

BK nodded in delight, clapping her hands together. 'Alright,' she said.

Tim made to escape, but lightning fast, BK had hold of his wrist—like a startled snake in summer, she latched on and refused to let go. Tim sighed theatrically and sat down.

'You guys suck,' he said, sending a glare at Freddie and me.

Still holding onto Tim's arm, BK pulled out a deck of Tarot cards. Zach's jaw dropped.

'Where the hell were you keeping those?' he asked, eyes bulging out of his head as he tried to imagine where they'd been hidden.

Ant shook his head. 'She hides them all sorts of places,' he said, as if this was perfectly normal.

She cleared the space in front of her, using her arm to sweep the poker game onto the floor. The chips clattered onto the tiles, some bouncing away into the lounge room and others spinning to a soft hum on the floor.

With the skill of someone who'd had years of practice, BK spread the cards across the table with only one hand. She stared at the cards, her green gaze focused.

Tim had a pained expression, his face scrunched up as he waited for bad news. He always drew cards like Death, or the Ten of Swords, or the Tower. Bad cards in bad positions.

Even good cards in bad positions. There was always something that seemed so catastrophic about his readings that it had become a running joke amongst us.

BK had once told our teacher that 'darkness was waiting to swallow the light'. The next day at school, that same teacher was arrested for drunk driving. She gave up six years of sobriety after failing to win a modelling contest.

Tim had avoided anymore fortune tellings after that incident, convinced BK could only predict horrible futures.

'Okay,' said BK, still holding onto Tim's arm. 'We're after a love reading, yes? Do you want to know *your* love? Or who loves you?'

Freddie and I shared another look, and I shook my head at him. I mouthed *'don't'*, but of course, Freddie didn't listen.

He stuck his hand up in the air, waving it around like a five year old trying to impress his teacher until he had BK's attention. With a wicked grin, he signed, *'Loves him,'* and pointed at Tim.

Tim rolled his eyes, his shoulders relaxing as some of his anxiety eased off. 'Alright then,' he said, grinning a little. 'I'm open for that. Just, hang on, someone get me a drink. I need booze to go with this thing.'

Freddie laughed and bounded up from the table. I shook my head. He was *hopeless*. Beside me, Ant was rigid, staring at the cards with a faint look of horror.

I leaned over and whispered as quiet as I could. 'Stop worrying. Most of it's just rubbish.'

Ant glanced sideways at me and for a moment I thought he would look away. 'But she *knows*.'

'She wouldn't tell him though.'

'Not on purpose.'

Ant had once told me he thought BK's readings were all subconscious. It was something they'd started together. Tim and Freddie had teased Ant for weeks when BK had mentioned it, ribbing him for becoming a gypsy or a carnival boy. Ant, with his usual quiet dignity, had ignored them and kept up with it.

He said you could twist any card into a positive or negative light. What BK did was different. Often, when she was doing a reading, the cards helped her realise something she hadn't figured out about someone. The cards gave a voice to some feeling or intuition she had.

She took in everything around her, but she didn't always know how to interpret what she saw, or how she felt. The cards helped her do that. That was how she'd figured out Ant was gay. Of course, she'd immediately blurted it out for everyone to hear.

Now, the worry was something else. Something deeper. I shook my head.

'You said it yourself,' I said. 'She *knows*. It's not a realisation that she'll just accidentally blurt out. And really, if he hasn't figured it out by now…'

I trailed off, seeing the look of hurt and frustration that crossed his face. 'I'm sorry…' I said. 'About before.'

Ant's gaze softened. 'Don't worry about it,' he said, and shrugged, a wry smile pulling at his lips. 'I guess I'm a bit biased, and I *do* tend to back him up. Even when I know he's wrong.'

He shifted, his gaze dropping away, back towards Tim—who was still being held in BK's vice-like grip.

'You know,' he said, glancing sideways at me. 'Tim didn't mean any of what he said.'

I sighed. 'I know.'

'Do you?'

I glanced up. He was staring at me, brows furrowed, blue eyes dark and earnest. 'You saved his life. Killing that man…that was something you had to do. It's not your fault.'

I swallowed, looking back down at the cards in my hand. The hallway swam before my eyes; splattered and painted in red.

'I feel like—,'

Freddie came back, cutting me off as he dumped a plate of leftover pizza on the table. Zach, Tim and Ant all reached for the plate simultaneously, ravenous as crocodiles at the start of monsoon season.

'Okay,' said BK. 'Let's begin.' She drew a card.

Tim's face scrunched again, and he squinted at the card through one eye.

'Oh,' said BK. 'I wasn't expecting that.'

Tim peered at it. 'Is that the Knight?'

'Knight of cups. Let's see, what else…The Two of Cups…okay, and oh…the Tower.'

'Again?' Tim groaned. 'I thought this was supposed to be a love reading?'

'This is interesting. It's almost like…' her gaze flickered away, not quite *at* Ant, but in his general direction.

I let my hands fall onto my lap then reached over and took one of Ant's under the table. He squeezed. I didn't have to look at him to know he'd be blushing. I could just about *feel* the heat coming off his face.

She pulled out one more card, and paused, staring at it in her hand and not placing it on the table with the rest. Her green eyes shifted, becoming unfocused and staring through the card.

'Oh,' she said in a soft voice.

'Oh what?' asked Tim, his voice high.

'Hm?' she asked, her gaze snapping back to him. Abruptly, she let go of his arm. Without warning she gathered up the rest of the cards, shuffling them about in her hands as Tim and Freddie objected. Freddie reached over to try and snatch at the last card, but it was too late. The cards were all mixed up, with no way to know which had been the last.

'What was the last card?' Tim asked.

BK stared at him for a moment and then laughed. 'Didn't I show you?'

'Er, no?'

'Oh gosh, I'm such a goose. It was the Ten of Cups,' she said, and then leaned close to whisper in a loud voice. 'I think someone in this room is in love with you.'

Tim stared at her. After a long tense moment, in which Ant almost broke my fingers, Tim snorted. 'Who, *Stevie?*' he asked, and then cracked up.

Ant relaxed, Zach grinned—looking baffled but amused —and Freddie started teasing Tim, pretending to fawn over him while keeping his gaze firmly away from Ant. BK laughed, folding up her cards and watching Freddie and Tim wreck their usual havoc. Except there was an element missing from BK's laugh. It never reached her eyes, which remained unfocused, mulling over whatever interpretation of the reading she wasn't telling us.

I turned to get a piece of pizza before the boys ate it all and noticed Stevie. She was rigid, her gaze was pinned on BK, wide and unwavering, as a faint hint of static prickled up my skin in the heat of the afternoon.

I swallowed. What exactly had BK just realised?

CHAPTER THIRTY-ONE

Zach

Zach's fingers drummed along the table top. They were on their third round of frozen pizza for the day and the smell was starting to make Zach queasy. He wondered how long they could live off the stuff, especially considering it was less frozen, and more defrosted.

Zach was fairly certain no amount of overcooking was going to make it any less likely to give them food poisoning —but then again, it wasn't as if they had much choice.

'Would you stop that?' Tim barked, his left eye twitching as he turned to glare at Zach.

'What?' Zach asked, sitting up straight as he refocused on the group. He glanced down at his drumming fingers and abruptly laid his hand flat on the table.

'Right,' he said, throwing Tim a sheepish smile. 'Sorry, nervous tick.'

'What're you nervous for?' Tim growled, reaching for more of the pizza.

The smell of processed meatballs and overcooked ham wafted over to Zach. His stomach lurched—part hunger, part nausea.

'We're going to run out of edible food soon,' he said. He wrinkled his nose and added, 'In fact, I think we already have.'

Tim scoffed. 'I've got a cast-iron stomach.'

'That doesn't surprise me,' Zach muttered, and leant his elbow on the edge of the table. 'We need to consider what we're going to do next.'

'Well I was planning on sleeping,' said Tim.

'He meant after that, smart-ass,' Ant said, rolling his eyes. 'And he's right. We should think about going home...' he trailed off, and glanced down at his hands.

'Home's a good idea,' said Tim. 'At least, maybe my place.' His dark eyes flicked over to Genie and back to Ant again. 'Although maybe we should wait a few days.'

Freddie—who, for some unfathomable reason, had gone for a half-hour run and was recovering on the kitchen floor —sat up, his brows furrowed and his head tilted to one side in question. He brought his right hand up to his right shoulder, his thumb just touching before he flicked his hand away.

Tim shrugged, and once again his gaze flicked to Genie. 'Are you gonna hit me again?' he asked.

She flushed, and crossed her arms. 'Why would I hit you again?'

Tim hesitated before speaking. Zach suspected he was less worried about being hit than he was about upsetting the grey-eyed girl. She hadn't quite recovered from their fight. Her shoulders hunched inwards and her eyes remained downcast, never meeting anyone's gaze for more than a second.

Tim opened his mouth to speak, but paused and shook his head, seeming to think better of whatever it was he was going to say. After a few moments, he tried again.

'I just don't think going home's a good idea,' he said. 'What if those people at school know we escaped? What if they know where we live? I think if we wanna survive we have to figure out what the hell is going on.'

'How?' BK asked.

Tim pointed.

Stevie blinked, her ears flushing in surprise at being singled out.

'Zach said you've got some sort of teacher, right? Someone here to help you? Why don't we go find him?'

Genie jolted, turning to look at Stevie. 'Einstein?'

Stevie shifted in her seat, the jacket she had borrowed

rustling against the chair.

'Yes,' she murmured.

'Right,' said Tim. 'That's where we need to go. To Einstein.'

A faint buzz tickled up Zach's spine, and a familiar itch crept across his skin. They *should* go find Einstein. It was the most logical solution. He would know what was happening and, with any luck, how to fix it.

But Einstein could just take the twins and go home—leaving them to this God forsaken planet with the rampaging plague.

'Maybe we should sleep on it?' he suggested.

Tim snorted. 'Well I wasn't exactly suggesting we take off right now. I mean, there's things to take care of first. We gotta figure out where we're going, how we'll get there, clothes, *food*. Not to mention…I'm still pretty buggered.'

Ant chuckled. 'You can't be saying that you're *tired*? You? The one who never stops?'

'Shut it, or you can sleep on the floor.'

Ant held his hands up in mock-surrender, yet, that didn't stop him from ending up on the floor later anyway. In all fairness, Tim did too.

***

Zach's sleep was plagued by dreams of viral infections and quarantine camps. He kept waking, Tim's description of the men who'd chased him and Genie through the halls of a school—a *school*—racing through his mind as he jerked awake. Scientists in hazmat suits poked and prodded at him, their faces slowly turning black and rage filled.

His breathing came in short gasps, the sound of running footsteps fading in his ears. As he woke he thought he heard a voice calling to him.

'You must hurry, Zach. You must take Stevie where she needs to go.'

He shook his head, feeling dizzy and disorientated. Soft snores brought him back to reality. He sighed, and rubbed at his face, trying to rub away the fading memory of nightmares. He wasn't being experimented on or studied, he was safe in a strangers house in Northern Queensland.

Zach snorted. Yeah, safe. With an alien and five strangers.

He shook his head, the movement slow and monotonous. His mouth felt dry and his head ached. His stood, swaying and reaching for the couch as his stomach lurched. He wasn't sure if he wanted to eat or throw up.

Half frozen food from the unpowered convenience store hadn't seemed like such a bad idea. At least, not when Tim was moaning about how hungry he was.

The tiled floors were cool on his feet, and he winced, rising up onto his tip toes as he snuck around Ant and Tim. Zach felt momentarily guilty he'd ended up on the couch while they slept on nothing more than cushions and blankets.

Not that Tim seemed too bothered. He was sprawled out on the ground in a small nest of pillows and cushions, passed out and snoring, lost to the depths of restful sleep.

In contrast Ant laid next to him curled up on his side and hugging a pillow. One hand was thrown over the pillow, reaching beyond it to snag at the hem of Tim's shirt sleeve.

Tim rolled as Zach crept passed, snorting in his sleep. His whole body flopped sideways toward Ant in a sudden burst of movement—though the boy was still out cold. His arm flung out as he rolled, crisscrossing over Ant's chest.

Ant shifted in sleep, as if sensing this closer contact with his friend. A faint smile touched his lips and Zach shook his head, no longer feeling guilty about the couch.

He felt for his lighter. Tiredness soaked his thoughts, and yet he felt heavy knowing they still had to find Einstein. Still had to find a way to find him.

Zach frowned. Who was he anyway? This *Einstein*. He shook his head, twirling a joint between his fingers as he exited the front of the house.

The night air was cool and refreshing, though not so much as to be cold. He breathed in, tilting his head to look back up at the sky.

Despite the heaviness, despite his dreams, he felt oddly at ease. Stevie and these humans she'd thrown her lot in with were actually alright. Zach *liked* them. It had been a long time since he'd liked anyone enough to consider them friends, and though he'd only known these people for two days, he felt a contentedness he hadn't felt in years.

He sucked on the joint, releasing the smoke in a long, slow breath. What was *wrong* with him? How on Earth could he possibly feel *content*? The world was ending. People were dying, and here he was smoking and playing poker and… well, doing nothing different he'd been doing before.

Three days ago, he'd been sitting in his house, smoking the same bag of weed he was still working on, and getting pretty damn close to rock bottom on the downward spiral he'd made of his life. He'd done everything he possibly could to destroy his relationships with everyone. He was angry. He was destructive.

He was adopted.

The secret he was never supposed to know, the one that had changed him from a straight A student, two years ahead of his grade, to being expelled. To being a disappointment.

That's what his mother had called him anyway, before she'd left for her trip. They'd been arguing. He remembered calling her fake. She called him useless and lazy and disappointing. He told her to send him back and get a refund. She'd slapped him.

It wasn't so bad, being slapped. He didn't even think she'd meant it. They hadn't realised he'd known, hadn't ever considered Zach might work it out without them telling him. He wanted to hurt her back.

Not physically, of course. Zach wasn't capable of hurting anyone physically. He was too much of a coward to try. Instead, he'd thrown words at her, trying to cut her emotionally as her secrets had scarred him.

'Yeah, I'm real important to you, aren't I?' he'd snarled, nursing a bruising cheekbone. 'I'm not your son. I'm just another trophy to put up on your shelf, all shiny and clever. You're not pissed off because I blew off uni. You're pissed off because I squandered all the genes you paid for. Maybe you'll get lucky, maybe you'll find some other smart baby to adopt while off enjoying your fucking cruise.'

In reality, he was more like her than he cared to admit. The words, the hurtful tone, his anger—he'd learnt it all from her. He'd watched the pain he'd inflicted flash across her face. The realisation that she'd hurt him more than anyone else ever had burned through her eyes and she'd left without ever saying another word. Incapable of even trying to fix things with him.

That was the last time he'd ever seen her. Now, he'd never see her again.

Why had he done that? So they wanted a smart baby, what did that matter? Was it so bad they'd wanted him to do well? To build a good life?

Yet they'd cancelled the free programming class he'd been taking, because it wasn't what they'd envisioned. They didn't want a geek for a son. They wanted a *doctor*.

Zach clenched his teeth, feeling the old anger rise up inside him, rising above the nervous energy in his gut. He felt hot. He thought about going for a walk. He thought about punching something.

Instead, he sat down on the gutter, and smoked his joint. Waiting for the rest of the world to fall victim to the plague, and wondering how the hell six teenagers and an alien were going to survive it all?

CHAPTER THIRTY-TWO

Genie

A cool breeze drifted through the window. BK had rummaged up some candles hidden away under the bathroom sink, and now my borrowed room smelt of jasmine and wood-fire. The combination of incense with the soft evening breeze lulled me into a half sleep. Until a faint grunt woke me.

Freddie's shadowy figure appeared near the end of my bed, feeling for the frame for guidance as he struggled to navigate the unfamiliar room.

I searched for an extra pillow out of habit. Luckily, whoever slept in the room was a pillow hugger, and I found one wedged down the side of the bed. I sat up to hand it to Freddie and he sucked in a sharp breath, jumping.

Moonlight lit his face, and I could almost hear what his expression was saying. *Jesus, Genie. You scared the crap outta me!'*

'Sorry.'

He hesitated as I handed him the pillow. Instead of dropping to the floor (as I'd expected) he crawled into the bed, nudging me over. I raised my eyebrows but didn't say anything, even as he stole half my blankets.

Freddie was like a wild horse. If he was spooked, you had to be gentle. Even with me he was twitchy, shying away if you got too close to the problem. I had to wait for him tell me.

So I scooted over, becoming more alert in the presence of Freddie's anxiety. The wall was cold against my back, seeping through the thin fabric of the pyjamas I'd borrowed as I turned to look at him.

He threw me a quick glance before snuggling down in the bed. *'Why are you awake?'*

'You weren't exactly quiet.'

'Sorry.'

His attention turned to the ceiling, his face disappearing into the shadow of the room. His jaw was tense, and he kept his eyes fixated on a single point. Another sign of his anxiousness. I sighed. I hated when he was like this. He was too hard to read. I never quite knew what he was thinking. I wished I could lend him my voice so we could talk, really *talk* to each other.

So I could ask him what was wrong. So I could ask him if he thought *I* was wrong. For what I'd done. For who I'd killed. I took a deep breath, squashing down the urge to cry that was bubbling up inside me.

I let the breath out and yanked on the blanket. 'I'd rather you apologise for blanket theft,' I said, trying to lighten the moment. 'Hog.'

There wasn't enough light to see his face properly. Still, I could picture the little frown that would be playing on his features as he remained silent. I stopped moving, keeping my sigh silent, and chewed my lip as I waited for him to tell me what was wrong.

He rolled onto his side, curling up even though there wasn't enough room for him to sleep that way. He yanked on the covers again. I retaliated with a small push, not quite hard enough to shove him off the bed.

'Hog,' I repeated.

It had been at least a year since Freddie had last made one of these visits. They'd been becoming more infrequent over the last few years, so much so that I'd begun to wonder if he'd outgrown them. Though, of course, they'd only begun after we'd been forced into seperate rooms. Even if Grandma *was* right (we really were getting too old to share a room), neither Freddie nor I seemed to do so well on our own. I at least had BK, Freddie hadn't had anyone. So, he'd come to us.

BK had never noticed when he snuck into our room to sleep on the floor—or if she did, she'd never mentioned it. Not his visits, not the extra pillows and blankets I kept on the end of my bed—just in case. She seemed to sense this was something that belonged to Freddie and I alone.

Freddie shifted, moonlight-silver eyes flashing up to mine. I sensed rather than saw the pleading look on his face. The question he couldn't ask (with his hands tucked up under the blankets as they were) and the answer that only I could give. The answer his own voice would never allow him to have.

I sighed, but relented. How could I not?

So I rolled over, closed my eyes, and begun to hum. Humming turned into a soft whisper of song. Light and soft and a little bit melancholy. Just the way he liked it. Just the way our mother used to sing it to us before she'd died. I only knew some of the words, and seeing as I'd never been able to find the song (no matter how hard I'd searched) I substituted the blanks with my own lyrics.

A few minutes later, Freddie's breathing evened out and he began to snore in soft fits and starts.

I smiled, humming a few more notes before stopping.

The door creaked. I shifted in the bed, trying to see who was at the door without jostling Freddie awake.

'Sorry,' a soft voice whispered from the hall. 'Just wanted to hear better. Didn't mean to make you stop.'

Squinting into the dark, I made out Ant's face poking around the door.

'It's alright,' I said. 'I was finished anyway.'

'Oh,' he said, his voice low as his gaze dropped to the floor. 'Sorry.'

He started to duck away, but I called out. He paused, eyes shinning hopeful in the dark.

'I can sing it again, if you like,' I whispered.

A faint, wistful smile emerged. 'Only if you want,' he said, his voice low and embarrassed. 'It's just…'

'It's kind of creepy here, isn't it?' I said. I was sitting up now, my back pressed against the wall and my legs curled up against my chest. 'Come sit with me.'

Ant hesitated, but then, like a baby bird rushing back to the safety of it's mother's wings, he gave in. He left the door open as he trotted into the room. He manoeuvred around Freddie as if he were smaller than a toddler—not the full grown man he was. He sat on the bed next to me, mirroring my pose, and took a deep breath.

'Where are the others?' I asked.

'BK's sharing the other room with Stevie,' he said. 'Me and Tim were in the lounge room with Zach.'

'He's kind of weird, isn't he?'

'Zach? He's alright. I think he likes BK.'

A soft laugh bubbled up. 'Of course he does,' I said, shaking my head. 'When don't they fall for her?'

'I think Tim and Freddie were giving him a hard time.'

'Of course they were. I hope they weren't too mean.'

Ant chuckled. 'I think he'll live. If anything, he seems more determined to prove he can handle her.'

I grinned. 'That'll be different.'

'I kind of like him.'

I nudged him. Ant rolled his eyes and nudged back, shoving my shoulder.

'Not like that,' he said, and I could hear the embarrassment underlying his voice. 'I mean, I hope he does stick it out. I think he'd suit BK.'

'They're so different,' I said. 'He's so smart. I mean, BK is too, but it's not the same. She's…special.'

'Yeah, she is,' he paused.

In the silence, Freddie's soft snores were oddly comforting.

'How is he?'

I shrugged. 'I'm not sure. He didn't really explain. I think it's just…'

'Everything?'

'Yeah.'

'Tim's not sleeping well either.'

'Oh?'

'He was having nightmares before Freddie got up. I thought maybe that's why Freddie wasn't sleeping.'

'What about you? Is that why you're not sleeping?'

'I…' Ant paused. 'I was thinking about Mum.'

I swallowed. We all had our demons. Freddie had James. Tim had me. Ant had his Mum. The silence filled us. I reached over and took Ant's hand, squeezing, knowing that words wouldn't help him right now. His mother could be dead, what could I say that would help? What was going through his mind right now? Was he sad? Was he angry? Was he relieved? Was he guilty for being relieved?

All of the above?

The wind rustled the curtains and moonlight flooded into the room. I breathed in the clear air, smelling a hint of rain.

'What about you?' asked Ant in a soft voice. 'Are you okay?'

The hollowness in my stomach returned and memories threatened to overwhelm me. How I wished I could forget the last two days. Josie's death. The woman who chose death over even a chance of infection. The man I had killed. And James. James down a red splattered corridor. I swallowed.

'I…am okay.'

He turned to look at me, squeezing my hand so I looked at him. 'Are you really?'

My heart-beat sped up and I took a deep, steadying breath. 'I don't know,' I whispered.

Ant said nothing. He squeezed my hand again, letting me know in his own way that he was there, and we sat together in the dark listening to Freddie's snores. Each too afraid of being alone with our own thoughts.

At some point I fell asleep. It came in fits and starts, in gusts and billows, seeming to rock me into dreams of comfort before jerking me awake, the feel of monsters reaching for me, clawing along my skin.

Freddie's presence kept the monsters in their corners as they surged on the edges of my dreams. Sickly, damaged monsters, always closing in. Chasing me into corners. Whispering my name. Calling for me.

'Come out, come out wherever you are.'

CHAPTER THIRTY-THREE

Zach

Pre-dawn bird calls echoed. Zach blinked slowly, coming back into consciousness as the high faded away. He wondered how long he'd been sitting there, out on the gutter.

The sky was fading from black to a dark navy, the faint hint of light not yet dispelling the darkness. Warmth surged up Zach's spine. It had been a long time since he'd seen a sunrise.

He stretched his arms up above his head, muscles stiff and sore from sleeping on a hard couch. He rubbed at his neck, trying to ease some of the tension. A cool morning breeze stirred through the leaves and bushes along the front of the garden. Across the road, the river was quiet. A quarter moon was still visible in the early morning sky, reflecting off the gentle flow of water.

Zach squinted, making out the dark shadow of the little blue car near the bank of the water, a new feature of the riverbed. He doubted anyone would be around to pull it out any time soon. It was now a permanent addition to the bank.

He leaned back on his palms and stared up at the lightening sky. 'What am I going to do?'

Something crunched behind him. Zach turned his head, expecting Tim or Ant to have followed him.

Hazel eyes met his, a slim figure crouching behind him in the dark of the morning. Teeth flashed in a smile.

'You're going to disappear.'

The words came as Zach caught the faint glint of

something sharp. He jerked, his movements far to sluggish to avoid the slash of the blade that struck, piercing through his clothing and his skin, slipping through muscle as easily as a carvers knife.

Zach gasped, sucking in air, wanting to cry out in pain but unable to. Agony tore through him as the blade was pulled out, seeming to tear a part of him away with it. He collapsed, clutching at his side as the figure rose above him.

'Who…?'

'Who am I?' the man asked, gazing down as Zach bled onto the ground. 'Just a fox, looking for a little rabbit.'

He turned and headed for the house, his footsteps crunching in the gravel footpath. Zach panted.

His mind flared, panic flooding through him, pumping adrenaline and blood through the hole in his side.

'Stevie!'

The image of her stuck in his mind, even as pain clouded his thoughts, his breathing raged, pins and needles and sharp spikes of terror throbbing through his side. Stevie. Small, alien, timid Stevie. In the house the stranger was walking toward.

'No,' he called, his voice rasping around the pain. 'Wait…'

The figure didn't pause. Didn't even wait. He peeked inside, paused, and then stepped back. Zach twisted, trying to see where the man was going. He slipped around the edge of the house, working his way down toward the back.

Stevie.

Zach reached out, clawing at the ground, trying to drag himself along the pavement.

'Stev-ah. Stevie!' His voice wavered. Sharp stabbing pains shot up to his mind. 'Stevie! *Help,* God…Stevie, he's coming… run. Stevie!'

The throbbing in his side migrated to his head, pounding, pounding, pounding in time to the slowing beat of his heart. His vision faded, even as light began to flood the yard.

'Please,' he gasped, squinting at the gravel in front of him, curling up on himself. 'Please…Stevie.'

More footsteps. Zach's heartbeat quickened. Was he coming back? Coming to finish off the job? Zach whimpered. His hands were slick, covered in blood. Blood that seeped through his fingers and soaked his shirt.

'Zach? What're you…Jesus!'

Rushing footsteps. The crash of someone falling to the ground. Hands pulling at him, grabbing at his arms, trying to unfurl him.

'Zach, Zach you have to let me see. *Zach*! Jesus, what the hell happened?'

'What's going on?'

'Zach's been hurt!'

'What? How…*shit!*'

The voices were too loud, too frightening, and yet something deep within Zach began to relax. He knew those voices. Ant…and Tim…they would help. They would make everything okay. Tim was brave—far braver than Zach—and strong. He could protect Stevie.

'Stevie…he…he went for…for Stevie…' he gasped, struggling to open his eyes.

'What?'

The hands pulling at him stopped. Zach heard something like a curse and feet spinning around on gravel. Too late. Far too late.

There was a scream, ear splitting and agonising, ripping through Zach's ears and mind and soul. He cried out, trying to shut the sound out with his hands.

An explosion of light. Blinding and static, like the after shock of lightning.

The world started to tilt. The throbbing in his head became a rampage of pain, thudding and surging behind his eyes.

There was squealing, the incessant hum of voices. Shouting. Lot's of shouting. Hands pulling at Zach, fighting against someone trying to hold onto him.

'No! *No!* Stop! He's hurt, leave him alone!'

More shouting followed by a loud burst of noise, and pain thrusting along the back of his head.

He groaned, feeling sick. Where was he? He blinked

hard, trying to clear away the haze. Trying to get some sort of bearing.

What was he doing again?

He was running? No, that wasn't right. Someone *else* was running. Lot's of someone's. He could hear them all, their feet thumping heavy on the ground around him, vibrating through the earth as if each tread was laden with lead.

He was supposed to be doing something? Fighting? Protecting…protecting someone? Who?

A hand reached into his thoughts, claws ripping away at the edges of his consciousness, and agony swelled into a titanic wave that crashed over him.

He stopped caring about the man with the knife. Stopped worrying about Stevie and the othes. Stopped thinking *anything* as darkness swamped in around him, obliterating everything in it's path.

CHAPTER THIRTY-FOUR

Genie

When I woke up next, it was just me and Freddie. There was a thin blanket over me—Freddie had succeeded in stealing all the covers—and Ant was gone. I stretched out, uncurling from the awkward position I'd fallen asleep in, and tried to curl back up under the cozy darkness.

The faint call of a bird echoed on the air. Morning. Or the start of morning, at least, as it was still dusky outside. I blinked, shifting, distracted by the odd stop and start of the trilling bird.

Something rustled in the leaves outside. The little bird sang in soft whispers, long calls and raucous melody. The sounds made the morning light, the soft breeze brought the smell of morning dew and wet grass. I breathed in deep, feeling calm.

Calmer than I had woken, on the tail end of nightmares.

It was a magpie, shifting about on the tree outside, looking for a morning meal or doing whatever else it was magpies did in the morning (searching for a kid on a bike to terrorise perhaps?). Though magpies frightened me, I loved their song. The trills and gargles and coos and whistles blending together in a beautiful sound that told me I was home. That I was safe.

The magpie cut off mid gargle and screeched. In a flurry of wings and leaves I heard it take flight, exploding out from the tree in a rush of air and fright.

I sat up, reaching for the curtain, and Freddie rolled

over. He huffed, his breath whooshing out, his brow furrowed as some dream tormented him. I began to hum, pulling the curtain out just enough to peak outside.

Of course, no one was there.

Freddie shifted again, distracting me from the window. His frown deepened and he rolled, fidgeting in his sleep. I reached out and smoothed the hair back from his face. At my touch, he stiffened. It only lasted a moment. The lines on his face disappeared, relaxing as whatever nightmare was plaguing him dissipated.

He went still, his breathing evening out, and he stretched out across the bed. I shook my head and decided to see if anyone else was up. He was hogging the whole bed anyway, and I didn't think I could get back to sleep. I'd had enough of nightmares for one night. Besides, it had been too long since I'd last seen a sunrise.

The floor was cool in the morning air. My eyes adjusted swiftly to the dark and I crept through the door, leaving it ajar so to not wake Freddie. He was already frowning again, and I paused, sighing as I debated whether or not to just wake him up.

'Sleeping like a baby.'

My breath stuck, my lungs forgetting how to function as my brain short circuited, confused by the man standing before me.

'J-James?' I asked, taking a half step back.

His smile was cool, expectant, amused. So different from the vicious glee I'd seen in him the day before, yet still so familiar. He'd been walking my dreams all night, tormenting me, so much so that I thought, for a brief moment, that I was still dreaming.

Something clattered behind me and thumped to the floor. I turned to look, distracted and disorientated. I was too confused to pay enough attention to James. Stupid, really.

Silver glinted in the growing morning light, catching my eye as I turned back toward the bedroom. Instinct drove me another step back. Too late. Far too late.

Not a dream.

Pain lanced down the side of my face. I staggered, my knees giving way as my vision went black. My back jammed into something hard, and my head smacked back.

Stars erupted around the pain. My vision blurred. Was it the stars or the blood? Blood…God, I could feel it, hot and flooding down my face. So much blood.

Another flash of silver.

'Oof!'

Freddie flew past me, not even grazing me as I stood stuck in the doorway. He slammed into James, sending them both sprawling into the hallway.

'Freddie!' I gasped and whimpered from the pain.

How could talking hurt so much?

Something clattered along the floor as my brothers wrestled. The knife! Where was the knife? I took a step forward, one hand pressed to the side of my face.

My foot kicked something, and I winced. Blinking blood out of my eyes, I saw the flash of silver. I dove on it.

As I stood, the door in front of me opened. BK took one look at me, blood soaked and holding a knife, and screamed.

I didn't—couldn't—pay her any mind. Fire was racing through my veins. Lightbulbs exploded in the hallway, erupting into too-bright light before shattering into a rain of glass. BK shrieked again. I staggered through the glass, crying out as I stepped on it with bare feet. It didn't matter. *None of it mattered.*

Freddie was still fighting James. Freddie was still in danger.

'Stop!'

I froze. Instinct took hold. I blinked my vision clear, one hand still pressed to my face, and the other holding the knife out in front of me.

James stood before me in the hallway. Freddie was on his knees, gasping as James held him in a choke-hold, pressing the tip of a knife against his throat. I whimpered, trying to hold back a sob.

He had *two* knives?

The one in my hand slipped, my grip loosening as I took

in the sight. Without needing to be asked, I let my knife clatter to the floor. Freddie made a noise, his eyes wild and furious and desperate.

He wanted me to fight, but what could I do? If I tried, if I even *moved*, I had no doubt what James would do.

'Good,' James said, nodding. 'Good now—what the hell?'

I turned, following the line of his gaze.

Stevie. Stevie standing behind me, with black eyes. *Black.* Pure black, with no ounce of the beautiful silver.

'Don't—,' James didn't finish.

Blue lightning erupted. Striking out, blasting straight past my face so close I felt the wind from the sudden attack. Electricity fizzed and sparked and banged, heading straight for my brothers.

I screamed, covering my ears as the sound rushed around me. My head throbbed. My face buzzed with fire.

When the light stopped, I looked up.

Freddie lay curled up on the ground, covering his head with his arms. James was crumpled next to him, his skin singed, his hair burning and his eyes wide open, but blank. I gaped at him. Stevie…had done *that?*

I turned to look at her. Her eyes were still black. She stood in the door of her room and swayed. A single spark of lightning tracing down one ear before she fell to the floor, folding in on herself like a deflated balloon; as if someone had struck her with a pin and all the air, all the light, had gone out of her.

'Stevie,' I whimpered.

I wanted to go to her. I wanted to help. But James was gone. James was unconscious or dead, and Freddie and BK were safe, and I was in so much pain.

The fire within me was spreading. I sunk to my knees.

Someone cried out. BK, probably.

I ignored it. I pressed my hands back to my face. Blood was trailing down my face and pooling around my neck. God, what had he done to me?

Something bounced down the hallway. There was a *pop* and smoke spewed out into the hall.

'*No!*' BK screamed.

Freddie was on his knees, groping at his neck. I tried to crawl toward him, but my arms and legs felt heavy. So heavy.

Someone stepped through the smoke, into the hallway. He stood tall. Confident. Imposing. His eyes focused on me, like they had so many years ago, when he'd told me I was strong. Strong enough to build a race upon.

'Ein-Einstein?'

He moved towards Freddie, becoming a hazy figure in the smoke, and I felt hope and betrayal and terror swirl within my mind, clamouring for my attention over the pain as the alien I'd dreamed of all these years bent toward my choking brother.

'No,' I said. 'Don't…don't hurt him.'

The figure in the fog paused, and I struggled against the darkness surging in on the outskirts of my mind. I reached out. Sparks and fizzles erupted around my fingertips. Was I being electrocuted? Was he doing to me what Stevie had just done to James?

'Don't…' I said, ignoring the lightning arcs, trying to focus on Freddie. 'Don't…you…you promised…' Words ceased making sense. My thoughts faded away to nothing as sleep, blissful sleep, drew me into its warm embrace.

CHAPTER THIRTY-FIVE

Zach

Light. The crackle of lightning. Blinding, never ending light. And pain. Pounding, pounding, pounding deep into his mind, shredding every thought, every tendril of being, every memory and feeling and dream and imagining.

Sizzling, screaming, shouting.

Nothing.

Still the agonising pain. Throbbing through his whole body. In time with his heartbeat. Did he still have a heart?

Nothing. A black nothing. Empty. Void.

Drifting in the silence. No, not silence. A faint hum echoed in the darkness.

'Wake up.'

He flinched away from the voice. It echoed, rippling away from him within the blackness.

'Wake up.'

The darkness receded. He floated up out of it, reemerging in the real world with a sudden gasp of breath, gulping at the air as if he'd been truly submerged within the inky blackness.

His eyes opened, blinking rapidly in the light. He lifted a hand, shielding his face, still breathing deeply.

'Shh,' a voice hushed, touching his arm and causing him to flinch again. 'It's okay.'

Blinking, Zach's vision swam, blurred and then focused on the face in front of him. A tendril of blonde curl tickled his nose and Zach sneezed.

'Whoops, sorry,' she smiled, leaning back away from him so her hair no longer brushed his face.

Zach struggled to push himself up onto his elbows. Bedsheets were tucked in tight around him, restricting his movements, and his chest grew tight as he tried to kick free. Yanking at the sheets, he began to gasp, his vision narrowing to pinpoints as he strained against the taut fabric keeping him in place. Hands reached out, deftly tugging the sheets loose, and a soft voice murmured to him as he calmed down.

Sitting cross legged, Zach took a deep breath and surveyed the situation he was in. He was sitting on a bed in a small, white room. There was another bed pressed against the opposite wall, and a bedside table sitting neatly in between. BK was kneeling on the floor next to him, fingers gripping at the sheets she'd pulled free as she looked up at him with those enormous green eyes.

'Hello,' she said.

'Hi.'

'You're awake.'

'Uh, yeah…I guess.'

'You were asleep a long time.'

'I was?' Zach scratched at his hair and BK's smile twitched back into place.

She giggled. 'Your hair's all mussed up.'

He flushed and tried to flatten his bed hair. 'How long was I asleep for?'

BK took a glass of water from the bedside table and handed it to him. 'Hm,' she said, thinking as he took a sip. 'About three days I think.'

Zach choked, sucking in water and erupting into a fit of useless coughing in an attempt to exhale the liquid from his lungs.

'Three,' he wheezed, his voice tapering out as he spoke. 'Three *days*?'

She nodded, pushing herself up onto her feet, wincing as she stood. She hopped from foot to foot. 'Ouch, ouch! Pins and needles!'

Zach was still holding the glass, trying to catch his breath, as she plopped down onto the bed beside him.

'Yes, three days,' she said, bouncing slightly on the mattress.

He was silent. BK tucked her legs up against her chest, pulling the blankets up around them and tucking them back in, her curls wild about her face.

'What…what happened?'

'What do you remember?'

He frowned, staring down at the tangled sheets and attempting to dig through his memories. Everything was hazy, as if someone had laid a film of fog over his memories of the last few days.

'It's all…jumbled. We were…in a house?'

'Yes. We were attacked. But these men came to get us.'

'Why?'

BK paused, seeming to think on this question before saying, 'I think they want our help.'

He frowned and looked down at himself. He felt…off.

'You were hurt,' said BK, sensing his thoughts.

Zach glanced up. 'I was?' he said, and shook his head, trying to shake his thoughts into order. 'I…I was stabbed?'

'Yes.'

Zach swallowed, his mouth going dry. 'Why was I stabbed?'

'A very bad man came to get Genie. But you saw him, so he hurt you so you couldn't warn them. But you're okay now. Ant found you. And then the men came, and they took us all away.'

'This…this was all three days ago?' Zach asked, prodding at his side where he remembered the sharp agony of a knife gliding through his flesh.

'I'm not sure. I was asleep, like you. I woke up three days ago.'

'Great…so really, we could've been here for weeks and we wouldn't even know?'

She tilted her head. 'I guess so.'

Zach gritted his teeth and tried to focus on breathing. Seeming to sense his unease, BK remained quiet next to him.

Bits and pieces of memories came to him slowly, like mud oozing from a tap that should have been flowing with water. Zach bit the inside of his mouth in frustration and wished he was high.

'Oh, I forgot,' BK said, and leaned over to the bedside table, dragging the covers loose again.

Zach shook his head, unable to help a little smile working it's way onto his face. She was so calm, so at ease despite their situation, and instead of putting Zach on edge, it calmed him.

He blinked in surprise when she turned back to him, a glint of silver in her hand. He stretched out his palm and she placed the lighter in it. The cool metal fell into his fingers easily and he felt a small knot of tension release. Not much, but enough for him to breathe a little easier.

'I rescued it for you,' she said. 'I thought maybe you'd want it back.'

'Yeah. Thanks,' he said, feeling gratitude but unable to find a way to express it.

She didn't seem to mind. She leant her head on his shoulder and said, 'I'm glad you're awake. It was so lonely by myself.'

'You haven't seen anyone else?'

'No. Well, sometimes these doctors in suits come to give us food, but other than that, no one else.'

'What about the others?'

As he asked the question, he realised that, yes, there were others. People he was hesitant to call friends, and yet his stomach clenched in worry as he thought about them being missing. A memory of Ant surfaced. The boy leaning over him with worried eyes, trying to stop the bleeding. Were they here, somewhere, in this unknown building, locked in a room as he and BK were?

She shook her head. 'I haven't seen them.'

'Do you think they're okay?'

She nodded.

'How can you be sure?'

She shrugged and smiled at him. 'I just am.'

Zach sighed and sat back again, shifting so BK's elbow didn't brush passed his bandages. 'How do you do it?' he asked. 'How do you stay so unerringly confident that everything will be okay? We've been captured by officials who will probably do all sorts of tests on us. We've been separated from our friends. Colluding with aliens. And, worst of all, we were exposed to the most deadly plague on the planet that has managed to wipe out huge amounts of the population in a matter of days.'

His own words didn't register until after he'd finished saying them. The blood drained from his face, and he felt his chest constrict again at the implications of what he'd just said. They *had* been exposed to a deadly plague. How had he forgotten that.

How had he forgotten *Stevie?*

Zach frowned and rubbed at his face. Was that why he was here? What if cooperating with Stevie, leading her across the country, had gotten them in trouble. Worse yet, what if he was right? What if they were about to be tested and prodded and experimented on. His breathing hitched.

BK placed one hand on his arm, her touch cool to his flushed skin. 'We aren't dead yet.'

The simplicity of her words caught him off guard, derailing the full blown panic attack that had been brewing in his chest. He sat still and contemplated her words. They *weren't* dead. If they really *had* been exposed, they should have been.

He turned and found himself much closer to her face than he was expecting. She blinked, and he could make out the little flecks of brown in her olive green eyes. There was a light smattering of freckles across her nose that made her shy smile rather endearing, and he relaxed, melting back into the wall and enjoying the warmth of her pressed up next to him.

She tilted her head to the side, her lips quirking up in a curious smile. 'What?' she asked, her tone soft and embarrassed.

'Nothing,' he grinned back, and then shook his head to stop himself from smiling, feeling like an idiot.

After a beat of uncomfortable silence, in which the space between them became awkward, he turned back to her, his mouth open with a question, but her finger—which came out of nowhere—pressed against his lips.

'Shh,' she said, and turned her gaze back to the door. 'He's listening.'

'Who?'

'The one who brought us all here. Stevie's mentor. The one keeping you asleep.'

'Keeping…*Stevie's* mentor? You mean an alien?'

She nodded, her voice dropping even lower as she leaned close to him, her lips almost pressed to his ear as she said, 'he's working on the plague.'

CHAPTER THIRTY-SIX

Genie

Waking up was like fighting my way through a lake of mud. It was slow and tiring and even the simplest act of opening my eyes took more energy than it should have.

When I did wake, emerging from the thick fog in my mind like a lost ghost, I felt sodden and detached. Sodden because I was covered in a cold sweat. My body shivered and, weighed down by my own skin and bones, a sense of helplessness filled my chest.

A memory struggled up into my mind of another time my own body had felt too heavy to move. I had been in a white room with lots of shiny silver objects and men in blue outfits sewing something thin and barely visible into my aching chest.

The memory came with a ghost of pain, and I struggled to lift a hand to touch the old scar. Only I couldn't move my hand. It wasn't the heaviness that kept me locked in place, but something covering the length of my arm.

I tried to raise my head, to see what was holding me down, only to find that I couldn't sit up either. What I *could* do was lift my head just enough to see the thick leather straps across my arms, chest and legs.

'What…?'

My head spun with the effort and implications of why I was strapped to a table. Was I hurt? No. Surely they wouldn't strap me down if I was hurt. Yet pain, not a memory this time, shivered down the side of my face and jaw. I winced, sucking in a sharp breath.

I twisted, trying to better see the room, or a person I could ask. I was too confused, too woozy to be panicked. That would come later. For now I just wanted answers.

Where was I? Why was I tied to a table? Why did my face hurt? What was being injected into my arm?

The little needle poked out of the back of my left hand, taped down by three pieces of thin, white, tape. If I wriggled my hand, the little needle jabbed about in my skin and stung.

I laid my head back down on the table, which was steadily becoming more uncomfortable.

'Hello?' I called, coughing in an effort to speak. 'Hello?'

The door, which I hadn't seen, clattered open in a hurry. A woman in a white coat hurried through, a soft smile on her pretty face.

'You're awake!' she said, hurrying to my side and checking the needle. 'How do you feel?'

I felt the world sway around me, though I hadn't moved. 'Um…heavy?'

'Ah, yes, of course,' she patted my hand where the needle was, and shook her head. 'I'll fix that up for you in a moment. How about your thoughts? How's your memory? Do you know your name?'

'Why wouldn't I know my name?' I asked.

Except…did I know my name? For the briefest moment, my vision restricted, my throat tightened and the sweat broke out anew on my forehead. What *was* my name?

'Genie.'

Recognition. Relief. Yes…yes *that* was my name.

'Genie,' I said, repeating the thought. 'Genie Hart. That's my name.'

'Genie?' the woman asked, frowning and looking down at a device she held that I hadn't noticed before.

'It's a nickname. Short for Genevieve.'

Yes. That was right. I looked up at the woman's face, repeating the words whispering through my mind.

Her face cleared, a pleased smile blossoming. 'You remember nicknames. Excellent. That's excellent. And what about your birthday?'

My birthday? Why did she need to know my birthday.

'It's in two weeks,' said the voice. *'On the seventh. We turn eighteen.'*

We? This confused me, and I frowned, trying to sort out the mess of thoughts in my mind. The woman was watching me though, waiting for an answer.

'Um…the seventh. It's in two weeks…we…I turn eighteen.'

This answer seemed to satisfy the woman. She nodded, not asking for anything more specific, for which I was grateful. Did I know anything more specific? Was it strange I couldn't even remember my own birthday?

'And what's the last thing you remember?' she asked, adjusting the needle in my arm.

I thought for a moment, tilting my head and waiting for the voice to whisper the answer to me again. He (how could it be a he?), the voice, was more hesitant, and somehow I knew there was fear behind this answer. Except when the thought came, he was angry, no longer a whisper but a growl of outrage.

'He was there. He hurt you. Then they *took us. They took us when we were hurt but they didn't help us!'*

Memory exploded. Images rushing in all at once as the sharp sting of remembrance drove away the fog of drugs.

'Einstein,' I said. How had I forgotten him? 'He came… He came after those men. We…we were hurt but…but they weren't helping us. You weren't helping us!'

At this, the woman's face became strained, her smile forced, and her pretty blue eyes peered at me in suspicious scrutiny. Blue eyes. Blue like the summer sky.

Summer blue. Ant. Looking up from Zach's crumpled form, blood soaking his hands. Zach, limp and lifeless, blue eyes wide in pain. BK struggling, trying to see if they were okay, screaming at them to stop, to *help*. Stevie being carried off by men in suits, completely ignored by Einstein. Why? Why weren't they helping us?

Anger swelled in my chest. I wanted to scream. I wanted to cry. I wanted to beg to be released, to be able to see my friends, to make sure they were okay.

Yet something stilled me. Some idea that this…*interview* wasn't finished yet. That there was more to be revealed.

'Did you find those answers on your own?' the woman finally asked. 'Did you think them yourself, or did someone else think them for you?'

For a long moment I didn't answer. What did my thoughts have to do with anything? What did it matter if someone gave me the answers? They were the right ones, weren't they?

My thoughts went still, quiet, waiting. Waiting for the voice. The male voice that…was mine, right? It occurred to me then that the idea of hearing someone else's thoughts should have alarmed me more than it did.

'Tell her she's crazy,' he said, back to a whisper. *'Ask her how someone else could give you the answers when you're all alone. Swear at her.'*

I hesitated. *'Who are you?'* I thought back at the voice and realised for the first time how strange it was my inner voice was male, was so different from me. I was a girl, so why wasn't he? *'Are you me?'*

When no response came, I focused back on the woman, on her expectant and watchful gaze. I frowned. I glared. I balled my fists and I felt for the anger, clutched at it.

'What d'you mean did I *think them myself*? How else would I think them? How else would I get the answers?' I asked, hearing my own voice rise into a yell. 'There's only two of us in this stupid room, isn't there? Or do you have other people watching me? Huh? What are you doing to me? Let me out! Let me go! What've you done to my friends? Where's my brother?'

My voice became a shriek, shouting and raging at the woman even as my insides remained confused and scared. Brother. His face came to me. Rising up out of the remnants of fog, grinning with that lopsided smile, winking back at me with my own eyes. Except his eyes were sharp and bright and fun.

Something like relief washed through me. Freddie. That was what I'd been waiting for. *Freddie*. He was the final piece. The part of my memory that hadn't yet clicked into place. With him came the rest. The school, the plague, the crash, the house, James and Stevie.

Stevie who'd tried to save us, as Einstein stood by and watched.

'Where is he?' I yelled. 'Where's Einstein? I want to talk to him. I want to see Freddie!'

My fingers felt hot. Burning hot, like they were about to explode into fire, and a sudden pressure came down on my mind.

'Wait,' came the voice, that inner consciousness I'd always imagined sounded like him. *'You have to wait. You have to be patient. If you don't give them what they want, they'll put you back to sleep. They'll make you numb. It's starting already. Don't you feel it?'*

I stopped screaming, stopped struggling against the leather to realise the woman was putting the needle back into my hand. I felt the cold seep up into my arm, felt the numbness he had warned me of (he, or me? I still couldn't tell).

My fingers stopped feeling hot and instead I felt a hint of pain travel along my face. The woman eyed me as I grew still again.

'I…' I paused, and tears welled in my eyes. I didn't blink them away, instead let them slip down my face, unable to wipe them off. 'I'm just scared. What's…what's wrong with my face? It hurts.'

The woman's suspicions cleared and she nodded her head in understanding. 'Of course you're scared,' she said. 'This is a shock. But don't worry. You *are* safe here. You were injured before you came in, but we've taken care of you. We've stitched you up. All you need to do now is heal, and then take a few tests.'

'Tests?'

'Nothing to worry about. Just some simple memory tests. Once we're sure you're better, you can go back to your room.'

'Can I see Freddie?'

'Your brother? Perhaps. If we get the tests done.'

Somehow I knew the voice was right. I would have to cooperate, I would have to do as I was told if I wanted to see my friends. I would have to wait.

My mind went back to the first time I'd been given anaesthetic. To the reason why. To the feel of a knife sliding through my skin, to running, to hiding.

I could wait. I had waited then, for someone to rescue me.

I would wait now, and when it was time, I would find my family. I would find Freddie.

CHAPTER THIRTY-SEVEN

Zach

When the door opened, Zach was pacing. If the floor had been carpet instead of tiles, there'd already be a worn patch trodden in by Zach's relentless walk between each wall. BK sat on the bed, legs crossed, and watched him with her head tilted to one side. She worried about his wound, but Zach found the walking helped. He was stiff and sore, but he itched. Walking helped.

'Zach, what are you thinking?'

He started to answer, to sort his thoughts into some sort of coherent response, when the door opened.

The man that entered, if he could be called a man (for he surely wasn't human), stood watching him with a narrowed gaze. He was both like Stevie and unlike her. He had the same purple skin and blue veins; his ears trailed back over his shoulders just like hers, though they were perhaps longer, and the ridges more pronounced.

Yet he stood straight backed. Assured. Confident in his abundance of knowledge as those calculative, silver eyes focused and thought through a dozen ideas and thoughts at once. Zach could sense this as they stared at one another.

He was old. Far older than Stevie. Far older than any human Zach had ever known.

'Who are you?'

'You have not guessed?' The creature's lips twitched, in a strange half smile that was at once sardonic and patronising.

Zach, without knowing why, bristled. 'Stevie's mentor,' he said.

'Yes. You may call me Einstein.'

'Einstein?' He struggled to keep the snide amusement out of his voice at the presumption of the creature comparing himself to one of Earth's most famous scientists. 'You're a little more purple than I'd have imagined Einstein to be.'

'Perhaps,' said Einstein. 'It is not a name I would have chosen for myself.'

'Oh?'

'I must confess, though, seeing as we are making observations. You are a little more … puny, than I had imagined.'

Zach rolled his eyes. 'Yeah, well, at least I'm human.'

'You say that like it is a good thing.'

'Isn't it?'

Einstein paused, some stray emotion flashing through those sharp silver eyes before he could catch it and shut it away. Those eyes, like liquid mercury, narrowed at Zach. 'Perhaps,' he said.

Zach raised his eyebrows but said nothing more. He wasn't playing this game. If this otherworldly Einstein wanted something, he'd have to get to the point.

Einstein's brows, hairless, just like Stevie's, rose. 'Well, I suppose I could get to the point, but I had rather thought you would prefer some preparation.'

Zach froze. He felt the beat of his heart in steady, heavy thumps and fought to keep his emotions (outrage, wariness, fear) off his face. His gaze flicked to BK and away again just as quick, seeing in her expression that, yes, the alien had just got that thought out of his mind.

Though he knew that Stevie possessed some telepathic ability—the image of Freddie's outrage as he realised Stevie was reading his mind resurfaced in Zach's memory—the idea that some foreign creature could so easily invade his inner thoughts filled him with an anger he'd never experienced before.

The expression of derisive amusement on Einstein's face

only served to fuel that anger and Zach broke eye contact, snapping his head away and trying not to think about anything at all. Seeing that strategy was quickly going to fail —Zach had never been very good at not thinking—he began thinking the lyrics of the first song that came to mind as loudly as he could.

'Twinkle, twinkle little star!'

Einstein flinched, hissing in pain, a hand rising to his temple. Even BK jumped, as if she, too, had heard his mental shout. He pushed that thought away for later, focusing on the lyrics.

'How I wonder what you are.'

'On Earth,' Zach said aloud, keeping the lyrics at the forefront of his thoughts, 'it's considered rude to read people's minds.'

He didn't mention that the few times Stevie had delved towards his thoughts, he'd had at least some notion that something was wrong. That there was something foreign entering his mind. How was it that Einstein could pluck a single thought from him without him knowing at all?

'Up above the world so high.'

Einstein glowered at him, still rubbing his temple.

'But since you mentioned it,' said Zach, 'Yes, I'd like you to get to the point.'

'Like a diamond in the sky.'

'Interesting choice of…distraction,' said the alien man. 'Though, you need not avoid my gaze. Eye contact is irrelevant to my ability to see within your mind.'

Zach scoffed and kept mentally singing the song. *'Twinkle, twinkle little star.'*

'Although,' said Einstein, 'I do find your aversion quite interesting.'

Zach turned, focusing on the point just above Einstein's shoulder, still unconvinced that eye contact wouldn't at least make the connection stronger. 'Really? You find it *interesting* that I don't like my privacy being invaded?'

'Indeed,' Einstein smirked, and Zach's song faltered at the smugness in his tone. 'If I recall, when one of your little friends had a similar reaction to…what do you call her?

Stevie, to her using her own ability, you told him it was possible she could not help it. To which, I might add, you were quite right. With the force of which you are singing that little *song* I cannot help but hear it.'

Zach let the song fade away. He remembered the incident Einstein referred to. Remembered Freddie's anger at being spied on, and Zach's own irritation at the accusation in Freddie's words. His own reprimand came back to him.

They communicate telepathically. It's perfectly normal for them to be in each others heads. It's also something she probably can't control. You can't un-hear me speaking to you. It's the same.'

Zach pursed his lips, but glanced to Einstein, meeting his gaze properly. Though the alien didn't say so, Zach knew by the expression on his face that he'd heard the memory, the same as Zach.

'Well, try a little harder,' said Zach. 'The very least you could do is not spy deliberately. Overhearing is one thing. Deliberately eavesdropping is another. Don't you people have any privacy?'

'That is a human term.'

Zach narrowed his gaze but said nothing further. Getting angry without understanding this creature wasn't going to help matters. It wasn't going to help him or BK. So Zach took a deep breath and asked a different question than the one he wanted.

'Where are we?'

'This is a facility my people have managed for many years. It is safe.'

'Safe?' Zach scoffed. 'Safe for who, you? What exactly are we doing here? You say you've managed this place for years. To do what…experiments?'

'Something to that effect, yes.'

Zach paused, taken off guard by the casual truth. 'And we're, what? New subjects for you?'

'You are an answer.'

'An answer to what.'

'Exactly.' Einstein smirked at the confusion on Zach's face, before gesturing to the hallway beyond. 'Come with me. I have something I think you will find interesting.'

Zach didn't move. He *was* curious. No doubt whatever the alien had to show Zach *would* be interesting. He couldn't help that part of him. The part that always wanted an answer. He suspected, in some small way, that he and Einstein were alike in that matter.

However, another part of him, the part that dominated his survival instinct, was telling him to get out. To not trust this strange creature from another planet that had been experimenting on humans for years. Decades, maybe.

He was struggling with this battle of wanting both the answer, and to run, when a touch to his arm brought him out of his thoughts.

BK tilted her head in Einstein's direction, her green eyes glued to Zach's face. 'I think we should go with him. It's not far. Just down the hall.'

Another memory came to him then. A conversation that could have occurred only days ago.

'*...It's like, we're all going in one direction, following the path that's set out in front of us, and BK's taking a short cut through a rabbit's hole and getting there before us.*'

As was becoming usual, Zach had the feeling BK was trying to tell him something more than she was saying. Squashing the urge to question her, he sighed and decided to listen to her.

'Alright,' he said, gesturing to Einstein in mock respect. 'Lead on.'

Einstein's smirk grew, unfazed by Zach's cynical antics, and he stepped out into the hallway. BK took Zach's hand and pulled him after the alien man, and as they followed him down the hall, Zach couldn't help but feel like he was being led straight into wonderland.

He could only wonder what on Earth he was going to find there.

CHAPTER THIRTY-EIGHT

Genie

Water and steam surrounded me, spewing from all directions. I gasped, shivering though the water was way too hot. It pierced my skin, splitting me open with a million tiny needle pricks. Stinging my back, my hands, my face—sharp bursts of pain travelling up my cheek, shocking me back into consciousness.

I tried to shield my face, tried to hide from the pressure and the heat and the pain. The feeling of exposure, the realisation I was *undressed* came later. After the water had stopped and I lay gasping and panting in a heap on the tiled floor.

Panic and anger. Where was I? What was happening? *Who had taken my clothes?*

Hands grasped my arms, pulling me up. My body wouldn't obey me. I tried to curl up, to hide myself from them, but I was still so *heavy*.

'What're you doing?' I asked, though the words came out slurred and mashed together. 'Warruing?'

'She's awake?'

'Yeah, the drugs don't last long enough, we have to keep double dosing her.'

'What about the damage? The collective won't be pleased if we harm her.'

'The Collective only wants her DNA; besides, we have to keep them under somehow, don't we?'

'What about the brother? Is he still docile?'

'Yeah.'

'Isn't that strange? Why would you have to double dose this one, when the twin is unresponsive? Do you think there's something wrong with him?'

'You'd better hope not. These two are our best chance. If they fail the tests, it's over for the Collective…and for us.'

I didn't understand any of the conversation. Confusion swirled amongst the words, turning them into gibberish. I knew I *should* understand, I knew that this was important and that I had to remember what they were saying—they were talking about me after all—yet I just couldn't process the conversation.

They pulled me down a corridor, uncaring to my dragging legs, or the aches in my shoulders as they held me up.

I wanted to scream. I wanted to cry. I wanted to ask for some God damn clothes! Didn't they care? Couldn't they at least give me some dignity?

Doors slipped open, the air hissing and sucking as we moved from the little corridor into a large open room. Somewhere warm and dry and not as frightening as the wet room.

The two men picked me up, shifting my small, unresisting limbs onto what looked and felt like a gurney. God, where they going to kill me?

A door banged open, hard enough to bounce off the wall and fling back at the person storming through.

'What is this?'

'Decontamination, sir. They wish to begin testing.'

Fury. Complete and utter fury. 'She is not an animal,' snarled the voice and the two men on either side of me flinched. 'Give her some dignity. Or are you so deep, so far beyond your own sense of being that common decency and compassion have forsaken you?'

'I…'

'Quiet!'

There was a sharp whip of fabric being shaken out, and a sheet was dropped over me. I didn't realise I had been shivering until I stopped. My eyes were open, but locked on the ceiling above. I swallowed, trying to work my mouth into opening. Trying to speak. Trying to thank this person. And to ask why the other men had been so awful, and didn't they have any *female* attendants?

And what, exactly, was I going to be tested for?

My breathing sharpened, and I felt a scream building. What was going on?

'Shh, just wait.'

I paused, the scream lodging in my throat.

'It's almost time. Just wait.'

The voice was comforting. Soothing in the way that the others had been cruel and careless. He eased my fears, and I felt myself slipping back into the drugs.

'Go back to sleep. I'll keep watch for a while.'

Somewhere in my mind, I thought to wonder about his voice. It was mine, and yet, it was male. Somehow, I knew this had always been the case. That I'd substituted my own inner voice with that of another.

Déjà vu struck me. I'd been down this train of thought before, hadn't I? I'd questioned my own subconscious. I had reached some sort of conclusion. What was it? Why couldn't I remember?

The voice was that of another, not mine. A voice I knew and yet had never heard. The voice of someone who *couldn't* speak.

Someone who…who…was waiting?

Waiting for what?

***

My first test was simple. A memory game. Something old and familiar from my childhood, something I knew instinctually how to play. Turn the cards over, remember their places and match them up.

Though I couldn't remember who I'd played with or where, I knew I'd always been good at this game. I sensed pride in my memories. Pleasure from someone I loved when I did well. I often did well. Competitions with another—who could be the best?

Similar games. Puzzle pieces, untangling locks, building things. Children's games. Things from my past I had forgotten. It was all so familiar, and yet it was all so forgotten.

When was the last time I'd played games like these?

'Before Mum died.'

His voice whispered out at me, startling me so badly that I knocked over the tower of thin blocks I'd been constructing into a bridge.

'Start again,' said a fuzzy voice over an intercom.

I looked up, but no one was in the room. Just me, and the puzzle games. At least I had clothes this time. Thin, and grey, but clothes none the less.

I began reconstructing my bridge, thinking about my mother. I didn't remember her well. Her face was nothing but a blurry outline in my mind. When had she died?

'When we were seven.'

Yes. I remembered waking up during the night, getting a glass of water. There was someone in the house…someone bad?

I remembered her turning to look at me. She was pretty, with long red hair and bright eyes that shinned in the dark. She'd touched my hair, trailing a hand down over the back of my head they way Mum often did. She put a finger to her lips. I nodded, and without a thought, I went back to bed. The next day, my parents were dead.

I paused, one hand holding a block over the rest, my breath coming in short gasps.

'Is something wrong?' asked the voice over the intercom.

'I…I think…'

'Are you confused about the objective?'

'No.'

'But something is bothering you?'

'I remembered something,' I said, still looking at the block in my hand but not really seeing it.

My mind was caught back in that night. How had I forgotten that woman?

'What did you remember?'

'I…I let my mother die.'

A long pause.

'You remember your mother?'

'She used to give me tests like these. Me and…and Freddie? Is…is Freddie okay? Can I see him yet?'

Another long pause.

'Do you remember anything else about your mother? You said you let her die, what do you mean?'

'There was a woman…please, when can I see my brother?' I put the block down and hugged myself, bringing my knees up to my chest. 'I really want to see him.'

'You may put the blocks away, you should rest before we continue.'

'And Freddie?' I asked, looking up and staring at the wall in front if me.

Though the wall was blank, the same white as the rest of my room, I could almost sense the indistinct person on the other side, watching me.

'No, not yet.'

CHAPTER THIRTY-NINE

Zach

'What do you see?'

Zach sighed, not answering the question. The lights above him were florescent, glowing an unnatural light that was beginning to give Zach a headache. A normal headache, rather than the aggressive onslaught from Einstein's attack at the house.

Einstein huffed and Zach narrowed his eyes. He kept his hand steady, letting a drop of red dye fall onto the slide before saying, 'If you don't like what you hear, don't listen to my thoughts.'

The red dye settled and, under the magnifying lens, the image became clearer. The dial clicked, ticking over rivets as Zach's fingers lightly adjusted the magnification.

He frowned, pulling away from the lens and shifting the position of the sample slide. When he pressed his eyes against the looking lens, it was the same.

'This is...' he trailed off, unsure of what it was he was seeing, trying to make sense of the information before him.

He stepped away, peering at the monitor to his left and studying the figures there. The protein markers, the numbers, they were all normal. Perfect health. Almost too perfect. Zach's frown deepened. It didn't match with the image he was seeing.

He glanced to his left where Stevie stood leaning against a bench top watching him, her fingers shredding apart a piece of paper. The one she'd shown him with the various test results of Freddie Hart.

She was trying too hard. Like a lost puppy, eager to please but not quite sure of itself to do anything more than wag its tail and follow its master.

Einstein paid her no attention and irritation bubbled in Zach's stomach. He shot a glare at the scientist, before scowling back down at the microscope.

With a mentor like Einstein, it was no wonder Stevie was terrified of everything. Someone so overbearing and cold could never be appeased. The way she'd spoken of him, with that kind of reverence one reserved for a father, had given Zach a different image of the creature that stood before him.

Zach scowled. Einstein didn't deserve her respect. Not when he had left her alone with only vague promises and commands to carry out. Not when he'd abandoned her. For that matter, hadn't he abandoned Genie too? Hadn't Zach heard talk about an alien who'd told her she was strong, that she would be cared for and protected.

Yet here he was, kidnapping them and subjecting them to tests.

Zach saw Einstein's shoulders stiffen. His ears went rigid and a faint blue spark traveled along the ridges on his head.

Zach smirked and focused more on the thought, turning it into a telepathic sneer aimed directly at Einstein. *You abandoned them.*

Einstein crossed his arms and said nothing. Satisfied with his minor attack, Zach turned back to the scope.

He shook his head. 'What exactly am I looking at?'

'What do you think you are looking at?' Einstein asked, his voice stiff and cold.

Zach drummed his fingers along the bench and wished for a smoke. 'It's almost like a blood sample. But it's not.'

'What makes you think it is not?'

Zach scoffed and pulled away from the microscope, pointing at it. 'Because no blood sample I've ever seen looks like *that*. Unless it's yours.'

'It is not mine,' said Einstein. His gaze flicked to Stevie

before he added. 'Nor is it hers. That came from a human. Tell me, what do you see?'

'I see the impossible,' said Zach, crossing his arms and leaning back against the bench. 'It's not human, it's…well… parasitic, almost. No, not that either. It's…it's a mutation. The cells have become like…like spores?'

Zach didn't mean for the words to come out like questions, but he was grasping at straws, trying to make sense of the mutated mess of cells on the slide. Still, Einstein didn't call him on it. He just smiled, giving a soft little nod.

'Exactly.'

Zach frowned. 'You're saying this was taken from a human?' he asked.

Einstein nodded.

'Then you did this, right?'

Einstein paused, and again he glanced at Stevie. She was watching them both, silver eyes wide and troubled as they swivelled back and forth between them.

BK stood opposite her, alternating between watching the conversation, and peering curiously at the slide. The two girls had remained silent throughout Zach's examination of the test slides, but BK was still her usual calm self, so Zach was content to look around until he could make sense of whatever it was Einstein was showing him.

'Not…exactly.'

'What does that mean?' Zach asked.

'This precise sample was not of my doing,' explained Einstein, without really explaining anything.

Zach sighed, sick of playing riddles. 'What the hell does *that* mean?'

Einstein grinned again, and reached for yet another slide.

The first two slides of blood cells moved like spores when introduced to a fresh sample of normal blood—Zach hadn't dared ask where Einstein had procured all these samples from—the spore-like sample would attack it, mutating the normal cells in rapid succession until they conformed to the rest.

Zach had never seen anything like it before. Hadn't thought it even possible for changes to be made on that level so suddenly without a virus or bacteria being involved. And yet, these weren't dangerous cells. They weren't deteriorating, they were…*improving*.

Zach sighed, and accepted the fourth slide, taking out the third and replacing it with the fresh sample. 'You know, just because you've got dozens of these slides, doesn't mean I'm going to believe you the more I see. Don't think I don't realise you're just using this as a diversion. You think you can — what the hell?'

He adjusted the zoom again, getting a better view of cells.

'This is the source of the spores,' he murmured, staring into the microscope at what was clearly an alien blood sample.

'Yes, it is the source. But it is not as alien as you think it to be.'

'I told you to stop reading my mind,' Zach said, still gazing at the sample. 'Are the results the same with this one?'

'Better. It is a perfected system, balanced to optimise all strengths, and reduce all weaknesses.'

Zach heard the hint of smugness, of pride, of wistfulness, but didn't understand it. Didn't even register it. Not then, anyway. He was too focused on the sample he was looking at.

He swapped it out with the previous slide, to better compare them. Now that he'd seen the parent cell, he could see where the cells of the previous slide had been human. How they'd mutated to become like, but unlike, the parent cell.

'You said this wasn't alien?'

'No.'

'But it's not human.'

A pause. 'No.'

Zach looked up. 'What is it?'

Einstein raised one brow, a very human expression on his inhuman face. It was odd. Stranger than seeing human expressions on Stevie's face.

'Humans. Such young, stupid creatures. Always jumping to conclusions. Never seeing what is right in front of you.'

'Don't avoid the question.'

'Why? It is the wrong question, after all.'

Zach's eyes narrowed and he straightened up. 'What's the right one?'

A smile spread across his face, revealing his teeth, sharp and gleaming white. 'Not what, but *who*?'

CHAPTER FORTY

Genie

The tests were always different. Sometimes they wanted me to run. Sometimes they wanted me to sit and breathe. Sometimes they wanted me to lift weights and do stretches and punch and kick until I ached all over and then do it all over again.

Sometimes they wanted me to write. They asked me questions, odd questions that didn't make sense but I somehow knew the answers to anyway. They set me down on a table and told me to lie flat, while they took pictures of my brain and samples of my blood.

I didn't fight. Didn't argue or disobey or resist. I did the tests, and I waited.

And in between I dreamt.

Strange dreams that echoed and swam and made me dizzy.

A red headed woman, petting my head. Blood dripping on the hallway. The creak of a door. A question. Big brother, asking what was wrong. *'You hurt, Evie?'*

A dark skinned boy, shoving back someone bigger and older, coal black eyes gleaming with a fierce, untameable fire as I sat on the ground and cried. *'Don't you call her crazy!'*

Swoosh.

Tumbling through darkness, slipping under the murky memory only to emerge somewhere deeper. Somewhere new. A memory, or a dream? Or something else?

'Are you gonna let me out?' Harsh and familiar, the

words tumble from my mouth…but no…not *my* mouth.

A dream from someone else's eyes. This body did not belong to me, this voice was not mine and those words, those were words that came from fire I did not have.

A pause in my body—or, this *other's* body—as if he can sense me there where I should not be.

But then the attendant by the door moved, catching my —our—attention. They wear a hazmat suit that is at once familiar and frightening. The cover is clear so we can see her face.

She takes a step back toward the door and as we take a step after her, a low growl emanates through the room. For the first time I see the dog on the thick chain the woman in the hazmat suit is holding. It sits at her heels, a large, short-haired shepherd that could have been cute if it wasn't baring it's fangs to attack.

Retreat. Back under the murky water. Back to the dreams.

Soft, smiling, blue eyes. A shy smile hidden by the steam of freshly made coffee. The tangy smell hanging in the air and tickling my nose. A reluctant grin as we compared notes on the cute boys passing by our table.

Swoosh.

Back within the deep. I open my eyes—not *my* eyes— and see wires. Bleeps and whirrs mark the use of machinery, and my heartbeat flutters in panic as footsteps near. *What're they going to do next? When are they going to stop?*

Another man in a hazmat suit. Our breathing quickens. Something small and sharp presses into the soft skin at our elbow. The numbness is familiar, but this body responds to it with fear. Knowing that with the numbness also comes pain.

'Initiating Test Number Seventeen. Introducing viral stimuli number twelve to the mutated blood cells: depth, bone.'

Blood rushing in our ears. Fear that made our heart thump so hard it *hurt*.

That pain was nothing, *nothing*, to the pain that followed, stabbing first into our arm, and then deeper. *Far* deeper. Cracking through muscle and flesh and *bone*.

Screaming. Screaming so loud I thought my head would explode.

Retreat. Retreat, retreat, retreat. I gasp, scrabbling at my sheets, trying to wake up, but I'm still tumbling through the water, through the muddled memories of my own mind. Is it still *my* mind?

Wild curls. She was always wild. Wild in thought, in words, in mannerisms. Yet also quiet. Comforting. As soft and malleable as a baby bird. She braids my hair, fingers coming through the tangles and knots with practised ease. *'You know, you're really very pretty.'*

Swoosh.

Sitting in a small room, watching a sandy haired boy sleep and waiting for him to wake up.

Waiting?

Who was I waiting for?

Swoosh.

Grey eyes stare at me from a mirror. Mine? No…the other part of me. The part of me that wasn't me, but someone else. Someone separate. Separate but the same? I wasn't sure anymore.

Something else prodding at my mind. Some other memory. Some other new place trying to catch my attention. Somewhere that was me…but not me.

'Stay.'

It's his voice. It echoes up from beneath the cloudy memories.

'But…'

'Shh…they can hear you. Just stay.'

The other place prods at me again. Except, I'm starting to understand. It's not a place…but a *person*. A mind. A mind beckoning for me to enter, to see from their eyes, to feel from their body, to hear from their ears.

The realisation frightens me further back within myself and I retreat away from the prodding mind, and the memories, and the confusing dreams. I bury myself within the darkness and try to forget, try to wait them out, try not to remember.

'Soon, Genie. Soon we can stop waiting.'

Except, I was beginning to fear that moment. Somewhere, deep down—where his voice came from—I knew that when I stopped waiting, when I could break free of the murky fog clouding my mind, everything would change.

There were things happening to me, happening *within* me that didn't make sense. The answers were there, hovering on the edges of the darkness, waiting—just like I was.

A shiver of nervousness gripped me, took hold of my chest and squeezed so I had to fight to breathe. I curled around myself, taking a deep breathe, and letting it out slow. *Not yet.*

For now, I was still waiting, and so I was still safe. For now.

CHAPTER FORTY-ONE

Zach

Zach frowned, both confused and weary of the question. 'Who's blood? You mean…we know who this is?'

'Of course,' said Einstein. 'That is why you are all here.'

'Wait…this is one of *us*? You…you said you didn't do this!'

'I said I was not the cause of the first two. The last is my work.'

'Your *work*? What exactly did you do to us? Hang on, give me a needle, I want to make sure this stuff isn't in *me*. BK, come here, I'll do yours too.'

Zach was scrounging through the draws, looking for a needle and syringe to take a sample from himself. His mind was racing, coming up with all sorts of horrible scenarios as to what Einstein's experiments could do to them.

'I am afraid that would only confuse matters further,' said Einstein, watching Zach in amusement.

'What?' Zach asked, fumbling to connect a needle into the head of a syringe.

'I can allow you to test your own blood, in fact, I encourage it. It will show you more of what I have planned here. But your friend is another matter. She will only confuse you.'

Zach straightened up at the odd note in Einstein's voice. He felt a prickle of unease along the back of his neck.

BK looked between them, her smile vacant and her eyes creased in worry. Zach had never seen her worried. Not like this. This wasn't fear for her friends, or sadness for others, this was self preservation. He knew it, because that's what he saw when he looked in a mirror.

She was afraid of what he was about to find out.

'Why would she confuse things?' Zach asked, keeping his gaze locked on hers.

Einstein didn't answer. Instead, BK spoke in a soft voice. Calm. Resigned.

'I'm an alien,' she said softly.

Zach shook his head, taking a single step back. 'But… but you're human.'

She shook her head, and her curls bounced gently around her face. 'No. I'm like Stevie'

'You can't be. You're human,' Zach repeated, feeling his head spin as he tried to focus on her face. Her *human* face. 'You *look* human. You don't look like Stevie, not even a little bit.'

'I don't look like this. Not really. Well, not before I came here.'

Zach slouched back against the bench, clutching at it with both hands. 'You don't…' he trailed off, too confused to finish the sentence.

How could it be possible she didn't really look like she did? How could she have been *different?*

BK took step toward him and then stopped, biting her lip. Her brows furrowed as she waited for him to accept what she was saying.

'She-She isn't l-l-lying,' said Stevie. Her stutter, bad even on a good day, had become more pronounced in Einstein's presence.

'Oh great,' said Zach, turning to give her a wild eyed glare. 'So you're telling me I'm the only human in here? And what about all those scientists you were parading about before? Are *they* human? Or are they all experiments too?'

'The guardian is not an experiment,' Einstein said, his voice cracking like a whip.

Zach jumped, and then glowered at the man. 'And what the hell is that supposed to mean? What guardian?'

'Me,' said BK.

Zach blinked a few times, looking between BK and Einstein.

'I…you're a guardian? Of what?' Something in Zach's mind clicked into place. A memory jostled out of the chaos of Zach's thoughts, and he heard Genie telling him about her encounter with Einstein. How he'd told her he was going to send someone to protect her. A guardian. 'The twins? Ant said…he said you've got good instincts. They listen to you. They all do.' Zach turned to Einstein. 'I suppose that's some form of mind control too, is it?'

'No,' BK exclaimed, 'I can't! I would never.'

Einstein waved a dismissive hand. 'She has a mild empath ability, but no more. She is merely insurance.'

'Insurance?' Zach sneered, 'What? Of your special *projects*? I suppose it's her job to keep them safe? To sacrifice herself should the need arise?'

'Yes,' said Einstein matter-of-factly.

'For what? Why are they so important to you? What are they to you?'

Zach's elbow hit the microscope, and he cursed, spinning to glare at the infuriating machine that had turned his whole world upside down. His gaze fell on the little slides scattered over the bench and he thought he might throw up.

'You said it was one of us. The samples…the spores. It's the twins, right? BK's here to protect them because you did something to them.'

'No, we did not *do* anything. We *created* them.'

'Created…' Zach trailed off.

'Zach—,'

He held up a hand to interrupt BK. 'And you just went along with it?' he asked her, ignoring the tears welling up in her gaze, the way her lips trembled as he glowered at her. 'What, you're older than you appear or something?'

'No,' she stammered, surprised by his anger. 'I'm just… I'm me. I'm just me. I'm eighteen, just like I told you. I swear!'

'Eighteen? So you were twelve when you were adopted, yeah?'

'Yes.'

'You told me all you remembered was being found by your first adopted parent in Scotland.'

'And that's true!' she cried, green eyes turning the colour of seaweed. 'I never lied! I never said what I am but I never lied!'

'Great,' said Zach and turned to Einstein with a snarl. 'So you, being *so* much better than us mere *humans*, plucked some poor alien kid from her parents and her *planet* and dumped her here on Earth *not even in the right place*, and expected her to raise two genetically engineered…what, mutants? And you thought it would all turn out fine and dandy?'

Surprise lifted Einstein's hairless brows and his amusement began to disperse from his face. 'You are angry.'

'Of course I'm angry!'

'No, you are angry about what I have done to the girl.'

'I'm angry about all of it! You're absurd. You're messing with things you shouldn't be messing with. You aren't *God*. You're not even a scientist. You're Hitler!'

Stevie and BK both gasped. Shock kept Einstein quiet a moment, giving Zach a chance to realise what he'd just compared Einstein to. He could only hope the alien didn't have a clue who Hitler was. Judging from the look of anger beginning to spread across his face and the dark, angry flush creeping up the creature's ears, Zach had the sinking feeling that he *did*.

'You think I would commit such heinous crimes?' said the alien in a low, quiet voice.

Zach swallowed and remained silent.

Einstein took a step forward, electricity crackling along his ears. Stevie made a small noise and darted out in front of him, holding her hands up.

'He d-d-doesn't under-understand,' she gasped out, stumbling over the words. She turned to Zach, silver eyes imploring. 'We-we are d-d-dying. Our p-people. We can't, can't- We cannot-'

She broke off, blinking several times in quick succession.

'Our species can no longer reproduce,' said Einstein, growling out the words. 'Through all our travels, we would take what we learned and try to apply it to our own genetics. Improving ourselves over and over again until we gave ourselves an incurable flaw.'

Zach snorted in derision. 'Of course you did,' he muttered. 'It's straight out of a bloody sci-fi movie. And now you're here, trying to fix your unfixable mistake, is that right?'

Einstein nodded, still stiff with anger.

'And I suppose it doesn't matter who you hurt in that process, does it? You don't care about the twins other than what they can do for you.'

'That is not true.'

'Oh? Then where are they? Have you even been to see them? Have you explained *any* of this to them?' Zach waved his hand around the small lab with its microscopes, blood samples and data reports. 'I bet you haven't. I bet their scared shitless because all you're doing is putting them through hell in order to save your own arse! If you cared even a little, you'd bring them here right now and tell them everything!'

'I...I cannot...'

'Bullshit! *Bullshit*,' Zach snarled. 'If they really meant anything to you at all, you'd have told them by now!'

'If I tell them, they'll die!' Einstein yelled, and a bulb in the far corner exploded. 'They will *die*!'

CHAPTER FORTY-TWO

Genie

I was lying on the floor of the puzzle room when the waiting came to an end. When the nurse first entered I thought she was going to yell at me. They didn't like it when I slacked off. I stood up—rolling over onto my stomach and pushing myself to my feet, bracing myself for being told off.

Instead, she smiled at me. The kind of smile you give to someone who has just won something amazing.

'We think you're finally ready,' she said.

'Ready for what?'

'Integration with the others.'

I perked up. 'Will Freddie be there?'

She paused, her eyes going cloudy as they often did when I mentioned my brother. 'No, not Freddie. He is still… undergoing testing.'

'Liar.'

I frowned, but I didn't argue. She laid out some fresh grey clothes, and gave me pat on the hand. Something she seemed to think would make me feel better.

'I'll let you get changed. Just knock on the door when you're ready.'

It was a relief to finally get some clarity from the drugs. So far, I hadn't been allowed to walk anywhere on my own. Instead, when they wanted to move me, they dosed me with something heavy and numbing. I hated waking up afterwards, with my thoughts all fuzzy and my memory in pieces.

Now, though, I'd been free from a dosing for at least half a day, and they were letting me out of my room!

'It's a test.'

I knew that, but I still couldn't help the excitement tingling up my spine. I was being let out.

We exited on a corner with a hallway leading straight ahead and another leading left. They were both short, both lined with three doors. She gestured, and we started down the corridor facing straight ahead. The floor was linoleum, and her shoes squeaked as we walked. I tried to look around, but there was just nothing to see aside from the doors, the walls were devoid of anything of substance.

A door ahead of us opened and a second nurse exited, a boy clad in the same grey clothes as me following on her heels. The lady beside me stiffened, her shoulders rolling back as she stopped in the hall. Ahead of us, the nurse looked up, eyes wide and startled. She glanced down at her wrist, as if to reaffirm she was on time.

She started to usher the boy back inside but it was too late. He had seen me. His eyes, dark blue and lined in shadow, were bright with hope.

'Genie?'

The word was muffled, frail, hoarse. Wrongness surged through me. Why was he so frail looking? This was a man who was meant to be strong. Strong and yet kind. His lean frame was made to be a comforting support, a friendly hug, a shoulder to lean on. Eyes that were now dull and terrified were supposed to be bright, and calm and blue. Ant. Sweet, beautiful, kind Ant. Looking at me like I was a ghost. Looking at me like I had come to save him.

My chest ached. I was breathing too fast. The dreams came back to me. Dreams of an agony so intense it clouded all else, piercing through skin to gouge away at something deep inside. God, had that been real? *Had that been Ant?*

My skin burned.

'Ant?' I asked, holding onto my arm where the ghostly pain still lingered—pain that hadn't been mine.

He opened his mouth tried to speak again, but his voice was raspy and he winced, falling silent. Tears pricked my eyes as I remembered dreams filled with screams. Had they been his?

'Ant…what've they done to you?'

My eyes felt too big and the hallway too small. I was gasping, struggling to breathe.

'Come now, Genie,' said my nurse, reaching for me, her tone impatient but with an edge of wariness.

As if I might turn and attack.

I stepped back, sharp and sure, glowering at her as my fists clenched again.

She hesitated, her hand still stretched out for me. 'You're safe here.'

'No,' I said, shaking my head. 'You're lying.'

'Genie, you know we—'

'You drugged me. How can I be safe when you drugged me?'

'We only want to protect you.'

'Why?' I asked, backing away from her, glancing behind me where Ant was watching us.

I turned to the woman. 'Why do you want to protect me?' I asked. 'For Einstein? Or for the Collective?'

Fear flashed across her face. 'How do you know about the Collective?'

'I've been listening,' I said and took several steps backwards toward Ant. 'I want to see Freddie. Now.'

'I'm afraid that's not possible.'

'He's sick,' Ant said.

He was inching forward, closing the gap between us closing, blue eyes dark with pain and despair, his voice still hoarse and filled with an intense worry.

Panic flooded through my chest. My heart began to beat faster, thumping hard and painful, as if it was going to burst through my chest at any moment.

'Sick?' my voice squeaked.

'He has become ill,' said the nurse. 'This is why we haven't been able to let you see him. We are waiting for him to get better before he can be tested. So you must wait…'

I stopped listening to her babble. Freddie was sick?

My thoughts raced, searching back through my mind.

This wasn't possible, was it? Freddie was strong. Freddie was invincible. He'd never been sick. Not once.

Yet…where was he? Loneliness crept through me. His voice, which had been with me so constantly while they'd been testing me, was now gone. Was it just the drugs or was something really wrong?

'Freddie?' I whispered.

'I'm here,' came his faint, weak whisper.

'You're sick?' horror and alarm and something deeper… something *angry*.

'I'm…'

A face flashed into my mind. James. James sitting beside me, smiling as he brushed a hand along my face, brushing back sweaty hair. Only it wasn't *me*.

The image was yanked away, and I staggered back. Hands grasped my shoulders, catching me. Familiar hands, strong and yet soothing.

'James is there?' I gasped.

'No. Gone now.'

'But he's…he's *hurt* you?'

'Gone now. Took him away…when I got…sick…'

'Freddie?'

'What're you doing?' whispered the nurse.

My gaze snapped up, losing sight of whatever images my mind had conjured. The nurse was gaping at me, her expression shocked and…frightened?

'Stay back.' Ant's grip on me became protective, one arm slipping around my shoulders, supporting me as he glowered back and forth between both nurse attendants.

I focused on one. The woman who'd told me I could see Freddie, and yet denied me at every turn.

'This is your fault,' I said.

She took a half step back.

Good. She should be afraid.

I straightened out of Ant's hold, staring at her, thinking of Freddie and Ant and their pain. Thinking of Tim and BK and Zach, and wondering what was happening to *them*. And Stevie. What would they be doing to Stevie?

'You can't…' the nurse whispered, taking another step

back. 'We tested you…you can't speak to him…'

'You hurt my brother,' I said, my voice sounding strange.

Something old was surging through me. Something primal. Something *hungry*. Bursting through me like a cyclone. It built up within me. Ancient and angry. Something I'd felt before, back in that corridor of red at school, and when I'd been reaching out for Einstein; reaching out to stop him from taking Freddie with lightning around my fingers.

I'd thought that was him. I'd thought he was the one producing the sparks of electricity…yet, I raised my hand in front of me, seeing the faint spark along my fingertips. There were no aliens here, and my fingers still sizzled and sparked. Void of pain, but full of fire.

'What…what are you?'

I glanced back up again, clenching my fist around the tickle of electricity.

'Stronger than you,' I said.

My ears rushed, my vision narrowed, and my mind went blank. A surge of *power* went straight from my toes, tingled up my spine and shot out through my raised hand. Light brighter than the sun exploded into the hallway.

CHAPTER FORTY-THREE

Zach

'What?' Zach asked, looking up at Einstein as all the anger drained away from him. 'Die? Just because you tell them the truth?'

Einstein said nothing, his lips thinning out in annoyance and displeasure.

'That doesn't make sense. Why would they die?'

'Things aren't what they appear here,' said BK.

Blonde curls, messy and incongruous as usual, were framing her porcelain face like a halo. Her lips were red, from where she'd been biting. She looked different without her smile. Less, somehow, yet still beautiful. Still imperfectly human.

He turned back to Einstein. 'What's really going on here? Are you just going to take what you need and leave us all here to rot?'

'Of course not,' Einstein snapped.

'We are n-not monsters,' Stevie stuttered. 'We d-do feel.'

Zach shifted. He crossed his arms and sighed. 'Yeah, I know you're not,' he said, directing his words to Stevie only.

There was a moment of silence where the tension lingered. Zach felt it prickle up his skin, making the hairs on his arms stand on end. He realised for the first time that Stevie had changed clothes. She'd discarded her borrowed human clothes, but not for the slim-fitting suit that Einstein wore, clearly alien in origin. Instead, she had on a pair of jeans that actually fit, and a tight, long sleeve shirt. She looked remarkably human in the outfit.

She tilted her head at him, her silver eyes flashing in question at his stare and Zach couldn't help the snort of amusement that worked it's way out. As easy as that, the tension was gone.

Einstein rolled his eyes, but his anger faded into irritation. It seemed to be a permanent state of being for the alien.

Stevie's face broke into a soft smile, her eyes flicking to Einstein and away again just as quick, as she turned her head to hide her smile. It was the first time Zach had ever felt like Stevie was really prying into his thoughts and yet, it didn't bother him as it had with Einstein. Especially not when Stevie's reaction had confirmed his thoughts so completely.

He resisted the urge to ask how someone as nice as Stevie handled working with someone as irritable as Einstein and instead refocused on the situation.

'Well then,' he said. 'What are you planning on doing? Why will the twins die if you tell them the truth?'

Einstein raised an eyebrow. His right ear twitched behind his back, a small current of electricity running up it. Zach noted the dull blue colour, and recalled seeing the bright blue of Stevie's lightning. He wondered if the colour had any significance.

'Before your rather childish outburst, I had been trying to explain,' Einstein drawled, sighing. 'There are…other forces at play here. Other factions. There are reasons I must keep things quiet for now.'

'So why tell me?'

'Your mind is shielded.'

Zach frowned. 'What? Shielded? Why would *my* mind be shielded? What does that even mean?'

Einstein gave him a short nod. 'That is not what is important right now. We have a limited window before I must act. Those samples,' Einstein flicked a dismissive hand toward the slides Zach had been looking at, 'were merely the beginning. There is more you must know.'

He went to one of the lab stations, the monitors and machines whirring softly in the background, and opened a draw. He pulled out two folders and handed both to Zach. One was red, the other was green.

On a hunch, Zach opened the red.

'Whoa,' he said, flicking through the comprehensive reports and graphs and results of various tests and studies. 'Is this the plague?'

He flicked through a few pages, glancing up to catch another short nod from Einstein. The alien's face was grim, and he watched Zach with an inscrutable expression.

'Jesus,' said Zach. 'No wonder it's wiping us out. Just take a look at its make up! It's…well, it's ingenious.' He couldn't keep the note of impressed marvel out of his voice.

Suspicion quickly followed on the heels of marvel. It *was* ingenious. As if it had been *made* to be ingenious. Zach closed his eyes. A memory jumped forth. The world map pinned up in the study of the house they'd broken into.

The map had been huge, spread out across the wall with pins stuck in various places. Zach—with the help of Freddie and Tim—had painstakingly rearranged those pins, forming a new pattern. One Zach saw more clearly now, with the red folder in his hands. He recalled six points on the map, six clusters where the first hints of the pandemic begun. Each one residing on a single continent, excepting Australia.

At first, Zach had thought travel was the cause of the spread. It only took one person with the sniffles to carry a disease across the ocean to a new country where it would grow and mutate and spread.

Now, however, he knew better.

'You made this?' he asked, opening his eyes to gaze hard at Einstein.

The alien's ears twitched and he rose one eyebrow. 'No.'

'But this…'

'I did not create this plague.'

'But it *was* engineered, wasn't it? Like your twins?'

Einstein dipped his chin down. 'Yes.'

Zach sighed, tilting his head back and staring at the ceiling. He recalled an older memory. His presentation on his thesis. He was the youngest by several years, and the whole class had laughed at him.

'Biological warfare? Could you get anymore sci-fi?'

Well, here was the proof he'd been right. Right here in the red folder in his hands. Biological warfare at its finest. Not to mention the aliens. Zach smirked. Guess he *could* have gotten more sci-fi.

'This was an act of savagery,' said Einstein, his expression morphing into disgust. 'It is unrefined and deliberately brutal. There is no regard to the life that is being destroyed. This thing was designed only with the end goal in mind. Kill.'

'Yeah,' said Zach, 'But it *was* designed. It's, well, actually, it's kind of cool. I wouldn't have thought we could make something like this.'

'Certainly not,' said Einstein.

Zach narrowed his eyes. 'I thought you said you didn't do this?' he said.

'It was not *me*.'

Zach rolled his eyes. 'That's just semantics,' he said, exasperated. 'It was your kind, right?'

Einstein remained silent, which was all the answer Zach needed.

'So what are you going to do about it then, other than putting together this?' Zach asked, slapping the red folder onto the bench and crossing his arms.

Einstein pointed at the at the green folder, which Zach had placed on the bench next to him. Zach snatched it up.

'What is this?' Zach asked, gaping at the first page. 'This…this is a cure, right?'

Einstein tilted his head, silver eyes regarding Zach with something close to approval and…expectation?

Zach flicked through the folder. 'It…this is…complete. Days ago. How did you even find the time to put this together?'

'I do not require as much sleep as humans,' Einstein said dryly.

'Even so,' said Zach, stopping at a section of the folder describing a breakdown in the virus' attack mechanisms. 'Creating this with so little time, it's amazing. But you haven't used it yet?'

'There is one final test I need to run.'

Einstein gestured to the slides, still scattered on the table next to the microscope. Zach glanced back at them. Without really thinking about it, he reached for the red folder again and opened it, leafing through the pages until he found an image of the virus. He left the page open on the bench and pulled the microscope back towards him.

It was one of the samples from the twins. Zach ignored the spore-like blood cell and swapped the slide out for one of the mutated blood samples. The ones from Ant and Tim.

There were remnants of the original blood type in there, and yet the spore quality of the twins' blood had altered it so much it was barely recognisable as human. Zach pulled away and looked at the picture of the virus. At the way it too had mutated the cells.

'They're similar,' he said. 'Not the same, but…similar enough.'

Einstein nodded.

'You think the cure will attack these cells too,' Zach guessed, gesturing to the microscope. 'Or even the twins. Or you, too, I suppose.'

'There is that possibility,' Einstein agreed.

'Alright,' said Zach, drumming his fingers along the bench. 'Guess we better find out then. You have samples of the cure?'

Einstein nodded, his face set in grim approval. 'You will help, then?'

'I don't approve of your methods,' said Zach. 'But I can see why you did it. You're out of time, and you need results. So let's go get them. The sooner we do this, the sooner we can all leave.'

Something flickered in Einstein's gaze, even as Stevie nodded beside him, her shy smile squashing the worry that had been building. Zach decided to ignore whatever it was that Einstein was still hiding. He'd had enough revelations to last him a life time, he could use a day to recuperate before they dumped anymore on him.

Hope filled Stevie's face as Einstein gestured to the door. Zach stepped out into the stark white hallway, the girls falling into step behind him as Einstein shut and locked the door. Zach wasn't sure why it needed locking. Who did he think was going to come and pry?

'What happens if your test fails?' Zach asked. 'If the cure does attack the alien blood types?'

Einstein's entire frame was stiff as he walked, but he glanced sideways at Zach with those steely silver eyes. 'Then you will have a decision to make.'

'*Me?*'

'There is more at stake here than you know. There are other reasons I have yet to act. There are-'

A shout from up ahead interrupted him. Zach stopped, head snapping up to peer down the corridor. Footsteps clattered, heels clacking frantically down the tiled floors. A woman rounded the corner, glancing back over her shoulder, her face pale.

As she straightened out, she refocused on her path and spotted them. Her eyes went wide, and she faltered, almost tripping as she missed a step.

'Sir!' she gasped, gaping at Einstein.

'What happened?' Einstein asked, his voice cracking like a whip as the air turned static around them.

Zach recognised the feeling and took a wary step back, pushing BK back behind him.

'It's…it's the boy,' she stammered, her hands shaking as she tired to get the words out. 'The telepathic twin…The mute one. He…we were conducting a test…he's sick.'

'Sick?'

'Wait,' Zach asked, a feeling of dread knotting up his stomach. Telepathic? Twin? *Mute.* 'Which boy?'

CHAPTER FORTY-FOUR

Genie

'Ant? Ant! Jesus, what——?'

A heavy weight lifted from my chest and air, sweet and burnt, filled my lungs.

'Tim?'

'What happened? Are you—is that *Genie*?'

'She's, she's hurt. I don't…I think…she won't wake up. I keep trying but I can't…Tim…What's happening?'

I retreated from the noise, trying to sink back down into the cool, numb darkness, but a touch to my aching hands pulled me back into consciousness.

My hands tingled. I wriggled my fingers, feeling pins and needles shiver up my arm. I winced, then winced again as my fingers reflexively closed. Ouch.

'Genie? Oh God, Genie! You…'

He collapsed back down on me, hiding a tear streaked face in the loose grey clothes I'd been fitted with.

Faint sobs shook his shoulders.

'Ant?' My own voice crackled, worn out, as if I'd been screaming for a very long time.

'I thought you were dead,' came his muffled voice. 'I thought you were all dead.'

His hands convulsed, clutching and releasing the cotton fabric.

'I'm okay,' I said, though I sure didn't sound like it.

'Ant,' came another voice, and my gaze shifted to the figure leaning over Ant's shoulder. 'C'mon, let her breathe.'

Tim. Covered in muck and blood, his own grey clothes stained with a pungent smell. His dark skin stood out against the grey and blended with the spray of blood. His hair was matted and his eyes were lacking their usual glint. They were fixed on my face, staring at me in a mix of shock and horror and relief.

Ant allowed himself to be pulled away. He scuttled backwards, half falling against the wall as soft sobs consumed him.

'Ant,' Tim said, his gaze shifting back and forth between us.

'I'm okay,' I said, my voice hoarse as I gestured to Ant.

Tim's black eyes fell back on me.

'But your face...' coal black eyes bored into mine, as if trying to convince himself I was real. 'Jesus, Genie...your face.'

I tried to touch it, to raise my hand, but the effort was exhausting. The pain still throbbed in my hands but I pushed it away. Tim took my raised wrist, staring at the blistered skin on my palms and fingertips.

'What's wrong with my face?' I asked.

He swallowed, coal eyes still staring at me as if I was going to disappear. He shook his head. He let go of me and reached out a hand, hesitated, and brushed one finger down the left side of my face.

His touch was hot and sparked a faint sting of pain, from the tip of my left eyebrow down to my jaw. I winced and he yanked his hand back, but just before his finger broke contact with my face a series of images rushed in.

Running. Cables and cords. Fighting, over and over again. An angry shepherd. A kind smile and warm words, followed by the same face, staring blanking up at him with empty eyes. Me, small and pale, grey eyes dull and confused and a scar making its way down my face in a red, razor thin line—my face carved in two like a Jack O'Lantern at halloween.

'What did they do to you?' Tim whispered.

'I...I'm not sure,' I said, startled by the images I'd somehow taken from him. 'Everything is...fuzzy.'

Something clattered and Tim's head jerked around. Wildness was etched into his face. He licked his lips, gaze darting back and forth across the hallway. He reached for me, his hands shaking as he pulled me up into a sitting position.

'It wasn't them,' Ant said, his voice shaking with swallowed tears. 'James…he…he got her. Before they came. Before they took us away.'

'James?'

'He stabbed Zach.'

Fear punched me in the gut. 'Zach?'

'That was James?' Tim asked, leaning toward Ant but not leaving my side. 'Is Zach alright?'

More tears flooded Ant's face. He shook his head, squeezing his eyes shut. 'I don't know,' he whispered. 'They came, and they took us all away. They had Genie, and there was so much blood. And they just walked passed us. And Zach…he was bleeding. So much blood. Always so much…'

This time Tim did leave my side. He crawled over to Ant and pulled him into a rough hug. Ant clung to him, his whole body trembling as he struggled to stop his tears.

'It's alright,' Tim soothed, his calm voice at odds with the violence splattered over his clothes. 'We're here. You're okay. It's alright.'

'I was…'

'I know. Me too.'

'I thought everyone was dead,' Ant gasped, his voice muffled as he pressed into Tim's shoulder. 'I thought you were dead. I thought you had left me.'

'Never,' said Tim, his voice a fierce and rough growl.

Ant's sobs began to quiet. I attempted to crawl toward them, wincing as I put pressure on my blistered hands. Tim flinched when I reached out for him. The two boys looked at me, black and blue eyes searching my face for reassurance.

'We're going to be okay,' I said.

Tim nodded. He released Ant, who had calmed down now, and glanced around the hallway again.

'We have to get outta here,' he said.

He blinked, taking in the scene. The blackened streaks

marring the walls, the two nurses lying prone in the hallway, their clothes smoking, their skin riddled with white angry marks of lightning.

'Man,' said Tim, 'what happened here?'

Ant glanced at me, blue eyes wide and unsure. His head tilted slightly toward Tim but he didn't say anything. He left it to me. I swallowed, studying the black marks on the wall.

'Tim,' I said, but instead of telling him what I'd done, I asked a different question. 'Are you okay?'

'Hm? Yeah.'

'You're covered in…blood…'

He glanced down at his ragged and bloody clothes, and a hollow smile quirked his lips. 'It's not mine,' he said.

'Oh.'

The woman's face came to me again. She had been Tim's attendant. She was kind of pretty, even through the film of the hazmat suit. With hazel eyes and blonde hair. I imagined him talking to her. Trying to smooth talk his way out of things in between the tests and the fighting. Tim never stopped struggling. It wasn't in him to sit down and admit defeat. He'd have done anything to get out and find the rest of us. Even if that meant fraternising with the enemy.

I wondered if it was her blood, splattered all over him.

Tim's gaze drifted back over me, resting on the side of my face. I reached up and touched it, feeling the raised skin that trailed down my cheek, thin but fresh. I swallowed, and touched the scar on my chest, hiding beneath my shirt. They both watched me, Tim's gaze inscrutable and Ant's soft and sad.

'Is it bad?' I asked, looking between them and knowing the answer already.

Ant glanced at Tim, his expression unsure and worried.

Tim shook his head. 'Not really. Whoever stitched it could've done better, but…it's not so bad. It's healing, at least. I…I'm sorry. I was there…I was trying to find him only, I didn't know it was James. I should have. We *saw* him. I should never have—'

'Tim,' I said, cutting him off and reaching out for him. 'It's okay.'

Tim frowned, his coal black eyes hard and furious. 'No, it's not. He hurt you.'

I shook my head. 'I'm okay. For the most part, anyway…I think.' I sighed and rubbed my tired eyes.

'Genie thinks he's here,' said Ant. 'He's been with Freddie, wherever they're keeping him.'

'With Freddie? Shit. For how long?'

Ant shrugged. 'However long we've been here, I guess.'

'What? The whole week?'

'A week? But…we haven't even been here for a week,' I said. 'Have we?'

Tim's brows furrowed, his eyes turning confused. 'What drugs were they feeding you?'

He asked it as a joke, but I answered anyway. 'Not sure, but there were lots.'

Tim blinked and I shrugged at the question in his eyes. I saw the blood on him again, the dried patches flaking away on his neck, and the brown stains in his grey clothes.

'Tim…what happened to you?'

His eyes dropped away and he shrugged. He pushed himself to his feet and reached out for Ant, pulling him easily into a stand.

He turned to me, sticking out his hand.

'C'mon,' he said. 'We need to find the others and get the hell outta here. Either of you know *where* they're keeping Freddie and James?'

My muscles ached and I tried to stretch out the stiffness in my back and shoulders as I stood. Everything hurt.

'No,' I said. 'But Freddie is sick.'

'Sick? You've seen him?'

'Not…exactly.'

Ant and I exchanged glances. I swallowed and nodded.

'Tim?'

'Yeah?'

'There's something wrong with me,' I said.

'What?' he asked, peering down the hall.

He crouched and rifled through the nurses' things. I looked away, focusing on a light fixture further up the hall. One of the black marks seared into the wall brushed passed it, barely leaving it intact.

'You see all this?' I said, and waved at the charred wall.

Tim's gaze flickered up and around. 'Yeah?' he said.

'I think I did it.'

Black eyes back on me. He swallowed and licked his lips, still crouched by the nurse.

'Oh,' he said and stood.

I shrugged, confused by his reaction to what I'd done, and was grateful Ant looked just as lost as I felt.

Tim nodded and started down the hall, not saying anything else, and Ant and I shared another look. I felt hot despair sloshing in my gut. Ant shuffled across the quiet floor and wrapped an arm around my shoulder.

There was nothing but our footsteps and the sound of our heavy breathing echoing down the hallway.

'Also,' I said as Tim led us around a corner. 'You should probably know I'm hearing voices.'

Tim glanced back at me, slowing his pace so we could catch up.

'Might be a side effects of the drugs?' he suggested.

I shook my head.

'I know about the dog,' I said, shifting so that Ant wasn't supporting so much of my weight. 'The one you had to kill. And I've been talking to someone. In my head. I think always have been.'

Ant gave me a sideways look, and glanced at Tim. Tim stopped in the hallway. Black eyes bored into mine. The image of the dog flashed into my mind again—not angry this time, but still and unmoving, splayed across the floor of white room as hurt and sadness filled my—*his*—chest.

'You mean Freddie's voice?' Tim asked.

I startled and gaped at him. 'How did you…?' I trailed off, and shot Ant an enquiring look. Had *he* realised?

Ant's face had gone expressionless as he glanced between us.

'Because,' Tim said, turning back to the corridor. 'I can hear him too.'

CHAPTER FORTY-FIVE

Zach

'Freddie!' BK gasped, taking a step backwards.

Stevie made a strange noise, halfway between a gasp and a whine, before dashing down the hallway. The still babbling woman flinched as Stevie passed, but Stevie paid her no mind, disappearing around the corner in a panicked rush.

Einstein strode off after her. He barked an order at the woman that Zach didn't hear. He was too busy staring after Stevie, trying to grasp what was happening. He ran a hand over his face.

'Jesus,' he muttered. 'Can't everyone just stop a moment?'

'Zach.'

He looked up into BK's anxious, imploring face.

'We have to go,' she whispered, though she remained rooted to the spot. 'Freddie…he's…we have to…'

Zach took a deep breath, ran a hand through his hair and prayed somcone would appear down the corridor with a lit joint for him to smoke. When, after a moment of silence, that didn't happen, Zach let out his breath in one big whoosh, and nodded.

'Alright,' he said. 'On to the next disaster.'

He grasped BK's hand, and hauled her after Stevie and Einstein. His sneakers squealed as he launched into a run. Déjà vu hit him as he vaulted around the corner into the corridor, feeling like he was back at the museum, racing toward Stevie.

Now he was chasing after a different alien. One he didn't particularly want to help.

They almost ran into them at the next turn, skidding to a frantic halt just short of Einstein. The alien was standing in the doorway, high voltage currents racing along the ridges of his head. They cackled and fizzed and the air smelt faintly burnt. Like lightning had struck nearby.

Zach swallowed, keeping his grip on BK's hand so she didn't get too close. When the alien stepped further into the room, Zach and BK followed at a cautious distance.

'No…' the whispered word was full of anguish, and Zach was startled to see tears pouring down Stevie's face.

BK groaned, her gaze riveted to the centre of the room, where a huddled form grasped the legs of a hospital bed, struggling to stay upright. She took a step forward, but Einstein thrust out his arm.

'Stay back,' he said in a hoarse voice.

Zach licked his lips. The boy before them was completely changed from when Zach had seen him last. His hair was limp and oily, hanging around his pale face lifelessly. There were big shadows under his eyes, and he was thin, far thinner than one should be after just one week.

Worse were his hands. Inky black markings stained his skin, creeping up his wrists. Zach cautiously crept forward, ignoring the warning glance from Einstein, and crouched before Freddie. Glassy grey eyes flicked up to his face and a faint hint of recognition crossed them, but Freddie made no move to communicate.

Zach hesitated to touch the hands clutching at the metal poles. The black markings weren't markings at all. They were his veins. Stained black by whatever was poisoning his body.

'What happened to him?' he asked.

'That is something I would like the answer to as well,' said Einstein, his cool tone not wavering a bit.

Zach glanced up at the alien. Einstien's face was a carefully controlled mask, and Zach fought the urge to gulp, sensing the rage hidden beneath that calm facade.

'*Get in here*, now.'

The words were so loud, so *heavy* that Zach almost fell over, crouched as he was before Freddie. Freddie shuddered, as if he too had been physically struck by the sentence. Zach blinked, momentarily stunned. The words, the *thought*, had come from Einstein. It must have. There was a distant quality to his eyes that Zach recognised.

Stevie had often worn that same expression. Not quite at the same intensity, but often enough that she must have been communicating with him. Or at the very least listening to the minds around her.

A scurry of frantic footfalls down the hallway distracted Zach from his thoughts and several people burst into the room at once. They could have come off the street for all Zach could tell. They were all dressed in casual clothes, the only sign they worked at the facility the were clipboards each of them seemed to hold in their hands.

Before any of them could speak, Einstein stepped forward and pressed one finger to the forehead of the closest man. The man gasped, his eyes rolling back as faint sparks of electricity crackled along Einstein's ears.

Stevie shuddered. Her ears twitched and her head tilted as if she was hearing something. Her silver eyes went wide and shocked and…angry? She opened her mouth, her throat working, trying and failing to speak. A damn burst, and suddenly the words shot out, loud and painful. 'How could you!' she shrieked.

'What?' Zach asked, 'What did they do?'

'The source,' Stevie said, her voice quiet and low and angrier than Zach ever thought she could be. 'They ex-exposed him to it.'

Her fury allowed her more control over her own voice, and she spat the words out in a flurry, her own ears lighting up in bright sparks of power. Zach shrunk back from her, realising for the first time just how dangerous she really could be.

Except her words registered to him, and shock overcame the fear. 'You have the source?' he asked, twisting to stare at Einstein.

He was ignored as Einstein continued his strange, supernatural interrogation. 'How long? Why was I not made aware of this sooner?'

'Wait! Please, we came for you as soon as we realised.'

'You should have come instantly!'

Zach, Freddie and BK all flinched in unison; the words echoed both within and outside their minds. Zach's head spun. It really was too much. He felt the information crowd within his mind. Overwhelming him.

'I should have been informed immediately! Yet you imbeciles waited! Why?'

Whatever answer he dug from the man's mind apparently wasn't satisfactory. A thick bolt of lightning struck out from Einstein's ears, striking the wall and leaving a large black welt in the paint.

'You l-left him!' Stevie said, her fists clenched. 'You l-l-*left* him! Al-lone!'

She spun away from the group of cowering scientists and hurried over to where Zach still crouched by Freddie. She ducked down next to him, even as Einstein still glowered at the scientists, digging through the man's mind as if he could change what they had done if he delved deep enough.

Zach turned his face away from the scene, seeing the twitch in the man's face, the nerves reacting to whatever was going on in his head. There was pain in that expression, and Zach didn't want to see what would happen if the alien went any deeper.

Instead, he watched Stevie. She peered at Freddie's face, tilting it up in a soft grip, studying the pale, sweaty skin with sharp silver eyes.

Dumbly, instead of asking how Freddie was, Zach could only repeat his last question. 'You have the source?'

Without looking at him, Stevie nodded. Zach cursed under his breath, wishing he hadn't been so careless, running about the facility with no means of protection. He'd supposed that since no one else was dressed up in hazmat suits he would be safe enough, yet to know the source of the plague was sitting around in this facility somewhere sent a wave of fear so strong over him, Zach almost threw up.

'Go and get him,' Einstein snarled, pushing the man away from him. 'I want to see him, now.'

The man staggered and one of his colleagues grasped his shoulders, helping to steady him.

'You…you want *us* to get him?'

At the look Einstein gave them, they all nodded quickly, muttering acquiescence as they turned and fled the room—pulling their mind-numbed friend along with them.

'He? The source is a person?' Zach supposed this really shouldn't surprise him, given all the other horrors he'd learnt over the last two hours.

Einstein didn't take his eyes off Freddie as he answered. 'I believe his name is James Hart.'

'Hart?' Zach asked in surprise. 'As in…' he looked at Freddie, at the way the boy's shoulders tensed and eyes blazed at the mention of the name. 'As in the twins?'

Zach looked to BK, who was still by the door, clutching at the frame and staring at her cousin in dazed horror. At his question, she nodded mutely.

'And he's the source?' Zach asked, directing this question back at Einstein.

'One of them, yes.'

'*One* of them?'

Einstein sighed, his eyes rolling up in a very human-like gesture. 'Do keep up,' said the alien. 'Yes, one of the sources. As in there are more than one. Spread amongst the seven continents like rats hiding in the sewers, creeping out to infect you all.'

Zach shuddered at this image. He'd never been particularly fond of rats.

'That's just perfect,' he snapped. 'And you didn't think to mention this sooner? You don't think it's a bit of a coincidence that the source *happens* to be related to your genetically engineered experiments?'

'No,' said Einstein darkly, his gaze hardening even further. 'I do not think that is a coincidence.'

CHAPTER FORTY-SIX

Genie

I pulled Tim to a stop. 'You can hear Freddie?'

Tim kept his gaze down the corridor. 'Yeah,' he said briskly. 'Yeah, the last few days.'

'He's…actually talking to you? I'm not insane?'

This time, Tim's eyes strayed to my face, flickering away again before I could catch sight of whatever emotion he was trying to keep from me.

'No,' he said. 'You're not insane.'

The way he said it, with that tight edge to his voice, echoed through me. That undertone seemed to reach inside me, curl up in a ball and settle deep within my gut. *Wrong*, it said. *This is wrong.*

What was wrong? Me? I wasn't crazy but…there was something else. Something I was missing.

'Tim?' I asked. 'What is it? What aren't you telling me?'

He cleared his throat and began pulling me down the hall again. 'C'mon. We gotta get the others. We have to—' he stopped, staring down the hall we had just entered.

'What?' Ant asked.

'That's my room,' said Tim, gesturing to the end of the hallway.

There was another left turn and an open door leading right. Red splattered the floor, and I took a hasty step back, memories trying to seep up from the fog of drugs that still clouded my mind. I shook my head, trying to clear them away.

'Are you sure?'

'Yep,' said Tim. 'That's my room. We heard the bangs. Must've been Genie doing whatever it was she did to those women. That's how I got out. She was distracted.'

Tim's gaze flicked my way again, and once again I wondered what he knew. What he was keeping from me. Ant shifted, leaning against the wall as he tried to hold back a grunt of pain.

'You alright?' Tim asked, his voice tight as he too saw just how haggard Ant was.

Ant nodded, rubbing the side of his leg. 'Yeah,' he said, his voice still raspy. 'Just a bit sore.'

Tim frowned, looking at Ant'a leg. 'What did they do?'

Ant shook his head. 'Nothing,' he said. His shoulders had that stubborn set to them. 'Let's find Freddie and the others.'

'You're hurt.'

'I'm *fine*, Tim. Freddie isn't. Let's keep moving.'

Tim sighed, his fists clenching and unclenching. He took two steps to Ant, his strides long and purposeful—just as stubborn as Ant—and before Ant could object, hooked Ant's arm around his shoulder.

'Alright,' he said, cutting off Ant's protests and pulling him down the end of the hallway.

We were about to pass Tim's room when one of the door's behind us was flung open and people rushed out into the hallway.

Tim stiffened. Without hesitation, he grabbed my arm and yanked me backwards into the blood soaked room. The room that had been his.

'Jesus,' Ant said, staring around the room in horror.

The woman whose face I'd seen in Tim's mind lay in a pile of pooling blood. The dog she'd used to keep Tim in check lay on the other side of the room, a syringe sticking out of its hide.

I sucked in a sharp breath, covering my mouth with my hands as I stared at the still form of the beautiful dog. Tim's face was hard, yet he kept his gaze fixed on the door.

More images threatened to overwhelm me. I knew why

he didn't want to look. I knew why he had to stay focused on something else.

I squeezed my eyes shut, willing myself not to remember, not to *see*. Not what I'd done, not what Tim had done. Not what we might still have to do to get out of here alive.

Alive.

That's what I focused on. We were alive. That was what was important. No matter what else happened, so long as we got out alive and together that was all that mattered.

Rustling papers made me open my eyes. Ant was staring down at a clipboard he'd picked up from a table.

'Is this…?' he hesitated, and then read down the page. 'Endurance level, high. Stamina level, high. Physical strength, exceptional. Pain tolerance, exceptional. Recovery, high. Recommendation: eligible for DNA transference.' He glanced up at Tim, who was still focused on the door. 'What is this?'

'Test results,' I murmured.

'DNA transference? What the hell does that mean? What were they doing to us?'

I shrugged.

'I say we don't stick around to find out,' said Tim, peering out the door.

'Yeah but…' he paused, and fear flashed through his eyes.

'What is it? Did they do something to you?'

To my dismay, Ant's expression shifted, closing off his real emotions under a mask, a pretence that he was okay. He shook his head and gestured to Tim.

'He's right. We have to find the others and get out of here.'

Tim started to speak and then paused. There was shouting echoing down both halls. We all froze. My heart hammered, and I felt the beat in my temple and at the tips of my fingers and in the fresh scar running down the side of my face.

My adrenaline was peaking again. A heat swept through me. A fire that was preparing my body to fight. We had to get out alive.

'*It's a square*,' came a voice, echoing out from my subconscious.

I stared down the hallway we had come down with a frown. I turned the other direction, hearing the shouting coming from both directions and noticed a faint marking on the far wall at the end of the hall. Black lines, like charred lightning and the smell of something burnt.

'It's a square,' I said, repeating my thought.

'Huh?' Tim asked.

'The corridors, they make a circle. They're all connected. You're here, Ant and I were down that way,' I said, stepping out into the hallway and pointing.

I looked back down the way we'd come. Where those people had come tearing out of a room, to disappear out of sight. Unless there were stairs somewhere, or an elevator, they would be in one of the rooms just around the corner. Everything was so close, much closer than I expected it to be.

'Freddie has to be down there,' I said, pointing back in the direction we'd originally come from. 'There aren't many doors, so he has to be in one of them.'

'Those people went that way,' Ant said, his voice small.

Tim stepped closer to him, grabbing one of his arms and looping it back around his shoulders again. 'Don't worry,' he said, his voice filled with forced cheerfulness. 'I'll beat the crap outta anyone who tries to stick us back in those rooms.'

CHAPTER FORTY-SEVEN

Zach

Despite the day's overwhelming flood of horrible information, Zach felt at ease for the first time since finding Stevie by the river in Brisbane.

The dots had finally connected. Everything was coming together to create an image that Zach could comprehend. This made him calm.

Seven points. Seven sources. Genie and Freddie had been engineered. *Created.* Their older brother was a source of a plague designed to kill humans. That was *not* a coincidence.

'Someone like you made the plague, right?' Zach said. 'One of your kind. I want an answer this time.'

Einstein looked back down at Freddie, eyes going cloudy and distant. 'My program has been running for many years with little result,' he said in that same quiet voice. 'There are some who do not believe it will work. They are focused on doing what good they can with the remainder of their days.'

'And, what, wiping out the human race is one of those "good deeds" is it?'

'Yes,' said Einstein, looking up with simple honesty.

Zach thought about Stevie. How soft and kind and gentle she was. Her interest in the plants. Her smile when BK had taken her out the back of their house to show her the birds before they'd had dinner. The simultaneous sadness that had clouded her eyes at the sight of them caged.

There were humans like Stevie and BK. People who loved nature and animals and the wild. They fought constantly to save it. They were alone in a sea of creatures that just wanted to consume everything before them until there was nothing left.

'You were destroying us, to save the rest of the planet,' said Zach, looking from Einstein to Stevie. 'Is that it?'

'I suspect so,' said Einstein.

Stevie's gaze snapped to him, even more bug eyed than usual. 'B-But...'

Einstein sighed. He closed his eyes and took a deep breath, nostrils closing briefly before he opened his eyes again and turned to his apprentice. 'I did not wish to upset you,' he said, his voice gentle in a way Zach hadn't expected. 'If this plague is, as I suspect, from our origin, then the principal organiser of a feat such as this would be your mother.'

Stevie went still, frozen in place by the shock of Einstein's words. Zach's eyebrows shot up. He glanced between Einstein and Stevie, watchful. Stevie's mother created the plague?

Though timid and shy, Zach had never seen her cry before. She covered her face with her hands, shoulders hunching forwards as a soft keening noise erupted from her.

'It is a misguided view, and one they never would have attempted had I succeeded here. Had I given them the time they needed to make subtle changes. You know your mother, you have seen her work. Never before has she acted so rashly as this. Yet she is desperate. She believes she is out of time.'

'Oh, great,' Zach muttered. 'So because she has to die, so do we?'

'It is not something I approve of.'

'Well that's really comforting, thanks. Hope you give her a good talking to.'

'The punishment for interference on this scale is death,' said Einstein, his voice cracking back into that sharp coldness.

Zach blinked, opened his mouth and then closed it again. He sighed, dropping his gaze and scowling at the floor. There wasn't anything he could say to that. If Einstein was telling the truth about the punishment, then he was also right about Stevie's mother being desperate.

'But…but she,' Stevie's gaze fell back to Freddie, and she touched his face with a tenderness Zach didn't understand.

Einstein's cool mask fell away for an instant as he surveyed his emotional apprentice. 'I am sorry. I am sure she did not realise what this would mean for you.'

The fury welled again, and Zach felt his fists clench, felt the urge to throw something so strong he shook with it. 'You're sorry? For *Stevie*? What about Freddie? He's the one sitting here falling apart!'

Einstein started to speak, but a noise from the doorway ceased their argument.

To his surprise, Zach felt a knot untangle in his gut as he saw the three of them walk into the room, worse for wear, but otherwise unharmed.

Tim came first, skulking into the room in that predatory walk of his, and Zach had no doubt that if the boy had the inclination, he would pounce on them with the same feline ferocity of any large cat. He was followed in by Ant, and then—

'Freddie!' Genie dashed in, her eyes locking in an instant on her twin brother.

She fell to her knees by Freddie, her gaze glued to his greying face. She reached out as if to touch him, but stopped.

'What happened?' Genie asked. 'What's wrong with him?'

No one answered. Zach, Einstein and Stevie all shifted away from her question. Zach wasn't sure why he felt the need to shy away, only that he had some notion of Einstein taking responsibility.

Tim stomped into the room further, glowering. 'She asked what's wrong with Freddie,' he snapped. 'What've you done?'

Einstein glowered. 'We did nothing.'

'Bullshit,' spat Tim.

'He was infected.'

'Infected by what?'

'The plague.'

'He was in contact with the source,' said Zach. 'One of the original carriers of the disease that's been killing everyone.'

Tim blinked, his fists balling at his sides as his black gaze narrowed at Einstein. 'You exposed him to the source?'

'I did not,' said Einstein. 'You were all already exposed.'

'What?' Ant asked, his face going so pale that Zach worried he might pass out.

'James Hart,' said Einstein. 'He's a carrier.'

Silence met his statement. For a moment, anyway. Then Tim started to swear. He turned and kicked at the table by the door, sending paperwork scattering all over the floor.

'He…he can infect us?' Ant asked, turning to stare at the twins. 'He…but if he has it, why isn't he dead?'

'Carriers don't have the disease,' said Zach. 'They're immune. They just…pass it on.'

'Bet that's how the prick got out of prison,' snarled Tim. 'And the school, with that kid. You remember Genie? The way the kid's face went blue. It was 'cause of James, wasn't it? He did it. He killed all of them.'

Zach was too startled over the revelation James had been in prison to respond to Tim's questions. He looked at the twins, surprised that neither of them had mentioned it before. A glint of light hit Genie's face in a way that shone off her cheek.

Zach froze, seeing the fresh scar for the first time. It traced down the side of her face, leaving a thin, pinkish-white arc, like a gutter grooved deep by the persistent rut of tears. The tip pulled at the end of her eyebrow, just barely missing those bright grey eyes.

'What…?'

'Where is he,' Tim growled, black eyes fixed on Einstein. 'I'll kill him myself.'

'Tim, you can't,' said Ant. 'He'll infect you.'

'I don't care,' said Tim. 'He's killed everyone we know. He's tried to kill Genie. You think he won't come after her again? Look what he did this time? I'm not gonna let him touch her again. Not ever.'

Zach started. *James* was responsible for the scar? Regardless of the fact he was the source of a plague, she was his *sister*. Tim's words echoed in Zach's head. *'Look what he did this time.'* This time.

Zach's eyes sought out Genie, dropping to her left shoulder where he knew the old scar would be visible. A wound like that, on someone as young as Genie, certainly would be enough to send the one responsible to jail.

'Jesus,' Zach whispered.

'He d-did it?'

Zach turned his head. Stevie's pupils were dilated, her ears twitching as she came to the same realisation as Zach—perhaps had even heard the thought from his mind. The air around them became thick and Zach felt the charge on his skin, raising the hairs all over his body. His clothing clung to the static racing along his skin as Stevie's gaze hardened.

'He h-hurt her.'

Stevie took a single step. Her ears rippled with lightning, her beautiful silver eyes no longer soft and sweet, but darkening to a furious black.

Einstein cut her off.

'No,' said Einstein. 'This is not for you to deal with.'

'Oh? Then who is it for?' Tim snapped. '*You?* Are you going to *deal* with us? Experiment on us? *Infect* us?'

'*You* are no concern of mine,' Einstein snapped, rolling his eyes as if he were talking to a child.

'Good,' Tim barked. 'Then we're leaving.' He turned to the twins, leaning over to help pull Freddie to his feet.

'I said *you* were not my concern. I never said they were not.'

Tim's gaze flicked over to Einstein and then back on the twins. He straightened.

'What do you want with them?' Ant asked.

'They are mine,' said Einstein.

Tim scoffed. 'Oh yeah? Your's eh? Wanna bet?'

'I made them, therefore, they are entirely my concern.'

'And what the fuck is that s'posed to mean?'

Tim's question was loud and angry, yet Zach thought not as surprised as it should have been. His gaze darted to Genie and Freddie, a hint of worry creeping into his expression. Zach narrowed his eyes. What did Tim know?

Before he could question Tim, Genie stood up. She turned slowly to Einstein, her own grey eyes wide and nervous and questioning.

'What does that mean?' she asked, repeating Tim—though with far less anger.

'You were created,' said BK, her soft voice echoing eerily around the lab. 'On another planet. Stevie made you. She grew you and looked after you until you were ready to be put inside your mother. Artificially inseminated in your mother's womb.'

Genie gaped at her, shaking her head. Even Tim hesitated, staring at BK as if she'd suddenly started talking in French.

'He's telling the truth,' said Zach. 'There are only three humans in this room, and you aren't one of them.'

CHAPTER FORTY-EIGHT

Genie

Created? I wasn't even *human*? *That's* why Einstein came to me? They…they made me?

Zach's words echoed around my head and I turned my gaze down to Freddie. To my twin brother. We weren't identical twins, we were fraternal. And yet, how often had people said how similar we were?

Was that because we were made? Had they *designed* us?

This was it, this was the answer I'd been waiting for. The explanation that would make sense of all the strangeness of the last week. We weren't human.

Freddie's head lurched up. His gaze swung around the room, grey eyes unfocused until he caught sight of my face and latched onto me. His expression shifted, twisting with the effort of focusing.

More than ever I wished he could speak. I wished he could tell me it was going to be okay. That we were human. That it didn't matter what they said about us because it didn't change anything. Nothing. We were the same.

'We are.'

His voice whispered through my mind. That voice that I had always thought was my subconscious. My subconscious that sounded like him. An imaginary voice. Not imaginary.

I sucked in a sharp breath. I knew this. I had known this for days. It had been coming to me, bit by bit, despite all the drugs. He was *talking* to me. He'd always been talking to me.

What did that mean? He was…telepathic? Like…Stevie?

Did that mean he knew? He knew what we were? He was so pale, so sick, he might not have even heard what they said, but…but he heard me, didn't he?

'Yes.'

I reached out a hand, felt him clutch at it, felt his clammy skin and shivered. God, he was so cold. I squeezed my eyes shut, trying to squash the sob caught in my throat. His hand tightened around mine and I opened my eyes to look straight into his. Grey into grey.

Images rushed in.

I was tumbling through them, racing through flashes of colour and trees and swing sets and quad bikes and laughter until I felt dizzy and sick and claustrophobic all at once.

It was just like before, under the haze of drugs, when I had dreamed that I was in other people's bodies. Now I was conscious, I was aware of what was happening. These were *memories*. But they weren't mine.

My chest constricted and I gasped, trying to turn my head, to shut my eyes against the flood but I couldn't. I was stuck. The images came faster.

Stevie, standing in the dark with blue arcs of lightning fizzing from her ears.

Zach shifting from foot to foot, a cigarette in one hand as he stuck out the other in an awkward gesture of peace.

Tim stealing firecrackers from the eccentric neighbour down the road.

Ant sitting in Sunday school with his head bowed and his fists clenched under the table as the teacher told us about the kind of people who went to hell.

BK with her hair flowing around her head in a golden halo, a glow about her face, almost like an image stuck upon another image.

Grandma reading us Freddie's favourite dragon book, smoothing his hair back.

Dressed all in black, standing at the edge of another coffin being lowered into the ground. Grandpa's name carved out in stone next to Mum and Dad.

Me sitting in a hospital bed with stitches across my chest, laughing at something Freddie had just signed to me.

Darkness.

It flooded into the absence of the memories.

Somewhere in the darkness, a figure stepped out before me.

His hair was mussed up and he wore a lopsided grin, his expression somewhat sheepish as he regarded me. Slowly, the darkness began to recede around him and a room took shape.

I recognised it instantly. Grandpa's garden shed. The one Freddie and Tim had taken over when Grandma had finally deemed them old enough and responsible enough to go through the tools without hurting themselves.

Freddie plopped down on one of the chairs, one hand resting on the bench top, staring at it as if he wasn't quite sure it was there.

'Well this is different.'

I started. Freddie cocked his head, one eyebrow raised.

'You're not gonna freak out, are you?' he asked.

He *asked*. I wasn't just imagining the words. His lips moved, making the shape of the words, expelling them forth for me to hear *outside* my head.

'Of course I asked,' he said. 'I can talk in here.'

'In…In here?'

'Well it is my head. Normally we always talk in yours. I've never seen my mindscape before. Not like this, anyway.'

The room tilted, and I sat down hard on one of the stools. 'Your head?'

'It's not so hard to believe, is it?' he asked, still watching me with that contemplative expression. Like he wasn't sure if I was going to curl up into a ball and start screaming.

'I…' I swallowed and licked my lips. 'What's a mindscape?'

Freddie considered this, tilting his head up and thinking. 'I guess it's kind of like your safe place. It's how your mind takes shape on the inside. Your's is the piano room. You feel safe there, so that's the shape your mind takes. I guess. I mean, I've never really bothered with the science of it, but that's what Stevie says.'

'Stevie?'

And like that, she was there with us, standing in the corner with a shy little smile, silver eyes shifting back and forth between us.

There were no memories as she entered, but there was a pressure, a strange popping in my ears.

'Genie?' Freddie asked, standing up, eyes creasing in worry.

He reached out a hand, but the space stretched out between us in an instant, pushing him too far from me to reach.

I couldn't breath. I clutched at my chest, taking big, rasping gulps of air as the room began spinning. Freddie ran towards me. He kept running and running, aiming straight for me in the spinning room but he not getting any closer.

My chest grew tighter and I gasped.

'Genie? Genie!'

I was wrenched to my feet in a sudden lurch, and the world stayed tilted on its axis for a moment too long. I staggered, grabbing tight to the hands holding me up, and then shoved away as the world righted.

Staggering, I grabbed onto to the desk pressed against the far wall, clutching onto the smooth, cold metal and trying to get my bearings, to put my head back on straight.

'Sorry!' someone was babbling. 'I'm s-s-sorry. I thought-thought it would h-help. T-to ex-explain!'

'What're you talking about?' Tim snapped. 'What would help? What did you do to her?'

'I'm okay,' I said, still hanging onto the desk.

There were little rivulets in the metal where someone had scraped something heavy across the surface. I touched them, the rough texture of the marks sending gooseflesh up my arms. I breathed in.

'I'm alright,' I said again, nodding to myself.

I told you, you are strong.'

I spun, whirling around from the desk and glowering at Freddie. 'You *told* me, did you?'

Anger surged through me in what was becoming a familiar burn, making my neck and face and ears hot and my words biting.

'You *told* me? Last I checked you couldn't *tell* me anything. Stay out of my head, Freddie! You didn't *tell* me anything! You knew! You knew what we were and you've *never* said anything! All this time? You've been talking to me all this time? How could you not tell me!'

He flinched and dropped his gaze to the ground. He was standing, clutching the bedhead next to him to steady his swaying. His Adam's apple bob up and down as he swallowed. Guilt flooded through me, washing away the anger. His fever was getting worse, the flush on his cheeks brighter against the greying tone of his skin. The inky black lines staining his arms had crept further along, even in the short time since I'd gotten there.

I sunk to the floor, staring at him. 'I'm sorry,' I whispered.

He shook his head, eyes still on the ground, but his voice remained absent from my mind. I shut my eyes. I reached for the spot in my mind where his voice had away surfaced from. Where it normally waited for me.

'I'm sorry,' I said tentatively, pushing the thoughts toward that spot.

Something stirred there. A whispering touch of something *moving* in my mind. I flinched away, snapping back into the safety of my own head.

'Oh,' I said, wrapping my arms around myself and shivering. 'God that…that's *you.*'

Ant stepped in front of me, crouching down to look me in the eye, his face filled with concern. 'What's going on?'

'They're talking,' said Tim bluntly. 'To each other. In their heads.'

'I…He's right. We aren't…I shocked those nurses. I *electrocuted* them,' I said, and looked down at my own hands. Little sparks of blue light were zapping off the tips of my fingers. 'And Freddie…I thought I was imagining it…I thought I'd made up that voice but it's him. It's always been him. He can…he speaks to me. In my head. God. We really aren't human, are we?'

Ant's brows creased even further but he said nothing. He didn't try to reassure me, didn't say that I was wrong, that *of course* we were human. He just stayed silent, his brows creased, his mouth set in a thin line, watching me with dark blue eyes.

'You are.'

My gaze snapped up, fixating on Zach in quiet hope.

'Mostly,' he added, his lips quirking in a wry smile. 'For the most part, you're still human.'

My heart sank, dipping down into the pit of my stomach.

'Is that supposed to make her feel better?' Tim barked, his voice hard.

Zach began to scowl and opened his mouth. He stopped, mid word, and frowned. I followed his gaze.

Stevie and Einstein had both become motionless. Even Freddie was quiet, gazing up at Einstein with blank eyes. I wanted to go to him, to help him, but I wasn't sure how.

Everything had shifted. I felt like someone had just come along and told me my whole perception of the world was wrong. That the sky was really pink, and, actually, there was no such thing as water and, oh, by the way, you've imagined this whole scenario for yourself and any moment now you're going to wake up in a mental hospital wrapped in a straight jacket.

The world seemed suddenly small and claustrophobic, as if there wasn't enough air for those of us left to share. I sucked in a sharp breath, trying to clear my mind, but unable to shake off the oppressive feeling.

Something heavy pressed down on my mind, and I gasped. I leant forward, ignoring the concerned question Ant was directing my way as I clutched at the sides of my head.

Gravity was shifting, was crushing down on top of me, blinding me to all else except trying to breathe in the now suffocating atmosphere.

Somewhere in the haze, I sensed Freddie. He was close. Closer than I thought and I had an idea that he was reaching out to me. I reached back trying to grab at him. If I could only get to him, we would be okay.

We would be okay.

Wouldn't we?

CHAPTER FORTY-NINE

Zach

Zach staggered back, his head in tatters, and would have fallen had someone not caught his shoulders and steadied him.

'What did you do to him?' someone shouted, the noise reverberating through the inside of Zach's head.

The hands were pulled away from his shoulders and he began to fall. He had just enough vision to see Einstein step in close to him, shoving away whichever of the boy's it was that had been steadying him. Einstein pressed something into Zach's hands, stepping in close so that only Zach could hear.

'This is the key,' he said. 'You are smart. You have all the pieces. Use your brain and you will fit the puzzle together.'

Somehow Einstein's voice penetrated through the noise in his mind. There was the clatter of metal and the floor rumbled beneath Zach's feet. He felt the weight of a thousand voices pressing down on him. Someone shrieked. It echoed close to Zach's ears, so loud he thought his head would explode. He moaned. God, would they all just shut up?

Einstein reached up with his other hand to press a cool finger to Zach's temple. Pain exploded, and Zach cried out, almost dropping the thing Einstein had given him. What was it? A vial? Somehow, in the depths of his mind, he knew it was important, that it was vital he did not loose it.

'You have all the pieces, Zach,' Einstein repeated.

Einstein's voice was louder than the others, pushing them further out of Zach's head. He shuddered in relief, unused to such violent, invasive telepathy, and had a vague appreciation for what Freddie's human doctor had gone through.

'Your mind is your most valuable asset,' said Einstein, and Zach *felt* the alien in his head, felt him reach in and clear away space in order to plant something else there. Something new.

For the briefest instant, Zach felt fear. What was it that Einstein had cleared away, what had Zach just lost?

'But what have you gained?'

Zach dug around, inspecting the knew information as Einstein retreated. The cure? He had the cure! All of it. Everything Einstein knew. More than just the green folder of reports.

Zach staggered back, reaching for his head. There was more. There was intent. Einstein's plans. His *plan*. The only plan. And the Collective…God, what *was* the Collective? It was too much. There was too much information in his head.

'What…what about the twins? It…it might hurt them?'

'You will have to test it. You will have to find the others. Stevie can help you, she knows where they are. She knows how to find them.'

'What if I can't?'

'You will.' Einstein turned, addressing Tim who was standing close by, watching their interaction with dark, wary eyes. 'You need to keep him alive. He is naturally immune to the plague. It is part of why I chose him, and you will need that. You will need him. This is not over.'

'You're bloody right it ain't,' Tim said, though his tone was more subdued, his expression more watchful than aggressive.

Einstein shook his head. 'Humans,' he muttered. 'You need to leave, now.'

Tim didn't move. 'You need to explain what the hell is going on.'

'Zach has the answers, I have given them to him. Right now, it is imperative that you retreat.'

'Why the hell should we?'

'Because it is not safe here. There are others coming.'

'What others?' Tim asked, still unmoving, but his whole body tensing, preparing itself for whatever fight would come next.

For the first time, Zach noticed the stains and—God, the *smell*—covering Tim's clothes. It seemed Tim had been doing plenty of fighting already. Zach tried not to breathe in the pungent smell, his stomach twisting in nausea now that he'd noticed it.

'You wish to protect them, do you not?' Einstein asked, gesturing at Genie and Freddie.

Ant and Genie were supporting Freddie, all three of them watching the exchange. Only BK, looking up toward the ceiling, seemed unconcerned with the conversation between the alien scientist and Tim.

'Yeah,' said Tim.

'So do I,' said Einstein, and his voice softened ever so slightly as he looked at Tim. 'You have done me a great service. You have stayed by their side for so long.'

'I didn't do it for you.'

'Regardless, it is not unappreciated. I need you to keep protecting them.' His silver eyes flickered to Genie. 'They are strong. They are special. There are things you think I have done wrong, but I assure you, I am not your enemy. I am sorry for what they did to you. It was not my intention when bringing you here. There are other powers at play. Powers much stronger than mine, and they are coming. Coming for them.' Einstein gestured to the twins. 'You must leave this place. Live today, and fight tomorrow.'

'Who are these people?' Tim asked, finally moving, taking one step backwards in the direction of Ant and the twins. 'Aliens?'

'The Collective,' said BK, her voice faint and her eyes gleaming as she stared up at the ceiling. 'They're very angry. Angry at you.'

Her head tilted back down from the ceiling, her gaze dropping to Einstein, though unfocused, as if she were seeing something very far away.

Einstein tensed. A ripple of electricity arcing between the tips of his ears.

Zach felt it again. The oppressive weight that had crashed over him when Einstein entered his mind. The weight hadn't been Einstein himself, but what he was *connected to*. It was huge. A huge, powerful, intelligent mass of interconnected minds.

How could they communicate across such distances?

'They've entered our solar system,' said BK, her gaze flashing back up to the ceiling. 'They're really very angry. They know what you've done now. They know you ruined their plans…' she trailed off, her eyes drifting back down as a forlorn expression crossed her face.

'We have to go, don't we?' said Genie, tears in her pretty silver eyes.

They looked so much like Stevie's. Zach thought he could see a bit of Einstein in them too. That sharpness, the strength, it was there, whether she knew it or not.

'Yes,' said Zach. 'We do.'

'I wish— I had questions,' she said, staring at Einstein.

'I know,' said Einstein, regret tightening his features.

The alien still stood in the centre of the room, his eyes flickering back and forth between Genie and Stevie. His back was stiff, his chin held high, yet Zach could now sense the weariness. The exhaustion of so many years. He saw a lifetime of trying to undo his ancestor's mistakes, trying to remedy the fate his predecessors had set for his species. He saw the countless attempts to save them. The sacrifices Einstein had made to be there. He saw the hard exterior of an intelligent man who knew he was doomed for failure.

'Take care of them,' said a voice inside his mind, gentle and soft and defeated. *'They are all I have left.'*

Zach swallowed, wondering, *aching,* to ask. 'Come with us,' he said.

Einstein smiled that sharp toothed, wry smile. *'There is something here I must yet see to. Take them, and take care with them.'*

A strange noise came from Stevie. She was looking between Zach and Einstein with an anxious frown, staring at them as if they were speaking a language she couldn't understand. Zach got the feeling Einstein's words had been for him, and him alone. He turned back to the others, the people he now considered friends.

'We have to go,' Zach repeated. 'He's not wrong. There's something else here worse than him.'

Stevie shook her head, taking a step toward Einstein, but Tim caught her arm. He was staring at Einstein with a hard frown, but something had changed. The anger had drained away. He looked back at his friends, black eyes focusing on the twins with new understanding.

Tim faced Einstein. He was no longer the predator, the hunter, the angry beast, but rather a boy. A teenager fighting against a world that was trying to destroy him and everyone else he cared about. He stood straight, his arms hanging by his side, his fists unclenched and his head raised but not defiant.

'I am going to protect them,' Tim said, eyes gleaming. 'But not because you asked me to.'

Despite the situation, a faint smirk pulled at Einstein's lips.

Tim was still holding onto Stevie's arm, and black eyes flickered her way, before refocusing on Einstein.

'I'm going to protect *all* of them. And I'll do it better than you did.'

'Humans have strange notions of the forces that control fate,' said Einstein, and his posture relaxed ever so slightly as he—just like BK had—tilted his head to stare up toward the ceiling. 'I have always had trouble understanding this idea that there is some other being at work controlling your lives. While *I* have controlled many things throughout their lives —' he gestured toward the twins, encompassing BK and Zach in the motion. 'You are the one thing I did not foresee. You are the one human who has made me think, for just a moment, that fate is, perhaps, possible. For I was unquestionably lucky, the day you entered their lives.'

A smile cracked Tim's lips. 'And don't you forget it,' he said.

Without another glance back, Tim turned and left, taking Ant and Stevie with him.

The others left, following their friend's lead, Genie casting one last longing look at the alien who had created her.

Zach took a few steps after them before stopping, one hand on the doorway. He stood half in, and half out of the room, knowing he had to go, but not quite ready. 'What about you?'

'I will be fine.'

Zach hesitated one last moment, taking the alien in.

He looked so lonely, in the nearly empty room. So small, after the weight of all those voices. Zach knew this was just a head start. That Einstein was going to buy them time. They'd come for the twins, surely; but first, they would come for *him*. The man who had tried to save them, and the man who had destroyed their plans

'Go,' Einstein whispered, his voice hoarse, choked tight with years of emotion.

Zach went. With a pang of regret lodging in his throat, he jogged after the others, knowing with a certainty that frightened him that he would never see Einstein again.

CHAPTER FIFTY

Genie

My head pounded.

Sweat had broken out over my entire body, though we weren't running. We couldn't. Not when Freddie could barely stand upright. Not when Ant was limping with every step, struggling to help Freddie while just managing to walk himself.

'How,' Ant panted, readjusting Freddie's arm over his shoulders. 'How do we get out?'

Tim glanced back, an answer on his lips that faded when he took Ant and Freddie in. He cursed and doubled back.

'Sorry,' he said, looping Freddie's other arm over his shoulder. 'Wasn't paying attention. I've got him. You have a break.'

'I'm okay.'

'You look like shit.'

'Yeah, well, you stink,' Ant said tiredly.

He really did. The smell hung around Tim, getting thicker and richer the longer we stood in the hallway. He was shivering too, his face pale and shining with sweat.

Yet it was nothing compared to Ant, who was almost as grey skinned as Freddie. There was fresh blood on the bandages on his arms and I was reminded of the dreams I'd had of Ant being stuck with needles.

I shuddered. Had those been real?

'There's an elevator,' said Zach, his voice strained as he rubbed at his temples. 'Somewhere around here.'

Tim snorted. 'Well, this place is small enough, won't take us long to find it. We'll just check all the rooms.'

'What about the other doctors?'

'Genie can fry them,' said Tim, shrugging awkwardly as he reached for the handle of the nearest door.

With the adrenaline fading out of my system, I wondered if I could fry anyone. I stared at my fingertips and tried to draw on the fire. My fingers stayed cold—the blistered tips a little numb.

'You've got to be kidding,' said Tim, gaping at the room beyond. 'They have a God damn waiting room.'

We stepped into the room after him, peering around at the only decorated space I'd seen so far. There was a large desk to the right and a row of chairs to our left. Directly in front of us were two large elevator doors that made my heart lurch in relief.

'SC,' said Ant, stopping to read the sign up behind what looked to be a receptionist's desk. '"Symbiotic Cybernetics. Where do you fit in society's future?"…What is this place?'

Tim, who had already hit the call button for the elevator, glanced over his shoulder as he helped Freddie lean up against the wall. 'Who cares,' he said. 'So long as we never see it again.'

BK stared at the sign, her head tilted on an angle.

'I know that name,' I said, as a faint feeling of familiarity trickled along my spine.

BK glanced back at me and trotted over to the desk, her quiet footsteps echoing along the floor. I realised she was the only one wearing shoes.

She ran a hand along the smooth, black, granite high-top bench as she walked around the desk. It was large, spanning almost the entire length of the wall and set high, so whoever normally sat behind the desk it was shielded from view.

BK picked up a picture frame, staring at it intently. 'She looks like you, Genie.'

She looked up, green eyes wide and confused as she held out the picture frame for me to look at.

There were a group of them, maybe a dozen, standing together like couples wearing serious expressions that I never got a chance to properly examine.

A low chuckle echoed from the doorway behind us.

'There you are.'

A faint yelp echoed through the room and I spun to once again see my big brother holding a knife to someone's throat.

He turned his head, murmuring softly into Zach's ear, though his gaze never left my face. 'Didn't I already kill you?' he asked.

Any energy I had left drained from my body. When would it be enough? When would it be over? When would he leave me alone?

Zach trembled, blue eyes bright and wide as his throat worked.

'Don't!' BK cried, her voice high and panicked, her hands flying to her mouth. 'Please, please don't hurt him.'

'And why should I listen to you?' asked James, his lips twisting in disgust. 'Aren't you an alien?'

Surprise jolted through me. BK didn't deny his claim, didn't argue, she just stared at him pleadingly.

'Let him go,' said Tim.

'No,' said James. 'I need a shield. I saw your handiwork. I don't intend to end up minced like that pretty little nurse you slaughtered.'

Tim's fists clenched, his teeth grinding as he glowered at James. A hint of shame flashed across his face, but he reigned it in, holding onto the fire that allowed him to fight his way out of any situation.

Hesitantly, as if testing the waters, I felt a presence enter my mind. Unfurling like soft petals in spring.

'*Fight,*' said Freddie, whispering the words into my mind, creeping out into my thoughts as if it belonged there.

I saw now how I'd thought that voice had belonged to me. He was so quiet, so unobtrusive. His voice emerged like a slow knowing, an understanding that eased up from my subconscious.

Except how could I fight when James had Zach in his grasp? How could I even fight *James?* He was my brother.

A tingle of pain winced along my face and once again I saw the image of myself I'd stollen from Tim's mind. In truth, I was lucky I could still see. Any closer and the blade would have carved out my eye.

Maybe I *had* loved him once, but he had never loved me. Not when we were young. Not when he pushed me and hit me and snarled at me. Not when he'd held me down and cut me.

Not now, when he'd come for me. To hurt me some more. There were no more excuses. I knew, with a certainty that went deep into my very soul, that James had come straight for me the moment he escaped prison. He'd come straight for me now, after escaping whoever held him. He would always come straight for me.

I saw it in his eyes. In the lust and hunger and anger that swirled there. A burning rage swept through my mind and I started, turning my head in surprise to stare not at Freddie, but at *Stevie*.

Lightning ran in lances down her long, slender ears. Her eyes were pure black and fixed straight on James. A strange, subdued kind of fury emanated from her. The anger of someone who'd had something precious mistreated.

When she unveiled her mind, it was like being struck by a wave of heat. I staggered back, gaping at her in awe. I realised I'd only ever seen a glimpse of what she was capable of. This was her true power. The power that had been contained by her timidness; crippled by her own uncertainty.

James had incited her into using it. Into reaching her full potential.

James went stiff. In one, abrupt movement, he flung the knife away. It whizzed through the air, jamming into the wall behind the reception desk with a faint thrum.

'Let him go,' Stevie said, her voice solid and powerful and furious.

CHAPTER FIFTY-ONE

Zach

Zach fell away, his centre of gravity thrown off balance the minute the sharp steel left his neck. He twisted, a clawing beast in his chest telling him to *get away*. He staggered, the hands on his arm slipping loose. He fell, his knees slamming into hard tile, jarring all the way up through him to his teeth.

The air was stale and hot and hard to breathe. Zach panted, sucking at air that didn't seem to want to enter his lungs, twisting around to find the threat he knew was still there.

Zach's vision narrowed, the pulse in his neck—where the knife had pressed against his skin—making it hard to concentrate. He felt like he was breathing underwater…or—his mind flashed back to that oppressive weight he had felt beyond Einstein's mind—breathing the vacuum that was space.

A cry of alarm echoed through the noise of panic, cutting through it, slicing it in half and giving Zach sudden clarity as the haze fell away.

Bubbles of light swam around James. He gaped. Zach rubbed at his eyes and stared, sure he was hallucinating, convinced they'd drugged him and he was having some sort of adverse reaction.

James was illuminated by light. Tiny little bubbles of brightness that began to engulf him. Zach searched out Stevie, wondering what on Earth it was she was doing.

Her gaze was silver, the black pupils reduced to

pinpricks as she stared at the sight in astonishment.

There was a faint *ding*, followed but the *shick* of the elevator doors opening. Freddie fell back through the opening, and Ant twisted, scrambling to catch hold of his friend.

'What're you doing?' James screeched, trying to brush the lights off himself. 'What're you doing to me? Get it off! You won't beat me! I'll find you! I'll come after you!'

They were all frozen. All staring. Ant and Freddie in the elevator, Tim in the doorway, BK and Genie by the receptionist's desk, and Stevie standing in the middle of the room, watching James get brighter and brighter, with a dawning look of horror.

There was a pause, pregnant with anticipation, with horror, with understanding, with fear.

'Run!' BK screamed, grasping Genie's hand in a sudden lurch and hauling her toward the open elevator doors.

Zach scrambled to his feet, his pounding heart lodged in his throat, needing no further invitation to get the hell out of there.

He dove passed Stevie, snatching her arm as he went and sending them crashing through the doors with BK and Genie.

James attempted to follow them, howling obscenities even as he became obscured by the bubbles of light crowding him.

'Shut the doors!' Ant yelled.

Tim was smashing the "close door" button, his gaze fixed on James, his teeth bared in a mixed expression.

James made a dive and Zach thought he might throw up. He was going to make it! He was going to wedge himself in the doorway and bar the only exit they had.

'Look out!' BK shrieked, turning her head and throwing her arms over Genie, shielding her face.

Zach ducked his head, seeing the others do the same out of the corner of his eye, instinctively obeying BK as James shot through the doors.

Except…he didn't.

The light erupted. Zach cried out, squeezing his eyes

shut, covering them with his hands but unable to blot out the unbearable brightness.

He was going to go blind. The light was going to sear away his cornea, leaving him only with the faint memory of sight. A memory the light was slowly obliterating, along with his entire being.

He felt as if he were floating in a pit of darkness. Darkness so deep and so long that he would never be able to crawl out of it again, never be able to find himself, never be able to—

Ding, 'Carpark 2.'

Zach blinked. In a rush of breathless exclamations and cries of relief they all tumbled out of the cramped elevator and onto the hard concrete floor of an underground carpark.

'What…what just happened?' Ant asked from somewhere to Zach's left.

Zach groaned, rubbing at his eyes, trying to push himself up from the cold, hard ground. He winced as someone kicked him in the shin and settled for kneeling, one hand waving about in front of him as the other shielded his eyes.

He kept one eye firmly shut and attempted to open the other. He twitched, expecting the feeling of "seeing" to burn. Instead, he found that the limited glow of carpark lights wasn't the least bit painful. He lowered his hand, unblinded, and found himself almost nose to nose with BK.

'Hello,' she said, blinking at him.

'Er…hi.'

'Where the hell are we?' Tim asked.

He was already on his feet, examining the carpark they'd fled to.

Ant was trying to get Freddie to his feet, but Freddie kept wobbling, as if he were playing the part of a drunkard on a swaying ship.

'We n-need to k-keep going,' said Stevie.

Zach turned to locate her. She, too, was on her feet— though instead of looking around like Tim, her silver eyes were fixed on the ceiling.

'How did they get so close?' BK whispered. 'I didn't think they could get us from there.'

'Get us?' asked Tim. 'You mean whatever that light thing was that got James? What was that? Did they kill him?'

Stevie shook her head. 'We have t-to g-g-go.'

'Alright, alright, keep your pants on,' Tim growled and stalked off toward the nearest row of cars.

Stevie paused, her head cocking to one side as she frowned after Tim, her brows furrowed. She glanced down at herself—back in her skin-tight space suit—with such a perplexed expression that Zach couldn't help the absurd, slightly hysterical giggle that erupted out of him, echoing through the carpark.

Tim glanced back, his dark eyes skirting over them, his lips moving as he did a quick head count before he disappeared through a row of cars.

'Tim!' Ant called, 'Where are—'

'I'll be back in a minute!' came Tim's annoyed shout. 'Stay there.'

'We c-c-can't stay,' Stevie said, wringing her hands and shifting about on her feet.

She moved to Ant's side, helping to pull Freddie to his feet, anxiety coming off her in waves. Faint currents of electricity were zapping in arcs out from her ears as the air grew static around them.

'What is it?' asked Genie, putting a hand on Stevie's shoulder to get her attention. 'What's wrong?'

'This place makes their technology stronger,' said BK. 'They can get us if we stay too close. Like they got James.'

'Wait,' said Zach, shaking his head. 'You mean…you're not saying they…they *beamed* him away…are you?'

'Yes,' said BK, turning to gaze at Zach with intense green eyes. 'And they're trying to get us, too.'

CHAPTER FIFTY-TWO

Genie

Tires screeched against the slippery car park floor, skidding as Tim careened out onto the wet street. Rain splattered down on the windscreen, turning the outside world into a haze as grey as our clothes. I hung onto Freddie, making sure he didn't catapult out of his seat, cursing as I tried to get his seatbelt on.

'Jesus, Tim, slow down!' Ant snapped, crashing into me as the car squealed around a corner.

I yelped as his elbow dug into my side, into the still tender skin over my ribs and, with a sudden jolt, memory slammed into me. A crash. Rising water. Tim unconscious.

'Tim, slow down!'

At the panicked, breathless pitch in my voice, Tim braked, glancing up into the rear view mirror sheepishly. 'Sorry,' he said. 'Stevie said go.'

'She also said don't die!' Ant snapped.

She hadn't said that, but I was pretty sure we all agreed. In the front passenger seat, Zach was nodding frantically. He had one hand on the dash and the other clutching at the door.

'Sorry, I was just—is this Main Street?' Tim said, cutting himself off.

I glanced out the window. The rain was coming down so heavy, it took a moment for my eyes to adjust. I turned back. The car park we had just left was one of many exits to the main shopping centre in town.

'How…' I twisted in my seat and even though I was stuck between Freddie and Ant, it was clear where we were.

'We were underneath the shopping centre?' Ant asked, staring out past the rivers running down the window. 'We were so close to home, all this time?'

I thought for a moment that Ant might cry, and I turned to him, ready to tell him that we were okay. That we were free now. After all, it wasn't so scary from the outside. It wasn't even *there* from the outside. It was just a shopping centre. Somewhere we'd been hundreds of times before. It almost made me feel stupid for being afraid.

I didn't get the chance to console Ant. Tim was still speeding, still going that little bit too fast. If he hadn't been, we'd have probably all died. The street lit up behind us, blasting away the grey wet world for a moment, just one, single moment.

Sound rushed in behind the bright flash of fire. *BOOM!*

The earth rumbled. The sky lit up in fire and smoke.

Tim swore.

The shopping centre—a place we'd fled to for fun and respite, a place we now fled in fear—expanded. It was as if it were a creature come to life, sucking in it's first breath, before the whole thing shattered in on itself.

Tim slammed on the breaks, swearing, trying to see behind us and trying not to drive the car off the road. My head hit the back of Tim's seat as the car tried to stop, but couldn't. Rubble exploded around us. Something smashed into the back of the car and we went fishtailing along the road.

My ears hurt. The air was thick, filled with pressure and the groaning sound of a building collapsing in on itself. All that concrete and steel bursting under its own weight.

A strange, strained sound erupted from Stevie, and she crumbled, hands flying up to her face.

'Stevie!' BK gasped.

Stevie cried out, speaking another language. I saw the flash of agony cross Freddie's face half a second before pain exploded in my mind. Stevie's wail of anguish echoed behind the pain. Bright sparks of electricity ran in rapid arcs along the ridges of her head.

A coldness seeped into me, a fog lifting from my mind as I gaped through the back window at the ruin.

A pang of loss settled deep into my chest, an ache for something I'd longed for half my life but never truly attained, as a single thought raced through my head.

Was Einstein dead?

The car jerked to a stop. The quiet rumbling of the engine almost echoed in the aftermath of what we'd just barely escaped.

Then, like a flock of cockatoos startled into flight, we all burst from the car.

'What the fuck? What the *fuck*!'

My thoughts echoed Tim's shout as we all scrambled around the back of the car to better see the building. The whole thing was a ruin. Crumbled pieces of concrete that had moments ago been whole and strong and were now nothing but dust and rubble.

'How?'

The bewildered question came from Ant. I didn't turn to him, didn't offer an opinion even as Tim speculated about bombs. Instead, I stared down at my hands.

Water pounded down on me and within moments I was soaked. It seeped into my hair, tickling my scalp and dripping down the long strands into the top of my shirt. Droplets slinked down my back and clung to my eyelashes and my fringe. It was cool. Refreshing. Like washing away the trauma of the last few days. Yet my fingers remained warm. Heated up. Ready for fire.

When I glanced back up, Zach was watching me, blue eyes electric in the rain. As if reflecting that part of me back at myself. Something in his sombre gaze told me he was thinking the same thing I was, if not something very similar.

It hadn't been a bomb. It was Einstein. And if Einstein could do that…I stared at my hands again, feeling the heat in my blistered fingertips. What in the world was I capable of?

A high keening broke me out of my own self pity.

Stevie was still in the back of the four wheel drive, having stayed glued to her seat, staring out the back windshield, as the rest of us hurried out into the downpour for a better view. She looked up at me when I climbed into the car. Water dripped everywhere but I pushed into the back, sitting next her despite my sodden clothes.

Her silver eyes were bright with tears, so like and unlike my own.

'I'm sorry,' I said.

She shook her head. 'I…they…' She stopped and shook her head again, bright tears spilling down her face. Currents raced back and forth along her ridges. 'All g-gone. All a-alone.'

I crouched down and took her hand. Volts of energy raced along her skin. I winced, feeling a faint shock go up my arms. How could I feel the zap of her electricity but not my own?

'I know I'm not like you,' I said. 'Not by much anyway. But you're not alone. We're here. BK is here. We might not be the same species, but we're family now, you and me.'

The currents died out but the tears increased. She blinked, several sets of eyelids flashing shut, and threw her arms around me. After a split second of surprise—she'd never touched me before—I squeezed her back, tightening my hold and feeling the pain in her grasp.

Einstein.

Since that first meeting when I was ten years old, I'd always wondered about him. Was he a dream? A ghost? An angel? Was he a God? Some other divine form sent down from the heavens?

That first visit was a vague memory, overshadowed by years of therapy that had tried to tell me it was a dream. That I'd created his existence as a way for me to deal with what James had done. But I hadn't. Einstein was real, and in some way, he'd cared about me. Or, at the very least, he'd cared that I was healthy. He'd wanted me protected, and he'd said I was strong. Strong enough to build a race upon.

His race? Stevie said they were dying. Was that why he'd cared about me? Was I nothing more than a cure for him?

Why? Why had he sent us away, fleeing from the building, from James and the scientists…from the Collective, only to blow it up? Was he gone? Judging from Stevie's reaction, he was.

Someone reached out, grasping at Stevie's hand.

Freddie. He was pale and shaking, his own eyes clouded in pain, but his gaze was sure, steady, determined. He grit his teeth and nodded, his gaze darting to me for just a moment. He nodded again.

'We are family.'

'Now what?' Tim asked, slouching down against the side of the car, looping his arms behind his head as he let the rain pour down on him. 'Where are we supposed to go from here?'

'Home,' I said. 'We go home.'

CHAPTER FIFTY-THREE

Zach

Tim's place was a small property five minutes further down the same bumpy dirt road Genie and Freddie lived on. The house was set back on the property in a way that seemed common in the area, yet Tim bypassed the small car port, instead following the narrow road down around a bend of trees clustered on the edge of a creek.

The little rickety bridge rattled as they crossed, and a flock of birds squawked indignantly, taking flight from the tops of the trees. On the other side of the bend was a large barn and a few fenced paddocks containing three horses. The car pulled to a stop and for a moment they all sat there, even after Tim had turned off the engine.

Ant was the first to move. He slid out of the backseat like a ghost, but instead of moving off to the barn, he wandered over to the paddock.

Without being called, the three horses turned their heads, watching Ant approach the fence with dark, unreadable eyes. The largest, a speckled grey, tossed it's head and whinnied loud enough for Zach to hear inside the car. As one, the three horses trotted over to the fence, greeting Ant like he were one of them.

'We're home,' Tim muttered, and with a sigh he pushed open his door.

He didn't follow Ant. Instead he trundled over to the paint peeled, faded red barn door, not glancing back to see if the others were following.

There were three clean, unused stables at the front of the barn before it opened up into a large space with a big round table and some hay bales. Plenty of storage racks lined the walls, holding an assortment of items from saddles, horse brushes, whiskey bottles and what looked like party streamers and board games.

At the back of the barn were two more stables with couches and cushioned chairs set up within them, and a set of wide wooden steps leading up to a second level.

Genie led them over to the stabled couches, collapsing into one as she watched Tim scrounge around in some of the storage boxes.

'What're you looking for?'

'Spare key.'

'It's in the flamingo,' said Genie, pointing to a large flamingo ornament in the centre of the table.

Tim straightened, rolling his eyes and muttering something under his breath as he stomped over to the table.

'How's Freddie's fever?' Zach asked.

Genie winced, glancing sideways at her brother who offered Zach a weak smile and a thumbs up.

'Not great,' she said.

'Hm. He could do with a shower,' said Zach.

'Why d'you think I'm looking for the key,' said Tim, turning and crossing back over to his friend. 'All yours.'

Freddie nodded, holding an open palm out for the key and attempting to stand, only to have one leg buckle under him. Tim caught him, pulling him back up to his feet with a roll of his eyes and a tense grin.

He threw Freddie's arm around his shoulders. 'You know, if you wanted to get me naked, all you had to do was ask.'

Freddie signed something even Zach could tell was rude, and Tim laughed.

'C'mon,' he said. 'You stink.'

When Ant wandered in a few minutes later there was a clang, followed by a string of muffled swear words.

Ant glanced upwards and Genie explained.

'Freddie is showering. Tim's helping.'

Ant snorted. 'Hope they're not killing each other,' he muttered.

'They won't be,' said BK, patting the seat next to her.

Ant sat, relaxing into the worn padding of the couch. BK tucked her legs up and lay down, resting her head on Ant's thigh. He glanced down at her as she curled up. Zach felt a twinge of jealousy curl in his chest. BK closed her eyes and slipped easily into sleep. Within seconds, she began to snore.

Some of the pain eased out of Ant's frame, and a soft smile replaced the worry.

'How does she do that?' he murmured.

'Beats me,' Genie whispered back. 'But I wish I could.'

'Has she always been that way?' asked Zach.

He moved to their stable and sat down on the floor, grabbing one of the cushions as he went. For once, he felt as young as he was. The adrenaline ridden panic that had engulfed their lives for the past…what was it? A week? It had all faded away. The need to survive was over, and it had stripped him of any and all energy.

'Yeah,' Genie said, answering Zach's question as he turned those electric blue eyes on her. 'She has. It's kinda reassuring, you know?'

He nodded. 'Makes sense,' he said. 'It's probably why they chose her.'

Genie jerked and Ant's eyes snapped to Zach's face. Zach swallowed. Genie stared at him as if he'd just thrown a pillow at her. He tucked his knees up to his chest and pressed his mouth into the cushion he was hugging.

'Sorry,' he muttered.

Like a silent ghost, Stevie appeared, manoeuvring through the scattered cushions to sit on the small couch next to Genie. She hesitated, then laid a soft, tentative hand on Genie's shoulder.

'He is right,' she said. 'That is why we ch-chose her. She is s-special. The others needed a pro-protector, b-but you n-needed someone *you* c-could protect.'

'Do…do you think she regrets coming here?' Genie asked.

Stevie squeezed her arm, her ears twitching over her shoulders.

'Einstein said she's never known anything else,' said Zach, shifting his cushion so his words weren't muffled. 'They took her before she was old enough to remember any of her home planet.'

'That's kind of sad,' Genie whispered.

Zach shrugged. 'Not really. To her, this is her home planet, and you're her family. That's all that really matters, isn't it?'

'I guess so,' she said.

'You still love her like family, don't you?'

'Of course!'

'Well, then who cares?' asked Zach. 'What matters is that we're all here. Together. Not where we're from or what we are.'

He swallowed, meaning the words but unsure if he really felt included in that statement. Would they be offended that he was lumping himself in with them, though they barely knew him? Already he felt more comfortable in this group than he ever had with people his own age, or with the older kids in his advanced classes, or with his own parents.

'Together,' she said, and looked down at her hands.

'Zach's right,' said Ant. 'We're...we're together. And we're gonna keep it that way. We won't lose anyone else.' His fists clenched on top of his knees. 'We won't ever lose anyone else again.'

'Damn right we won't.'

Zach jumped and glanced up to see Tim, still looking rather drenched, sauntering over to them from the bottom of the stairs.

'Freddie's asleep on your bed,' Tim said, glancing at Ant as he tossed Genie a towel. 'Figured you wouldn't mind.'

'"Course not,' said Ant. 'How is he?'

Tim shrugged and repeated Genie's earlier assessment. 'Not great.'

Genie stiffened, took the towel and headed for the stairs. Stevie followed, her small, alien frame growing tense with concern for her dying patient. Her creation.

Zach wondered how involved she'd been in the twin's growth. For that matter, he wondered how old she was. It was something he'd never thought to ask, and he ached to question her, but she'd already gone.

They went one by one, slowly washing away the grit and the grim and the stress of the last few days. Zach opted to go last, seeing in the faces of the others that their stresses had been worse than his. Genie spent a long time in her shower while their little group grew quiet.

Tim pulled out a deck of cards and tried to teach Stevie some games while BK watched. Ant pulled out a box full of what looked to Zach like scraps and junk and began tinkering with them.

Zach snooped around, found an old, dusty book someone had hidden between monopoly and a box of stuffed animals and started to read.

When it was his turn, Zach stepped into the shower with a sigh of relief. Hot water burned out, scorching his fair skin red in minutes. He didn't care. The warmth spread through him, easing his muscles and washing away the grit and grime. He hadn't realised how gross he'd felt until the water was cascading over his head.

There about five different soap options and at least four shampoos. Zach grabbed one at random and scrubbed with gusto. He washed his hair three times and understood why Tim had come back from his shower looking so relieved. It was complete bliss.

At least Zach hadn't been covered in blood like Tim had.

With regret, he shut off the taps and stepped out into the steamy room. The towel was rough, nothing like the luxurious soft towels his parents bought, but Zach didn't care. It was still like heaven.

Now, all that was left was to curl up in a proper bed and sleep for a week.

And to work out how to tell the others about the vial of bluish liquid he'd been hiding in the pockets of his pants. The vial Einstein had given him and tasked him to protect.

The vial that had the potential to save Freddie.

CHAPTER FIFTY-FOUR

Genie

Tim dragged the three spare sleep-over mattresses out. Rather than setting them up downstairs like usual, he squished them all onto the floor of Ant's room in the loft.

Without argument, I dropped into a cleared space and let exhaustion claim me.

When I woke up next, it was eight hours later and someone had draped a blanket over me. Freddie was next to me and Stevie was brushing his brow with a damp towel. Kind, silver eyes gazing at him with a wistful longing I was beginning to make sense of.

Zach had told me Stevie wasn't just an apprentice to Einstein, but that she'd overseen Freddie and me specifically.

Sometimes, amongst the small, quiet looks of affection and longing, I thought she was especially fond of Freddie. A small well of disappointment crept through me that I tried and failed to squash.

Of course she was more connected to him; they could talk to each other in a way I couldn't—or didn't know how to. Besides, Freddie had never met Einstein. Now, I had an idea of how he'd felt whenever I'd spoken of the alien. He'd always believed me, and I realised this was why. He'd known what we were.

What was that like for him? To know, and yet to have missed the chance for answers? Answers I hadn't even known to ask for. How frustrating must that have been for him?

Was that why he wasn't talking to me now? Those thoughts that had once come with such ease were silent. Was it because the disguise had been lost? Or was it my reaction? Had I banished him from my mind forever when I had shut him out? The thought of hurting him, of actually causing my strong, wilful brother pain, made me sick. But the thought of letting him in, of letting him see me, was frightening. He'd always had such faith. He'd always believed I was strong.

How could he say that when he'd seen inside my mind? When he'd seen how weak and scared I really was?

Even now, I half expected him to talk to me, to chide me for my lack of self worth. But nothing came.

What if he wasn't speaking to me because he wasn't strong enough?

The thought twisted in my stomach. Was his sickness that bad?

Curling up around my pillow, I cast the thoughts from my mind and buried myself in dreamless sleep. Sleeping was surprisingly easy. I half expected to walk through nightmares and memories of Einstein's lab. Instead, I fell into darkness, my body claiming the rest it desperately craved.

For two days I (and the others, I guess) slept like the dead, only waking to eat like ravenous beasts or to go to the bathroom.

On the second day I woke to a muffled crash from the next room. Blinking sleep out of my eyes, I squinted into the dusky light.

No one else stirred, and after a moment of quiet I settled back down into my blankets and attempted to drift back into sleep.

Until, like distant fireworks, the shouting began.

I scrambled to my feet, my heart jumping straight into overdrive, pounding hard against my fragile, recovering chest as I flung blankets everywhere.

Images flashed through my mind as I staggered across the creaky wooden floor. Masked men in hazmat suits. Women with needles full of mind numbing, poisonous liquid. Blood soaked hallways filled with bodies and glassy eyes. Always glassy, and hazel and filled with a terror I can't begin to understand.

I almost tripped over BK as she sat up in a flurry of blankets, a startled cry on her lips. I fell through the bedroom door, my hands hot and ready to face whatever new threat was waiting for me.

Tim was thrown out of the bathroom door, landing on his backside in the small, narrow hallway as Ant slammed the door behind him. Tim was back on his feet in less time than it took me to comprehend what I was seeing. He bashed against the door, still shouting, swearing obscenities I'd never even heard before.

'God damnit Ant, open this bloody door before I break it down myself!'

Tim took two steps back—almost crashing into me—leaned back and kicked at the door.

Ant's voice echoed back, stilted and choked and not at all like him. 'Go away!'

'Ant-!'

'Go away Tim!'

'Not until you let me see!'

'Fuck off!'

My short breathing evened out, but my heart continued to hammer, confused by what was happening.

A hand touched my shoulder and I jumped, yelping and causing Tim to turn in a flurry of startled swear words.

BK blinked back at me, giving me an apologetic half smile. 'What's going on?'

'I'm not sure,' I said, turning to look back at Tim.

He glowered at us and I was tempted to take a step back. 'Ant's hurt.' Without explaining, he turned his attention back to the door.

He kicked at the door two more times. I'd been up in the loft enough times before to know all that held the door in place was a simple little latch, nailed into the frame.

Wood splintered and the door smashed inwards. Next to me BK jumped, her hand flying to my wrist, gripping it. Digging her nails in so hard I think she might've drawn blood, but I didn't care.

I didn't care because Tim was tumbling through the doorway and surging across the room toward Ant. Ant who had managed to get dressed in the time it had taken for Tim to bash through the door—but it was a pointless effort. There's a fury in Tim I didn't understand and he grabbed hold of Ant's shirt, tugging at it.

'What're you doing?' Ant shouted, shoving at Tim, but Tim was strong and angry and unrelenting.

Like a cornered animal Tim scrabbled at the thin, cotton shirt. 'Take it off!' he shouted back, slapping away Ant's hands. 'I want to see, take it off!'

'Stop it! Tim, back off! Leave me alone!'

'Stop it!' BK cried, and her voice was choked. She started to cry, big fat tears cascading down her cheeks in a sudden downpour. 'Stop it! Tim, you're hurting him!'

I wanted to join in. To shout at Tim to stop. To rush in and help pull Ant free. But I couldn't. Because something had just occurred to me.

I'd been too focused on Tim falling through the door to pay enough attention to Ant. I recalled the image of him flinging the door shut. He hadn't had a shirt on, yet something wasn't right.

Something was very, very wrong.

They tumbled to the ground and Ant cried out, half a gasp, half a sob of pain. Tim was on top of him, taking advantage of Ant's reflexive stillness to yank the shirt clear off him.

BK gasped, her hands flying to her mouth.

My knees felt weak. BK's grip on my arm was tight and painful, but didn't keep me on my feet. I sunk to the ground, staring as my breath was sucked away, only to be replaced by the taste of bile.

Ant cringed. He pulled free of Tim, sliding backwards to sit against the bathroom wall, his chest heaving as he tried to reign in his sobs.

His chest was no longer a healthy, sun-kissed tan. It was a patchwork of black and blue and red. The marks covered his stomach, his chest and parts of his arms, and, I suspected, a good portion of his back.

There were small, circular red marks on his arms the size of my pinky nail. When he scrambled to his feet I saw more —dozens more—on his back. The bruising wasn't as bad, yet there were more of the little red marks, lining up along his spine. The realisation came like a punch to the gut.

Needle marks.

I wanted to throw up. I wanted to cry. I wanted to wrap him up in a hug and never let anyone hurt him again.

Instead I sat there. I felt hot. My fingertips burned— though BK didn't pull away.

'Christ, Ant…what happened?'

Ant looked down at Tim, fury and pain and shame mingling in his kind blue eyes. 'None of your business,' he growled. He snatched another shirt from the cabinet and stormed past us.

BK tried to reach out for him, but he flinched away.

'Shit…*shit.*'

'Why did you do that?' BK asked, turning bright green eyes accusingly on Tim. 'Why would you attack him like that?'

'I didn't attack him,' said Tim, startled by BK's anger.

'Yes you did! You can't treat people like that! You can't just make them do what you want. We're all hurting, Tim! We're all trying to deal with it however we can. We can't all heal and forget as easily as you can!'

'You think I've forgotten?'

'Stop it!' I shouted and the light fixture above us exploded.

'Great,' snapped Tim. 'Now I'll have to fix that.'

'Try not to break it any further,' I said, launching to my feet with a glare. 'Isn't that what you do when you fix things?'

Following Ant's lead, I turned and fled the bathroom. Zach was downstairs, hurrying through the barn with a look of alarm on his face.

'Genie, what's happened? I just saw Ant and…Genie?'

I tried to brush the tears away. Emotion and confusion and exhaustion mixed together in a dangerous combination. My hands still burned. I wanted to set something on fire. I wanted to light up the room with a thousand sparks. I wanted to scream and to cry and to wipe away all the memories and the hurt and the pain.

Instead, my gaze caught on the flash of light glinting off of whatever Zach was holding. I took a shaky breath, focusing on the object.

It was a thin vial of blueish looking liquid, corked with a silver topper. I stared at it and instead of answering Zach's question, I asked one of my own.

'What's that?'

Zach glanced down. He made a face, worry and weariness flashing through his eyes as they rose to meet mine. He weighed the vial in his hand, bobbing the thing up and down so the liquid sloshed.

He sighed. 'Einstein gave it to me,' he said, his voice low and uncertain. 'I…I think it can cure Freddie.'

CHAPTER FIFTY-FIVE

Zach

They were all staring at him. It was to be expected, really. After all, he'd just dropped a bomb shell on them. Again.

Of course, it was Tim who broke the silence first.

'*What?*' Tim asked, pushing up from the make-shift table and knocking back his chair. 'You…You've had a cure? *All* this time?'

Zach winced, dropping his gaze to the table. He tried to think of something to say but before he had time to respond, Ant spoke up.

'All this time?' Ant asked, and Zach's gaze snapped up at the exasperated tone. 'Really?'

Zach winced. Genie had filled him in on what had happened, and BK had told them—after she had found him out in the field with the horses—what had caused the injuries Ant had sustained at the lab.

It took BK three hours to convince Ant to come back into the barn, and Zach suspected he'd only come for Freddie. He sat opposite Tim, and the two of them had glowered at each other until Zach started talking.

Tim flushed. 'Well he has!'

'It's been barely three days, Tim!'

'So?'

'So, maybe Zach had a good reason to not tell us?' Ant's eyes slid back to Zach, one eyebrow raised in question.

Now that Zach knew they were there, he could just make out the mottled bruises peeking out from the shoulder of the loose shirt Ant wore. Every time he moved, he twitched. A flicker of pain jolting over his entire body. From what Zach could guess, it sounded like they'd taken bone marrow…amongst other things. He shuddered.

Zach fidgeted. 'It'll save everyone else,' he said. 'All the other humans. The ones who aren't immune, anyway.'

'But?' asked Genie, her voice subdued—as if she already knew the answer.

'But it might not fix Freddie,' said Zach. Before Tim could interject, before he could tell them to give it to Freddie anyway, Zach added, 'In fact, it could kill him. It could kill all of you.'

Silence. The faint pitter of infrequent raindrops on the tin roof told them the rain was on it's way. It was a good chance to get fresh water (which they desperately needed) but none of them moved.

'What do you mean it might kill us?' asked Tim, his tone bewildered rather than angry. 'It's a cure.'

'For the plague,' said Zach.

'And we ain't got the plague! We're immune…aren't we?' his confidence and bewilderment melted away into uncertainty.

'No. You're…different. Your blood has been mutated. Changed. By the twins.'

Genie's gaze fixed on Zach, zeroing in, pinning him in place as she absorbed his words. 'Changed…by us?'

Zach nodded, swallowing. 'Yes,' he said. 'You're blood acts like a spore. It can latch onto normal blood cells and mutate them. I don't really know how to describe it without seeing the process. I don't know how it happened. My cells are unaffected, but…'

'But Ant and Tim's are.'

'Yes.'

'We infected them?'

Zach rubbed his hands over his face, scrubbing his fingers through his hair as he took a deep breath and sighed. He lowered his hands, dropping them back onto the table with a thud, and followed up with a shrug. 'For lack of a better word, yeah.'

'Hang on...what?' Tim asked, shaking his head, still leaning over the table. 'You're saying that our blood has somehow changed? Because of Freddie and Genie?'

'Yes,' said Zach, his knee jigging up and down. 'It's... stronger. It's why you haven't gotten sick yet. You're not immune, you're just...resistant.'

'But...' Ant's gaze drifted over to Freddie and the black veins creeping along his skin like a sickly spider web. 'Then how come Freddie is...'

'That's different. They did something, back in the lab. What's happening to Freddie isn't normal. That's why this cure might not work. It might not save him. In fact, it'll probably make him worse.'

BK bit her lip, staring at her cousin with wide green eyes.

'Why?' asked Ant, his voice quiet. 'Why will it make him worse?'

'The plague mutates human blood to destroy itself. The cure attacks the mutated blood cells, protecting the remaining cells from mutation and destroying the ones that have been altered.'

'So?'

'So, you *all* have mutated blood cells,' said Zach.

Genie slumped, her shoulders hunching inwards as she realised what this meant. 'So because of us, Ant and Tim can't have the cure?' she murmured.

'Actually, because of you, they're still alive,' said Zach, tapping his fingers in time to the rain. 'If it weren't for their resistance, they'd have caught the plague by now.'

There was another moment of silence.

'Tim would have gotten it for sure at the school,' said Ant, his gaze flashing to his friend's face before dropping back to his hands.

'So, what, we have super healing powers or something?' asked Tim, turning around with his arms crossed in skepticism.

'Er...no,' said Zach. 'You're just...stronger, I guess.'

'You guess?'

'Well...when was the last time you got sick?'

'Freddie and Genie don't get sick,' said BK, contributing to the conversation for the first time. Her gaze shied away from her cousins, but her words were strong and sure and confident.

Tim stopped scowling, his expression morphing into surprised realisation. Above them, the pitter patter of rain became more frequent, more demanding of their attention.

Ant frowned. 'Of course they do.'

'No…' said Tim, his voice low and wondrous. 'They don't. Don't you remember? We had that pox party when we were kids, but Genie and Freddie never got it. And that virus that went around school in year ten, right during exams, they didn't get that either. BK's right…they've never gotten sick.'

Ant frowned.

'And you…you used to get migraines. Even your Mum was talking about taking you to get scans before they stopped.'

'So I grew out of it.'

'I remember the last one,' said Tim. 'Six months ago. The day before the suspension.'

Realisation dawned on their faces. A look of horror flashed through Genie's eyes a second before full comprehension. Her gaze dropped to her open palm.

'The pact,' she said. 'Our blood it…that was when it infected you.'

'Pact?' Zach asked, looking back and forth between them.

'Blood pact,' said Genie, still staring at her empty palm. 'We made a blood pact six months ago.'

'You did *what?* Are you insane? Do you even realise how dangerous that is?' Zach exploded in astonished bewilderment.

'Apparently not at all,' Tim said as he surveyed his friends with a contemplative expression. 'Apparently it saved our lives.'

Wind strained against the barn walls, pounding rain into the silence that had filled the inside.

'But…the cure…' said Genie, turning those storm grey eyes on Zach. 'It destroys mutations.'

Zach nodded, his hands clenching around the vial of bluish liquid.

'It could kill us,' said Ant, his eyes faraway, his voice faint.

'Yeah,' said Zach. 'There's a pretty good chance that it will.'

More silence. The rain became heavier, picking up in frequency so it was a steady thrum against the tin awning. Kookaburra's laughed and squawked in the distance, the barn walls thin enough to hear them playing amongst the water drops.

'What do we do?' Genie asked, her voice small.

Tim began pacing. Next to Zach, Stevie began to fidget. She played with the hem on the pocket of her jacket, fiddling with a fraying thread. Her ears were twitching and Zach wondered how much of their thoughts she was picking up on. A faint trickle of electricity ran down the length of one ear as her gaze flicked his way.

Tim made another turn of the table. 'What we do,' he said, not slowing his pace at all. 'Is give Freddie the cure. Right?'

'What if…?'

'You said it's a cure?'

'Yes, but—'

'And Einstein was supposed to be super smart and all, right?'

'Well, yeah but—'

'So then, we give Freddie the cure. He's dying anyway, so what's the difference if it's the cure or the virus?' Tim's eyes were hard and unreadable, his voice flat and emotionless.

Zach had to give him credit though, he was right. Freddie *was* dying.

'It's not that simple,' sighed Zach.

'Why not?'

'Einstein's cure is designed to spread, just like the plague does,' Zach explained. 'If we inject Freddie with it, it'll be in each of us within hours. We can't isolate him. If we do this, if…if *you* do this. Either it works and Freddie lives, or it doesn't and you *all* die.'

Tim stopped pacing. Coal black eyes glittered at Zach, a sheen of tears threatening to fall. Zach's throat worked, his chest feeling tight and restricted as he realised he was the cause of those tears. He'd managed to make this tough, hardened boy cry.

Tim sat down next to Ant. He nodded. He took a deep breath and nodded again.

'I'll do it,' he said, his voice soft. No hint of the anger or the fire or the aggression. Just simple submission.

Ant stared at him. He glanced up, staring first at BK, at Stevie, and then at Genie and Freddie.

Freddie gazed right back, his fevered grey eyes wide and shocked and for the first time in hours, Zach thought he was listening.

Ant sucked in a sharp breath and nodded. Without looking away from Freddie, he whispered,

'Me too.'

Genie's gaze snapped up.

'Me too,' said BK, leaning forward to stare earnestly at her cousins, nodding firmly.

Her gaze shifted sideways to Stevie, green eyes questioning her alien friend. Without a word, Stevie dipped her head, reaching out and resting her soft skinned hand in the middle of the table.

Without hesitation Tim added his hand to hers—BK half a second behind him. Ant, too, added his hand to the growing pile.

A small, shaky sob burst forth from Genie and she turned, wrapping her arms around Freddie, gripping him in a fervent hug. Freddie was staring at the hands piled on the table before him. He kept opening his mouth, closing it and swallowing. His chest rose and fell in sharp movements.

Zach took a deep breath, trying to squash the hollow feeling growing in his gut. If the cure didn't work—if it attacked any non-human cells as Einstein suspected—then Zach would…he squashed the thought, swallowing the heavy lump in his throat.

No. He glanced at BK, feeling the warmth radiate out from her. At her gaze fixed assuredly on her cousins, no doubt or fear in her decision.

Zach wanted to have that selfless confidence. He wanted to be like her.

So he took a deep breath, sighed and nodded. 'Alright,' he said. 'When do you want to do this?'

'No time like the present,' said Tim, glancing sideways at Freddie.

Freddie, looking more aware than he had in days, nodded lifted a hand in a thumbs up.

'Let's do it.'

CHAPTER FIFTY-SIX

Genie

The morning air was crisp and cold, seeping into my bones. Making me still and breathless and frozen. Numbness crept along my skin, my muscles stiff and unmoving.

It felt good.

It kept the bad thoughts at bay.

It made me want to sleep.

The ground was damp and rocky and sharp things jabbed up at my back and legs and head as I lay staring up at the dawning sky.

Somewhere out there Einstein's…enemies? Friends? Co-workers?…They were flying towards us at speeds I couldn't even comprehend.

But I wasn't thinking about the Collective. I wasn't thinking about anything except the cold sinking into my soul.

Footsteps crunched in the grass and I turned my head, startled as someone flopped down onto the grass behind me.

He matched my pose, stretched out, arms spread wide in the morning frost, head next to mine but upside down. He didn't look at me, just stared up into that expanse of sky.

I turned my gaze back up and refused to contemplate anything except the dark and the cold.

In the frosted silence I grew sleepy and my eyes drifted shut. Everything was still and quiet and in that singular moment of space I could pretend. Pretend that none of it happened. That nothing else would happen. That I was less broken.

'Do you see them?'

His voice was soft and low, breaking through the silence in a whisper that felt like a shout. I didn't startle though. My eyes drifted back open.

'Who?' I asked, but I was pretty sure I knew, so before he could explain, before he could utter those words that I didn't want to hear, I answered. 'Yes.'

'Did you sleep at all?'

'No. You?'

He took a deep breath and answered with a sigh. 'No. I…I kept seeing her face. And that bloody dog…'

He trailed off, and I kept up my game of pretence. Saying nothing about the catch in his voice or the sharp intake of breathe.

But I couldn't not see them then. My own demons. My own ghosts. Ghosts I made.

'Do you…do you think they were dead? The nurses… the ones I fried when you found us.'

There was a long moment of silence and even before he said it I knew what his answer would be. Because he wouldn't have taken so long to say it otherwise. Because he never lied just to make me feel better.

'Yeah…' he said. 'I'm sorry.'

'I don't even remember…I don't think I meant to…'

'I know.'

'Do you think I'm like James?'

'What?' His voice came out sharp, his head turning in the grass to glare at me.

I kept my eyes fixed on the faint stars above, though I could see him out of the corner of my eye.

'I killed them without even meaning to,' I said, clenching my hands in the ground—feeling the heat in them evaporate the wet dew clinging to the grass around me. 'Just because I was angry. Just because they had what I wanted.'

I expected him to get angry. I waited for him to start shouting. To yell at me and tell me I was stupid. My body tensed in anticipation, my fists clenching around the fragile strands of grass.

I remembered the last time we'd spoken about killing. How I'd slapped him. Felt the sting of memory crawl across my palm. He'd yelled at me then.

It never came, though. He was quiet, and worry clenched in my gut. My heart sped up, the numbing cold dissipating under the heat of my pounding heart.

'Depends,' he said, turning to stare up at the sky again, his jaw tight. 'Do you think *I'm* like James.'

'No! No you…you're *nothing* like him.'

He let out a faint breath, a relieved sigh I didn't realise he'd been holding in. 'Good,' he said. 'And no. You ain't like him. He hurts for fun. Because he *likes* it. You would only ever hurt to protect.'

Tears pricked my eyes but I held them back, searching for the numbness, willing it to seep back into my body.

'I was just so angry,' I said. 'I was so scared.'

'Me too.'

I turned my head, my eyes snapping open, staring at the side of his face with my mouth open.

He glanced my way and a scowl curved his lips. 'What?'

'Nothing…just…you didn't seem scared.'

'Neither did you,' he retorted.

I laughed, tight and without mirth. 'I was terrified.'

'Yeah, well, so was I.'

'Oh.'

'We did the right thing. Well, maybe not the *right* thing. But we did what we had to. To survive. To live. To be here right now. And I won't say sorry for that. We did what we had to. Right?'

I tried to swallow the lump in my throat so I could get the words out. I wanted to agree with him. I wanted to think that we had to do it. That I had to strike those nurses, and I had to shoot that man. But their faces swam in my mind.

The woman in the hazmat suit, whose mask I'd ripped away. I'd goaded her, throwing her own words back at her, terrifying her into making the worst possible choice. I had done that. And I wasn't sure that was something I could just brush away. That I could move on from simply because my actions had kept me alive. Me, instead of them.

'It's over, isn't it?' I asked, countering his question with one of my own. 'We don't have to kill anyone else?'

'I…I don't know,' he said, and then—after a long pause —in a quiet voice that barely broke the hushed, frosty air, he added, 'I hope so. I don't want to have to kill anyone else.'

To have to. Because he would, if he had to. I supposed I would too. If it meant that Tim would live. Or BK, or Ant, or Zach, or Stevie. Or Freddie.

Almost instinctively my mind reached out, dredging itself out of the cold and searching for that place deep within my mind that I was becoming familiar with. The place that was Freddie's. As I reached, I also withdrew. Frightened of what I would find there.

'I think Ant hates me,' said Tim.

I glanced sideways, but he was still staring up at the sky. I rolled my eyes, exasperation stirring within the cold.

'He doesn't hate you,' I said. 'He loves you.'

A heart beat of silence. He didn't answer, and I clenched my teeth.

'I know you know,' I said. 'Stop pretending you can't see it.'

He sighed. His posture relaxed, as if all his worry and tension melted away under my accusation. Under my *knowing*.

'You sound like Freddie.'

'Freddie's talked to you about it?'

'Of course he has. Mind reading asshole.'

I snorted, but as soon as it came the laughter died. 'You need to apologise.'

'I tried!'

'Well keep trying! You've known how he's felt for so long and you never answered him. You never responded!'

'It's not like he's actually said any—'

'Shut up! That's not the point! If you knew you should've said something. You know what he's like. You know what his mother put him through. And now you've hurt him and you need to make it right.'

Tim sat up, surging out of the wet grass in a sudden burst. 'What do you want me to do? I didn't mean to upset him. I didn't mean to do anything. I was just surprised. He didn't even *tell* us what they did to him. And I saw the bruises and I just panicked, alright? You think I'd ever do that on purpose? You think I'd ever want to hurt him? I've tried to say sorry. I've tried—'

He cut off and with a start I realised he was crying. Tim. Tim was crying.

He was trying to hold it back. Trying to keep it quiet so I couldn't hear but I knew him. I knew him better than anyone else, except maybe Freddie.

I rolled over, pushing myself to my knees and wrapping my arms around him. He stiffened, like I knew he would, and scrubbed at his face with clenched hands.

'We need to stick together now,' I said, leaning my chin on his shoulder the way he so often did to me. 'We can't fall apart. I know you. So why are you holding back?'

He sniffed, short and rough. 'I can't disappoint him.'

I pulled away and moved so I was sitting next to him. So I could see his face. Fresh rocks jabbed into my knees and dew seeped into my clothes but I didn't care.

'Why would you?'

He stared at me, a silhouette in the growing morning light. 'I haven't ever told you why I hate BK's tarot readings.'

Confused by the change of subject, I said, 'because they're always bad?'

Tim shook his head. He bent his knees and looped his arms around them, leaning forward and staring out at nothing and everything. He looked smaller. Quieter. Younger. No longer the fierce warrior I'd always known.

'I'm pretty sure she doesn't remember, but the first time we met she told I'd die…for you.'

It took a moment for his words to sink in. For the meaning behind them to make sense.

'You know, I don't really believe in psychics or any of that shit. And even if you and Freddie and Stevie and whoever else can read minds, I still don't think it's possible that BK can see the future, but,' he picked at some grass, his voice soft. 'I think about it a lot. I think it was one of those things that she knows. Not because it's the future but 'cause it's a possibility. 'Cause of who I am. That's what I figure, anyway. When we were in that facility…I thought a lot about it and I think I came to terms with the fact that I might die. That I wasn't gonna make it out of there.'

'Tim…' I didn't know what else to say.

'I have a job. And I'm always going to do that job. No matter what. It's always going to come first.'

'You mean me.'

Dark eyes that glowed like amber in the rising sun flicked my way before darting off again.

'I can protect myself,' I said. 'I…I'm stronger now.'

'Yeah,' Tim scoffed. 'I'll believe you when you can say that like you mean it.'

I flushed and clenched my hands. 'I don't want to be the reason you miss out.'

'Who says I'm missing out?'

'Don't you love him?'

'Ant?' Tim shrugged, staring out at the field stretching beyond the barn. 'Maybe. I've never really let myself think about it.'

Sun filtered down into the morning haze, lifting fog up from the dewy grasses and casting strange shadows out of trees and rocks.

'I think you should,' I said. 'I think you should decide how you feel, and then tell him. Don't use me as an excuse not to.'

He glanced my way, black eyes sharper this time.

'And you?' he asked. 'Are you gonna face how *you* feel?'

'What're you talking about?'

He was quiet, chewing on his words before speaking them. 'You've talked about Ant, and about killing, and even about James. But you haven't mentioned Freddie.'

I flinched, shying away from the truth in his words.

'You haven't spoken to him since you found out. You can't tell me I'm being unfair, when you won't even let him speak to you the only way he can.'

'That's different.'

'It is not! He's *dying*! He's hurting and Zach's stupid cure isn't working and you can't even *look* at him. Instead you're out here, letting yourself freeze to death.'

'What do you want me to do?' I shouted, on my feet before I even realised I was reacting the same way he had—proving his point. 'You want me to watch him die? I have these stupid abilities and they're nothing! They're useless! *I'm* useless! I can't do anything except watch and I hate it! I hate it.' Sobs worked their way out of my chest, fighting to be free. 'I can't. I *can't*. What if…it gets worse…and then…and he…I can't. I can't do it.'

'Shit.'

His arms wrapped around me, pulling me in, and I'm ten years old again. I'm hiding in a corner of the barn, praying James doesn't find me and then he's there. Tim. Wrapping me up. Calling for help. Saving me. He'd never left me. Never let me go. Not then, and not since. Not now.

'How about we do it together?' he mumbled into the tangled mess that was my hair. 'He's ours, after all. We're the only ones who can understand, you and me. So, we'll go in together, alright? And we'll let him talk. We'll let him see us. Even if it's scary.'

Sniffling, trying to push down the sobs, I nodded. 'Okay.'

He pulled away, turning his head and swiping at his eyes in an attempt to stop me from seeing that he was crying again. I felt stupid, but I also felt better knowing I wasn't the only one who was a mess.

He bumped my shoulder, making me stumble as he always did, and cracked a grin as I recovered my footing. I rolled my eyes and just like that, we weren't fighting anymore.

Together, as a united front, we headed back toward the barn with renewed purpose—renewed strength—as the sunlight warmed our backs.

CHAPTER FIFTY-SEVEN

Zach

The cure wasn't working.

Zach knew it would take longer than a day to take effect, but three? Three days with nothing. No fever reduction, no temperature shift…just…nothing.

At least he wasn't getting any *worse*. The others though? They *were* getting worse.

Stevie, who attended Freddie almost every minute of the day, was so sleep deprived Zach wondered how she was functioning. Her skin was dry—almost flakey—the smooth texture now rough and parched. As if all the moisture had been sucked out of her.

'You need to have a break,' said Zach, wondering how often she needed to absorb moisture to stay healthy. 'You won't do Freddie any good if you burn yourself out.'

Although he had a feeling she already had.

'Just lay down for a while. There's a tub in the house if you need it…?'

Stevie shook her head, her movements delayed and slow, as if his words weren't reaching her.

'I… have to…k-k-keep…going. He is…mine to…to…'

Stevie trailed off, eyes drifting shut for a moment too long and panic filled Zach's chest.

He got up, quietly navigated through the pillows and blankets and pitfalls before racing down the stairs, his footsteps loud and clattering.

He jogged to the couches where the others had been

sorting through the canned food collected from the house.

'Stevie is sick,' he said, blurting the words out before he really took stock of the situation.

BK looked up at him, her face pink and flushed, her hair damp from sweat.

'So is Ant,' said Tim, though he didn't move, didn't even look up from where he cradled Ant's head in his lap.

'It's the cure isn't it?' Genie said, staring at her unconscious friend. 'It's killing him.'

Zach swallowed hard. Ant was covered in a thin layer of perspiration, and his brow furrowed in a restless sleep.

'I think so,' Zach sighed and rubbed a hand over his face. 'Let's get him upstairs.'

It took them minutes of awkward co-ordination between Zach and Tim to get Ant up the stairs. BK trudged up behind them with heavy footsteps.

Upstairs, Stevie was already asleep, her head resting on the mound of blankets and pillows that was Freddie. Zach swallowed hard against the lump in his throat and helped Tim lower Ant onto one of the mattresses on the floor.

Once settled, Tim slumped down next to Ant, swiping sweat from his forehead. He was panting heavier than Zach, his boundless stamina and energy seeming to have lost all steam and will.

He sat staring at his friend, brooding from his spot against the wall until he fell asleep. He didn't wake up. His dark skin was flushed red with the heat, though the day was cooler than a winter afternoon on a dune layered beach.

'We need more antibiotics or something,' said Zach, laying a cool towel over Stevie's forehead.

'I'll see what's in the house,' said Genie, pushing up from where she'd been sitting cross legged in the doorway.

'Be careful,' said Zach, his words coming out sharper than he'd intended. 'You're looking a bit pink yourself.'

'I'm okay,' she said. 'Watch out for BK.'

'I'm alright,' said BK, sitting up straighter as she jerked out of a doze.

Genie met Zach's eye, and they shared a grim expression.

The room went still when Genie left. Zach sighed, leaning back to stare at them all as silence fell over the room. Until Tim's mutterings started up again.

There was a whisper of movement next to him, and Zach jerked, startled out of his thoughts.

'Oh, sorry, I didn't mean to startle you,' BK whispered, leaning over to rest her head on his shoulder. 'You just looked so lonely.'

'I think I will be feeling pretty lonely soon enough,' Zach mumbled, a hollow feeling settling into his gut. He shook himself and offered BK a wan smile. 'But not yet. You're still here.'

'We're all going to get sick, aren't we?'

'Not quite. I won't. I'm the only one with normal human blood cells.'

'Oh,' she said, and her voice was so sad Zach felt a wave of darkness sweep over him.

His breathing shortened, his pulse quickened, and as his vision blurred as he fought the urge to burst into tears. In an effort to distract himself he asked the first thing he could think of.

'What do you really look like?'

She looked up, eyes wide with surprise.

'I mean, you don't really look like us, do you?' he rambled, scrunching up a towelette and laying it flat again. 'Human, that is.'

'I … No. I guess I don't.'

She felt hot against him, like there was a fire raging beneath her skin. Her cheek burned on his shoulder as she rested her head back down.

'So, what do you look like?'

'I don't really know,' she said, her words slow and tired. 'I've never thought about it. I wonder…'

'I bet you'd still be pretty,' he said, feeling his chest constrict as her voice petered out.

Again, her face filled with surprise. 'You think?'

'Well, yeah. I mean,' he licked his lips, his eyes loosing focus as he fought off tears. 'You're attractive. For an alien.'

A smile blossomed on her face. 'You're pretty too. If I were human, I'd kiss you. You...you seem like...a good person to kiss.'

She was out before Genie made it back from the house. He sat waiting for her, surrounded by people and yet completely alone.

Genie came back sweating and out of breath, but holding three packets of panadol. It wasn't much, but it was more than they'd had, so Zach was grateful.

Genie helped him distribute the pills. Making sure none of the others choked as they tried to make them swallow the little, powdery tablets.

'Can Stevie have these?' Genie asked, her voice going hoarse.

Zach shrugged, brushing BK's hair out of her face. 'I'm not sure. But, at this point, it's not likely to make her worse.'

Genie was trying to fight, to stay awake. She slumped next to him, exhausted. 'You...aren't alone,' she said, her voice surprisingly strong. 'I won't...leave...you...alone...'

'Thanks,' he said. 'I appreciate that.'

Her brows furrowed together and she reached out a hand. Zach grasped it. Her skin was clammy, but not as hot as the others'.

'Tell me...about...Einstein...'

'I think you could tell me more about him. I never did hear how you met him.'

'You didn't? I was...almost eleven. Six...six years ago. They all thought...I was crazy. Except Freddie. He knew. He came when I was alone...like a ghost...like a beautiful ghost...'

She drifted off, leaving Zach to stare down at her, his heart lodged in his throat so he couldn't breathe. Tears pricked at his eyes and he tried to blink away the sharp sting.

Zach got up. 'You guys are going to wake up,' he said, looking around at the six of them. 'And when you do, I'll be here. So don't give up on me, okay? I'm waiting...so just... don't leave me alone.'

BK shifted, a faint smile lifting her flushed pink cheeks. Zach didn't believe in signs, but at this point, he'd have got down on his knees and prayed if it meant they would wake up. BK's smile gave him a small measure of hope. He squared his shoulders and got to work.

CHAPTER FIFTY-EIGHT

Freddie

Strange dreams melted away under the heat of the morning. Dreams that were really memories seeped out of my subconscious while I slept, avoiding the remnants of the drug haze my mind had been in the last few days. Or was it weeks? It was hard to tell.

I rubbed my face, blinking away images of frogs as the echo of high pitched giggles faded into the quiet hum of morning.

Somewhere in the distance I could hear birds. Magpies, cockatoos and kookaburras. The sound was familiar and comforting and I wondered if it was the cause of the warm memories easing away the darkness in my mind.

I tried to open my eyes and winced, squinting into the sunlight that assaulted me. I grunted. Or…I tried to. Like all the times I've tried before, nothing happened. Nothing except a faint puff of air exhaling from a throat that refused to speak.

I sighed.

Next to me, someone shifted in restless sleep, startling me a little. I turned my jhead and it was like seeing myself laying next to me. Only if I'd been a girl. Except now this face is more different from mine than it had ever been. The pink, puckered scar tracing it's way down, almost gentle in its thinness.

My fists clenched, but I reminded myself she was still alive, and she was stronger. Stronger than she knew.

An itch ran through my muscles to get up and stretch. To do something other than lay there. To *run*.

Careful not to wake Genie, I sat up, wriggling out of the massive pile of blankets plastered over me.

Sunlight poured into the familiar room through large, high arching windows I recognised at once.

I was home. Well, not home exactly. In reality, it was more Ant's home than anyone else's but the space was as familiar and safe as home ever was. More so now, I supposed.

The barn loft was still the same, unmarred by the chaos of the outside world. For a moment I wondered if I imagined the whole ordeal. If the last few days were just some strange fevered dream I'd had.

Movement in the corner of my eye caught my attention on the other side of the room. Stevie murmured something in a strange language, her hairless brows scrunched together in worry.

I sighed. Not a dream.

She's on the edge of the the giant, mashed together bed Tim was so fond of making for sleepovers. With two extra people, it was unusually crowded in the loft, yet, somehow cosier.

I counted them up. One, two, three…six bright points of light, glowing in the morning sun. My stomach unclenched. They're all there. All safe.

Tim's snores emanated on my other side, and I glanced that way to see him and Ant sprawled in their usual tangle of limbs, wedged between me and the wall. I shook my head, knowing that Ant would wake up before Tim, like he always did, and pretend they hadn't just spent the night curled around each other; and Tim, oblivious as he ever was, would never realise.

I snorted and debated waking Tim up, just to see how he'd handle it. But the bright spark that was his mind was, for once, a calm blue—with none of the restless red that usually jittered through his light.

So instead, I pushed myself up to my feet. Stevie and Einstein couldn't see other people's minds like I did. They didn't get the bright glow of colours that I did. Instead, they saw something else. Einstein called it a "network of minds". They didn't know why I saw something different.

More unanswered questions.

I shook my head, trying to drag myself out of my thoughts. It was no use dwelling on it. I'd figured out plenty on my own, and I'd keep figuring things out. For now though, it was time to stretch my legs.

As I headed for the door, I almost tripped over a lump that turned out—to my surprise—to be BK and Zach. They were similarly entangled, and I wondered when that had happened. I paused, half wanting to wake Genie, to talk to her about the developments between our friends, and what had happened when I was sick, but I wasn't sure where we stood.

Was she still mad at me? Did she hate me for being in her mind so often? For invading her privacy so thoroughly. I wanted to explain to her that I'd never spied. Not on purpose, anyway. It was hard. She didn't feel the connection like I did. She didn't see the sparks. She didn't see me.

Not like I saw her.

Her mind was bright, even in my peripheral. Visible through blankets, through walls and doors and even buildings. Traceable even when we were in thick crowds; even when we were apart, so I always knew what she was feeling or thinking the minute I cast my mind toward her.

She was dreaming something pleasant. Her thoughts were a warm orange, like sunrise. Flashes of images tried to jump out at me, but I turned away, focusing hard on the feel of the grainy wooden steps beneath my feet.

The itch in my muscles turned into an ache and, trying to ignore the thoughts that attempted to follow me like music trailing down a hallway, I made my way down into the barn below.

Summer was fading, though the heat still lingered.

After a quick stretch that made me feel light and relaxed, I began to run. The thud of the dirt road under my feet kept in rhythm with my heartbeat. It was steady and familiar and I relished in the exercise. In the burn that started far sooner than it should.

Man, I was unfit. I vaguely remembered getting sick and the fever that had stollen my ability to see and think clearly. I shook my head, my breath puffing out silently as I thought of *why* I'd gotten sick.

James.

I didn't remember what had happened to him. Had we beaten him? Was he gone? Could I stop worrying?

I didn't know.

Adrenaline flowed into my legs, and I sprinted, pushing myself as hard as I could. Trees flew passed, my feet barely touching the ground as I ran flat out, trying to outrun the demons in my thoughts.

The air was fresh and light and tasted like freedom. Not like the sterile taste I'd been breathing at the facility.

My lungs burned. My legs ached. Yet I ran. I put my head down and panted my way up the long, steep hill halfway down our street. I slipped and slid down the other side, wincing as sharp rocks jabbed into the soft underside of my bare feet.

Why hadn't I put on shoes?

Absurdly, it's at the end of the street—in the final forty metres of actual paved road—that I fell on my face. Something sharp struck me on the ball of my foot and I staggered, going down with a yelp. Well, sort of a yelp. Air burst out of my lungs the way it should yet without the accompanying sound. I slammed into the hard ground.

I didn't get up. There were no cars to worry about, so for a while I just laid there, panting and sore, but grinning.

Adrenaline pumped through me, making my chest heave and filling me with a euphoria that cast away the pain. I huffed out a silent laugh, at once annoyed and amused by my inability to laugh at myself.

A face appeared above me and my huffing laugh cut off.

'Alright there mate?'

Again I tried to yelp. In my surprise, the sound echoed out away from me, but mentally, instead of physically. I wondered if he heard it?

I scrambled to my feet—my already hammering heart doubling its pace as I backed up—and stood a few feet away as I attempted to catch my breath.

'Easy,' said the boy, hands raised in a gesture of peace. 'Easy,' he said again. 'I saw you trip. Gave me a fright, I'll tell you. Wasn't expecting to see nobody out in these parts.'

He had a strange accent. A lilt to his voice I wasn't familiar with. Genie would know, but I'd always had trouble identifying accents. While the mind's voice was generally the same as the physical, there were slight differences that made it difficult for me to ever place anyone's origin.

His mind's voice matched the bright light that glowed there. It was a warm green, like his eyes, and I relaxed, an impression of summer afternoons and sunlight washing away the leftover adrenaline.

'You live out here?' he asked.

I nodded, still staring at the spark lighting up his mind. There's a thought there, bright and excited, that I tried to catch.

Looks a bit banged up but he'll clean up alright once we're back at camp. Wonder what's for dinner tonight? He looks like he could use a decent feed. Least he's my age. I'll finally have someone to talk to. Wonder if Ayana knows who he is?'

Ayana? I pulled out of his mind, blinking rapidly as I tried to unravel the energetic, fast flowing thoughts. His mind was more chaotic than Tim's and it took me a moment to resettle within myself.

Ayana…I knew that name.

'You got anyone else with you? I thought we'd already rounded up everyone still left in this area, but out in this bush it's hard to tell.'

A bell jangled, and the boy and I both looked back toward the general store as someone stepped out through the doorway. The minute I saw her, the minute her mind's spark lit up the street, a heaviness I hadn't realised I was holding onto lifted off my shoulders.

My feet kicked off, and it was like I hadn't ever fallen. I ran.

'Hey, what're you—'

Recognition lit her face as I sprinted toward her. She dropped the armful of cans and food and other things she was holding and met me in the park. I flung my arms around her, never feeling so relieved to see an adult in my entire life.

Tim got his height from his Mum. He might've been taller than her, but I was short enough that when I crashed into her in the carpark of Joe's Corner, she was able to wrap me up with ease.

'Freddie!'

Emotion swelled in my chest. Emotion I tried to hang onto, to keep locked away where it belonged.

Ayana Holt pulled away, staring at me with my best friend's eyes. She cupped my face with her hands.

'Good heavens, boy you look like you've gone ten rounds with a bull,' she said, tears and laughter mixing in her voice as she pulled me in for another hug. 'But oh, I've never been happier to see you. Are you alright? What about…what about Tim? Is he okay?'

I pulled away again, nodding so hard I thought I'd shake my brains loose.

Bright tears overflowed from warm, melted chocolate eyes. She dashed them from her eyes but more replaced them. She gasped, a huge smile breaking over her relieved face as she started to fire off questions.

'Oh thank God. He's okay? Thank *God*. I was so worried! What happened? What about the others? Genie? And Ant and BK? Are they all okay?'

I kept nodding, grinning as her face brightened with delight. She was darker than Tim, her skin coloured bronze, her hair flaring out around her face in a chaotic mess.

'Where are they? Are they here?'

I pointed back up the road, and made a single sign. Home.

'I'm guessing you two know each other then?'

Mrs Holt laughed. 'Yes. Freddie, this is Travis. He was helping me gather supplies for our camp. It's a place for survivors of the plague. Travis, this is my son's best friend, Freddie. He's just told me my boy is alright. They came home after all.'

I grinned over at her. Images were pouring out from her. Mostly images of Tim, but also images of the camp she'd mentioned. There were people, lots of them, all working together to help find family and friends, to get supplies, to survive.

She started telling me about it as we walked, and I contemplated telling her about everything that had happened to me and the others. About what we had been through. I got the feeling I could have entered her mind, and she wouldn't have even been surprised. She'd always treated Genie and me like family, especially after Mum died. She said it was her duty as Mum's friend to look out for us.

She was a lot like Tim, that way. Only, more level headed.

Her mind shone bright with excitement as she and Travis overloaded me with information while we walked. It took longer than usual, mostly because I was limping now. Travis offered to patch me up but I was too excited to stop and I knew that Mrs Holt was desperate to see Tim.

When we stepped into the barn a rush of hope swelled in my chest. It might've been the run, or the fresh morning air, or the bright, intense relief that washed over Tim's face the minute he saw his mother, or even the fact that I wasn't sick anymore. Probably it was all of those things.

I watched Tim, followed by Ant, latch onto Mrs Holt like they were little kids again. I saw a flash of blonde curls hurtling toward me and I was swamped in a hug of my own —BK and Genie almost knocking me over.

Over Genie's shoulder I saw Travis staring bug-eyed, like a kid overwhelmed at Christmas, at Stevie. She was hiding behind Zach (who was trying his best to look intimidating and failing miserably) fidgeting under the new kid's scrutiny. I grinned and sent a wave of calm towards them. Letting Stevie know that it was okay. That we were safe now.

So maybe the Collective was still out there somewhere. Probably on their way here even. They'd sure made a dent in our numbers. They'd pulled down our society in a single day and turned us into an endangered species.

I reckon they expected us to crumble, to tear at the remnants of our existence and destroy each other just as they themselves had tried to do.

But maybe we were fighting back. Maybe we were pulling together, stronger than we'd ever been. Maybe we were going to survive.

And maybe, just maybe, humanity wasn't as easy to extinguish as the Collective thought.

The End

Want more?

Genie and the gang often pop back up in my thoughts while I'm writing, so if you enjoyed Extinguish feel free to check out my website at:

jhmitchell.com/extinguish/

Here you can find more free content such as:
Backstories
Pre-novel short stories
The Freddie Monologues (short series)
Somewhat Serendipitous (10,000 Novella)

I'd also love to hear your thoughts. Write a review at goodreads or amazon, or send me an email at:

jhmitchell.writing@gmail.com